CHARLES DICKENS

THE BEDSIDE DICKENS

Classics for Pleasure

CHANCELLOR
PRESS

The following first published in Great Britain in book form:
The Pickwick Papers 1837
Oliver Twist 1838
Nicholas Nickleby 1839
The Old Curiosity Shop 1841
Barnaby Rudge 1841
A Christmas Carol 1843
Martin Chuzzlewit 1844
Dombey and Son 1848
David Copperfield 1850
Bleak House 1853
Hard Times 1854
Little Dorrit 1857
A Tale of Two Cities 1859
Great Expectations 1861
Our Mutual Friend 1865
The Mystery of Edwin Drood 1870

This edition published in Great Britain 1993
by Chancellor Press
an imprint of Reed Consumer Books Limited
Michelin House, 81 Fulham Road, London SW3 6RB
and Auckland, Melbourne, Singapore and Toronto

ISBN 1 851 52313 8

A CIP catalogue record for this book is available
from the British Library

Printed in Great Britain by William Clowes, Beccles.

Contents

THE PICKWICK PAPERS

On their travels, Messrs Pickwick, Snodgrass, Tupman and Winckle encounter an acquaintance, Mr Wardle, who invites them to sojourn at Manor Farm, his home at Dingley Dell in Kent. He lives there with his aged mother, his unmarried sister and his two daughters, and is attended by a fat boy whom he calls 'a natural curiosity'. The day after their arrival, having received a slight injury in a shooting accident, Mr Tupman is left in the care of the ladies while his companions attend a cricket match …

The quiet seclusion of Dingley Dell, the presence of so many of the gentler sex, and the solicitude and anxiety they evinced in his behalf, were all favourable to the growth and development of those softer feelings which nature had implanted deep in the bosom of Mr Tracy Tupman, and which now appeared destined to centre in one lovely object. The young ladies were pretty, their manners winning, their dispositions unexceptionable; but there was a dignity in the air, a touch-me-not-ishness in the walk, a majesty in the eye of the spinster aunt, to which, at their time of life, they could lay no claim, which distinguished her from any female on whom Mr Tupman had ever gazed. That there was something kindred in their nature, something congenial in their souls, something mysteriously sympathetic in their bosoms, was evident. Her name was the first that rose to Mr Tupman's lips as he lay wounded on the grass; and her hysteric laughter was the first sound that fell upon his ear when he was supported to the house. But had her agitation arisen from an amiable and feminine sensibility which would have been equally irrepressible in any case; or had it been called forth by a more ardent and passionate feeling, which he, of all men living, could alone awaken? These were the doubts which racked his brain as he lay extended on the sofa: these were the doubts which he determined should be at once and for ever resolved.

It was evening. Isabella and Emily had strolled out with Mr Trundle; the deaf old lady had fallen asleep in her chair; the snoring of the fat boy, penetrated in a low and monotonous sound from the distant kitchen; the buxom servants were lounging at the side door, enjoying the pleasantness of the hour, and the delights of a flirtation, on first principles, with certain unwieldy animals attached to the farm; and there sat the interesting pair, uncared for by all, caring for none, and dreaming only of themselves; there they sat, in short, like a pair of carefully-folded kid-gloves—bound up in each other.

'I have forgotten my flowers,' said the spinster aunt.

'Water them now,' said Mr Tupman, in accents of persuasion.

'You will take cold in the evening air,' urged the spinster aunt, affectionately.

'No, no,' said Mr Tupman, rising; 'it will do me good. Let me accompany you.'

The lady paused to adjust the sling in which the left arm of the youth was placed, and taking his right arm led him to the garden.

There was a bower at the farther end, with honeysuckle, jessamine, and creeping plants—one of those sweet retreats which humane men erect for the accommodation of spiders.

The spinster aunt took up a large watering-pot which lay in one corner, and was about to leave the arbour. Mr Tupman detained her, and drew her to a seat beside him.

'Miss Wardle!' said he.

The spinster aunt trembled, till some pebbles which had accidentally found their way into the large watering-pot shook like an infant's rattle.

'Miss Wardle,' said Mr Tupman, 'you are an angel.'

'Mr Tupman!' exclaimed Rachael, blushing as red as the watering-pot itself.

'Nay,' said the eloquent Pickwickian—'I know it but too well.'

'All women are angels, they say,' murmured the lady, playfully.

'Then what can *you* be; or to what, without presumption, can I compare you?' replied Mr Tupman. 'Where was the woman ever seen who resembled you? Where else could I hope to find so rare a combination of excellence and beauty? Where else could I seek to—Oh!' Here Mr Tupman paused, and pressed the hand which clasped the handle of the happy watering-pot.

The lady turned aside her head. 'Men are such deceivers,' she softly whispered.

'They are, they are,' ejaculated Mr Tupman; 'but not all men. There lives at least one being who can never change—one being who would be content to devote his whole existence to your happiness—who lives but in your eyes—who breathes but in your smiles—who bears the heavy burden of life itself only for you.'

'Could such an individual be found,' said the lady—

'But he *can* be found,' said the ardent Mr Tupman, interposing. 'He *is* found. He is here, Miss Wardle.' And ere the lady was aware of his intention, Mr Tupman had sunk upon his knees at her feet.

'Mr Tupman, rise,' said Rachael.

'Never!' was the valorous reply. 'Oh, Rachael!'—He seized her passive hand, and the watering-pot fell to the ground as he pressed it to his lips.—'Oh, Rachael! say you love me.'

'Mr Tupman,' said the spinster aunt, with averted head—'I can hardly speak the words; but—but—you are not wholly indifferent to me.'

Mr Tupman no sooner heard this avowal, than he proceeded to do what his enthusiastic emotions prompted, and what, for aught we know (for we are but little acquainted with such matters), people so circumstanced always do. He jumped up, and, throwing his arm around the neck of the spinster aunt, imprinted upon her lips numerous kisses, which after a due show of struggling and resistance, she received so passively, that there is no telling how many more Mr Tupman might have bestowed, if the lady had not given a very unaffected start, and exclaimed in an affrighted tone—

'Mr Tupman, we are observed!—we are discovered!'

Mr Tupman looked round. There was the fat boy, perfectly motionless, with his large circular eyes staring into the arbour, but without the slightest expression on his face that the most expert physiognomist could have referred to astonishment, curiosity, or any other known passion that agitates the human breast. Mr Tupman gazed on the fat boy, and the fat boy stared at him; and the longer Mr Tupman observed the utter vacancy of the fat boy's countenance, the more convinced he became that he either did not know, or did not understand, anything that had been going forward. Under this impression, he said with great firmness—

'What do you want here, sir?'

'Supper's ready, sir,' was the prompt reply.

'Have you just come here, sir?' inquired Mr Tupman, with a piercing look.

'Just,' replied the fat boy.

Mr Tupman looked at him very hard again; but there was not a wink in his eye, or a curve in his face.

Mr Tupman took the arm of the spinster aunt, and walked towards the house; the fat boy followed behind.

'He knows nothing of what has happened,' he whispered.

'Nothing,' said the spinster aunt.

There was a sound behind them, as of an imperfectly suppressed chuckle. Mr Tupman turned sharply round. No; it could not have been the fat boy; there was not a gleam of mirth, or anything but feeding in his whole visage.

'He must have been fast asleep,' whispered Mr Tupman.

'I have not the least doubt of it,' replied the spinster aunt.

They both laughed heartily.

Mr Tupman was wrong. The fat boy, for once, had not been fast asleep. He was awake—wide awake—to what had been going forward.

The supper passed off without any attempt at a general conversation. The old lady had gone to bed; Isabella Wardle devoted herself exclusively to Mr Trundle; the spinster's attentions were reserved for Mr Tupman; and Emily's thoughts appeared to be engrossed by some distant object—possibly they were with the absent Snodgrass.

Eleven—twelve—one o'clock had struck, and the gentlemen had not arrived. Consternation sat on every face. Could they have been waylaid and robbed? Should they send men and lanterns in every direction by which they could be supposed likely to have travelled home? or should they—Hark! there they were. What could have made them so late? A strange voice, too! To whom could it belong? They rushed into the kitchen whither the truants had repaired, and at once obtained rather more than a glimmering of the real state of the case.

Mr Pickwick, with his hands in his pockets and his hat cocked completely over his left eye, was leaning against the dresser, shaking his head from side to side, and producing a constant succession of the blandest and most benevolent smiles without being moved thereunto by any discernible cause or pretence whatsoever; old Mr Wardle, with a highly-inflamed countenance, was grasping the hand of a strange gentleman muttering protestations of eternal friendship; Mr Winkle, supporting himself by the eight-day clock, was feebly invoking destruction upon the head of any member of the family who should suggest the propriety of his retiring for the night; and Mr Snodgrass had sunk into a chair, with an expression of the most abject and hopeless misery that the human mind can imagine, portrayed in every lineament of his expressive face.

'Is anything the matter?' inquired the three ladies.

'Nothing the matter,' replied Mr Pickwick. 'We—we're—all right.—I say, Wardle, we're all right, ain't we?'

'I should think so,' replied the jolly host.—'My dears, here's my friend, Mr Jingle—Mr Pickwick's friend, Mr Jingle, come 'pon—little visit.'

'Is anything the matter with Mr Snodgrass, sir?' inquired Emily, with great anxiety.

'Nothing the matter, ma'am,' replied the stranger. 'Cricket dinner—glorious party—capital songs—old port—claret—good—very good—wine, ma'am—wine.'

'It wasn't the wine,' murmured Mr Snodgrass, in a broken voice. 'It was the salmon.' (Somehow or other, it never *is* the wine, in these cases.)

'Hadn't they better go to bed, ma'am?' inquired Emma. 'Two of the boys will carry the gentlemen up-stairs.'

'I won't go to bed,' said Mr Winkle, firmly.

'No living boy shall carry me,' said Mr Pickwick, stoutly; and he went on smiling as before.

'Hurrah!' gasped Mr Winkle, faintly.

'Hurrah!' echoed Mr Pickwick, taking off his hat and dashing it on the floor, and insanely casting his spectacles into the middle of the kitchen.—At this humorous feat he laughed outright.

'Let's—have—'nother—bottle,' cried Mr Winkle, commencing in a very loud key, and ending in a very faint one. His head dropped upon his breast; and, muttering his invincible determination not to go to his bed, and a sanguinary regret that he had not 'done for old Tupman' in the morning, he fell fast asleep; in which condition he was borne to his apartment by two young giants under the personal superintendence of the fat boy, to whose protecting care Mr Snodgrass shortly afterwards confided his own person. Mr Pickwick accepted the proffered arm of Mr Tupman and quietly disappeared, smiling more than ever; and Mr Wardle, after taking as affectionate a leave of the whole family as if he were ordered for immediate execution, consigned to Mr Trundle the honour of conveying him up-stairs, and retired, with a very futile attempt to look impressively solemn and dignified.

'What a shocking scene!' said the spinster aunt.

'Dis—gusting!' ejaculated both the young ladies.

'Dreadful—dreadful!' said Jingle, looking very grave: he was about a bottle and a half ahead of any of his companions. 'Horrid spectacle—very!'

'What a nice man!' whispered the spinster aunt to Mr Tupman.

'Good-looking, too!' whispered Emily Wardle.

'Oh, decidedly,' observed the spinster aunt.

Mr Tupman thought of the window at Rochester: and his mind was troubled. The succeeding half-hour's conversation was not of a nature to calm his perturbed spirit. The new visitor was very talkative, and the number of his anecdotes was only to be exceeded by the extent of his politeness. Mr Tupman felt that as Jingle's popularity increased, he (Tupman) retired further into the shade. His laughter was forced—his merriment feigned; and when at last he laid his aching temples between the sheets, he thought, with horrid delight, on the satisfaction it would afford him to have Jingle's head at that moment between the feather bed and the mattress.

The indefatigable stranger rose betimes next morning, and, although his companions remained in bed overpowered with the dissipation of the previous night, exerted himself most successfully to promote the hilarity of the breakfast-table. So successful were his efforts, that even the deaf old lady insisted on having one or two of his best jokes retailed through the trumpet; and even she condescended to observe to the spinster aunt, that 'he' (meaning Jingle) 'was an impudent young fellow:' a sentiment in which all her relations then and there present thoroughly coincided.

It was the old lady's habit on the fine summer mornings to repair to the arbour in which Mr Tupman had already signalised himself, in form and manner following: first, the fat boy fetched from a peg behind the old lady's bedroom door, a close black satin bonnet, a warm cotton shawl, and a thick stick with a capacious handle; and the old lady, having put on the bonnet and shawl at her leisure, would lean one hand on the stick and the other on the fat boy's shoulder, and walk leisurely to the arbour, where the fat boy would leave her to enjoy the fresh air for the space of half an hour; at the expiration of which time he would return and reconduct her to the house.

The old lady was very precise and very particular; and as this ceremony had been observed for three successive summers without the slightest deviation from the accustomed form, she was not a little surprised on this particular morning to see the fat boy, instead of leaving the arbour, walk a few paces out of it, look carefully round him in every direction, and return towards her with great stealth and an air of the most profound mystery.

The old lady was timorous—most old ladies are—and her first impression was that the bloated lad was about to do her some grievous bodily harm with the view of possessing himself of her loose coin. She would have cried for assistance, but age and infirmity had long ago deprived her of the power of screaming; she, therefore, watched his motions with feelings of intense terror, which were in no degree diminished by his coming close up to her, and shouting in her ear in an agitated, and as it seemed to her, a threatening tone —

'Missus!'

Now it so happened that Mr Jingle was walking in the garden close to the arbour at that moment. He too heard the shout of 'Missus,' and stopped to hear more. There were three reasons for his doing so. In the first place, he was idle and curious; secondly, he was by no means scrupulous; thirdly, and lastly, he was concealed from view by some flowering shrubs. So there he stood, and there he listened.

'Missus!' shouted the fat boy.

'Well, Joe,' said the trembling old lady. 'I'm sure I have been a good mistress to you, Joe. You have invariably been treated very kindly. You have never had too much to do; and you have always had enough to eat.'

This last was an appeal to the fat boy's most sensitive feelings. He seemed touched, as he replied, emphatically —

'I knows I has.'

'Then what can you want to do now?' said the old lady, gaining courage.

'I wants to make your flesh creep,' replied the boy.

This sounded like a very bloodthirsty mode of showing one's gratitude; and as the old lady did not precisely understand the process by which such a result was to be attained, all her former horrors returned.

'What do you think I see in this very arbour last night?' inquired the boy.

'Bless us! What?' exclaimed the old lady, alarmed at the solemn manner of the corpulent youth.

'The strange gentleman—him as had his arm hurt—a kissin' and huggin'—'

'Who, Joe? None of the servants, I hope.'

'Worser than that,' roared the fat boy, in the old lady's ear.

'Not one of my grand-da'aters?'

'Worser than that.'

'Worse than *that*, Joe!' said the old lady, who had thought this the extreme limit of human atrocity. 'Who was it, Joe? I insist upon knowing.'

The fat boy looked cautiously round, and having concluded his survey, shouted in the old lady's ear:

'Miss Rachael.'

'What!' said the old lady, in a shrill tone. 'Speak louder.'

'Miss Rachael,' roared the fat boy.

'My da'ater!'

The train of nods which the fat boy gave by way of assent, communicated a *blanc-mange* like motion to his fat cheeks.

'And she suffered him!' exclaimed the old lady.

A grin stole over the fat boy's features as he said:

'I see her a kissin' of him agin.'

If Mr Jingle, from his place of concealment, could have beheld the expression which the old lady's face assumed at this communication, the probability is that a sudden burst of laughter would have betrayed his close vicinity to the summer-house. He listened attentively. Fragments of angry sentences such as, 'Without my permission!'—'At her time of life'—'Miserable old 'ooman like me'—'Might have waited till I was dead,' and so forth, reached his ears; and then he heard the heels of the fat boy's boots crunching the gravel, as he retired and left the old lady alone.

It was a remarkable coincidence perhaps, but it was nevertheless a fact, that Mr Jingle within five minutes of his arrival at Manor Farm on the preceding night, had inwardly resolved to lay siege to the heart of the spinster aunt, without delay. He had observation enough to see, that his off-hand manner was by no means disagreeable to the fair object of his attack; and he had more than a strong suspicion that she possessed that most desirable of all requisites, a small independence. The imperative necessity of ousting his rival by some means or other, flashed quickly upon him, and he immediately resolved to adopt certain proceedings tending to that end and object, without a moment's delay. Fielding tells us that man is fire, and woman tow, and the Prince of Darkness sets a light to 'em. Mr Jingle knew that young men, to spinster aunts, are as lighted gas to gunpowder, and he determined to essay the effect of an explosion without loss of time.

Full of reflections upon this important decision, he crept from his place of concealment, and, under cover of the shrubs before mentioned, approached the house. Fortune seemed determined to favour his design. Mr Tupman and the rest of the gentlemen left the garden by the side gate just as he obtained a view of it; and the young ladies, he knew, had walked out alone, soon after breakfast. The coast was clear.

The breakfast-parlour door was partially open. He peeped in. The spinster aunt was knitting. He coughed; she looked up and smiled. Hesitation formed no part of Mr Alfred Jingle's character. He laid his finger on his lips mysteriously, walked in, and closed the door.

'Miss Wardle,' said Mr Jingle, with affected earnestness, 'forgive intrusion—short acquaintance—no time for ceremony—all discovered.'

'Sir!' said the spinster aunt, rather astonished by the unexpected apparition and somewhat doubtful of Mr Jingle's sanity.

'Hush!' said Mr Jingle, in a stage-whisper—'large boy—dumpling face—round eyes—rascal!' Here he shook his head expressively, and the spinster aunt trembled with agitation.

'I presume you allude to Joseph, sir?' said the lady, making an effort to appear composed.

'Yes, ma'am—damn that Joe!—treacherous dog, Joe—told the old lady—old lady furious—wild—raving—arbour—Tupman—kissing and hugging—all that sort of thing—eh, ma'am—eh?'

'Mr Jingle,' said the spinster aunt, 'if you come here, sir, to insult me—'

'Not at all—by no means,' replied the unabashed Mr Jingle;—'overheard the tale—came to warn you of your danger—tender my services—prevent the hubbub. Never mind—think it an insult—leave the room'—and he turned, as if to carry the threat into execution.

'What *shall* I do!' said the poor spinster, bursting into tears. 'My brother will be furious.'

'Of course he will,' said Mr Jingle pausing—'outrageous.'

'Oh, Mr Jingle, what *can* I say!' exclaimed the spinster aunt, in another flood of despair.

'Say he dreamt it,' replied Mr Jingle, coolly.

A ray of comfort darted across the mind of the spinster aunt at this suggestion. Mr Jingle perceived it, and followed up his advantage.

'Pooh, pooh!—nothing more easy—blackguard boy—lovely woman—fat boy horsewhipped—you believed—end of the matter—all comfortable.'

Whether the probability of escaping from the consequences of this ill-timed discovery was delightful to the spinster's feelings, or whether the hearing herself described as a 'lovely woman' softened the asperity of her grief, we know not. She blushed slightly, and cast a grateful look on Mr Jingle.

That insinuating gentleman sighed deeply, fixed his eyes on the spinster aunt's face for a couple of minutes, started melodramatically, and suddenly withdrew them.

'You seem unhappy, Mr Jingle,' said the lady, in a plaintive voice. 'May I show my gratitude for your kind interference, by inquiring into the cause, with a view, if possible, to its removal?'

'Ha!' exclaimed Mr Jingle, with another start—'removal! remove *my* unhappiness, and your love bestowed upon a man who is insensible to the blessing—who even now contemplates a design upon the affections of the niece of the creature who—but no; he is my friend; I will not expose his vices. Miss Wardle—farewell!' At the conclusion of this address, the most consecutive he was ever known to utter, Mr Jingle applied to his eyes the remnant of a handkerchief before noticed, and turned towards the door.

'Stay, Mr Jingle!' said the spinster aunt emphatically. 'You have made an allusion to Mr Tupman—explain it.'

'Never!' exclaimed Jingle, with a professional (*i.e.* theatrical) air. 'Never!' and, by way of showing that he had no desire to be questioned further, he drew a chair close to that of the spinster aunt and sat down.

'Mr Jingle,' said the aunt, 'I entreat—I implore you, if there is any dreadful mystery connected with Mr Tupman, reveal it.'

'Can I,' said Mr Jingle, fixing his eyes on the aunt's face—'can I see—lovely creature—sacrificed at the shrine—heartless avarice!' He appeared to be struggling with various conflicting emotions for a few seconds, and then said in a low voice —

'Tupman only wants your money.'

'The wretch!' exclaimed the spinster, with energetic indignation. (Mr Jingle's doubts were resolved. She *had* money.)

'More than that,' said Jingle—'loves another.'

'Another!' ejaculated the spinster. 'Who?'

'Short girl—black eyes—niece Emily.'

There was a pause.

Now, if there was one individual in the whole world, of whom the spinster aunt entertained a mortal and deep-rooted jealousy, it was this identical niece. The colour rushed over her face and neck, and she tossed her head in silence with an air of ineffable contempt. At last, biting her thin lips, and bridling up, she said —

'It can't be. I won't believe it.'

'Watch 'em,' said Jingle.

'I will,' said the aunt.

'Watch his looks.'

'I will.'

'His whispers.'

'I will.'

'He'll sit next her at table.'

'Let him.'

'He'll flatter her.'

'Let him.'

'He'll pay her every possible attention.'

'Let him.'

'And he'll cut you.'

'Cut *me!*' screamed the spinster aunt. '*He* cut *me;—will* he!' and she trembled with rage and disappointment.

'You will convince yourself?' said Jingle.

'I will.'

'You'll show your spirit?'

'I will.'

'You'll not have him afterwards?'

'Never.'

'You'll take somebody else?'

'Yes.'

'You shall.'

Mr Jingle fell on his knees, remained thereupon for five minutes thereafter; and rose the accepted lover of the spinster aunt: conditionally upon Mr Tupman's perjury being made clear and manifest.

The burden of proof lay with Mr Alfred Jingle; and he produced his evidence that very day at dinner. The spinster aunt could hardly believe her eyes. Mr Tracy Tupman was established at Emily's side, ogling, whispering, and smiling, in opposition to Mr Snodgrass. Not a word, not a look, not a glance, did he bestow upon his heart's pride of the evening before.

'Damn that boy!' thought old Mr Wardle to himself.—He had heard the story from his mother. 'Damn that boy! He *must* have been asleep. It's all imagination.'

'Traitor!' thought the spinster aunt. 'Dear Mr Jingle was not deceiving me. Ugh! how I hate the wretch!'

The following conversation may serve to explain to our readers this apparently unaccountable alteration of deportment on the part of Mr Tracy Tupman.

The time was evening; the scene the garden. There were two figures walking in a side path; one was rather short and stout; the other rather tall and slim. They were Mr Tupman and Mr Jingle. The stout figure commenced the dialogue.

'How did I do it?' he inquired.

'Splendid—capital—couldn't act better myself—you must repeat the part to-morrow—every evening, til further notice.'

'Does Rachael still wish it?'

'Of course—she don't like it—but must be done—avert suspicion—

afraid of her brother—says there's no help for it—only a few days more—when old folks blinded—crown your happiness.'

'Any message?'

'Love—best love—kindest regards—unalterable affection. Can I say anything for you?'

'My dear fellow,' replied the unsuspicious Mr Tupman, fervently grasping his 'friend's' hand—'carry my best love—say how hard I find it to dissemble—say anything that's kind: but add how sensible I am of the necessity of the suggestion she made to me, through you, this morning. Say I applaud her wisdom and admire her discretion.'

'I will. Anything more?'

'Nothing; only add how ardently I long for the time when I may call her mine, and all dissimulation may be unnecessary.'

'Certainly, certainly. Anything more?'

'Oh, my friend!' said poor Mr Tupman, again grasping the hand of his companion, 'receive my warmest thanks for your disinterested kindness; and forgive me if I have ever, even in thought, done you the injustice of supposing that you *could* stand in my way. My dear friend, can I ever repay you?'

'Don't talk of it,' replied Mr Jingle. He stopped short, as if suddenly recollecting something, and said—'By the bye—can't spare ten pounds, can you?—very particular purpose—pay you in three days.'

'I dare say I can,' replied Mr Tupman, in the fulness of his heart. 'Three days, you say?'

'Only three days—all over then—no more difficulties.'

Mr Tupman counted the money into his companion's hand, and he dropped it piece by piece into his pocket, as they walked towards the house.

'Be careful,' said Mr Jingle—'not a look.'

'Not a wink,' said Mr Tupman.

'Not a syllable.'

'Not a whisper.'

'All your attentions to the niece—rather rude, than otherwise, to the aunt—only way of deceiving the old ones.'

'I'll take care,' said Mr Tupman aloud.

'And *I'll* take care,' said Mr Jingle internally; and they entered the house.

The scene of that afternoon was repeated that evening, and on the three afternoons and evenings next ensuing. On the fourth, the host was in high spirits, for he had satisfied himself that there was no ground for the charge against Mr Tupman. So was Mr Tupman, for Mr Jingle had told him that his affair would soon be brought to a crisis. So was Mr Pickwick, for he was seldom otherwise. So was not Mr Snodgrass, for he had grown jealous of Mr Tupman. So was the old lady, for she had been winning at whist. So were Mr Jingle and Miss Wardle, for reasons of sufficient importance in this eventful history to be narrated in another chapter.

The supper was ready laid, the chairs were drawn round the table, bottles, jugs, and glasses were arranged upon the sideboard, and everything betokened the approach of the most convivial period in the whole four-and-twenty hours.

'Where's Rachael?' said Mr Wardle.

'Ay, and Jingle?' added Mr Pickwick.

'Dear me,' said the host, 'I wonder I haven't missed him before. Why, I don't think I've heard his voice for two hours at least. Emily, my dear, ring the bell.'

The bell was rung, and the fat boy appeared.

'Where's Miss Rachael?' He couldn't say.

'Where's Mr Jingle, then?' He didn't know.

Everybody looked surprised. It was late—past eleven o'clock. Mr Tupman laughed in his sleeve. They were loitering somewhere, talking about *him*. Ha, ha! capital notion that—funny.

'Never mind,' said Wardle, after a short pause. 'They'll turn up presently, I dare say. I never wait supper for anybody.'

'Excellent rule, that,' said Mr Pickwick, 'admirable.'

'Pray, sit down,' said the host.

'Certainly' said Mr Pickwick: and down they sat.

There was a gigantic round of cold beef on the table, and Mr Pickwick was supplied with a plentiful portion of it. He had raised his fork to his lips, and was on the very point of opening his mouth for the reception of a piece of beef, when the hum of many voices suddenly arose in the kitchen. He paused, and laid down his fork. Mr Wardle paused too, and insensibly released his hold of the carving-knife, which remained inserted in the beef. He looked at Mr Pickwick. Mr Pickwick looked at him.

Heavy footsteps were heard in the passage; the parlour door was suddenly burst open; and the man who had cleaned Mr Pickwick's boots on his first arrival, rushed into the room, followed by the fat boy, and all the domestics.

'What the devil's the meaning of this?' exclaimed the host.

'The kitchen chimney ain't a-fire, is it, Emma?' inquired the old lady.

'Lor, grandma! No,' screamed both the young ladies.

'What's the matter?' roared the master of the house.

The man gasped for breath, and faintly ejaculated —

'They ha' gone, Mas'r!—gone right clean off, sir!' (At this juncture Mr Tupman was observed to lay down his knife and fork, and to turn very pale.)

'Who's gone?' said Mr Wardle, fiercely.

'Mus'r Jingle and Miss Rachael, in a po'-chay, from Blue Lion, Muggleton. I was there; but I couldn't stop 'em; so I run off to tell'ee.'

'I paid his expenses!' said Mr Tupman, jumping up frantically. 'He's got ten pounds of mine!—stop him!—he's swindled me!—I won't bear it!—I'll have justice, Pickwick!—I won't stand it!' and with sundry incoherent exclamations of the like nature, the unhappy gentleman spun round and round the apartment, in a transport of frenzy.

'Lord preserve us!' ejaculated Mr Pickwick, eyeing the extraordinary gestures of his friend with terrified surprise. 'He's gone mad! What shall we do!'

'Do!' said the stout old host, who regarded only the last words of the sentence. 'Put the horse in the gig! I'll get a chaise at the Lion, and follow 'em instantly. Where'—he exclaimed, as the man ran out to execute the commission—'Where's that villain Joe?'

'Here I am; but I han't a willin,' replied a voice. It was the fat boy's.

'Let me get at him, Pickwick,' cried Wardle, as he rushed at the ill-starred youth. 'He was bribed by that scoundrel, Jingle, to put me on a wrong scent, by telling a cock-and-bull story of my sister and your friend Tupman!' (Here Mr Tupman sank into a chair.) 'Let me get at him!'

'Don't let him!' screamed all the women, above whose exclamations the blubbering of the fat boy was distinctly audible.

'I won't be held!' cried the old man. 'Mr Winkle, take your hands off. Mr Pickwick, let me go, sir!'

It was a beautiful sight, in that moment of turmoil and confusion, to behold the placid and philosophical expression of Mr Pickwick's face, albeit somewhat flushed with exertion, as he stood with his arms firmly clasped round the extensive waist of their corpulent host, thus restraining the impetuosity of his passion, while the fat boy was scratched, and pulled, and pushed from the room by all the females congregated therein. He had no sooner released his hold, than the man entered to announce that the gig was ready.

'Don't let him go alone!' screamed the females. 'He'll kill somebody!'

'I'll go with him,' said Mr Pickwick.

'You're a good fellow, Pickwick,' said the host, grasping his hand. 'Emma, give Mr Pickwick a shawl to tie round his neck—make haste. Look after your grandmother, girls; she has fainted away. Now then, are you ready?'

Mr Pickwick's mouth and chin having been hastily enveloped in a large shawl: his hat having been put on his head, and his great coat thrown over his arm, he replied in the affirmative.

They jumped into the gig. 'Give her her head, Tom,' cried the host; and away they went, down the narrow lanes: jolting in and out of the cart-ruts, and bumping up against the hedges on either side, as if they would go to pieces every moment.

'How much are they a-head?' shouted Wardle, as they drove up to the door of the Blue Lion, round which a little crowd had collected, late as it was.

'Not above three-quarters of an hour,' was everybody's reply.

'Chaise-and-four directly!—out with 'em! Put up the gig afterwards.'

'Now, boys!' cried the landlord—'chaise-and-four out—make haste—look alive there!'

Away ran the hostlers, and the boys. The lanterns glimmered, as the men ran to and fro; the horses' hoofs clattered on the uneven paving of the yard; the chaise rumbled as it was drawn out of the coach-house; and all was noise and bustle.

'Now then!—is that chaise coming out to-night?' cried Wardle.

'Coming down the yard now, sir,' replied the hostler.

Out came the chaise—in went the horses—on sprang the boys—in got the travellers.

'Mind—the seven-mile stage in less than half an hour!' shouted Wardle.

'Off with you!'

The boys applied whip and spur, the waiters shouted, the hostlers cheered, and away they went, fast and furiously.

'Pretty situation,' thought Mr Pickwick, when he had had a moment's time for reflection. 'Pretty situation for the General Chairman of the Pickwick Club. Damp chaise—strange horses—fifteen miles an hour—and twelve o'clock at night!'

For the first three or four miles, not a word was spoken by either of the gentlemen, each being too much immersed in his own reflections to address any observations to his companion. When they had gone over that much ground, however, and the horses getting thoroughly warmed began to do their work in really good style, Mr Pickwick became too much exhilarated with the rapidity of the motion, to remain any longer perfectly mute.

'We're sure to catch them, I think,' said he.

'Hope so,' replied his companion.

'Fine night,' said Mr Pickwick, looking up at the moon, which was shining brightly.

'So much the worse,' returned Wardle; 'for they'll have had all the advantage of the moonlight to get the start of us, and we shall lose it. It will have gone down in another hour.'

'It will be rather unpleasant going at this rate in the dark, won't it?' inquired Mr Pickwick.

'I dare say it will,' replied his friend drily.

Mr Pickwick's temporary excitement began to sober down a little, as he reflected upon the inconveniences and dangers of the expedition in which he had so thoughtlessly embarked. He was roused by a loud shouting of the post-boy on the leader.

'Yo-yo-yo-yo-yoe!' went the first boy.

'Yo-yo-yo-yoe!' went the second.

'Yo-yo-yo-yoe!' chimed in old Wardle himself, most lustily, with his head and half his body out of the coach window.

'Yo-yo-yo-yoe!' shouted Mr Pickwick, taking up the burden of the cry, though he had not the slightest notion of its meaning or object. And amidst the yo-yoing of the whole four, the chaise stopped.

'What's the matter?' inquired Mr Pickwick.

'There's a gate here,' replied old Wardle. 'We shall hear something of the fugitives.'

After a lapse of five minutes, consumed in incessant knocking and shouting, an old man in his shirt and trousers emerged from the turnpike-house, and opened the gate.

'How long is it since a post-chaise went through here?' inquired Mr Wardle.

'How long?'

'Ah!'

'Why, I don't rightly know. It worn't a long time ago, nor it worn't a short time ago—just between the two, perhaps.'

'Has any chaise been by at all?'

'Oh, yes, there's been a shay by.'

'How long ago, my friend,' interposed Mr Pickwick, 'an hour?'

'Ah, I dare say it might be,' replied the man.

'Or two hours?' inquired the post-boy on the wheeler.

'Well, I shouldn't wonder if it was,' returned the old man doubtfully.

'Drive on, boys,' cried the testy old gentleman; 'don't waste any more time with that old idiot!'

'Idiot!' exclaimed the old man with a grin, as he stood in the middle of the road with the gate half-closed, watching the chaise which rapidly diminished in the increasing distance. 'No—not much o' that either; you've lost ten minutes here, and gone away as wise as you came, arter all. If every man on the line as has a guinea give him, earns it half as well, you won't catch t'other shay this side Mich'lmas, old short-and-fat.' And with another prolonged grin, the old man closed the gate, re-entered his house, and bolted the door after him.

Meanwhile the chaise proceeded, without any slackening of pace, towards the conclusion of the stage. The moon, as Wardle had foretold, was rapidly on the wane; large tiers of dark heavy clouds, which had been gradually overspreading the sky for some time past, now formed one black mass over head; and large drops of rain which pattered every now and then against the windows of the chaise, seemed to warn the travellers of the rapid approach of a stormy night. The wind, too, which was directly against them, swept in furious gusts down the narrow road, and howled dismally through the trees which skirted the pathway. Mr Pickwick drew his coat closer about him, coiled himself more snugly up into the corner of the chaise, and fell into a sound sleep, from which he was only awakened by the stopping of the vehicle, the sound of the hostler's bell, and a loud cry of 'Horses on directly!'

But here another delay occurred. The boys were sleeping with such mysterious soundness, that it took five minutes a-piece to wake them. The hostler had somehow or other mislaid the key of the stable, and even when that was found, two sleepy helpers put the wrong harness on the wrong horses, and the whole process of harnessing had to be gone through afresh. Had Mr Pickwick been alone, these multiplied obstacles would have completely put an end to the pursuit at once, but old Wardle was not to be so easily daunted; and he laid about him with such hearty good-will, cuffing this man, and pushing that; strapping a buckle here, and taking in a link there, that the chaise was ready in a much shorter time than could reasonably have been expected, under so many difficulties.

They resumed their journey; and certainly the prospect before them was by no means encouraging. The stage was fifteen miles long, the night was dark, the wind high, and the rain pouring in torrents. It was impossible to make any great way against such obstacles united: it was hard upon one o'clock already; and nearly two hours were consumed in getting to the end of the stage. Here, however, an object presented itself, which rekindled their hopes, and re-animated their drooping spirits.

'When did this chaise come in?' cried old Wardle, leaping out of his own vehicle, and pointing to one covered with wet mud, which was standing in the yard.

'Not a quarter of an hour ago, sir,' replied the hostler, to whom the question was addressed.

'Lady and gentleman?' inquired Wardle, almost breathless with impatience.

'Yes, sir.'

'Tall gentleman—dress coat—long legs—thin body?'

'Yes, sir.'

'Elderly lady—thin face—rather skinny—eh?'

'Yes, sir.'

'By heavens, it's the couple, Pickwick,' exclaimed the old gentleman.

'Would have been here before,' said the hostler, 'but they broke a trace.'

'It is!' said Wardle, 'it is by Jove! Chaise and four instantly! We shall catch them yet, before they reach the next stage. A guinea a-piece, boys—be alive there—bustle about—there's good fellows.'

And with such admonitions as these, the old gentleman ran up and down the yard, and bustled to and fro, in a state of excitement which communicated itself to Mr Pickwick also; and under the influence of which, that gentleman got himself into complicated entanglements with harness, and mixed up with horses and wheels of chaises, in the most surprising manner, firmly believing that by so doing he was materially forwarding the preparations for their resuming their journey.

'Jump in—jump in!' cried old Wardle, climbing into the chaise, pulling up the steps, and slamming the door after him. 'Come along! Make haste!' And before Mr Pickwick knew precisely what he was about, he felt himself forced in at the other door, by one pull from the old gentleman, and one push from the hostler; and off they were again.

'Ah! we *are* moving now,' said the old gentleman exultingly. They were indeed, as was sufficiently testified to Mr Pickwick, by his constant collisions either with the hard woodwork of the chaise, or the body of his companion.

'Hold up!' said the stout old Mr Wardle, as Mr Pickwick dived head foremost into his capacious waistcoat.

'I never did feel such a jolting in my life,' said Mr Pickwick.

'Never mind,' replied his companion, 'it will soon be over. Steady, steady.'

Mr Pickwick planted himself into his own corner, as firmly as he could; and on whirled the chaise faster than ever.

They had travelled in this way about three miles, when Mr Wardle, who had been looking out of the window for two or three minutes, suddenly drew in his face, covered with splashes, and exclaimed in breathless eagerness —

'Here they are!'

Mr Pickwick thrust his head out of his window. Yes: there was a chaise and four, a short distance before them, dashing along at full gallop.

'Go on, go on,' almost shrieked the old gentleman. 'Two guineas a-piece, boys—don't let 'em gain on us—keep it up—keep it up.'

The horses in the first chaise started on at their utmost speed; and those in Mr Wardle's galloped furiously behind them.

'I see his head,' exclaimed the choleric old man; 'Damme, I see his head.'

'So do I,' said Mr Pickwick, 'that's he.'

Mr Pickwick was not mistaken. The countenance of Mr Jingle, completely coated with mud thrown up by the wheels, was plainly discernible at the window of his chaise; and the motion of his arm, which was waving violently towards the postilions, denoted that he was encouraging them to increased exertion.

The interest was intense. Fields, trees, and hedges, seemed to rush past them with the velocity of a whirlwind, so rapid was the pace at which they tore along. They were close by the side of the first chaise. Jingle's voice could be plainly heard, even above the din of the wheels, urging on the boys. Old Mr Wardle foamed with rage and excitement. He roared out scoundrels and villains by the dozen, clenched his fist and shook it expressively at the object of his indignation; but Mr Jingle only answered with a contemptuous smile, and replied to his menaces by a shout of triumph, as his horses, answering the increased application of whip and spur, broke into a faster gallop, and left the pursuers behind.

Mr Pickwick had just drawn in his head, and Mr Wardle, exhausted with shouting, had done the same, when a tremendous jolt threw them forward against the front of the vehicle. There was a sudden bump—a loud crash—away rolled a wheel, and over went the chaise.

After a very few seconds of bewilderment and confusion, in which nothing but the plunging of horses and breaking of glass could be made out, Mr Pickwick felt himself violently pulled out from among the ruins of the chaise; and as soon as he had gained his feet, and extricated his head from the skirts of his great coat, which materially impeded the usefulness of his spectacles, the full disaster of the case met his view.

Old Mr Wardle without a hat, and his clothes torn in several places, stood by his side, and the fragments of the chaise lay scattered at their feet. The post-boys, who had succeeded in cutting the traces, were standing, disfigured with mud and disordered by hard riding, by the horses' heads. About a hundred yards in advance was the other chaise, which had pulled up on hearing the crash. The postilions, each with a broad grin convulsing his countenance, were viewing the adverse party from their saddles, and Mr Jingle was contemplating the wreck from the coach-window, with evident satisfaction. The day was just breaking, and the whole scene was rendered perfectly visible by the grey light of the morning.

'Hallo!' shouted the shameless Jingle, 'anybody damaged?—elderly gentlemen—no light weights—dangerous work—very.'

'You're a rascal!' roared Wardle.

'Ha! ha!' replied Jingle; and then he added, with a knowing wink, and a jerk of the thumb towards the interior of the chaise—'I say—she's very well—desires her compliments—begs you won't trouble yourself—love to *Tuppy*—won't you get up behind?—drive on, boys.'

The postilions resumed their proper attitudes, and away rattled the chaise, Mr Jingle fluttering in derision a white handkerchief from the coach-window.

Nothing in the whole adventure, not even the upset, had disturbed the calm and equable current of Mr Pickwick's temper. The villainy, however, which could first borrow money of his faithful follower, and then abbreviate his name to 'Tuppy,' was more than he could patiently bear. He drew his breath hard, and coloured up to the very tips of his spectacles, as he said, slowly and emphatically —

'If ever I meet that man again, I'll—'

'Yes, yes,' interrupted Wardle, 'that's all very well: but while we stand talking here, they'll get their licence, and be married in London.'

Mr Pickwick paused, bottled up his vengeance, and corked it down.

'How far is it to the next stage?' inquired Mr Wardle, of one of the boys.

'Six mile, a'nt it, Tom?'

'Rayther better.'

'Rayther better nor six mile, sir.'

'Can't be helped,' said Wardle, 'we must walk it, Pickwick.'

'No help for it,' replied that truly great man.

So sending forward one of the boys on horseback, to procure a fresh chaise and horses, and leaving the other behind to take care of the broken one, Mr Pickwick and Mr Wardle set manfully forward on the walk, first tying their shawls round their necks, and slouching down their hats to escape as much as possible from the deluge of rain, which after a slight cessation had again begun to pour heavily down.

There are in London several old inns, once the head-quarters of celebrated coaches in the days when coaches performed their journeys in a graver and more solemn manner than they do in these times; but which have now degenerated into little more than the abiding and booking places of country waggons. The reader would look in vain for any of these ancient hostelries, among the Golden Crosses and Bull and Mouths, which rear their stately fronts in the improved streets of London. If he would light upon any of these old places, he must direct his steps to the obscurer quarters of the town; and there in some secluded nooks he will find several, still standing with a kind of gloomy sturdiness, amidst the modern innovations which surround them.

In the Borough especially, there still remain some half dozen old inns, which have preserved their external features unchanged, and which have escaped alike the rage for public improvement, and the encroachments of private speculation. Great, rambling, queer, old places they are, with galleries, and passages, and staircases, wide enough and antiquated enough to furnish materials for a hundred ghost stories, supposing we should ever be reduced to the lamentable necessity of inventing any, and that the world should exist long enough to exhaust the innumerable veracious legends connected with old London Bridge, and its adjacent neighbourhood on the Surrey side.

It was in the yard of one of these inns—of no less celebrated a one than the White Hart—that a man was busily employed in brushing the dirt off a pair of boots, early on the morning succeeding the events narrated in the last chapter. He was habited in a coarse-striped waistcoat, with black calico sleeves, and blue glass buttons; drab breeches and leggings. A bright red handkerchief was wound in a very loose and unstudied style round his neck, and an old white hat was carelessly thrown on one side of his head. There were two rows of boots before him, one cleaned and the other dirty, and at every addition he made to the clean row, he paused from his work, and contemplated its results with evident satisfaction.

The yard presented none of that bustle and activity which are the usual characteristics of a large coach inn. Three or four lumbering waggons, each with a pile of goods beneath its ample canopy, about the height of the second-floor window of an ordinary house, were stowed away beneath a lofty roof which extended over one end of the yard; and another, which was probably to commence its journey that morning, was drawn out into the open space. A double tier of bedroom galleries, with old clumsy balustrades, ran round two sides of the straggling area, and a double row of bells to correspond, sheltered from the weather by a little sloping roof, hung over the door leading to the bar and coffee-room. Two or three gigs and chaise-carts were wheeled up under different little sheds and pent-houses; and the occasional heavy tread of a cart-horse, or rattling of a chain at the further end of the yard, announced to anybody who cared about the matter, that the stable lay in that direction. When we add that a few boys in smock frocks were lying asleep on heavy packages, woolpacks, and other articles that were scattered about on heaps of straw, we have described as fully as need be the general appearance of the yard of the White Hart Inn, High Street, Borough, on the particular morning in question.

A loud ringing of one of the bells, was followed by the appearance of a smart chambermaid in the upper sleeping gallery, who, after tapping at one of the doors, and receiving a request from within, called over the balustrades —

'Sam!'

'Hallo,' replied the man with the white hat.

'Number twenty-two wants his boots.'

'Ask number twenty-two, wether he'll have 'em now, or wait till he gets 'em,' was the reply.

'Come, don't be a fool, Sam,' said the girl coaxingly, 'the gentleman wants his boots directly.'

'Well, you *are* a nice young 'ooman for a musical party, you are,' said the boot-cleaner. 'Look at these here boots—eleven pair o' boots; and one shoe as b'longs to number six, with the wooden leg. The eleven boots is to be called at half-past eight and the shoe at nine. Who's number twenty-two, that's to put all the others out? No, no; reg'lar rotation, as Jack Ketch said, wen he tied the men up. Sorry to keep you a waitin', sir, but I'll attend to you directly.'

Saying which, the man in the white hat set to work upon a top-boot with increased assiduity.

There was another loud ring; and the bustling old landlady of the White Hart made her appearance in the opposite gallery.

'Sam,' cried the landlady, 'where's that lazy, idle—why, Sam—oh, there you are; why don't you answer?'

'Wouldn't be gen-teel to answer, 'till you'd done talking,' replied Sam, gruffly.

'Here, clean these shoes for number seventeen directly, and take 'em to private sitting-room, number five, first floor.'

The landlady flung a pair of lady's shoes into the yard, and bustled away.

'Number 5,' said Sam, as he picked up the shoes, and taking a piece of chalk from his pocket, made a memorandum of their destination on the soles—'Lady's shoes and private sittin' room! I suppose *she* didn't come in the waggin.'

'She came in early this morning,' cried the girl, who was still leaning over the railing of the gallery, 'with a gentleman in a hackney-coach, and it's him as wants his boots, and you'd better do 'em, that's all about it.'

'Vy didn't you say so before?' said Sam, with great indignation, singling out the boots in question from the heap before him. 'For all I know'd he vas on o' the regular three-pennies. Private room! and a lady too! If he's anything of a gen'lm'n, he's vorth a shillin' a day, let alone the arrands.'

Stimulated by this inspiring reflection, Mr Samuel brushed away with such hearty good will, that in a few minutes the boots and shoes, with a polish which would have struck envy to the soul of the amiable Mr Warren (for they used Day and Martin at the White Hart), had arrived at the door of number five.

'Come in,' said a man's voice, in reply to Sam's rap at the door.

Sam made his best bow, and stepped into the presence of a lady and gentleman seated at breakfast. Having officiously deposited the gentleman's boots right and left at his feet, and the lady's shoes right and left at hers, he backed towards the door.

'Boots,' said the gentleman.

'Sir,' said Sam, closing the door, and keeping his hand on the knob of the lock.

'Do you know—what's a-name—Doctors' Commons?'

'Yes, sir.'

'Where is it?'

'Paul's Church-yard, sir; low archway on the carriage-side bookseller's at one corner, hot-el on the other, and two porters in the middle as touts for licences.'

'Touts for licences!' said the gentleman.

'Touts for licences,' replied Sam. 'Two coves in vhite aprons—touches their hats wen you walk in—'Licence, sir, licence?' Queer sort, them, and their mas'rs too, sir—Old Baily Proctors—and no mistake.'

'What do they do?' inquired the gentleman.

'Do! *You*, sir! That a'nt the wost on it, neither. They puts things into old gen'lm'n's heads as they never dreamed of. My father, sir, wos a coachman. A widower he wos, and fat enough for anything—uncommon fat, to be sure. His missus dies, and leaves him four hundred pound. Down he goes to the Commons, to see the lawyer and draw the blunt—wery smart—top boots on—nosegay in his button-hole—broad-brimmed tile—green shawl—quite the gen'lm'n. Goes through the archvay, thinking how he should inwest the money—up comes the touter, touches his hat—"Licence, sir, licence?'—"What's that?" says my father.—"Licence, sir," says he.—"What licence?" says my father.—"Marriage licence," says the touter.—"Dash my veskit," says my father, "I never thought o' that."—"I think you wants one, sir," says the touter. My father pulls up, and thinks abit—"No," says he, "damme, I'm too old, b'sides I'm a many sizes too large," says he.—"Not a bit on it, sir," says the touter.—"Think not?" says my father.—"I'm sure not," says he; "we married a gen'lm'n twice your size, last Monday."—"Did you, though," said my father.—"To be sure we did," says the touter, "you're a babby to him—this way, sir—this way!"—and sure enough my father walks arter him, like a tame monkey behind a horgan, into a little back office, vere a feller sat among dirty papers and tin boxes, making believe he was busy. "Pray take a seat, vile I makes out the affidavit, sir," says the lawyer.—"Thankee, sir," says my father, and down he sat, and stared with all his eyes, and his mouth vide open, at the names on the boxes. "What's your name, sir," says the lawyer.—"Tony Weller," says my father.—"Parish?" says the lawyer. "Belle Savage," says my father; for he stopped there wen he drove up, and he know'd nothing about parishes, *he* didn't.—"And what's the lady's name?" says the lawyer. My father was struck all of a heap. "Blessed if I know," says he.—"Not know!" says the lawyer.—"No more nor you do," says my father, "can't I put that in arterwards?"—"Impossible!" says the lawyer.—"Wery well," says my father, after he'd thought a moment, "put down Mrs Clarke."—"What Clarke?" says the lawyer, dipping his pen in the ink.—"Susan Clarke, Markis o' Granby, Dorking," says my father; "she'll have me, if I ask. I des-say—I never said nothing to her, but she'll have me, I know." The licence was made out, and she *did* have him, and what's more she's got him now; and *I* never had any of the four hundred pound, worse luck. Beg your pardon, sir,' said Sam, when he had concluded, 'but wen I gets on this here grievance, I runs on like a new barrow vit the wheel greased.' Having said which, and having paused for an instant to see whether he was wanted for anything more, Sam left the room.

'Half-past nine—just the time—off at once;' said the gentleman, whom we need hardly introduce as Mr Jingle.

'Time—for what?' said the spinster aunt, coquettishly.

'Licence, dearest of angels—give notice at the church—call you mine, to-morrow'—said Mr Jingle, and he squeezed the spinster aunt's hand.

'The licence!' said Rachael, blushing.

'The licence,' repeated Mr Jingle —

'In hurry, post-haste for a licence,
In hurry, ding dong I come back.'

'How you run on,' said Rachael.

'Run on—nothing to the hours, days, weeks, months, years, when we're united—*run* on—they'll fly on—bolt—mizzle—steam-engine—thousand-horse power—nothing to it.'

'Can't—can't we be married before to-morrow morning?' inquired Rachael.

'Impossible—can't be—notice at the church—leave the licence to-day—ceremony come off to-morrow.'

'I am so terrified, lest my brother should discover us!' said Rachael.

'Discover—nonsense—too much shaken by the breakdown—besides—extreme caution—gave up the post-chaise—walked on—took a hackney coach—came to the Borough—last place in the world that he'd look in—ha! ha!—capital notion that—very.'

'Don't be long,' said the spinster affectionately, as Mr Jingle stuck the pinched-up hat on his head.

'Long away from *you*?—Cruel charmer,' and Mr Jingle skipped playfully up to the spinster aunt, imprinted a chaste kiss upon her lips, and danced out of the room.

'Dear man!' said the spinster as the door closed after him.

'Rum old girl,' said Mr Jingle, as he walked down the passage.

It is painful to reflect upon the perfidy of our species; and we will not, therefore, pursue the thread of Mr Jingle's meditations, as he wended his way to Doctors' Commons. It will be sufficient for our purpose to relate, that escaping the snares of the dragons in white aprons, who guard the entrance to that enchanted region, he reached the Vicar General's office in safety, and having procured a highly flattering address on parchment, from the Archbishop of Canterbury, to his 'trusty and well-beloved Alfred Jingle and Rachael Wardle, greeting,' he carefully deposited the mystic document in his pocket, and retraced his steps in triumph to the Borough.

He was yet on his way to the White Hart, when two plump gentlemen and one thin one entered the yard, and looked round in search of some authorised person of whom they could make a few inquiries. Mr Samuel Weller happened to be at that moment engaged in burnishing a pair of painted tops, the personal property of a farmer who was refreshing himself with a slight lunch of two or three pounds of cold beef and a pot or two of porter, after the fatigues of the Borough market; and to him the thin gentleman straightway advanced.

'My friend,' said the thin gentleman.

'You're one o' the adwice gratis order,' thought Sam, 'or you wouldn't be so werry fond o' me all at once.' But he only said—'Well, sir.'

'My friend,' said the thin gentleman, with a conciliatory hem—'Have you got many people stopping here, now? Pretty busy. Eh?'

Sam stole a look at the inquirer. He was a little high-dried man, with a dark squeezed-up face, and small restless black eyes, that kept winking and twinkling on each side of his little inquisitive nose, as if they were playing a perpetual game of peep-bo with that feature. He was dressed all in black, with boots as shiny as his eyes, a low white neckcloth, and a clean shirt with a frill to it. A gold watch-chain, and seals, depended from his fob. He carried his black kid gloves *in* his hands, not *on* them; and as he spoke, thrust his wrists beneath his coat-tails, with the air of a man who was in the habit of propounding some regular posers.

'Pretty busy, eh?' said the little man.

'Oh, werry well, sir,' replied Sam, 'we shan't be bankrupts, and we shan't make our fort'ns. We eats our biled mutton without capers, and don't care for horse-radish wen ve can get beef.'

'Ah,' said the little man, 'you're a wag, a'nt you?'

'My eldest brother was troubled with that complaint,' said Sam; 'it may be catching—I used to sleep with him.'

'This is a curious old house of yours,' said the little man, looking round him.

'If you'd sent word you was a coming, we'd ha' had it repaired;' replied the imperturbable Sam.

The little man seemed rather baffled by these several repulses and a short consultation took place between him and the two plump gentlemen. At its conclusion, the little man took a pinch of snuff from an oblong silver box, and was apparently on the point of renewing the conversation, when one of the plump gentlemen, who in addition to a benevolent countenance, possessed a pair of spectacles, and a pair of black gaiters, interfered —

'The fact of the matter is,' said the benevolent gentleman, 'that my friend here (pointing to the other plump gentleman) will give you half a guinea, if you'll answer one or two—'

'Now, my dear sir—my dear sir,' said the little man, 'pray, allow me—my dear sir, the very first principle to be observed in these cases, is this: if you place a matter in the hands of a professional man, you must in no way interfere in the progress of the business; you must repose implicit confidence in him. Really, Mr (he turned to the other plump gentleman, and said)—I forget your friend's name.'

'Pickwick,' said Mr Wardle, for it was no other than that jolly personage.

'Ah, Pickwick—really Mr Pickwick, my dear sir, excuse me—I shall be happy to receive any private suggestions of yours, as *amicus curioe*, but you must see the impropriety of your interfering with my conduct in this case, with such an *ad captandum* argument as the offer of half a guinea. Really, my dear sir, really;' and the little man took an argumentative pinch of snuff, and looked very profound.

'My only wish, sir,' said Mr Pickwick, 'was to bring this very unpleasant matter to as speedy a close as possible.'

'Quite right—quite right,' said the little man.

'With which view,' continued Mr Pickwick, 'I made use of the argument which my experience of men has taught me is the most likely to succeed in any case.'

'Ay, ay,' said the little man, 'very good, very good, indeed; but you should have suggested it to *me*. My dear sir, I'm quite certain you cannot be ignorant of the extent of confidence which must be placed in professional men. If any authority can be necessary on such a point, my dear sir, let me refer you to the well-known case in Barnwell and—'

'Never mind George Barnwell,' interrupted Sam, who had remained a wondering listener during this short colloquy; 'every body knows what sort of a case his was, tho' it's always been my opinion, mind you, that the young 'ooman deserved scragging a precious sight more than he did. Hows'ever, that's neither here nor there. You want me to except of half a guinea. Werry well, I'm agreeable: I can't say no fairer than that, can I, sir? (Mr Pickwick smiled.) Then the next question is, what the devil do you want with me, as the man said wen he see the ghost?'

'We want to know—' said Mr Wardle.

'Now, my dear sir—my dear sir,' interposed the busy little man.

Mr Wardle shrugged his shoulders, and was silent.

'We want to know,' said the little man solemnly; 'and we ask the question of you, in order that we may not awaken apprehensions inside—we want to know who you've got in this house, at present?'

'Who there is in the house!' said Sam, in whose mind the inmates were always represented by that particular article of their costume, which came under his immediate superintendence. 'There's a vooden leg in number six; there's a pair of Hessians in thirteen; there's two pair of halves in the commercial; there's these here painted tops in the snuggery inside the bar; and five more tops in the coffee-room.'

'Nothing more?' said the little man.

'Stop a bit,' replied Sam, suddenly recollecting himself. 'Yes; there's a pair of Wellingtons a good deal worn, and a pair o' lady's shoes, in number five.'

'What sort of shoes?' hastily inquired Wardle, who, together with Mr Pickwick, had been lost in bewilderment at the singular catalogue of visitors.

'Country make,' replied Sam.

'Any maker's name?'

'Brown.'

'Where of?'

'Muggleton.'

'It *is* them,' exclaimed Wardle. 'By heavens, we've found them.'

'Hush!' said Sam. 'The Wellington has gone to Doctors' Commons.'

'No,' said the little man.

'Yes, for a licence.'

'We're in time,' exclaimed Wardle. 'Show us the room; not a moment is to be lost.'

'Pray, my dear sir—pray,' said the little man; 'caution, caution.' He drew from his pocket a red silk purse, and looked very hard at Sam as he drew out a sovereign.

Sam grinned expressively.

'Show us into the room at once, without announcing us,' said the little man, 'and it's yours.'

Sam threw the painted tops into a corner, and led the way through a dark passage, and up a wide staircase. He paused at the end of a second passage, and held out his hand.

'Here it is,' whispered the attorney, as he deposited the money in the hand of their guide.

The man stepped forward for a few paces, followed by the two friends and their legal adviser. He stopped at a door.

'Is this the room?' murmured the little gentleman.

Sam nodded assent.

Old Wardle opened the door; and the whole three walked into the room just as Mr Jingle, who had that moment returned, had produced the licence to the spinster aunt.

The spinster uttered a loud shriek, and, throwing herself in a chair, covered her face with her hands. Mr Jingle crumpled up the licence, and thrust it into his coat-pocket. The unwelcome visitors advanced into the middle of the room.

'You—you are a nice rascal, arn't you?' exclaimed Wardle, breathless with passion.

'My dear sir, my dear sir,' said the little man, laying his hat on the table, 'Pray, consider—pray. Defamation of character: action for damages. Calm yourself, my dear sir, pray—'

'How dare you drag my sister from my house?' said the old man.

Ay—ay—very good,' said the little gentleman, 'you may ask that. How dare you, sir?—eh, sir?'

'Who the devil are you?' inquired Mr Jingle, in so fierce a tone, that the little gentleman involuntarily fell back a step or two.

'Who is he, you scoundrel,' interposed Wardle. 'He's my lawyer, Mr Perker, of Gray's Inn. Perker, I'll have this fellow prosecuted—indicted—I'll—I'll—I'll ruin him. And you,' continued Mr Wardle, turning abruptly round to his sister, 'you, Rachael, at a time of life when you ought to know better, what do *you* mean by running away with a vagabond, disgracing your family, and making yourself miserable. Get on your bonnet, and come back. Call a hackney-coach there, directly, and bring this lady's bill, d'ye hear—d'ye hear?'

'Cert'nly, sir,' replied Sam, who had answered Wardle's violent ringing of the bell with a degree of celerity which must have appeared marvellous to anybody who didn't know that his eye had been applied to the outside of the keyhole during the whole interview.

'Get on your bonnet,' repeated Wardle.

'Do nothing of the kind,' said Jingle. 'Leave the room, sir—no business here—lady's free to act as she pleases—more than one-and-twenty.'

'More than one-and-twenty!' ejaculated Wardle, contemptuously. 'More than one-and-forty!'

'I a'nt' said the spinster aunt, her indignation getting the better of her determination to faint.

'You are,' replied Wardle, 'you're fifty if you're an hour.'

Here the spinster aunt uttered a loud shriek, and became senseless.

'A glass of water,' said the humane Mr Pickwick, summoning the landlady.

'A *glass* of water!' said the passionate Wardle. 'Bring a bucket, and throw it all over her; it'll do her good, and she richly deserves it.'

'Ugh, you brute!' ejaculated the kind-hearted landlady. 'Poor dear.' And with sundry ejaculations, of 'Come now, there's a dear—drink a little of this—it'll do you good—don't give way so—there's a love,' &c., &c., the landlady, assisted by a chamber-maid, proceeded to vinegar the forehead, beat the hands, titillate the nose, and unlace the stays of the spinster aunt, and to administer such other restoratives as are usually applied by compassionate females to ladies who are endeavouring to ferment themselves into hysterics.

'Coach is ready, sir,' said Sam, appearing at the door.

'Come along,' cried Wardle. 'I'll carry her down stairs.'

At this proposition, the hysterics came on with redoubled violence.

The landlady was about to enter a very violent protest against this proceeding, and had already given vent to an indignant inquiry whether Mr Wardle considered himself a lord of the creation, when Mr Jingle interposed —

'Boots,' said he, 'get me an officer.'

'Stay, stay,' said little Mr Perker. 'Consider, sir, consider.'

'I'll *not* consider,' replied Jingle. 'She's her own mistress—see who dares to take her away—unless she wishes it.'

'I *won't* be taken away,' murmured the spinster aunt. 'I *don't* wish it.' (Here there was a frightful relapse.)

'My dear sir,' said the little man, in a low tone, taking Mr Wardle and Mr Pickwick apart: 'My dear sir, we're in a very awkward situation. It's a distressing case—very; I never knew one more so; but really, my dear sir, really we have no power to control this lady's actions. I warned you before we came, my dear sir, that there was nothing to look to but a compromise.'

There was a short pause.

'What kind of compromise would you recommend?' inquired Mr Pickwick.

'Why, my dear sir, our friend's in an unpleasant position—very much so. We must be content to suffer some pecuniary loss.'

'I'll suffer any, rather than submit to this disgrace, and let her, fool as she is, be made miserable for life,' said Wardle.

'I rather think it can be done,' said the bustling little man. 'Mr Jingle, will you step with us into the next room for a moment?'

Mr Jingle assented, and the quartette walked into an empty apartment.

'Now, sir,' said the little man, as he carefully closed the door, 'is there no way of accommodating this matter—step this way, sir, for a moment—into this window, sir, where we can be alone—there, sir, there, pray sit down, sir. Now, my dear sir, between you and I, we know very well, my dear sir, that you have run off with this lady for the sake of her money. Don't frown, sir, don't frown; I say, between you and I, *we* know it. We are both men of the world, and *we* know very well that our friends here, are not—eh?'

Mr Jingle's face gradually relaxed; and something distantly resembling a wink quivered for an instant in his left eye.

'Very good, very good,' said the little man, observing the impression he had made. 'Now, the fact is, that beyond a few hundreds, the lady has little or nothing till the death of her mother—fine old lady, my dear sir.'

'*Old*,' said Mr Jingle briefly but emphatically.

'Why, yes,' said the attorney, with a slight cough. 'You are right, my dear sir, she is *rather* old. She comes of an old family though, my dear sir; old in every sense of the word. The founder of that family came into Kent, when Julius Cæsar invaded Britain;—only one member of it, since, who hasn't lived to eighty-five, and *he* was beheaded by one of the Henrys. The old lady is not seventy-three now, my dear sir.' The little man paused, and took a pinch of snuff.

'Well,' cried Mr Jingle.

'Well, my dear sir—you don't take snuff!—ah! so much the better—expensive habit—well, my dear sir, you're a fine young man, man of the world—able to push your fortune, if you had capital, eh?'

'Well,' said Mr Jingle again.

'Do you comprehend me?'

'Not quite.'

'Don't you think—now, my dear sir, I put it to you, *don't* you think—that fifty pounds and liberty, would be better than Miss Wardle and expectation?'

'Won't do—not half enough!' said Mr Jingle rising.

'Nay, nay, my dear sir,' remonstrated the little attorney, seizing him by the button. 'Good round sum—a man like you could treble it in no time—great deal to be done with fifty pounds, my dear sir.'

'More to be done with a hundred and fifty,' replied Mr Jingle coolly.

'Well, my dear sir, we won't waste time in splitting straws,' resumed the little man, 'say—say—seventy.'

'Won't do,' said Mr Jingle.

'Don't go away, my dear sir—pray don't hurry,' said the little man. 'Eighty; come: I'll write you a cheque at once.'

'Won't do,' said Mr Jingle.

'Well, my dear sir, well,' said the little man, still detaining him; 'just tell me what *will* do.'

'Expensive affair,' said Mr Jingle. 'Money out of pocket—posting, nine pounds; licence, three—that's twelve—compensation, a hundred—hundred and twelve—Breach of honour—and loss of the lady—'

'Yes, my dear sir, yes,' said the little man, with a knowing look, 'never mind the last two items. That's a hundred and twelve—say a hundred—come.'

'And twenty,' said Mr Jingle.

'Come, come, I'll write you a cheque,' said the little man; and down he sat at the table for that purpose.

'I'll make it payable the day after to-morrow,' said the little man, with a look towards Mr Wardle; 'and we can get the lady away, meanwhile.' Mr Wardle sullenly nodded assent.

'A hundred,' said the little man.

'And twenty,' said Mr Jingle.

'My dear sir,' remonstrated the little man.

'Give it him,' interposed Mr Wardle, 'and let him go.'

The cheque was written by the little gentleman, and pocketed by Mr Jingle.

'Now, leave this house instantly!' said Wardle, starting up.

'My dear sir,' urged the little man.

'And mind,' said Mr Wardle, 'that nothing should have induced me to make this compromise—not even a regard for my family—if I had not known that the moment you got any money in that pocket of yours, you'd go to the devil faster, if possible, than you would without it—'

'My dear sir,' urged the little man again.

'Be quiet, Perker,' resumed Wardle. 'Leave the room, sir.'

'Off directly,' said the unabashed Jingle. 'Bye bye, Pickwick.'

If any dispassionate spectator could have beheld the countenance of the illustrious man, whose name forms the leading feature of the title of this work, during the latter part of this conversation, he would have been almost induced to wonder that the indignant fire which flashed from his eyes, did not melt the glasses of his spectacles—so majestic was his wrath. His nostrils dilated, and his fists clenched involuntarily, as he heard himself addressed by the villain. But he restrained himself again—he did *not* pulverise him.

'Here,' continued the hardened traitor, tossing the licence at Mr Pickwick's feet; 'get the name altered—take home the lady—do for Tuppy.'

Mr Pickwick was a philosopher, but philosophers are only men in armour, after all. The shaft had reached him, penetrated through his philosophical harness, to his very heart. In the frenzy of his rage he hurled the inkstand madly forward, and followed it up himself. But Mr Jingle had disappeared, and he found himself caught in the arms of Sam.

'Hallo,' said that eccentric functionary, 'furniter's cheap where you come from, sir. Self-acting ink, that 'ere; it's wrote your mark upon the wall, old gen'lm'n. Hold still, sir; wot's the use o' runnin' arter a man as has made his lucky, and got to t' other end of the Borough by this time?'

Mr Pickwick's mind, like those of all truly great men, was open to conviction. He was a quick and powerful reasoner; and a moment's reflection sufficed to remind him of the impotency of his rage. It subsided as quickly as it had been roused. He panted for breath, and looked benignantly round upon his friends.

Shall we tell the lamentations that ensued, when Miss Wardle found herself deserted by the faithless Jingle? Shall we extract Mr Pickwick's masterly description of that heart-rending scene? His note-book, blotted with the tears of sympathising humanity, lies open before us; one word, and it is in the printer's hands. But, no! we will be resolute! We will not wring the public bosom, with the delineation of such suffering!

Slowly and sadly did the two friends and the deserted lady, return next day in the Muggleton heavy coach. Dimly and darkly had the sombre shadows of a summer's night fallen upon all around, when they again reached Dingley Dell, and stood within the entrance to Manor Farm.

OLIVER TWIST

Oliver Twist is born in the workhouse, his mother having been picked up half dead in the street and carried there, where she dies giving birth to him. He spends his first nine years in a 'branch workhouse', then he is taken to the workhouse proper by Mr Bumble, the parish beadle. After daring to 'ask for more', Oliver is apprenticed to the undertaker, Mr Sowerberry, but the harsh treatment he receives causes him to run away ...

Oliver reached the stile at which the by-path terminated; and once more gained the high-road. It was eight o'clock now. Though he was nearly five miles away from the town, he ran, and hid behind the hedges, by turns, till noon: fearing that he might be pursued and overtaken. Then he sat down to rest by the side of the milestone, and began to think, for the first time, where he had better go and try to live.

The stone by which he was seated, bore, in large characters, an intimation that it was just seventy miles from that spot to London. The name awakened a new train of ideas in the boy's mind. London!—that great large place!—nobody—not even Mr Bumble—could ever find him there! He had often heard the old men in the workhouse, too, say that no lad of spirit need want in London; and that there were ways of living in that vast city, which those who had been bred up in country parts had no idea of. It was the very place for a homeless boy, who must die in the streets unless some one helped him. As these things passed through his thoughts, he jumped upon his feet, and again walked forward.

He had diminished the distance between himself and London by full four miles more, before he recollected how much he must undergo ere he could hope to reach his place of destination. As this consideration forced itself upon him, he slackened his pace a little, and meditated upon his means of getting there. He had a crust of bread, a coarse shirt, and two pairs of stockings, in his bundle. He had a penny too—a gift of Sowerberry's after some funeral in which he had acquitted himself more than ordinarily well—in his pocket. 'A clean shirt,' thought Oliver, 'is a very comfortable thing; and so are two pairs of darned stockings; and so is a penny; but they are small helps to a sixty-five miles' walk in winter time.' But Oliver's thoughts, like those of most other people, although they were extremely ready and active to point out his difficulties, were wholly at a loss to suggest any feasible mode of surmounting them; so, after a good deal of thinking to no particular purpose, he changed his little bundle over to the other shoulder, and trudged on.

Oliver walked twenty miles that day; and all that time tasted nothing but the crust of dry bread, and a few draughts of water, which he begged at the cottage-doors by the roadside. When the night came, he turned into a meadow; and, creeping close under a hay-rick, determined to lie there, till morning. He felt frightened at first, for the wind moaned dismally over the empty fields: and he was cold and hungry, and more alone than he had ever felt before. Being very tired with his walk, however, he soon fell asleep and forgot his troubles.

He felt cold and stiff, when he got up next morning, and so hungry that he was obliged to exchange the penny for a small loaf, in the very first village through which he passed. He had walked no more than twelve miles, when night closed in again. His feet were sore, and his legs so weak that they trembled beneath him. Another night passed in the bleak damp air, made him worse; when he set forward on his journey next morning, he could hardly crawl along.

He waited at the bottom of a steep hill till a stage-coach came up, and then begged of the outside passengers; but there were very few who took any notice of him: and even those told him to wait till they got to the top of the hill, and then let them see how far he could run for a halfpenny. Poor Oliver tried to keep up with the coach a little way, but was unable to do it, by reason of his fatigue and sore feet. When the outsides saw this, they put their halfpence back into their pockets again, declaring that he was an idle young dog, and didn't deserve anything; and the coach rattled away and left only a cloud of dust behind.

In some villages, large painted boards were fixed up: warning all persons who begged within the district, that they would be sent to jail. This frightened Oliver very much, and made him glad to get out of those villages with all possible expedition. In others, he would stand about the inn-yards, and look mournfully at every one who passed: a proceeding which generally terminated in the landlady's ordering one of the post-boys who were lounging about, to drive that strange boy out of the place, for she was sure he had come to steal something. If he begged at a farmer's house, ten to one but they threatened to set the dog on him; and when he showed his nose in a shop, they talked about the beadle—which brought Oliver's heart into his mouth,—very often the only thing he had there, for many hours together.

In fact, if it had not been for a good-hearted turnpike-man, and a benevolent old lady, Oliver's troubles would have been shortened by the very same process which had put an end to his mother's; in other words, he would most assuredly have fallen dead upon the king's highway. But the turnpike-man gave him a meal of bread and cheese; and the old lady, who had a shipwrecked grandson wandering barefoot in some distant part of the earth, took pity upon the poor orphan, and gave him what little she could afford—and more—with such kind and gentle words, and such tears of sympathy and compassion, that they sank deeper into Oliver's soul, than all the sufferings he had ever undergone.

Early on the seventh morning after he had left his native place, Oliver limped slowly into the little town of Barnet. The window-shutters were closed; the street was empty; not a soul had awakened to the business of the day. The sun was rising in all its splendid beauty; but the light only served to show the boy his own lonesomeness and desolation, as he sat, with bleeding feet and covered with dust, upon a door-step.

By degrees, the shutters were opened; the window-blinds were drawn up; and people began passing to and fro. Some few stopped to gaze at Oliver for a moment or two, or turned round to stare at him as they hurried by; but none relieved him, or troubled themselves to inquire how he came there. He had no heart to beg. And there he sat.

He had been crouching on the step for some time: wondering at the great number of public-houses (every other house in Barnet was a tavern, large or small), gazing listlessly at the coaches as they passed through, and thinking how strange it seemed that they could do, with ease, in a few hours, what it had taken him a whole week of courage and determination beyond his years to accomplish: when he was roused by observing that a boy, who had passed him carelessly some minutes before, had returned, and was now surveying him most earnestly from the opposite side of the way. He took little heed of this at first; but the boy remained in the same attitude of close observation so long, that Oliver raised his head, and returned his steady look. Upon this, the boy crossed over; and, walking close up to Oliver, said,

'Hullo, my covey! What's the row?'

The boy who addressed this inquiry to the young wayfarer, was about his own age: but one of the queerest looking boys that Oliver had ever seen. He was a snub-nosed, flat-browed, common-faced boy enough; and as dirty a juvenile as one would wish to see; but he had about him all the airs and manners of a man. He was short of his age: with rather bow-legs, and little, sharp, ugly eyes. His hat was stuck on the top of his head so lightly, that it threatened to fall off every moment—and would have done so, very often, if the wearer had not had a knack of every now and then giving his head a sudden twitch, which brought it back to its old place again. He wore a man's coat, which reached nearly to his heels. He had turned the cuffs back, half-way up his arm, to get his hands out of the sleeves: apparently with the ultimate view of thrusting them into the pockets of his corduroy trousers; for there he kept them. He was, altogether, as roystering and swaggering a young gentleman as ever stood four feet six, or something less, in his bluchers.

'Hullo, my covey! What's the row?' said this strange young gentleman to Oliver.

'I am very hungry and tired,' replied Oliver: the tears standing in his eyes as he spoke. 'I have walked a long way. I have been walking these seven days.'

'Walking for sivin days!' said the young gentleman. 'Oh, I see. Beak's order, eh? But,' he added, noticing Oliver's look of surprise, 'I suppose you don't know what a beak is, my flash com-pan-i-on.'

Oliver mildly replied, that he had always heard a bird's mouth described by the term in question.

'My eyes, how green!' exclaimed the young gentleman. 'Why, a beak's a madgst'rate; and when you walk by a beak's order, it's not straight forerd, but always a going up, and nivir a coming down agin. Was you never on the mill?'

'What mill?' inquired Oliver.

'What mill! Why, *the* mill—the mill as takes up so little room that it'll work inside a Stone Jug; and always goes better when the wind's low with people, than when it's high; acos then they can't get workmen. But come,' said the young gentleman; 'you want grub, and you shall have it. I'm at low-water-mark myself—only one bob and a magpie; but, *as* far *as* it goes; I'll fork out and stump. Up with you on your pins. There! Now then! Morrice!'

Assisting Oliver to rise, the young gentleman took him to an adjacent chandler's shop, where he purchased a sufficiency of ready-dressed ham and a half-quartern loaf, or, as he himself expressed it, 'a fourpenny bran!' the ham being kept clean and preserved from dust, by the ingenious expedient of making a hole in the loaf by pulling out a portion of the crumb, and stuffing it therein. Taking the bread under his arm, the young gentleman turned into a small public-house, and led the way to a tap-room in the rear of the premises. Here, a pot of beer was brought in, by direction of the mysterious youth; and Oliver, falling to, at his new friend's bidding, made a long and hearty meal, during the progress of which, the strange boy eyed him from time to time with great attention.

'Going to London?' said the strange boy, when Oliver had at length concluded.

'Yes.'

'Got any lodgings?'

'No.'

'Money?'

'No.'

The strange boy whistled; and put his arms into his pockets, as far as the big coat sleeves would let them go.

'Do you live in London?' inquired Oliver.

'Yes. I do, when I'm at home,' replied the boy. 'I suppose you want some place to sleep in to-night, don't you?'

'I do, indeed,' answered Oliver. 'I have not slept under a roof since I left the country.

'Don't fret your eyelids on that score,' said the young gentleman. 'I've got to be in London to-night; and I know a 'spectable old genelman as lives there, wot'll give you lodgings for nothink, and never ask for the change—that is, if any genelman he knows interduces you. And don't he know me? Oh, no! Not in the least! By no means. Certainly not!'

The young gentleman smiled, as if to intimate that the latter fragments of discourse were playfully ironical; and finished the beer as he did so.

This unexpected offer of shelter was too tempting to be resisted; especially as it was immediately followed up, by the assurance that the old gentleman referred to, would doubtless provide Oliver with a comfortable place, without loss of time. This led to a more friendly and confidential dialogue; from which Oliver discovered that his friend's name was Jack Dawkins, and that he was a peculiar pet and *protégé* of the elderly gentleman before mentioned.

Mr Dawkins's appearance did not say a vast deal in favour of the comforts which his patron's interest obtained for those whom he took under his protection; but, as he had a rather flighty and dissolute mode of conversing, and furthermore avowed that among his intimate friends he was better known by the *sobriquet* of 'The artful Dodger,' Oliver concluded that, being of a dissipated and careless turn, the moral precepts of his benefactor had hitherto been thrown away upon him. Under this impression, he secretly resolved to cultivate the good opinion of the old gentleman as quickly as possible; and, if he found the Dodger incorrigible, as he more than half suspected he should, to decline the honour of his farther acquaintance.

As John Dawkins objected to their entering London before nightfall, it was nearly eleven o'clock when they reached the turnpike at Islington. They crossed from the Angel into St. John's Road; struck down the small street which terminates at Sadler's Wells Theatre; through Exmouth Street and Coppice Row; down the little court by the side of the workhouse; across the classic ground which once bore the name of Hockley-in-the-Hole; thence into Little Saffron Hill; and so into Saffron Hill the Great: along which the Dodger scudded at a rapid pace, directing Oliver to follow close at his heels.

Although Oliver had enough to occupy his attention in keeping sight of his leader, he could not help bestowing a few hasty glances on either side of the way, as he passed along. A dirtier or more wretched place he had never seen. The street was very narrow and muddy, and the air was impregnated with filthy odours. There were a good many small shops; but the only stock in trade appeared to be heaps of children, who, even at that time of night, were crawling in and out at the doors, or screaming from the inside. The sole places that seemed to prosper amid the general blight of the place, were the public-houses; and in them, the lowest orders of Irish were wrangling with might and main. Covered ways and yards, which here and there diverged from the main street, disclosed little knots of houses, where drunken men and women were positively wallowing in filth; and from several of the door-ways, great ill-looking fellows were cautiously emerging, bound, to all appearance, on no very well-disposed or harmless errands.

Oliver was just considering whether he hadn't better run away, when they reached the bottom of the hill. His conductor, catching him by the arm, pushed open the door of a house near Field Lane; and, drawing him into the passage, closed it behind them.

'Now, then!' cried a voice from below, in reply to a whistle from the Dodger.

'Plummy and slam!' was the reply.

This seemed to be some watchword or signal that all was right; for the light of a feeble candle gleamed on the wall at the remote end of the passage; and a man's face peeped out, from where a balustrade of the old kitchen staircase had been broken away.

'There's two on you,' said the man, thrusting the candle farther out, and shading his eyes with his hand. 'Who's the t'other one?'

'A new pal,' replied Jack Dawkins, pulling Oliver forward.

'Where did he come from?'

'Greenland. Is Fagin up stairs?'

'Yes, he's a sortin' the wipes. Up with you!' The candle was drawn back, and the face disappeared.

Oliver, groping his way with one hand, and having the other firmly grasped by his companion, ascended with much difficulty the dark and broken stairs: which his conductor mounted with an ease and expedition that showed he was well acquainted with them. He threw open the door of a back-room, and drew Oliver in after him.

The walls and ceiling of the room were perfectly black with age and dirt. There was a deal table before the fire: upon which were a candle, stuck in a ginger-beer bottle, two or three pewter pots, a loaf and butter, and a plate. In a frying-pan, which was on the fire, and which was secured to the mantelshelf by a string, some sausages were cooking; and standing over them, with a toasting-fork in his hand, was a very old shrivelled Jew, whose villainous-looking and repulsive face was obscured by a quantity of matted red hair. He was dressed in a greasy flannel gown, with his throat bare; and seemed to be dividing his attention between the frying-pan and a clothes-horse, over which a great number of silk handkerchiefs were hanging. Several rough beds made of old sacks, were huddled side by side on the floor. Seated round the table were four or five boys, none older than the Dodger, smoking long clay pipes, and drinking spirits with the air of middle-aged men. These all crowded about their associate as he whispered a few words to the Jew; and then turned round and grinned at Oliver. So did the Jew himself, toasting-fork in hand.

'This is him, Fagin,' said Jack Dawkins; 'my friend Oliver Twist.'

The Jew grinned; and, making a low obeisance to Oliver, took him by the hand, and hoped he should have the honour of his intimate acquaintance. Upon this, the young gentlemen with the pipes came round him, and shook both his hands very hard—especially the one in which he held his little bundle. One young gentleman was very anxious to hang up his cap for him; and another was so obliging as to put his hands in his pockets, in order that, as he was very tired, he might not have the trouble of emptying them, himself, when he went to bed. These civilities would probably have been extended much farther, but for a liberal exercise of the Jew's toasting-fork on the heads and shoulders of the affectionate youths who offered them.

'We are very glad to see you, Oliver, very,' said the Jew. 'Dodger, take off the sausages; and draw a tub near the fire for Oliver. Ah! you're a-staring at the pocket-handkerchiefs! eh, my dear! There are a good many of 'em, ain't there? We've just looked 'em out, ready for the wash; that's all, Oliver; that's all. Ha! ha! ha!'

The latter part of this speech, was hailed by a boisterous shout from all the hopeful pupils of the merry old gentleman. In the midst of which, they went to supper.

Oliver ate his share, and the Jew then mixed him a glass of hot gin and water: telling him he must drink it off directly, because another gentleman wanted the tumbler. Oliver did as he was desired. Immediately afterwards he felt himself gently lifted on to one of the sacks; and then he sunk into a deep sleep.

It was late next morning when Oliver awoke, from a sound, long sleep. There was no other person in the room but the old Jew, who was boiling some coffee in a saucepan for breakfast, and whistling softly to himself as he stirred it round and round, with an iron spoon. He would stop every now and then to listen when there was the least noise below: and when he had satisfied himself, he would go on, whistling and stirring again, as before.

Although Oliver had roused himself from sleep, he was not thoroughly awake. There is a drowsy state, between sleeping and waking, when you dream more in five minutes with your eyes half open, and yourself half conscious of everything that is passing around you, than you would in five nights with your eyes fast closed, and your senses wrapt in perfect unconsciousness. At such times, a mortal knows just enough of what his mind is doing, to form some glimmering conception of its mighty powers, its bounding from earth and spurning time and space, when freed from the restraint of its corporeal associate.

Oliver was precisely in this condition. He saw the Jew with his half-closed eyes; heard his low whistling; and recognised the sound of the spoon grating against the saucepan's sides; and yet the self-same senses were mentally engaged, at the same time, in busy action with almost everybody he had ever known.

When the coffee was done, the Jew drew the saucepan to the hob. Standing, then, in an irresolute attitude for a few minutes as if he did not well know how to employ himself, he turned round and looked at Oliver, and called him by his name. He did not answer, and was to all appearances asleep.

After satisfying himself upon this head, the Jew stepped gently to the door: which he fastened. He then drew forth: as it seemed to Oliver, from some trap in the floor: a small box, which he placed carefully on the table. His eyes glistened as he raised the lid, and looked in. Dragging an old chair to the table, he sat down; and took from it a magnificent gold watch, sparkling with jewels.

'Aha!' said the Jew, shrugging up his shoulders, and distorting every feature with a hideous grin. 'Clever dogs! Clever dogs! Staunch to the last! Never told the old parson where they were. Never peached upon old Fagin! And why should they? It wouldn't have loosened the knot, or kept the drop up, a minute longer. No, no, no! Fine fellows! Fine fellows!'

With these, and other muttered reflections of the like nature, the Jew once more deposited the watch in its place of safety. At least half a dozen more were severally drawn forth from the same box, and surveyed with equal pleasure; besides rings, brooches, bracelets, and other articles of jewellery, of such magnificent materials, and costly workmanship, that Oliver had no idea, even of their names.

Having replaced these trinkets, the Jew took out another: so small that it lay in the palm of his hand. There seemed to be some very minute inscription on it; for the Jew laid it flat upon the table, and, shading it with his hand, pored over it, long and earnestly. At length he put it down, as if despairing of success; and, leaning back in his chair, muttered:

'What a fine thing capital punishment is! Dead men never repent; dead men never bring awkward stories to light. Ah! it's a fine thing for the trade! Five of 'em strung up in a row, and none left to play booty, or turn white-livered!'

As the Jew uttered these words, his bright dark eyes, which had been staring vacantly before him, fell on Oliver's face; the boy's eyes were fixed on his in mute curiosity; and although the recognition was only for an instant—for the briefest space of time that can possibly be conceived—it was enough to show the old man that he had been observed. He closed the lid of the box with a loud crash; and, laying his hand on a bread knife which was on the table, started furiously up. He trembled very much though; for, even in his terror, Oliver could see that the knife quivered in the air.

'What's that?' said the Jew. 'What do you watch me for? Why are you awake? What have you seen? Speak out, boy! Quick—quick! for your life!'

'I wasn't able to sleep any longer, sir,' replied Oliver, meekly. 'I am very sorry if I have disturbed you, sir.'

'You were not awake an hour ago?' said the Jew, scowling fiercely on the boy.

'No! No, indeed!' replied Oliver.

'Are you sure?' cried the Jew: with a still fiercer look than before: and a threatening attitude.

'Upon my word I was not, sir,' replied Oliver, earnestly. 'I was not, indeed, sir.'

'Tush, tush, my dear!' said the Jew, abruptly resuming his old manner, and playing with the knife a little, before he laid it down; as if to induce the belief that he had caught it up, in mere sport. 'Of course I know that, my dear. I only tried to frighten you. You're a brave boy. Ha! ha! you're a brave boy, Oliver!' The Jew rubbed his hands with a chuckle, but glanced uneasily at the box, notwithstanding.

'Did you see any of these pretty things, my dear?' said the Jew, laying his hand upon it after a short pause.

'Yes, sir,' replied Oliver.

'Ah!' said the Jew, turning rather pale. 'They—they're mine, Oliver; my little property. All I have to live upon, in my old age. The folks call me a miser, my dear. Only a miser; that's all.'

Oliver thought the old gentleman must be a decided miser to live in such a dirty place, with so many watches; but, thinking that perhaps his fondness for the Dodger and the other boys, cost him a good deal of money, he only cast a deferential look at the Jew, and asked if he might get up.

'Certainly, my dear, certainly,' replied the old gentleman. 'Stay. There's a pitcher of water in the corner by the door. Bring it here; and I'll give you a basin to wash in, my dear.'

Oliver got up; walked across the room; and stooped for an instant to raise the pitcher. When he turned his head, the box was gone.

He had scarcely washed himself, and made everything tidy, by emptying the basin out of the window, agreeably to the Jew's directions, when the Dodger returned: accompanied by a very sprightly young friend, whom Oliver had seen smoking on the previous night, and who was now formally introduced to him as Charley Bates. The four sat down, to breakfast, on the coffee, and some hot rolls and ham which the Dodger had brought home in the crown of his hat.

'Well,' said the Jew, glancing slyly at Oliver, and addressing himself to the Dodger, 'I hope you've been at work this morning, my dears?'

'Hard,' replied the Dodger.

'As Nails,' added Charley Bates.

'Good boys, good boys!' said the Jew. 'What have *you* got Dodger?'

'A couple of pocket-books,' replied that young gentleman.

'Lined?' inquired the Jew, with eagerness.

'Pretty well,' replied the Dodger, producing two pocket-books; one green, and the other red.

'Not so heavy as they might be,' said the Jew, after looking at the insides carefully; 'but very neat and nicely made. Ingenious workman, ain't he, Oliver?'

'Very, indeed, sir,' said Oliver. At which Mr Charles Bates laughed uproariously; very much to the amazement of Oliver, who saw nothing to laugh at, in anything that had passed.

'And what have you got, my dear?' said Fagin to Charley Bates.

'Wipes,' replied Master Bates; at the same time producing four pocket-handkerchiefs.

'Well,' said the Jew, inspecting them closely; 'they're very good ones, very. You haven't marked them well, though, Charley; so the marks shall be picked out with a needle, and we'll teach Oliver how to do it. Shall us, Oliver, eh? Ha! ha! ha!'

'If you please, sir,' said Oliver.

'You'd like to be able to make pocket-handkerchiefs as easy as Charley Bates, wouldn't you, my dear?' said the Jew.

'Very much, indeed, if you'll teach me, sir,' replied Oliver.

Master Bates saw something so exquisitely ludicrous in this reply, that he burst into another laugh; which laugh, meeting the coffee he was drinking, and carrying it down some wrong channel, very nearly terminated in his premature suffocation.

'He is so jolly green!' said Charley when he recovered, as an apology to the company for his unpolite behaviour.

The Dodger said nothing, but he smoothed Oliver's hair over his eyes, and said he'd know better, by-and-bye; upon which the old gentleman, observing Oliver's colour mounting, changed the subject by asking whether there had been much of a crowd at the execution that morning? This made him wonder more and more; for it was plain from the replies of the two boys that they had both been there; and Oliver naturally wondered how they could possibly have found time to be so very industrious.

When the breakfast was cleared away, the merry old gentleman and the two boys played at a very curious and uncommon game, which was performed in this way. The merry old gentleman, placing a snuff-box in one pocket of his trousers, a note-case in the other, and a watch in his waistcoat pocket, with a guard-chain round his neck, and sticking a mock diamond pin in his shirt: buttoned his coat tight round him, and putting his spectacle-case and handkerchief in his pockets, trotted up and down the room with a stick, in imitation of the manner in which old gentlemen walk about the streets any hour in the day. Sometimes he stopped at the fire-place, and sometimes at the door, making believe that he was staring with all his might into shop-windows. At such times, he would look constantly round him, for fear of thieves, and would keep slapping all his pockets in turn, to see that he hadn't lost anything, in such a very funny and natural manner, that Oliver laughed till the tears ran down his face. All this time, the two boys followed him closely about: getting out of his sight, so nimbly, every time he turned round, that it was impossible to follow their motions. At last, the Dodger trod upon his toes, or ran upon his boot accidentally, while Charley Bates stumbled up against him behind; and in that one moment they took from him, with the most extraordinary rapidity, snuff-box, note-case, watch-guard, chain, shirt-pin, pocket-handkerchief, even the spectacle-case. If the old gentleman felt a hand in any one of his pockets, he cried out where it was; and then the game began all over again.

When this game had been played a great many times, a couple of young ladies called to see the young gentlemen; one of whom was named Bet, and the other Nancy. They wore a good deal of hair, not very neatly turned up behind, and were rather untidy about the shoes and stockings. They were not exactly pretty, perhaps; but they had a great deal of colour in their faces, and looked quite stout and hearty. Being remarkably free and agreeable in their manners, Oliver thought them very nice girls indeed. As there is no doubt they were.

These visitors stopped a long time. Spirits were produced, in consequence of one of the young ladies complaining of a coldness in her inside; and the conversation took a very convivial and improving turn. At length, Charley Bates expressed his opinion that it was time to pad the hoof. This, it occurred to Oliver, must be French for going out; for, directly afterwards, the Dodger, and Charley, and the two young ladies, went away together, having been kindly furnished by the amiable old Jew with money to spend.

'There, my dear,' said Fagin. 'That's a pleasant life, isn't it? They have gone out for the day.'

'Have they done work, sir?' inquired Oliver.

'Yes,' said the Jew; 'that is, unless they should unexpectedly come across any, when they are out; and they won't neglect it, if they do, my dear, depend upon it. Make 'em your models, my dear. Make'em your models,' tapping the fireshovel on the hearth to add force to his words; 'do everything they bid you, and take their advice in all matters—especially the Dodger's, my dear. He'll be a great man himself, and will make you one too, if you take pattern by him.—Is my handkerchief hanging out of my pocket, my dear?' said the Jew, stopping short.

'Yes, sir,' said Oliver.

'See if you can take it out, without my feeling it: as you saw them do, when we were at play this morning.'

Oliver held up the bottom of the pocket with one hand, as he had seen the Dodger hold it, and drew the handkerchief lightly out of it with the other.

'Is it gone?' cried the Jew.

'Here it is, sir,' said Oliver, showing it in his hand.

'You're a clever boy, my dear,' said the playful old gentleman, patting Oliver on the head approvingly. 'I never saw a sharper lad. Here's a shilling for you. If you go on, in this way, you'll be the greatest man of the time. And now come here, and I'll show you how to take the marks out of the handkerchiefs.'

Oliver wondered what picking the old gentleman's pocket in play, had to do with his chances of being a great man. But, thinking that the Jew, being so much his senior, must know best, he followed him quietly to the table, and was soon deeply involved in his new study.

NICHOLAS NICKLEBY

Nicholas Nickleby, along with his mother and his sister Kate, is left penniless when his father dies. He appeals for help to his unscrupulous uncle Ralph Nickleby who proposes that Nicholas obtain a position as an assistant teacher at Wackford Squeers's school at Dotheboys Hall in Yorkshire. Ralph and Nicholas go together to Snow Hill to meet Mr Squeers ...

Snow Hill! What kind of place can the quiet town's-people who see the words emblazoned, in all the legibility of gilt letters and dark shading, on the north-country coaches, take Snow Hill to be? All people have some undefined and shadowy notion of a place whose name is frequently before their eyes, or often in their ears. What a vast number of random ideas there must be perpetually floating about regarding this same Snow Hill. The name is such a good one. Snow Hill—Snow Hill too, coupled with a Saracen's Head: picturing to us by a double association of ideas something stern and rugged! A bleak desolate tract of country, open to piercing blasts and fierce wintry storms—a dark, cold, gloomy heath, lonely by day, and scarcely to be thought of by honest folks at night—a place which solitary wayfarers shun, and where desperate robbers congregate;—this, or something like this, should be the prevalent notion of Snow Hill in those remote and rustic parts, through which the Saracen's Head, like some grim apparition, rushes each day and night with mysterious and ghost-like punctuality; holding its swift and headlong course in all weathers, and seeming to bid defiance to the very elements themselves.

The reality is rather different, but by no means to be despised notwithstanding. There, at the very core of London, in the heart of its business and animation, in the midst of a whirl of noise and motion: stemming as it were the giant currents of life that flow ceaselessly on from different quarters and meet beneath its walls: stands Newgate;

and in that crowded street on which it frowns so darkly—within a few feet of the squalid tottering houses—upon the very spot on which the venders of soup and fish and damaged fruit are now plying their trades—scores of human beings, amidst a roar of sounds to which even the tumult of a great city is as nothing, four, six, or eight strong men at a time, have been hurried violently and swiftly from the world, when the scene has been rendered frightful with excess of human life; when curious eyes have glared from casement, and house-top, and wall and pillar; and when, in the mass of white and upturned faces, the dying wretch, in his all-comprehensive look of agony, has met not one—not one—that bore the impress of pity or compassion.

Near to the jail, and by consequence near to Smithfield also, and the Compter, and the bustle and noise of the city; and just on that particular part of Snow Hill where omnibus horses going eastward seriously think of falling down on purpose, and where horses in hackney cabriolets going westward not unfrequently fall by accident, is the coach-yard of the Saracen's Head Inn; its portal guarded by two Saracens' heads and shoulders, which it was once the pride and glory of the choice spirits of this metropolis to pull down at night, but which have for some time remained in undisturbed tranquillity; possibly because this species of humour is now confined to Saint James's parish, where door knockers are preferred as being more portable, and bell-wires esteemed as convenient tooth-picks. Whether this be the reason or not, there they are, frowning upon you from each side of the gateway. The inn itself garnished with another Saracen's Head, frowns upon you from the top of the yard; while from the door of the hind boot of all the red coaches that are standing therein, there glares a small Saracen's Head, with a twin expression to the large Saracens' Heads below, so that the general appearance of the pile is decidedly of the Saracenic order.

When you walk up this yard, you will see the booking-office on your left, and the tower of St. Sepulchre's church, darting abruptly up into the sky, on your right, and a gallery of bedrooms on both sides. Just before you, you will observe a long window with the words 'coffee-room' legibly painted above it; and looking out of that window, you would have seen in addition, if you had gone at the right time, Mr Wackford Squeers with his hands in his pockets.

Mr Squeers's appearance was not prepossessing. He had but one eye, and the popular prejudice runs in favour of two. The eye he had was unquestionably useful, but decidedly not ornamental: being of a greenish grey, and in shape resembling the fan-light of a street door.

The blank side of his face was much wrinkled and puckered up, which gave him a very sinister appearance, especially when he smiled, at which times his expression bordered closely on the villainous. His hair was very flat and shiny, save at the ends, where it was brushed stiffly up from a low protruding forehead, which assorted well with his harsh voice and coarse manner. He was about two or three and fifty, and a trifle below the middle size; he wore a white neckerchief with long ends, and a suit of scholastic black; but his coat sleeves being a great deal too long, and his trousers a great deal too short, he appeared ill at ease in his clothes, and as if he were in a perpetual state of astonishment at finding himself so respectable.

Mr Squeers was standing in a box by one of the coffee-room fire-places, fitted with one such table as is usually seen in coffee-rooms, and two of extraordinary shapes and dimensions made to suit the angles of the partition. In a corner of the seat was a very small deal trunk, tied round with a scanty piece of cord; and on the trunk was perched—his lace-up half-boots and corduroy trousers dangling in the air—a diminutive boy, with his shoulders drawn up to his ears, and his hands planted on his knees, who glanced timidly at the schoolmaster from time to time, with evident dread and apprehension.

'Half-past three,' muttered Mr Squeers, turning from the window, and looking sulkily at the coffee-room clock. 'There will be nobody here to-day.'

Much vexed by this reflection, Mr Squeers looked at the little boy to see whether he was doing anything he could beat him for. As he happened not to be doing anything at all, he merely boxed his ears, and told him not to do it again.

'At Midsummer,' muttered Mr Squeers, resuming his complaint, 'I took down ten boys; ten twentys is two hundred pound. I go back at eight o'clock to-morrow morning, and have got only three—three oughts is an ought—three twos is six—sixty pound. What's come of all the boys? what's parents got in their heads? what does it all mean?'

Here the little boy on the top of the trunk gave a violent sneeze.

'Halloa, sir!' growled the schoolmaster, turning round. 'What's that, sir?'

'Nothing, please sir,' said the little boy.

'Nothing, sir!' exclaimed Mr Squeers.

'Please sir, I sneezed,' rejoined the boy, trembling till the little trunk shook under him.

'Oh! sneezed, did you?' retorted Mr Squeers. 'Then what did you say "nothing" for, sir?'

In default of a better answer to this question, the little boy screwed a couple of knuckles into each of his eyes and began to cry, wherefore Mr Squeers knocked him off the trunk with a blow on one side of his face, and knocked him on again with a blow on the other.

'Wait till I get you down into Yorkshire, my young gentleman,' said Mr Squeers, 'and then I'll give you the rest. Will you hold that noise, sir?'

'Ye—ye—yes,' sobbed the little boy, rubbing his face very hard with the Beggar's Petition in printed calico.

'Then do so at once, sir,' said Squeers. 'Do you hear?'

As this admonition was accompanied with a threatening gesture, and uttered with a savage aspect, the little boy rubbed his face harder, as if to keep the tears back; and, beyond alternately sniffing and choking, gave no further vent to his emotions.

'Mr Squeers,' said the waiter, looking in at this juncture; 'here's a gentleman asking for you at the bar.'

'Show the gentleman in, Richard,' replied Mr Squeers, in a soft voice. 'Put your handkerchief in your pocket, you little scoundrel, or I'll murder you when the gentleman goes.'

The schoolmaster had scarcely uttered these words in a fierce whisper, when the stranger entered. Affecting not to see him, Mr Squeers feigned to be intent upon mending a pen, and offering benevolent advice to his youthful pupil.

'My dear child,' said Mr Squeers, 'all people have their trials. This early trial of yours that is fit to make your little heart burst, and your very eyes come out of your head with crying, what is it? Nothing; less than nothing. You are leaving your friends, but you will have a father in me, my dear, and a mother in Mrs Squeers. At the delightful village of Dotheboys, near Greta Bridge in Yorkshire, where youth are boarded, clothed, booked, washed, furnished with pocket-money, provided with all necessaries—'

'It *is* the gentleman,' observed the stranger, stopping the schoolmaster in the rehearsal of his advertisement. 'Mr Squeers, I believe, sir?'

'The same, sir,' said Mr Squeers, with an assumption of extreme surprise.

'The gentleman,' said the stranger, 'that advertised in the Times newspaper?'

'—Morning Post, Chronicle, Herald, and Advertiser, regarding the Academy called Dotheboys Hall at the delightful village of Dotheboys, near Greta Bridge in Yorkshire,' added Mr Squeers. 'You come on business, sir. I see by my young friends. How do you do, my little gentleman? and how do *you* do, sir?' With this salutation Mr Squeers patted the heads of two hollow-eyed, small-boned little boys, whom the applicant had brought with him, and waited for further communications.

'I am in the oil and colour way. My name is Snawley, sir,' said the stranger.

Squeers inclined his head as much as to say, 'And a remarkably pretty name, too.'

The stranger continued. 'I have been thinking, Mr Squeers, of placing my two boys at your school.'

'It is not for me to say so, sir,' replied Mr Squeers, 'but I don't think you could possibly do a better thing.'

'Hem!' said the other. 'Twenty pounds per annewum, I believe, Mr Squeers?'

'Guineas,' rejoined the schoolmaster, with a persuasive smile.

'Pounds for two, I think, Mr Squeers,' said Mr Snawley, solemnly.

'I don't think it could be done, sir,' replied Squeers, as if he had never considered the proposition before. 'Let me see; four fives is twenty, double that, and deduct the—well, a pound either way shall not stand betwixt us. You must recommend me to your connection, sir, and make it up that way.'

'They are not great eaters,' said Mr Snawley.

'Oh! that doesn't matter at all,' replied Squeers. 'We don't consider the boys' appetites at our establishment.' This was strictly true; they did not.

'Every wholesome luxury, sir, that Yorkshire can afford,' continued Squeers; 'every beautiful moral that Mrs Squeers can instil; every—in short, every comfort of a home that a boy could wish for, will be theirs, Mr Snawley.'

'I should wish their morals to be particularly attended to,' said Mr Snawley.

'I am glad of that, sir,' replied the schoolmaster, drawing himself up. 'They have come to the right shop for morals, sir.'

'You are a moral man yourself,' said Mr Snawley.

'I rather believe I am, sir,' replied Squeers.

'I have the satisfaction to know you are, sir,' said Mr Snawley. 'I asked one of your references, and he said you were pious.'

'Well, sir, I hope I am a little in that line,' replied Squeers.

'I hope I am also,' rejoined the other. 'Could I say a few words with you in the next box?'

'By all means,' rejoined Squeers with a grin. 'My dears, will you speak to your new playfellow a minute or two? That is one of my boys, sir. Belling his name is,—a Taunton boy that, sir.'

'Is he, indeed?' rejoined Mr Snawley, looking at the poor little urchin as if he were some extraordinary natural curiosity.

'He goes down with me to-morrow, sir,' said Squeers. 'That's his luggage that he is a sitting upon now. Each boy is required to bring, sir, two suits of clothes, six shirts, six pair of shoes, two hats, and a razor.'

'A razor!' exclaimed Mr Snawley, as they walked into the next box. 'What for?'

'To shave with,' replied Squeers, in a slow and measured tone.

There was not much in these three words, but there must have been something in the manner in which they were said, to attract attention; for the schoolmaster and his companion looked steadily at each other for a few seconds, and then exchanged a very meaning smile. Snawley was a sleek, flat-nosed man, clad in sombre garments, and long black gaiters, and bearing in his countenance an expression of much mortification and sanctity; so, his smiling without any obvious reason was the more remarkable.

'Up to what age do you keep boys at your school then?' he asked at length.

'Just as long as their friends make the quarterly payments to my agent in town, or until such time as they run away,' replied Squeers. 'Let us understand each other; I see we may safely do so. What are these boys;—natural children?'

'No,' rejoined Snawley, meeting the gaze of the schoolmaster's one eye. 'They ain't.'

'I thought they might be,' said Squeers, coolly. 'We have a good many of them; that boy's one.'

'Him in the next box?' said Snawley.

Squeers nodded in the affirmative; his companion took another peep at the little boy on the trunk, and turning round again, looked as if he were quite disappointed to see him so much like other boys, and said he should hardly have thought it.

'He is,' cried Squeers. 'But about these boys of yours; you wanted to speak to me?'

'Yes,' replied Snawley. 'The fact is, I am not their father, Mr Squeers. I'm only their step-father.'

'Oh! Is that it?' said the schoolmaster. 'That explains it at once. I was wondering what the devil you were going to send them to Yorkshire for. Ha! ha! Oh, I understand now.'

'You see I have married the mother,' pursued Snawley; 'it's expensive keeping boys at home, and as she has a little money in her own right, I am afraid (women are so very foolish, Mr Squeers) that she might be led to squander it on them, which would be their ruin, you know.'

'*I* see,' returned Squeers, throwing himself back in his chair, and waving his hand.

'And this,' resumed Snawley, 'has made me anxious to put them to some school a good distance off, where there are no holidays—none of those ill-judged comings home twice a year that unsettle children's minds so—and where they may rough it a little—you comprehend?'

'The payments regular, and no questions asked,' said Squeers, nodding his head.

'That's it, exactly,' rejoined the other. 'Morals strictly attended to, though.'

'Strictly,' said Squeers.

'Not too much writing home allowed, I suppose?' said the step-father, hesitating.

'None, except a circular at Christmas, to say they never were so happy, and hope they may never be sent for,' rejoined Squeers.

'Nothing could be better,' said the step-father, rubbing his hands.

'Then, as we understand each other,' said Squeers, 'will you allow me to ask you whether you consider me a highly virtuous, exemplary, and well-conducted man in private life; and whether, as a person whose business it is to take charge of youth, you place the strongest confidence in my unimpeachable integrity, liberality, religious principles, and ability?'

'Certainly I do,' replied the step-father, reciprocating the schoolmaster's grin.

'Perhaps you won't object to say that, if I make you a reference?'

'Not the least in the world.'

'That's your sort!' said Squeers, taking up a pen; 'this is doing business, and that's what I like.'

Having entered Mr Snawley's address, the schoolmaster had next to perform the still more agreeable office of entering the receipt of the first quarter's payment in advance, which he had scarcely completed, when another voice was heard inquiring for Mr Squeers.

'Here he is,' replied the schoolmaster; 'what is it?'

'Only a matter of business, sir,' said Ralph Nickleby, presenting himself, closely followed by Nicholas. 'There was an advertisement of yours in the papers this morning?'

'There was, sir. This way, if you please,' said Squeers, who had by this time got back to the box by the fire-place. 'Won't you be seated?'

'Why, I think I will,' replied Ralph, suiting the action to the word, and placing his hat on the table before him. 'This is my nephew, sir, Mr Nicholas Nickleby.'

'How do you do, sir?' said Squeers.

Nicholas bowed, said he was very well, and seemed very much astonished at the outward appearance of the proprietor of Dotheboys Hall: as indeed he was.

'Perhaps you recollect me?' said Ralph, looking narrowly at the schoolmaster.

'You paid me a small account at each of my half-yearly visits to town, for some years, I think, sir,' replied Squeers.

'I did,' rejoined Ralph.

'For the parents of a boy named Dorker, who unfortunately—'

'—unfortunately died at Dotheboys Hall,' said Ralph, finishing the sentence.

'I remember very well, sir,' rejoined Squeers. 'Ah! Mrs Squeers, sir, was as partial to that lad as if he had been her own; the attention, sir, that was bestowed upon that boy in his illness! Dry toast and warm tea offered him every night and morning when he couldn't swallow anything—a candle in his bed-room on the very night he died—the best dictionary sent up for him to lay his head upon—I don't regret it though. It is a pleasant thing to reflect that one did one's duty by him.'

Ralph smiled, as if he meant anything but smiling, and looked at the strangers present.

'These are only some pupils of mine,' said Wackford Squeers, pointing to the little boy on the trunk and the two little boys on the floor, who had been staring at each other without uttering a word, and writhing their bodies into most remarkable contortions, according to the custom of little boys when they first become acquainted. 'This gentleman, sir, is a parent who is kind enough to compliment me upon the course of education adopted at Dotheboys Hall, which is situated, sir, at the delightful village of Dotheboys, near Greta Bridge in Yorkshire, where youth are boarded, clothed, booked, washed, furnished with pocket-money—'

'Yes, we know all about that, sir,' interrupted Ralph, testily. 'It's in the advertisement.'

'You are very right, sir; it *is* in the advertisement,' replied Squeers.

'And in the matter of fact besides,' interrupted Mr Snawley. 'I feel bound to assure you, sir, and I am proud to have this opportunity *of* assuring you, that I consider Mr Squeers a gentleman highly virtuous, exemplary, well-conducted, and—'

'I make no doubt of it, sir,' interrupted Ralph, checking the torrent of recommendation; 'no doubt of it at all. Suppose we come to business?'

'With all my heart, sir,' rejoined Squeers. ' "Never postpone business," is the very first lesson we instil into our commercial pupils. Master Belling, my dear, always remember that; do you hear?'

'Yes, sir,' repeated Master Belling.

'He recollects what it is, does he?' said Ralph.

'Tell the gentleman,' said Squeers.

' "Never," ' repeated Master Belling.

'Very good,' said Squeers; 'go on.'

'Never,' repeated Master Belling again.

'Very good indeed,' said Squeers. 'Yes.'

'P,' suggested Nicholas, good-naturedly.

'Perform—business!' said Master Belling. 'Never—perform—business!'

'Very well, sir,' said Squeers, darting a withering look at the culprit. 'You and I will perform a little business on our private account by and bye.'

'And just now,' said Ralph, 'we had better transact our own, perhaps.'

'If you please,' said Squeers.

'Well,' resumed Ralph, 'it's brief enough; soon broached; and I hope easily concluded. You have advertised for an able assistant, sir?'

'Precisely so,' said Squeers.

'And you really want one?'

'Certainly,' answered Squeers.

'Here he is!' said Ralph. 'My nephew Nicholas, hot from school, with everything he learnt there fermenting in his head, and nothing fermenting in his pocket, is just the man you want.'

'I am afraid,' said Squeers, perplexed with such an application from a youth of Nicholas's figure,' 'I am afraid the young man won't suit me.'

'Yes, he will,' said Ralph; 'I know better. Don't be cast down, sir; you will be teaching all the young noblemen in Dotheboys Hall in less than a week's time, unless this gentleman is more obstinate than I take him to be.'

'I fear, sir,' said Nicholas, addressing Mr Squeers, 'that you object to my youth, and to my not being a Master of Arts?'

'The absence of a college degree *is* an objection,' replied Squeers, looking as grave as he could, and considerably puzzled, no less by the contrast between the simplicity of the nephew and the worldly manner of the uncle, than by the incomprehensible allusion to the young noblemen under his tuition.

'Look here, sir,' said Ralph; 'I'll put this matter in its true light in two seconds.'

'If you'll have the goodness,' rejoined Squeers.

'This is a boy, or a youth, or a lad, or a young man, or a hobbledehoy, or whatever you like to call him, of eighteen or nineteen, or thereabouts,' said Ralph.

'That I see,' observed the schoolmaster.

'So do I,' said Mr Snawley, thinking it as well to back his new friend occasionally.

'His father is dead, he is wholly ignorant of the world, has no resources whatever, and wants something to do,' said Ralph. 'I recommend him to this splendid establishment of yours as an opening which will lead him to fortune if he turns it to proper account. Do you see that?'

'Everybody must see that,' replied Squeers, half imitating the sneer with which the old gentleman was regarding his unconscious relative.

'I do, of course,' said Nicholas, eagerly.

'He does, of course, you observe,' said Ralph, in the same dry, hard manner. 'If any caprice of temper should induce him to cast aside this golden opportunity before he has brought it to perfection, I consider myself absolved from extending any assistance to his mother and sister. Look at him, and think of the use he may be to you in half a dozen ways! Now, the question is, whether, for some time to come at all events, he won't serve your purpose better than twenty of the kind of people you would get under ordinary circumstances. Isn't that a question for consideration?'

'Yes, it is,' said Squeers, answering a nod of Ralph's head with a nod of his own.

'Good,' rejoined Ralph. 'Let me have two words with you.'

The two words were had apart; in a couple of minutes Mr Wackford Squeers announced that Mr Nicholas Nickleby was, from that moment, thoroughly nominated to, and installed in, the office of first assistant master at Dotheboys Hall.

'Your uncle's recommendation has done it, Mr Nickleby,' said Wackford Squeers.

Nicholas, overjoyed at his success, shook his uncle's hand warmly, and could almost have worshipped Squeers upon the spot.

'He is an odd-looking man,' thought Nicholas. 'What of that? Porson was an odd-looking man, and so was Doctor Johnson; all these bookworms are.'

'At eight o'clock to-morrow morning, Mr Nickleby,' said Squeers, 'the coach starts. You must be here at a quarter before, as we take these boys with us.'

'Certainly, sir,' said Nicholas.

'And your fare down, I have paid,' growled Ralph. 'So, you'll have nothing to do but keep yourself warm.'

Here was another instance of his uncle's generosity! Nicholas felt his unexpected kindness so much that he could scarcely find words to thank him; indeed, he had not found half enough, when they took leave of the schoolmaster, and emerged from the Saracen's Head gateway.

'I shall be here in the morning to see you fairly off,' said Ralph. 'No skulking!'

'Thank you, sir,' replied Nicholas; 'I never shall forget this kindness.'

'Take care you don't,' replied his uncle. 'You had better go home now, and pack up what you have got to pack. Do you think you could find your way to Golden Square first?'

'Certainly,' said Nicholas. 'I can easily inquire.'

'Leave these papers with my clerk, then,' said Ralph, producing a small parcel, 'and tell him to wait till I come home.'

Nicholas cheerfully undertook the errand, and bidding his worthy uncle an affectionate farewell, which that warm-hearted old gentleman acknowledged by a growl, hastened away to execute his commission.

He found Golden Square in due course; Mr Noggs, who had stepped out for a minute or so to the public-house, was opening the door with a latch-key as he reached the steps.

'What's that?' inquired Noggs, pointing to the parcel.

'Papers from my uncle,' replied Nicholas; 'and you're to have the goodness to wait till he comes home, if you please.'

'Uncle!' cried Noggs.

'Mr Nickleby,' said Nicholas in explanation.

'Come in,' said Newman.

Without another word he led Nicholas into the passage, and thence into the official pantry at the end of it, where he thrust him into a chair, and mounting upon his high stool, sat, with his arms hanging straight down by his sides, gazing fixedly upon him, as from a tower of observation.

'There is no answer,' said Nicholas, laying the parcel on a table beside him.

Newman said nothing, but folding his arms, and thrusting his head forward so as to obtain a nearer view of Nicholas's face, scanned his features closely.

'No answer,' said Nicholas, speaking very loud, under the impression that Newman Noggs was deaf.

Newman placed his hands upon his knees, and, without uttering a syllable, continued the same close scrutiny of his companion's face.

This was such a very singular proceeding on the part of an utter stranger, and his appearance was so extremely peculiar, that Nicholas, who had a sufficiently keen sense of the ridiculous, could not refrain from breaking into a smile as he inquired whether Mr Noggs had any commands for him.

Noggs shook his head and sighed; upon which Nicholas rose, and remarking that he required no rest, bade him good morning.

It was a great exertion for Newman Noggs, and nobody knows to this day how he ever came to make it, the other party being wholly unknown to him, but he drew a long breath and actually said, out loud, without once stopping, that if the young gentleman did not object to tell, he should like to know what his uncle was going to do for him.

Nicholas had not the least objection in the world, but on the contrary was rather pleased to have an opportunity of talking on the subject which occupied his thoughts; so, he sat down again, and (his sanguine imagination warming as he spoke) entered into a fervent and glowing description of all the honours and advantages to be derived from his appointment at that seat of learning, Dotheboys Hall.

'But, what's the matter—are you ill?' said Nicholas, suddenly breaking off, as his companion, after throwing himself into a variety of uncouth attitudes, thrust his hands under the stool, and cracked his finger-joints as if he were snapping all the bones in his hands.

Newman Noggs made no reply, but went on shrugging his shoulders and cracking his finger-joints; smiling horribly all the time, and looking steadfastly at nothing out of the tops of his eyes, in a most ghastly manner.

At first, Nicholas thought the mysterious man was in a fit, but, on further consideration, decided that he was in liquor, under which circumstances he deemed it prudent to make off at once. He looked back when he had got the street-door open. Newman Noggs was still indulging in the same extraordinary gestures, and the crackling of his fingers sounded louder than ever.

If tears dropped into a trunk were charms to preserve its owner from sorrow and misfortune, Nicholas Nickleby would have commenced his expedition under most happy auspices. There was so much to be done, and so little time to do it in; so many kind words to be spoken, and such bitter pain in the hearts in which they rose to impede their utterance; that the little preparations for his journey were made mournfully indeed. A hundred things which the anxious care of his mother and sister deemed indispensable for his comfort, Nicholas insisted on leaving behind, as they might prove of some after use, or might be convertible into money if occasion required. A hundred affectionate contests on such points as these took place on the sad night which preceded his departure; and, as the termination of every angerless dispute brought them nearer and nearer to the close of their slight preparations, Kate grew busier and busier, and wept more silently.

The box was packed at last, and then there came supper, with some little delicacy provided for the occasion, and as a set-off against the expense of which, Kate and her mother had feigned to dine when Nicholas was out. The poor lad nearly choked himself by attempting to partake of it, and almost suffocated himself in affecting a jest or two, and forcing a melancholy laugh. Thus, they lingered on till the hour of separating for the night was long past; and then they found that they might as well have given vent to their real feelings before, for they could not suppress them, do what they would. So they let them have their way, and even that was a relief.

Nicholas slept well till six next morning; dreamed of home, or of what was home once—no matter which, for things that are changed or gone will come back as they used to be, thank God! in sleep—and rose quite brisk and gay. He wrote a few lines in pencil to say the good bye which he was afraid to pronounce himself, and laying them, with half his scanty stock of money, at his sister's door, shouldered his box and crept softly down stairs.

[…]By the time he had found a man to carry his box it was only seven o'clock, so he walked slowly on, a little in advance of the porter, and very probably with not half as light a heart in his breast as the man had, although he had no waistcoat to cover it with, and had evidently, from the appearance of his other garments, been spending the night in a stable, and taking his breakfast at a pump.

Regarding, with no small curiosity and interest, all the busy preparations for the coming day which every street and almost every house displayed; and thinking, now and then, that it seemed rather hard that so many people of all ranks and stations could earn a livelihood in London, and that he should be compelled to journey so far in search of one; Nicholas speedily arrived at the Saracen's Head, Snow Hill.

Having dismissed his attendant, and seen the box safely deposited in the coach-office, he looked into the coffee-room in search of Mr Squeers.

He found that learned gentleman sitting at breakfast, with the three little boys before noticed, and two others who had turned up by some lucky chance since the interview of the previous day, ranged in a row on the opposite seat. Mr Squeers had before him a small measure of coffee, a plate of hot toast, and a cold round of beef; but he was at that moment intent on preparing breakfast for the little boys.

'This is twopenn'orth of milk, is it, waiter?' said Mr Squeers, looking down into a large blue mug, and slanting it gently, so as to get an accurate view of the quantity of liquid contained in it.

'That's twopenn'orth, sir,' replied the waiter.

'What a rare article milk is, to be sure, in London!' said Mr Squeers with a sigh. 'Just fill that mug up with lukewarm water, William, will you?'

'To the wery top, sir?' inquired the waiter. 'Why, the milk will be drownded.'

'Never you mind that,' replied Mr Squeers. 'Serve it right for being so dear. You ordered that thick bread and butter for three, did you?'

'Coming directly, sir.'

'You needn't hurry yourself,' said Squeers; 'there's plenty of time. Conquer your passions, boys, and don't be eager after vittles.' As he uttered this moral precept, Mr Squeers took a large bite out of the cold beef, and recognised Nicholas.

'Sit down, Mr Nickleby,' said Squeers. 'Here we are, a breakfasting you see!'

Nicholas did *not* see that anybody was breakfasting, except Mr Squeers; but he bowed with all becoming reverence, and looked as cheerful as he could.

'Oh! that's the milk and water, is it, William?' said Squeers. 'Very good; don't forget the bread and butter presently.'

At this fresh mention of the bread and butter, the five little boys looked very eager, and followed the waiter out, with their eyes; meanwhile Mr Squeers tasted the milk and water.

'Ah!' said that gentleman, smacking his lips, 'here's richness! Think of the many beggars and orphans in the streets that would be glad of this, little boys. A shocking thing hunger is, isn't it, Mr Nickleby?'

'Very shocking, sir,' said Nicholas.

'When I say number one,' pursued Mr Squeers, putting the mug before the children, 'the boy on the left hand nearest the window may take a drink; and when I say number two, the boy next him will go in, and so till we come to number five, which is the last boy. Are you ready?'

'Yes, sir,' cried all the little boys with great eagerness.

'That's right,' said Squeers, calmly getting on with his breakfast; 'keep ready till I tell you to begin. Subdue your appetites, my dears, and you've conquered human natur. This is the way we inculcate strength of mind, Mr Nickleby,' said the schoolmaster, turning to Nicholas, and speaking with his mouth very full of beef and toast.

Nicholas murmured something—he knew not what—in reply; and the little boys, dividing their gaze between the mug, the bread and butter (which had by this time arrived), and every morsel which Mr Squeers took into his mouth, remained with strained eyes in torments of expectation.

'Thank God for a good breakfast,' said Squeers when he had finished. 'Number one may take a drink.'

Number one seized the mug ravenously, and had just drunk enough to make him wish for more, when Mr Squeers gave the signal for number two, who gave up at the same interesting moment to number three; and the process was repeated until the milk and water terminated with number five.

'And now,' said the schoolmaster, dividing the bread and butter for three into as many portions as there were children, 'you had better look sharp with your breakfast, for the horn will blow in a minute or two, and then every boy leaves off.'

Permission being thus given to fall to, the boys began to eat voraciously, and in desperate haste: while the schoolmaster (who was in high good humour after his meal) picked his teeth with a fork, and looked smilingly on. In a very short time, the horn was heard.

'I thought it wouldn't be long,' said Squeers, jumping up and producing a little basket from under the seat; 'put what you haven't had time to eat, in here, boys! You'll want it on the road!'

Nicholas was considerably startled by these very economical arrangements; but he had no time to reflect upon them, for the little boys had to be got up to the top of the coach, and their boxes had to be brought out and put in, and Mr Squeers's luggage was to be seen carefully deposited in the boot, and all these offices were in his department. He was in the full heat and bustle of concluding these operations, when his uncle, Mr Ralph Nickleby, accosted him.

'Oh! here you are, sir!' said Ralph. 'Here are your mother and sister, sir.'

'Where!' cried Nicholas, looking hastily round.

'Here!' replied his uncle. 'Having too much money and nothing at all to do with it, they were paying a hackney coach as I came up, sir.'

'We were afraid of being too late to see him before he went away from us,' said Mrs Nickleby, embracing her son, heedless of the unconcerned lookers-on in the coach-yard.

'Very good, ma'am,' returned Ralph; 'you're the best judge of course. I merely said that you were paying a hackney coach. *I* never pay a hackney coach, ma'am, I never hire one. I haven't been in a hackney coach of my own hiring, for thirty years, and I hope I shan't be for thirty more, if I live as long.'

'I should never have forgiven myself if I had not seen him,' said Mrs Nickleby. 'Poor dear boy—going away without his breakfast too, because he feared to distress us!'

'Mighty fine certainly,' said Ralph, with great testiness. 'When I first went to business, ma'am, I took a penny loaf and a ha'porth of milk for my breakfast as I walked to the city every morning; what do you say to that, ma'am? Breakfast! Bah!'

'Now, Nickleby,' said Squeers, coming up at the moment buttoning his great-coat; 'I think you'd better get up behind. I'm afraid of one of them boys falling off, and then there's twenty pound a year gone.'

'Dear Nicholas,' whispered Kate, touching her brother's arm, 'who is that vulgar man?'

'Eh!' growled Ralph, whose quick ears had caught the inquiry. 'Do you wish to be introduced to Mr Squeers, my dear?'

'That the schoolmaster! No, uncle. Oh no!' replied Kate, shrinking back.

'I'm sure I heard you say as much, my dear,' retorted Ralph in his cold sarcastic manner. 'Mr Squeers, here's my niece: Nicholas's sister!'

'Very glad to make your acquaintance, miss,' said Squeers, raising his hat an inch or two. 'I wish Mrs Squeers took gals, and we had you for a teacher. I don't know, though, whether she mightn't grow jealous if we had. Ha! ha! ha!'

If the proprietor of Dotheboys Hall could have known what was passing in his assistant's breast at that moment, he would have discovered, with some surprise, that he was as near being soundly pummelled as he had ever been in his life. Kate Nickleby, having a quicker perception of her brother's emotions, led him gently aside, and thus prevented Mr Squeers from being impressed with the fact in a peculiarly disagreeable manner.

'My dear Nicholas,' said the young lady, 'who is this man? What kind of place can it be that you are going to?'

'I hardly know, Kate,' replied Nicholas, pressing his sister's hand. 'I suppose the Yorkshire folks are rather rough and uncultivated; that's all.'

'But this person,' urged Kate.

'Is my employer, or master, or whatever the proper name may be,' replied Nicholas quickly, 'and I was an ass to take his coarseness ill. They are looking this way, and it is time I was in my place. Bless you, love, and good bye! Mother; look forward to our meeting again some day! Uncle, farewell! Thank you heartily for all you have done and all you mean to do. Quite ready, sir!'

With these hasty adieux, Nicholas mounted nimbly to his seat, and waved his hand as gallantly as if his heart went with it.

At this moment, when the coachman and guard were comparing notes for the last time before starting on the subject of the way-bill; when porters were screwing out the last reluctant sixpences, itinerant newsmen making the last offer of a morning paper, and the horses giving the last impatient rattle to their harness; Nicholas felt somebody pulling softly at his leg. He looked down, and there stood Newman Noggs, who pushed up into his hand a dirty letter.

'What's this?' inquired Nicholas.

'Hush!' rejoined Noggs, pointing to Mr Ralph Nickleby, who was saying a few earnest words to Squeers, a short distance off. 'Take it. Read it. Nobody knows. That's all.'

'Stop!' cried Nicholas.

'No,' replied Noggs.

Nicholas cried stop, again, but Newman Noggs was gone.

A minute's bustle, a banging of the coach doors, a swaying of the vehicle to one side, as the heavy coachman, and still heavier guard, climbed into their seats; a cry of all right, a few notes from the horn, a hasty glance of two sorrowful faces below and the hard features of Mr Ralph Nickleby—and the coach was gone too, and rattling over the stones of Smithfield.

Mr Squeers, being safely landed, left Nicholas and the boys standing with the luggage in the road, to amuse themselves by looking at the coach as it changed horses, while he ran into the tavern and went through the leg-stretching process at the bar. After some minutes, he returned, with his legs thoroughly stretched, if the hue of his nose and a short hiccup afforded any criterion; and at the same time there came out of the yard a rusty pony-chaise, and a cart, driven by two labouring men.

'Put the boys and the boxes into the cart,' said Squeers, rubbing his hands; 'and this young man and me will go on in the chaise. Get in, Nickleby.'

Nicholas obeyed. Mr Squeers with some difficulty inducing the pony to obey also, they started off, leaving the cart-load of infant misery to follow at leisure.

'Are you cold, Nickleby?' inquired Squeers, after they had travelled some distance in silence.

'Rather, sir, I must say.'

'Well, I don't find fault with that,' said Squeers; 'it's a long journey this weather.'

'Is it much farther to Dotheboys Hall, sir?' asked Nicholas.

'About three mile from here,' replied Squeers. 'But you needn't call it a Hall down here.'

Nicholas coughed, as if he would like to know why.

'The fact is, it ain't a Hall,' observed Squeers drily.

'Oh, indeed!' said Nicholas, whom this piece of intelligence much astonished.

'No,' replied Squeers. 'We call it a Hall up in London, because it sounds better, but they don't know it by that name in these parts. A man may call his house an island if he likes; there's no act of Parliament against that, I believe?'

'I believe not, sir,' rejoined Nicholas.

Squeers eyed his companion slily at the conclusion of this little dialogue, and finding that he had grown thoughtful and appeared in nowise disposed to volunteer any observations, contented himself with lashing the pony until they reached their journey's end.

'Jump out,' said Squeers. 'Hallo there! come and put this horse up. Be quick, will you!'

While the schoolmaster was uttering these and other impatient cries, Nicholas had time to observe that the school was a long, cold-looking house, one story high, with a few straggling outbuildings behind, and a barn and stable adjoining. After the lapse of a minute or two, the noise of somebody unlocking the yard-gate was heard, and presently a tall lean boy, with a lantern in his hand, issued forth.

'Is that you, Smike?' cried Squeers.

'Yes, sir,' replied the boy.

'Then why the devil didn't you come before?'

'Please, sir, I fell asleep over the fire,' answered Smike, with humility.

'Fire! what fire? Where's there a fire?' demanded the schoolmaster, sharply.

'Only in the kitchen, sir,' replied the boy. 'Missus said as I was sitting up, I might go in there for a warm.'

'Your Missus is a fool,' retorted Squeers. 'You'd have been a deuced deal more wakeful in the cold, I'll engage.'

By this time Mr Squeers had dismounted; and after ordering the boy to see to the pony, and to take care that he hadn't any more corn that night, he told Nicholas to wait at the front door a minute while he went round and let him in.

A host of unpleasant misgivings, which had been crowding upon Nicholas during the whole journey, thronged into his mind with redoubled force when he was left alone. His great distance from home and the impossibility of reaching it, except on foot, should he feel ever so anxious to return, presented itself to him in most alarming colours; and as he looked up at the dreary house and dark windows, and upon the wild country round, covered with snow, he felt a depression of heart and spirit which he had never experienced before.

'Now then!' cried Squeers, poking his head out at the front door. 'Where are you, Nickleby?'

'Here, sir,' replied Nicholas.

'Come in, then,' said Squeers, 'the wind blows in at this door fit to knock a man off his legs.'

Nicholas sighed, and hurried in. Mr Squeers, having bolted the door to keep it shut, ushered him into a small parlour scantily furnished with a few chairs, a yellow map hung against the wall, and a couple of tables; one of which bore some preparations for supper; while, on the other, a tutor's assistant, a Murray's grammar, half a dozen cards of terms, and a worn letter directed to Wackford Squeers, Esquire, were arranged in picturesque confusion.

They had not been in this apartment a couple of minutes, when a female bounced into the room, and, seizing Mr Squeers by the throat, gave him two loud kisses: one close after the other, like a postman's knock. The lady, who was of a large raw-boned figure, was about half a head taller than Mr Squeers, and was dressed in a dimity night-jacket; with her hair in papers; she had also a dirty nightcap on, relieved by a yellow cotton handkerchief which tied it under the chin.

'How is my Squeery?' said this lady in a playful manner, and a very hoarse voice.

'Quite well, my love,' replied Squeers. 'How's the cows?'

'All right, every one of 'em,' answered the lady.

'And the pigs?' said Squeers.

'As well as they were when you went away.'

'Come; that's a blessing,' said Squeers, pulling off his great-coat. 'The boys are all as they were, I suppose?'

'Oh, yes, they're well enough,' replied Mrs Squeers, snappishly. 'That young Pitcher's had a fever.'

'No!' exclaimed Squeers. 'Damn that boy, he's always at something of that sort.'

'Never was such a boy, I do believe,' said Mrs Squeers; 'whatever he has is always catching too. I say it's obstinacy, and nothing shall ever convince me that it isn't. I'd beat it out of him; and I told you that, six months ago.'

'So you did, my love,' rejoined Squeers. 'We'll try what can be done.'

Pending these little endearments, Nicholas had stood, awkwardly enough, in the middle of the room: not very well knowing whether he was expected to retire into the passage, or to remain where he was. He was now relieved from his perplexity by Mr Squeers.

'This is the new young man, my dear,' said that gentleman.

'Oh,' replied Mrs Squeers, nodding her head at Nicholas, and eyeing him coldly from top to toe.

'He'll take a meal with us to-night,' said Squeers, 'and go among the boys to-morrow morning. You can give him a shake-down here to-night, can't you?'

'We must manage it somehow,' replied the lady. 'You don't much mind how you sleep, I suppose, sir?'

'No, indeed,' replied Nicholas, 'I am not particular.'

'That's lucky,' said Mrs Squeers. And as the lady's humour was considered to lie chiefly in retort, Mr Squeers laughed heartily, and seemed to expect that Nicholas should do the same.

After some further conversation between the master and mistress relative to the success of Mr Squeers's trip, and the people who had paid, and the people who had made default in payment, a young servant girl brought in a Yorkshire pie and some cold beef, which being set upon the table, the boy Smike appeared with a jug of ale.

Mr Squeers was emptying his great-coat pockets of letters to different boys, and other small documents, which he had brought down in them. The boy glanced, with an anxious and timid expression, at the papers, as if with a sickly hope that one among them might relate to him. The look was a very painful one, and went to Nicholas's heart at once; for it told a long and very sad history.

It induced him to consider the boy more attentively, and he was surprised to observe the extraordinary mixture of garments which formed his dress. Although he could not have been less than eighteen or nineteen years old, and was tall for that age, he wore a skeleton suit, such as is usually put upon very little boys, and which, though most absurdly short in the arms and legs, was quite wide enough for his attenuated frame. In order that the lower part of his legs might be in perfect keeping with this singular dress, he had a very large pair of boots, originally made for tops, which might have been once worn by some stout farmer, but were now too patched and tattered for a beggar. Heaven knows how long he had been there, but he still wore the same linen which he had first taken down; for, round his neck, was a tattered child's frill, only half concealed by a coarse, man's neckerchief. He was lame; and as he feigned to be busy in arranging the table, glanced at the letters with a look so keen, and yet so dispirited and hopeless, that Nicholas could hardly bear to watch him.

'What are you bothering about there, Smike?' cried Mrs Squeers; 'let the things alone, can't you?'

'Eh!' said Squeers, looking up. 'Oh! it's you, is it?'

'Yes, sir,' replied the youth, pressing his hands together, as though to control, by force, the nervous wandering of his fingers ; 'Is there—'

'Well!' said Squeers.

'Have you—did anybody—has nothing been heard—about me?'

'Devil a bit,' replied Squeers testily.

The lad withdrew his eyes, and, putting his hand to his face, moved towards the door.

'Not a word,' resumed Squeers, 'and never will be. Now, this is a pretty sort of thing, isn't it, that you should have been left here, all these years, and no money paid after the first six—nor no notice taken, nor no clue to be got who you belong to? It's a pretty sort of thing that I should have to feed a great fellow like you, and never hope to get one penny for it, isn't it?'

The boy put his hand to his head as if he were making an effort to recollect something, and then, looking vacantly at his questioner, gradually broke into a smile, and limped away.

'I'll tell you what, Squeers,' remarked his wife as the door closed, 'I think that young chap's turning silly.'

'I hope not,' said the schoolmaster; 'for he's a handy fellow out of doors, and worth his meat and drink, anyway. I should think he'd have wit enough for us though, if he was. But come; let's have supper, for I am hungry and tired, and want to get to bed.'

The reminder brought in an exclusive steak for Mr Squeers, who speedily proceeded to do it ample justice. Nicholas drew up his chair, but his appetite was effectually taken away.

'How's the steak, Squeers?' said Mrs S.

'Tender as a lamb,' replied Squeers. 'Have a bit.'

'I couldn't eat a morsel,' replied his wife. 'What'll the young man take, my dear?'

'Whatever he likes that's present,' rejoined Squeers, in a most unusual burst of generosity.

'What do you say, Mr Knuckleboy?' inquired Mrs Squeers.

'I'll take a little of the pie, if you please,' replied Nicholas. 'A very little, for I'm not hungry.'

'Well, it's a pity to cut the pie if you're not hungry, isn't it?' said Mrs Squeers. 'Will you try a bit of the beef?'

'Whatever you please,' replied Nicholas, abstractedly; 'it's all the same to me.'

Mrs Squeers looked vastly gracious on receiving this reply; and nodding to Squeers, as much as to say that she was glad to find the young man knew his station, assisted Nicholas to a slice of meat with her own fair hands.

'Ale, Squeery?' inquired the lady, winking and frowning to give him to understand that the question propounded, was, whether Nicholas should have ale, and not whether he (Squeers) would take any.

'Certainly,' said Squeers, re-telegraphing in the same manner. 'A glassful.'

So Nicholas had a glassful, and, being occupied with his own reflections, drank it, in happy innocence of all the foregone proceedings.

'Uncommon juicy steak that,' said Squeers, as he laid down his knife and fork, after plying it, in silence, for some time.

'It's prime meat,' rejoined his lady, 'I bought a good large piece of it myself on purpose for—'

'For what!' exclaimed Squeers hastily. 'Not for the—'

'No, no; not for them,' rejoined Mrs Squeers; 'on purpose for you against you came home. Lor! you didn't think I could have made such a mistake as that.'

'Upon my word, my dear, I didn't know what you were going to say,' said Squeers, who had turned pale.

'You needn't make yourself uncomfortable,' remarked his wife, laughing heartily. 'To think that I should be such a noddy! Well!'

This part of the conversation was rather unintelligible; but popular rumour in the neighbourhood asserted that Mr Squeers, being amiably opposed to cruelty to animals, not unfrequently purchased for boy consumption the bodies of horned cattle who had died a natural death; possibly he was apprehensive of having unintentionally devoured some choice morsel intended for the young gentlemen.

Supper being over, and removed by a small servant girl with a hungry eye, Mrs Squeers retired to lock it up, and also to take into safe custody the clothes of the five boys who had just arrived, and who were half-way up the troublesome flight of steps which leads to death's door, in consequence of exposure to the cold. They were then regaled with a light supper of porridge, and stowed away, side by side, in a small bedstead, to warm each other, and dream of a substantial meal with something hot after it, if their fancies set that way: which it is not at all improbable they did.

Mr Squeers treated himself to a stiff tumbler of brandy and water, made on the liberal half-and-half principle, allowing for the dissolution of the sugar; and his amiable helpmate mixed Nicholas the ghost of a small glassful of the same compound. This done, Mr and Mrs Squeers drew close up to the fire, and sitting with their feet on the fender, talked confidentially in whispers; while Nicholas, taking up the tutor's assistant, read the interesting legends in the miscellaneous questions, and all the figures into the bargain, with as much thought or consciousness of what he was doing as if he had been in a magnetic slumber.

At length, Mr Squeers yawned fearfully, and opined that it was high time to go to bed; upon which signal, Mrs Squeers and the girl dragged in a small straw mattress and a couple of blankets, and arranged them into a couch for Nicholas.

'We'll put you into your regular bed-room to-morrow, Nickleby,' said Squeers. 'Let me see! Who sleeps in Brooks's bed, my dear?'

'In Brooks's,' said Mrs Squeers, pondering. 'There's Jennings, little Bolder, Graymarsh, and what's his name.'

'So there is,' rejoined Squeers. 'Yes! Brooks is full.'

'Full!' thought Nicholas. 'I should think he was.'

'There's a place somewhere, I know,' said Squeers; 'but I can't at this moment call to mind where it is. However, we'll have that all settled to-morrow. Good night, Nickleby. Seven o'clock in the morning, mind.'

'I shall be ready, sir,' replied Nicholas. 'Good night.'

'I'll come in myself and show you where the well is,' said Squeers. 'You'll always find a little bit of soap in the kitchen window; that belongs to you.'

Nicholas opened his eyes, but not his mouth; and Squeers was again going away, when he once more turned back.

'I don't know, I am sure,' he said, 'whose towel to put you on; but if you'll make shift with something to-morrow morning, Mrs Squeers will arrange that, in the course of the day. My dear, don't forget.'

'I'll take care,' replied Mrs Squeers; 'and mind *you* take care, young man, and get first wash. The teacher ought always to have it; but they get the better of him if they can.'

Mr Squeers then nudged Mrs Squeers to bring away the brandy bottle, lest Nicholas should help himself in the night; and the lady having seized it with great precipitation, they retired together.

Nicholas, being left alone, took half a dozen turns up and down the room in a condition of much agitation and excitement; but, growing gradually calmer, sat himself down in a chair, and mentally resolved that, come what come might, he would endeavour, for a time, to bear whatever wretchedness might be in store for him, and that remembering the helplessness of his mother and sister, he would give his uncle no plea for deserting them in their need. Good resolutions seldom fail of producing some good effect in the mind from which they spring. He grew less desponding, and—so sanguine and buoyant is youth—even hoped that affairs at Dotheboys Hall might yet proved better than they promised.

He was preparing for bed, with something like renewed cheerfulness, when a sealed letter fell from his coat pocket. In the hurry of leaving London, it had escaped his attention, and had not occurred to him since, but it at once brought back to him the recollection of the mysterious behaviour of Newman Noggs.

'Dear me!' said Nicholas; 'what an extraordinary hand!'

It was directed to himself, was written upon very dirty paper, and in such cramped and crippled writing as to be almost illegible. After great difficulty and much puzzling, he contrived to read as follows: —

'My dear young Man.

'I know the world. Your father did not, or he would not have done me a kindness when there was no hope of return. You do not, or you would not be bound on such a journey.

'If ever you want a shelter in London (don't be angry at this, *I* once thought I never should), they know where I live, at the sign of the Crown, in Silver Street, Golden Square. It is at the corner of Silver Street and James Street, with a bar door both ways. You can come at night. Once, nobody was ashamed—never mind that. It's all over.

'Excuse errors. I should forget how to wear a whole coat now. I have forgotten all my old ways. My spelling may have gone with them.

'NEWMAN NOGGS.

'P. S. If you should go near Barnard Castle, there is good ale at the King's Head. Say you know me, and I am sure they will not charge you for it. You may say *Mr* Noggs there, for I was a gentleman then. I was indeed.'

It may be a very undignified circumstance to record, but after he had folded this letter and placed it in his pocket-book, Nicholas Nickleby's eyes were dimmed with a moisture that might have been taken for tears.

A ride of two hundred and odd miles in severe weather is one of the best softeners of a hard bed that ingenuity can devise. Perhaps it is even a sweetener of dreams for those which hovered over the rough couch of Nicholas and whispered their airy nothings in his ear, were of an agreeable and happy kind. He was making his fortune very fast indeed, when the faint glimmer of an expiring candle shone before his eyes, and a voice he had no difficulty in recognising as part and parcel of Mr Squeers, admonished him that it was time to rise.

'Past seven, Nickleby,' said Mr Squeers.

'Has morning come already?' asked Nicholas, sitting up in bed.

'Ah! that has it,' replied Squeers, 'and ready iced too. Now, Nickleby, come; tumble up, will you?'

Nicholas needed no further admonition, but 'tumbled up' at once, and proceeded to dress himself by the light of the taper, which Mr Squeers carried in his hand.

'Here's a pretty go,' said that gentleman; 'the pump's froze.'

'Indeed!' said Nicholas, not much interested in the intelligence.

'Yes,' replied Squeers. 'You can't wash yourself this morning.'

'Not wash myself!' exclaimed Nicholas.

'No, not a bit of it,' rejoined Squeers tartly. 'So you must be content with giving yourself a dry polish till we break the ice in the well, and can get a bucketful out for the boys. Don't stand staring at me, but do look sharp, will you?'

Offering no further observation, Nicholas huddled on his clothes. Squeers, meanwhile, opened the shutters and blew the candle out;

when the voice of his amiable consort was heard in the passage, demanding admittance.

'Come in, my love,' said Squeers.

Mrs Squeers came in, still habited in the primitive night-jacket which had displayed the symmetry of her figure on the previous night, and further ornamented with a beaver bonnet of some antiquity, which she wore, with much ease and lightness, on the top of the nightcap before mentioned.

'Drat the things,' said the lady, opening the cupboard; 'I can't find the school spoon anywhere.'

'Never mind it, my dear,' observed Squeers in a soothing manner; 'it's of no consequence.'

'No consequence, why how you talk!' retorted Mrs Squeers sharply; 'isn't it brimstone morning?'

'I forgot, my dear,' rejoined Squeers; 'yes, it certainly is. We purify the boys' bloods now and then, Nickleby.'

'Purify fiddlesticks' ends,' said his lady. 'Don't think, young man, that we go to the expense of flower of brimstone and molasses, just to purify them; because if you think we carry on the business in that way, you'll find yourself mistaken, and so I tell you plainly.'

'My dear,' said Squeers frowning. 'Hem!'

'Oh! nonsense,' rejoined Mrs Squeers. 'If the young man comes to be a teacher here, let him understand, at once, that we don't want any foolery about the boys. They have the brimstone and treacle, partly because if they hadn't something or other in the way of medicine they'd be always ailing and giving a world of trouble, and partly because it spoils their appetites and comes cheaper than breakfast and dinner. So, it does them good and us good at the same time, and that's fair enough, I'm sure.'

Having given this explanation, Mrs Squeers put her hand into the closet and instituted a stricter search after the spoon, in which Mr Squeers assisted. A few words passed between them while they were thus engaged, but as their voices were partially stifled by the cupboard, all that Nicholas could distinguish was, that Mr Squeers said what Mrs Squeers had said, was injudicious, and that Mrs Squeers said what Mr Squeers said, was 'stuff.'

A vast deal of searching and rummaging ensued, and it proving fruitless, Smike was called in, and pushed by Mrs Squeers, and boxed by Mr Squeers; which course of treatment brightening his intellects, enabled him to suggest that possibly Mrs Squeers might have the spoon in her pocket, as indeed turned out to be the case. As Mrs Squeers had previously protested, however, that she was quite certain she had not got it, Smike received another box on the ear for presuming to contradict his mistress, together with a promise of a sound thrashing if he were not more respectful in future; so that he took nothing very advantageous by his motion.

'A most invaluable woman, that, Nickleby,' said Squeers when his consort had hurried away, pushing the drudge before her.

'Indeed, sir!' observed Nicholas.

'I don't know her equal,' said Squeers; 'I do not know her equal. That woman, Nickleby, is always the same—always the same bustling, lively, active, saving creetur that you see her now.'

Nicholas sighed involuntarily at the thought of the agreeable domestic prospect thus opened to him; but Squeers was, fortunately, too much occupied with his own reflections to perceive it.

'It's my way to say, when I am up in London,' continued Squeers, 'that to them boys she is a mother. But she is more than a mother to them; ten times more. She does things for them boys, Nickleby, that I don't believe half the mothers going, would do for their own sons.'

'I should think they would not, sir,' answered Nicholas.

Now, the fact was, that both Mr and Mrs Squeers viewed the boys in the light of their proper and natural enemies; or, in other words, they held and considered that their business and profession was to get as much from every boy as could by possibility be screwed out of him. On this point they were both agreed, and behaved in unison accordingly. The only difference between them was, that Mrs Squeers waged war against the enemy openly and fearlessly, and that Squeers covered his rascality, even at home, with a spice of his habitual deceit; as if he really had a notion of some day or other being able to take himself in, and persuade his own mind that he was a very good fellow.

'But come,' said Squeers, interrupting the progress of some thoughts to this effect in the mind of his usher, 'let's go to the school-room; and lend me a hand with my school coat, will you?'

Nicholas assisted his master to put on an old fustian shooting-jacket, which he took down from a peg in the passage; and Squeers, arming himself with his cane, led the way across a yard, to a door in the rear of the house.

'There,' said the schoolmaster as they stepped in together; 'this is our shop, Nickleby!'

It was such a crowded scene, and there were so many objects to attract attention, that, at first, Nicholas stared about him, really without seeing anything at all. By degrees, however, the place resolved itself into a bare and dirty room, with a couple of windows, whereof a tenth part might be of glass, the remainder being stopped up with old copybooks and paper. There were a couple of long old rickety desks, cut and notched, and inked, and damaged, in every possible way; two or three forms; a detached desk for Squeers; and another for his assistant. The ceiling was supported, like that of a barn, by cross beams and rafters; and the walls were so stained and discoloured that it was impossible to tell whether they had ever been touched with paint or whitewash.

But the pupils—the young noblemen! How the last faint traces of hope, the remotest glimmering of any good to be derived from his efforts in this den, faded from the mind of Nicholas as he looked in dismay around! Pale and haggard faces, lank and bony figures, children with the countenances of old men, deformities with irons upon their limbs, boys of stunted growth, and others whose long meagre legs would hardly bear their stooping bodies, all crowded on the view together; there were the bleared eye, the hare-lip, the crooked foot, and every ugliness or distortion that told of unnatural aversion conceived by parents for their offspring, or of young lives which, from the earliest dawn of infancy, had been one horrible endurance of cruelty and neglect. There were little faces which should have been handsome, darkened with the scowl of sullen, dogged suffering; there was childhood with the light of its eye quenched, its beauty gone, and its helplessness alone remaining; there were vicious-faced boys, brooding, with leaden eyes, like malefactors in a jail; and there were young creatures on whom the sins of their frail parents had descended, weeping even for the mercenary nurses they had known, and lonesome even in their loneliness. With every kindly sympathy and affection blasted in its birth, with every young and healthy feeling flogged and starved down, with every revengeful passion that can fester in swollen hearts eating its evil way to their core in silence, what an incipient Hell was breeding here!

And yet this scene, painful as it was, had its grotesque features, which, in a less interested observer than Nicholas, might have provoked a smile. Mrs Squeers stood at one of the desks, presiding over an immense basin of brimstone and treacle, of which delicious compound she administered a large instalment to each boy in succession: using for the purpose a common wooden spoon, which might have been originally manufactured for some gigantic top, and which widened every young gentleman's mouth considerably; they being all obliged, under heavy corporal penalties, to take in the whole of the bowl at a gasp. In another corner, huddled together for companionship, were the little boys who had arrived on the preceding night, three of them in very large leather breeches, and two in old trousers, a something tighter fit than drawers are usually worn; at no great distance from these was seated the juvenile son and heir of Mr Squeers—a striking likeness of his father—kicking, with great vigour, under the hands of Smike, who was fitting upon him a pair of new boots that bore a most suspicious resemblance to those which the least of the little boys had worn on the journey down—as the little boy himself seemed to think, for he was regarding the appropriation with a look of most rueful amazement. Besides these, there was a long row of boys waiting, with countenances of no pleasant anticipation, to be treacled; and another file, who had just escaped from the infliction, making a variety of wry mouths indicative of anything but satisfaction. The whole were attired in such motley, ill-sorted, extraordinary garments, as would have been irresistibly ridiculous, but for the foul appearance of dirt, disorder, and disease, with which they were associated.

'Now,' said Squeers, giving the desk a great rap with his cane, which made half the little boys nearly jump out of their boots, 'is that physicking over?'

'Just over,' said Mrs Squeers, choking the last boy in her hurry, and tapping the crown of his head with the wooden spoon to restore him. 'Here, you Smike; take away now. Look sharp!'

Smike shuffled out with the basin, and Mrs Squeers having called up a little boy with a curly head and wiped her hands upon it, hurried out after him into a species of wash-house, where there was a small fire and a large kettle, together with a number of little wooden bowls which were arranged upon a board.

Into these bowls, Mrs Squeers, assisted by the hungry servant, poured a brown composition which looked like diluted pincushions without the covers, and was called porridge. A minute wedge of brown bread was inserted in each bowl, and when they had eaten their porridge by means of the bread, the boys ate the bread itself, and had finished their breakfast; whereupon Mr Squeers said, in a solemn voice, 'For what we have received, may the Lord make us truly thankful!'—and went away to his own.

Nicholas distended his stomach with a bowl of porridge, for much the same reason which induces some savages to swallow earth—lest they should be inconveniently hungry when there is nothing to eat. Having further disposed of a slice of bread and butter, allotted to him in virtue of his office, he sat himself down to wait for school-time.

He could not but observe how silent and sad the boys all seemed to be. There was none of the noise and clamour of a school-room; none of its boisterous play, or hearty mirth. The children sat crouching and shivering together, and seemed to lack the spirit to move about. The only pupil who evinced the slightest tendency towards locomotion or playfulness was Master Squeers, and as his chief amusement was to tread upon the other boys' toes in his new boots, his flow of spirits was rather disagreeable than otherwise.

After some half-hour's delay, Mr Squeers reappeared, and the boys took their places and their books, of which latter commodity the average might be about one to eight learners. A few minutes having elapsed, during which Mr Squeers looked very profound, as if he had a perfect apprehension of what was inside all the books, and could say every word of their contents by heart if he only chose to take the trouble, that gentleman called up the first class.

Obedient to this summons there ranged themselves in front of the schoolmaster's desk, half-a-dozen scarecrows, out at knees and elbows, one of whom placed a torn and filthy book beneath his learned eye.

'This is the first class in English spelling and philosophy, Nickleby,' said Squeers, beckoning Nicholas to stand beside him. 'We'll get up a Latin one, and hand that over to you. Now, then, where's the first boy?'

'Please, sir, he's cleaning the back parlour window,' said the temporary head of the philosophical class.

'So he is, to be sure,' rejoined Squeers. 'We go upon the practical mode of teaching, Nickleby; the regular education system. C-l-e-a-n, clean, verb active, to make bright, to scour. W-i-n, win, d-e-r, der, winder, a casement. When the boy knows this out of book, he goes and does it. It's just the same principle as the use of the globes. Where's the second boy!'

'Please, sir, he's weeding the garden,' replied a small voice.

'To be sure,' said Squeers, by no means disconcerted. 'So he is. B-o-t, bot, t-i-n, tin, bottin, n-e-y, ney, bottinney, noun substantive, a knowledge of plants. When he has learned that bottinney means a knowledge of plants, he goes and knows 'em. That's our system, Nickleby; what do you think of it?'

'It's a very useful one, at any rate,' answered Nicholas.

'I believe you,' rejoined Squeers, not remarking the emphasis of his usher. 'Third boy, what's a horse?'

'A beast, sir,' replied the boy.

'So it is,' said Squeers. 'Ain't it, Nickleby?'

'I believe there is no doubt of that, sir,' answered Nicholas.

'Of course there isn't,' said Squeers. 'A horse is a quadruped, and quadruped's Latin for beast, as every body that's gone through the grammar, knows, or else where's the use of having grammars at all?'

'Where, indeed!' said Nicholas abstractedly.

'As you're perfect in that,' resumed Squeers, turning to the boy, 'go and look after *my* horse, and rub him down well, or I'll rub you down. The rest of the class go and draw water up, till somebody tells you to leave off, for it's washing-day to-morrow, and they want the coppers filled.'

So saying, he dismissed the first class to their experiments in practical philosophy, and eyed Nicholas with a look, half cunning and half doubtful, as if he were not altogether certain what he might think of him by this time.

'That's the way we do it, Nickleby,' he said, after a pause.

Nicholas shrugged his shoulders in a manner that was scarcely perceptible, and said he saw it was.

'And a very good way it is, too,' said Squeers. 'Now, just take them fourteen little boys and hear them some reading, because, you know, you must begin to be useful. Idling about here, won't do.'

Mr Squeers said this, as if it had suddenly occurred to him, either that he must not say too much to his assistant, or that his assistant did not say enough to him in praise of the establishment. The children were arranged in a semicircle round the new master, and he was soon listening to their dull, drawling, hesitating recital of those stories of engrossing interest which are to be found in the more antiquated spelling books.

In this exciting occupation, the morning lagged heavily on. At one o'clock, the boys, having previously had their appetites thoroughly taken away by stir-about and potatoes, sat down in the kitchen to some hard salt beef, of which Nicholas was graciously permitted to take his portion to his own solitary desk, to eat it there in peace. After this, there was another hour of crouching in the school-room and shivering with cold, and then school began again.

It was Mr Squeers's custom to call the boys together and make a sort of report, after every half-yearly visit to the metropolis, regarding the relations and friends he had seen, the news he had heard, the letters he had brought down, the bills which had been paid, the accounts which had been left unpaid, and so forth. This solemn proceeding always took place in the afternoon of the day succeeding his return; perhaps, because the boys acquired strength of mind from the suspense of the morning, or, possibly, because Mr Squeers himself acquired greater sternness and inflexibility from certain warm potations in which he was wont to indulge after his early dinner. Be this as it may, the boys were recalled from house-window, garden, stable, and cow-yard, and the school were assembled in full conclave, when Mr Squeers, with a small bundle of papers in his hand, and Mrs S. following with a pair of canes, entered the room and proclaimed silence.

'Let any boy speak a word without leave,' said Mr Squeers mildly, 'and I'll take the skin off his back.'

This special proclamation had the desired effect, and a death-like silence immediately prevailed, in the midst of which Mr Squeers went on to say:

'Boys, I've been to London, and have returned to my family and you, as strong and well as ever.'

According to half-yearly custom, the boys gave three feeble cheers at this refreshing intelligence. Such cheers! Sighs of extra strength with the chill on.

'I have seen the parents of some boys,' continued Squeers, turning over his papers, 'and they're so glad to hear how their sons are getting on, that there's no prospect at all of their going away, which of course is a very pleasant thing to reflect upon, for all parties.'

Two or three hands went to two or three eyes when Squeers said this, but the greater part of the young gentlemen having no particular parents to speak of, were wholly uninterested in the thing one way or other.

'I have had disappointments to contend against,' said Squeers, looking very grim; 'Bolder's father was two pound ten short. Where is Bolder?'

'Here he is, please sir,' rejoined twenty officious voices. Boys are very like men to be sure.

'Come here, Bolder,' said Squeers.

An unhealthy-looking boy, with warts all over his hands, stepped from his place to the master's desk, and raised his eyes imploringly to Squeers's face; his own, quite white from the rapid beating of his heart.

'Bolder,' said Squeers, speaking very slowly, for he was considering, as the saying goes, where to have him. 'Bolder, if your father thinks that because—why, what's this, sir?'

As Squeers spoke, he caught up the boy's hand by the cuff of his jacket, and surveyed it with an edifying aspect of horror and disgust.

'What do you call this, sir?' demanded the schoolmaster, administering a cut with the cane to expedite the reply.

'I can't help it, indeed, sir,' rejoined the boy, crying. 'They will come; it's the dirty work I think, sir—at least I don't know what it is, sir, but it's not my fault.'

'Bolder,' said Squeers, tucking up his wristbands, and moistening the palm of his right hand to get a good grip of the cane, 'you are an incorrigible young scoundrel, and as the last thrashing did you no good, we must see what another will do towards beating it out of you.'

With this, and wholly disregarding a piteous cry for mercy, Mr Squeers fell upon the boy and caned him soundly: not leaving off indeed, until his arm was tired out.

'There,' said Squeers, when he had quite done; 'rub away as hard as you like, you won't rub that off in a hurry. Oh! you won't hold that noise, won't you? Put him out, Smike.'

The drudge knew better from long experience, than to hesitate about obeying, so he bundled the victim out by a side door, and Mr Squeers perched himself again on his own stool, supported by Mrs Squeers, who occupied another at his side.

'Now let us see,' said Squeers. 'A letter for Cobbey. Stand up, Cobbey.'

Another boy stood up, and eyed the letter very hard while Squeers made a mental abstract of the same.

'Oh!' said Squeers: 'Cobbey's grandmother is dead, and his uncle John has took to drinking, which is all the news his sister sends, except eighteenpence, which will just pay for that broken square of glass. Mrs Squeers, my dear, will you take the money?'

The worthy lady pocketed the eighteenpence with a most business-like air, and Squeers passed on to the next boy, as coolly as possible.

'Graymarsh,' said Squeers, 'he's the next. Stand up, Graymarsh.'

Another boy stood up, and the schoolmaster looked over the letter as before.

'Graymarsh's maternal aunt,' said Squeers, when he had possessed himself of the contents, 'is very glad to hear he's so well and happy, and sends her respectful compliments to Mrs Squeers, and thinks she must be an angel. She likewise thinks Mr Squeers is too good for this world; but hopes he may long be spared to carry on the business. Would have sent the two pair of stockings as desired, but is short of money, so forwards a tract instead, and hopes Graymarsh will put his trust in Providence. Hopes, above all, that he will study in everything to please Mr and Mrs Squeers, and look upon them as his only friends; and that he will love Master Squeers; and not object to sleeping five in a bed, which no Christian should. Ah!' said Squeers, folding it up, 'a delightful letter. Very affecting indeed.'

It was affecting in one sense, for Graymarsh's maternal aunt was strongly supposed, by her more intimate friends, to be no other than his maternal parent; Squeers, however, without alluding to this part of the story (which would have sounded immoral before boys), proceeded with the business by calling out 'Mobbs,' whereupon another boy rose, and Graymarsh resumed his seat.

'Mobbs's step-mother,' said Squeers, 'took to her bed on hearing that he wouldn't eat fat, and has been very ill ever since. She wishes to know, by an early post, where he expects to go to if he quarrels with his vittles; and with what feelings he could turn up his nose at the cow's liver broth, after his good master had asked a blessing on it. This was told her in the London newspapers—not by Mr Squeers, for he is too kind and too good to set anybody against anybody—and it has vexed her so much, Mobbs can't think. She is sorry to find he is discontented, which is sinful and horrid, and hopes Mr Squeers will flog him into a happier state of mind; with this view, she has also stopped his halfpenny a week pocket-money, and given a double-bladed knife with a corkscrew in it to the Missionaries, which she had bought on purpose for him.'

'A sulky state of feeling,' said Squeers, after a terrible pause, during which he had moistened the palm of his right hand again, 'won't do. Cheerfulness and contentment must be kept up. Mobbs, come to me!'

Mobbs moved slowly towards the desk, rubbing his eyes in anticipation of good cause for doing so; and he soon afterwards retired by the side door, with as good cause as a boy need have.

Mr Squeers then proceeded to open a miscellaneous collection of letters; some enclosing money, which Mrs Squeers 'took care of;' and others referring to small articles of apparel, as caps and so forth, all of which the same lady stated to be too large, or too small, and calculated for nobody but young Squeers, who would appear indeed to have had most accommodating limbs, since everything that came into the school fitted him to a nicety. His head, in particular, must have been singularly elastic, for hats and caps of all dimensions were alike to him.

This business despatched, a few slovenly lessons were performed, and Squeers retired to his fireside, leaving Nicholas to take care of the boys in the school-room, which was very cold, and where a meal of bread and cheese was served out shortly after dark.

There was a small stove at that corner of the room which was nearest to the master's desk, and by it Nicholas sat down, so depressed and self-degraded by the consciousness of his position, that if death could have come upon him at that time he would have been almost happy to meet it. The cruelty of which he had been an unwilling witness, the coarse and ruffianly behaviour of Squeers even in his best moods, the filthy place, the sights and sounds about him, all contributed to this state of feeling; but when he recollected that, being there as an assistant, he actually seemed—no matter what unhappy train of circumstances had brought him to that pass—to be the aider and abettor of a system which filled him with honest disgust and indignation, he loathed himself, and felt, for the moment, as though the mere consciousness of his present situation must, through all time to come, prevent his raising his head again.

But, for the present, his resolve was taken, and the resolution he had formed on the preceding night remained undisturbed. He had written to his mother and sister, announcing the safe conclusion of his journey, and saying as little about Dotheboys Hall, and saying that little as cheerfully, as he possibly could. He hoped that by remaining where he was, he might do some good, even there; at all events, others depended too much on his uncle's favour to admit of his awakening his wrath just then.

One reflection disturbed him far more than any selfish considerations arising out of his own position. This was the probable destination of his sister Kate. His uncle had deceived him, and might he not consign her to some miserable place where her youth and beauty would prove a far greater curse than ugliness and decrepitude? To a caged man, bound hand and foot, this was a terrible idea;—but no, he thought, his mother was by; there was the portrait-painter, too—simple enough, but still living in the world, and of it. He was willing to believe that Ralph Nickleby had conceived a personal dislike to himself. Having pretty good reason, by this time, to reciprocate it, he had no great difficulty in arriving at this conclusion, and tried to persuade himself that the feeling extended no farther than between them.

As he was absorbed in these meditations, he all at once encountered the upturned face of Smike, who was on his knees before the stove, picking a few stray cinders from the hearth and planting them on the fire. He had paused to steal a look at Nicholas, and when he saw that he was observed, shrunk back, as if expecting a blow.

'You need not fear me,' said Nicholas kindly. 'Are you cold?'

'N-n-o.'

'You are shivering.'

'I am not cold,' replied Smike quickly. 'I am used to it.'

There was such an obvious fear of giving offence in his manner, and he was such a timid, broken-spirited creature, that Nicholas could not help exclaiming, 'Poor fellow!'

If he had struck the drudge, he would have slunk away without a word. But, now, he burst into tears.

'Oh dear, oh dear!' he cried, covering his face with his cracked and horny hands. 'My heart will break. It will, it will.'

'Hush!' said Nicholas, laying his hand upon his shoulder. 'Be a man; you are nearly one by years, God help you.'

'By years!' cried Smike. 'Oh dear, dear, how many of them! How many of them since I was a little child, younger than any that are here now! Where are they all?'

'Whom do you speak of?' inquired Nicholas, wishing to rouse the poor half-witted creature to reason. 'Tell me.'

'My friends,' he replied, 'myself—my—oh! what sufferings mine have been!'

'There is always hope,' said Nicholas; he knew not what to say.

'No,' rejoined the other, 'no; none for me. Do you remember the boy that died here?'

'I was not here, you know,' said Nicholas gently; 'but what of him?'

'Why,' replied the youth, drawing closer to his questioner's side, 'I was with him at night, and when it was all silent he cried no more for friends he wished to come and sit with him, but began to see faces round his bed that came from home; he said they smiled, and talked to him; and he died at last lifting his head to kiss them. Do you hear?'

'Yes, yes,' rejoined Nicholas.

'What faces will smile on me when I die!' cried his companion, shivering. 'Who will talk to me in those long nights! They cannot come from home; they would frighten me, if they did, for I don't know what it is, and shouldn't know them. Pain and fear, pain and fear for me, alive or dead. No hope, no hope!'

The bell rang to bed: and the boy, subsiding at the sound into his usual listless state, crept away as if anxious to avoid notice. It was with a heavy heart that Nicholas soon afterwards—no, not retired; there was no retirement there—followed—to his dirty and crowded dormitory.

When Mr Squeers left the school-room for the night, he betook himself, as has been before remarked, to his own fireside, which was situated—not in the room in which Nicholas had supped on the night of his arrival, but in a smaller apartment in the rear of the premises, where his lady wife, his amiable son, and accomplished daughter, were in the full enjoyment of each other's society; Mrs Squeers being engaged in the matronly pursuit of stocking-darning; and the young lady and gentleman being occupied in the adjustment of some youthful differences, by means of a pugilistic contest across the table, which, on the approach of their honoured parent, subsided into a noiseless exchange of kicks beneath it.

And, in this place, it may be as well to apprise the reader, that Miss Fanny Squeers was in her three-and-twentieth year. If there be any one grace or loveliness inseparable from that particular period of life, Miss Squeers may be presumed to have been possessed of it, as there is no reason to suppose that she was a solitary exception to a universal rule. She was not tall like her mother, but short like her father; from the former she inherited a voice of harsh quality; from the latter a remarkable expression of the right eye, something akin to having none at all.

Miss Squeers had been spending a few days with a neighbouring friend, and had only just returned to the parental roof. To this circumstance may be referred, her having heard nothing of Nicholas, until Mr Squeers himself now made him the subject of conversation.

'Well, my dear,' said Squeers, drawing up his chair, 'what do you think of him by this time?'

'Think of who?' inquired Mrs Squeers; who (as she often remarked) was no grammarian, thank Heaven.

'Of the young man—the new teacher—who else could I mean?'

'Oh! that Knuckleboy,' said Mrs Squeers impatiently. 'I hate him.'

'What do you hate him for, my dear?' asked Squeers.

'What's that to you?' retorted Mrs Squeers. 'If I hate him, that's enough, ain't it?'

'Quite enough for him, my dear, and a great deal too much, I dare say, if he knew it,' replied Squeers in a pacific tone. 'I only asked from curiosity, my dear.'

'Well, then, if you want to know,' rejoined Mrs Squeers, 'I'll tell you. Because he's a proud, haughty, consequential, turned-up-nosed peacock.'

Mrs Squeers, when excited, was accustomed to use strong language, and, moreover, to make use of a plurality of epithets, some of which were of a figurative kind, as the word peacock, and furthermore the allusion to Nicholas's nose, which was not intended to be taken in its literal sense, but rather to bear a latitude of construction according to the fancy of the hearers.

Neither were they meant to bear reference to each other so much as to the object on whom they were bestowed, as will be seen in the present case; a peacock with a turned-up nose being a novelty in ornithology, and a thing not commonly seen.

'Hem!' said Squeers, as if in mild deprecation of this outbreak. 'He is cheap, my dear; the young man is very cheap.'

'Not a bit of it,' retorted Mrs Squeers.

'Five pound a year,' said Squeers.

'What of that; it's dear if you don't want him, isn't it?' replied his wife.

'But we *do* want him,' urged Squeers.

'I don't see that you want him any more than the dead,' said Mrs Squeers. 'Don't tell me. You can put on the cards and in the advertisements, 'Education by Mr Wackford Squeers and able assistants,' without having any assistants, can't you? Isn't it done every day by all the masters about? I've no patience with you.'

'Haven't you!' said Squeers, sternly. 'Now I'll tell you what, Mrs Squeers. In this matter of having a teacher, I'll take my own way, if you please. A slave-driver in the West Indies is allowed a man under him, to see that his blacks don't run away, or get up a rebellion; and I'll have a man under me to do the same with *our* blacks, till such time as little Wackford is able to take charge of the school.'

'Am I to take care of the school when I grow up a man, father?' said Wackford junior, suspending, in the excess of his delight, a vicious kick which he was administering to his sister.

'You are, my son,' replied Mr Squeers, in a sentimental voice.

'Oh my eye, won't I give it to the boys!' exclaimed the interesting child, grasping his father's cane. 'Oh, father, won't I make 'em squeak again!'

It was a proud moment in Mr Squeers's life, when he witnessed that burst of enthusiasm in his young child's mind, and saw in it a foreshadowing of his future eminence. He pressed a penny into his hand, and gave vent to his feelings (as did his exemplary wife also), in a shout of approving laughter. The infantine appeal to their common sympathies, at once restored cheerfulness to the conversation, and harmony to the company.

'He's a nasty stuck-up monkey, that's what I consider him,' said Mrs Squeers, reverting to Nicholas.

'Supposing he is,' said Squeers, 'he is as well stuck up in our school-room as anywhere else, isn't he?—especially as he don't like it.'

'Well,' observed Mrs Squeers, 'there's something in that. I hope it'll bring his pride down, and it shall be no fault of mine if it don't.'

Now, a proud usher in a Yorkshire school was such a very extraordinary and unaccountable thing to hear of,—any usher at all being a novelty; but a proud one, a being of whose existence the wildest imagination could never have dreamed—that Miss Squeers, who seldom troubled herself with scholastic matters, inquired with much curiosity who this Knuckleboy was, that gave himself such airs.

'Nickleby,' said Squeers, spelling the name according to some eccentric system which prevailed in his own mind; 'your mother always calls things and people by their wrong names.'

'No matter for that,' said Mrs Squeers, 'I see them with right eyes, and that's quite enough for me. I watched him when you were laying on to little Bolder this afternoon. He looked as black as thunder, all the while, and, one time started up as if he had more than got it in his mind to make a rush at you. *I* saw him, though he thought I didn't.'

'Never mind that, father,' said Miss Squeers, as the head of the family was about to reply. 'Who is the man?'

'Why, your father has got some nonsense in his head that he's the son of a poor gentleman that died the other day,' said Mrs Squeers.

'The son of a gentleman!'

'Yes; but I don't believe a word of it. If he's a gentleman's son at all, he's a fondling, that's my opinion.'

Mrs Squeers intended to say 'foundling,' but, as she frequently remarked when she made any such mistake, it would be all the same a hundred years hence; with which axiom of philosophy, indeed, she was in the constant habit of consoling the boys when they laboured under more than ordinary ill usage.

'He's nothing of the kind,' said Squeers, in answer to the above remark, 'for his father was married to his mother, years before he was born, and she is alive now. If he was, it would be no business of ours, for we make a very good friend by having him here; and if he likes to learn the boys anything besides minding them, I have no objection, I am sure.'

'I say again, I hate him worse than poison,' said Mrs Squeers, vehemently.

'If you dislike him, my dear,' returned Squeers, 'I don't know anybody who can show dislike better than you, and of course there's no occasion, with him, to take the trouble to hide it.'

'I don't intend to, I assure you,' interposed Mrs S.

'That's right,' said Squeers; 'and if he has a touch of pride about him, as I think he has, I don't believe there's a woman in all England that can bring anybody's spirit down, as quick as you can, my love.'

Mrs Squeers chuckled vastly on the receipt of these flattering compliments, and said, she hoped she had tamed a high spirit or two, in her day. It is but due to her character to say, that in conjunction with her estimable husband, she had broken many and many a one.

Miss Fanny Squeers carefully treasured up this, and much more conversation on the same subject, until she retired for the night, when she questioned the hungry servant, minutely, regarding the outward appearance and demeanour of Nicholas; to which queries the girl returned such enthusiastic replies, coupled with so many laudatory remarks touching his beautiful dark eyes, and his sweet smile, and his straight legs—upon which last-named articles she laid particular stress; the general run of legs at Dotheboys Hall being crooked—that Miss Squeers was not long in arriving at the conclusion that the new usher must be a very remarkable person, or, as she herself significantly phrased it, 'something quite out of the common.' And so Miss Squeers made up her mind that she would take a personal observation of Nicholas the very next day.

In pursuance of this design, the young lady watched the opportunity of her mother being engaged, and her father absent, and went accidentally into the school-room to get a pen mended: where, seeing nobody but Nicholas presiding over the boys, she blushed very deeply, and exhibited great confusion.

'I beg your pardon,' faltered Miss Squeers; 'I thought my father was—or might be—dear me, how very awkward!'

'Mr Squeers is out,' said Nicholas, by no means overcome by the apparition, unexpected though it was.

'Do you know will he be long, sir?' asked Miss Squeers, with bashful hesitation.

'He said about an hour,' replied Nicholas—politely of course but without any indication of being stricken to the heart by Miss Squeer's charms.

'I never knew anything happen so cross,' exclaimed the young lady. 'Thank you! I am very sorry I intruded, I am sure. If I hadn't thought my father was here, I wouldn't upon any account have—it is very provoking—must look so very strange,' murmured Miss Squeers, blushing once more, and glancing, from the pen in her hand, to Nicholas at his desk, and back again.

'If that is all you want,' said Nicholas, pointing to the pen, and smiling, in spite of himself, at the affected embarrassment of the schoolmaster's daughter, 'perhaps I can supply his place.'

Miss Squeers glanced at the door, as if dubious of the propriety of advancing any nearer to an utter stranger; then round the schoolroom, as though in some measure reassured by the presence of forty boys; and finally sidled up to Nicholas and delivered the pen into his hand, with a most winning mixture of reserve and condescension.

'Shall it be a hard or a soft nib?' inquired Nicholas, smiling to prevent himself from laughing outright.

'He *has* a beautiful smile,' thought Miss Squeers.

'Which did you say?' asked Nicholas.

'Dear me, I was thinking of something else for the moment, I declare,' replied Miss Squeers—'Oh! as soft as possible, if you please.' With which words, Miss Squeers sighed. It might be, to give Nicholas to understand that her heart was soft, and that the pen was wanted to match.

Upon these instructions Nicholas made the pen; when he gave it to Miss Squeers, Miss Squeers dropped it; and when he stooped to pick it up, Miss Squeers stooped also, and they knocked their heads together; whereat five-and-twenty little boys laughed aloud: being positively for the first and only time that half year.

'Very awkward of me,' said Nicholas, opening the door for the young lady's retreat.

'Not at all, sir,' replied Miss Squeers; 'it was my fault. It was all my foolish—a—a—good morning!'

'Good bye,' said Nicholas. 'The next I make for you, I hope will be made less clumsily. Take care! You are biting the nib off now.'

'Really,' said Miss Squeers; 'so embarrassing that I scarcely know what I—very sorry to give you so much trouble.'

'Not the least trouble in the world,' replied Nicholas, closing the school-room door.

'I never saw such legs in the whole course of my life!' said Miss Squeers, as she walked away.

In fact, Miss Squeers was in love with Nicholas Nickleby.

To account for the rapidity with which this young lady had conceived a passion for Nicholas, it may be necessary to state, that the friend from whom she had so recently returned, was a miller's daughter of only eighteen, who had contracted herself unto the son of a small corn-factor, resident in the nearest market town. Miss Squeers and the miller's daughter, being fast friends, had covenanted together some two years before, according to a custom prevalent among young ladies, that whoever was first engaged to be married, should straightway confide the mighty secret to the bosom of the other, before communicating it to any living soul, and bespeak her as bridesmaid without loss of time; in fulfilment of which pledge the miller's daughter, when her engagement was formed, came out express, at eleven o'clock at night as the corn-factor's son made an offer of his hand and heart at twenty-five minutes past ten by the Dutch clock in the kitchen, and rushed into Miss Squeers's bed-room with the gratifying intelligence. Now, Miss Squeers being five years older, and out of her teens (which is also a great matter), had, since, been more than commonly anxious to return the compliment, and possess her friend with a similar secret; but, either in consequence of finding it hard to please herself, or harder still to please anybody else, had never had an opportunity so to do, inasmuch as she had no such secret to disclose. The little interview with Nicholas had no sooner passed, as above described, however, than Miss Squeers, putting on her bonnet, made her way, with great precipitation, to her friend's house, and, upon a solemn renewal of divers old vows of secrecy, revealed how that she was—not exactly engaged, but going to be—to a gentleman's son—(none of your corn-factors, but a gentleman's son of high descent)—who had come down as teacher to Dotheboys Hall, under most mysterious and remarkable circumstances—indeed, as Miss Squeers more than once hinted she had good reason to believe, induced, by the fame of her many charms, to seek her out, and woo and win her.

'Isn't it an extraordinary thing?' said Miss Squeers, emphasising the adjective strongly.

'Most extraordinary,' replied the friend. 'But what has he said to you?'

'Don't ask me what he said, my dear,' rejoined Miss Squeers. 'If you had only seen his looks and smiles! I never was so overcome in all my life.'

'Did he look in this way?' inquired the miller's daughter, counterfeiting, as nearly as she could, a favourite leer of the corn-factor.

'Very like that—only more genteel,' replied Miss Squeers.

'Ah!' said the friend, 'then he means something, depend on it.'

Miss Squeers, having slight misgivings on the subject, was by no means ill pleased to be confirmed by a competent authority; and, discovering, on further conversation and comparison of notes, a great many points of resemblance between the behaviour of Nicholas and that of the corn-factor, grew so exceedingly confidential, that she intrusted her friend with a vast number of things Nicholas had *not* said, which were all so very complimentary as to be quite conclusive. Then, she dilated on the fearful hardship of having a father and mother strenuously opposed to her intended husband; on which unhappy circumstance she dwelt at great length; for the friend's father and mother were quite agreeable to her being married, and the whole courtship was in consequence as flat and common-place an affair as it was possible to imagine.

'How I should like to see him!' exclaimed the friend.

'So you shall, 'Tilda,' replied Miss Squeers. 'I should consider myself one of the most ungrateful creatures alive, if I denied you. I think mother's going away for two days to fetch some boys; and when she does, I'll ask you and John up to tea, and have him to meet you.'

This was a charming idea, and having fully discussed it, the friends parted.

It so fell out, that Mrs Squeers's journey, to some distance, to fetch three new boys, and dun the relations of two old ones for the balance of a small account, was fixed, that very afternoon, for the next day but one; and on the next day but one, Mrs Squeers got up outside the coach, as it stopped to change at Greta Bridge, taking with her a small bundle containing something in a bottle and some sandwiches, and carrying besides a large white top coat to wear in the night-time; with which baggage she went her way.

Whenever such opportunities as these occurred, it was Squeers's custom to drive over to the market town every evening, on pretence of urgent business, and stop till ten or eleven o'clock at a tavern he much affected. As the party was not in his way, therefore, but rather afforded a means of compromise with Miss Squeers, he readily yielded his full assent hereunto, and willingly communicated to Nicholas that he was expected to take his tea in the parlour that evening, at five o'clock.

To be sure Miss Squeers was in a desperate flutter as the time approached, and to be sure she was dressed out to the best advantage: with her hair—it had more than a tinge of red, and she wore it in a crop—curled in five distinct rows, up to the very top of her head, and arranged dexterously over the doubtful eye; to say nothing of the blue sash which floated down her back, or the worked apron, or the long gloves, or the green gauze scarf, worn over one shoulder and under the other; or any of the numerous devices which were to be as so many arrows to the heart of Nicholas. She had scarcely completed these arrangements to her entire satisfaction, when the friend arrived with a whitey-brown parcel—flat and three-cornered—containing sundry small adornments which were to be put on up stairs, and which the friend put on, talking incessantly. When Miss Squeers had 'done' the friend's hair, the friend 'did' Miss Squeers's hair, throwing in some striking improvements in the way of ringlets down the neck; and then, when they were both touched up to their entire satisfaction, they went down stairs in full state with the long gloves on, all ready for company.

'Where's John, 'Tilda?' said Miss Squeers.

'Only gone home to clean himself,' replied the friend. 'He will be here by the time the tea's drawn.'

'I do so palpitate,' observed Miss Squeers.

'Ah! I know what it is,' replied the friend.

'I have not been used to it, you know, 'Tilda,' said Miss Squeers, applying her hand to the left side of her sash.

'You'll soon get the better of it, dear,' rejoined the friend. While they were talking thus, the hungry servant brought in the tea things, and, soon afterwards, somebody tapped at the room door.

'There he is!' cried Miss Squeers. 'Oh 'Tilda!'

'Hush!' said 'Tilda. 'Hem! Say, come in.'

'Come in,' cried Miss Squeers faintly. And in walked Nicholas.

'Good evening,' said that young gentleman, all unconscious of his conquest. 'I understood from Mr Squeers that—'

'Oh yes; it's all right,' interposed Miss Squeers. 'Father don't tea with us, but you won't mind that, I dare say.' (This was said archly.)

Nicholas opened his eyes at this, but he turned the matter off very coolly—not caring, particularly, about anything just then—and went through the ceremony of introduction to the miller's daughter with so much grace, that that young lady was lost in admiration.

'We are only waiting for one more gentleman,' said Miss Squeers, taking off the tea-pot lid, and looking in to see how the tea was getting on.

It was matter of equal moment to Nicholas whether they were waiting for one gentleman or twenty, so he received the intelligence with perfect unconcern; and, being out of spirits, and not seeing any especial reason why he should make himself agreeable, looked out of the window and sighed involuntarily.

As luck would have it, Miss Squeers's friend was of a playful turn, and hearing Nicholas sigh, she took it into her head to rally the lovers on their lowness of spirits.

'But if it's caused by my being here,' said the young lady, 'don't mind me a bit, for I'm quite as bad. You may go on just as you would if you were alone.'

' 'Tilda,' said Miss Squeers, colouring up to the top row of curls, 'I am ashamed of you;' and here the two friends burst into a variety of giggles, and glanced, from time to time, over the tops of their pocket-handkerchiefs, at Nicholas, who from a state of unmixed astonishment, gradually fell into one of irrepressible laughter—occasioned, partly by the bare notion of his being in love with Miss Squeers, and partly by the preposterous appearance and behaviour of the two girls. These two causes of merriment, taken together, struck him as being so keenly ridiculous, that, despite his miserable condition, he laughed till he was thoroughly exhausted.

'Well,' thought Nicholas, 'as I am here, and seem expected, for some reason or other, to be amiable, it's of no use looking like a goose. I may as well accommodate myself to the company.'

We blush to tell it; but his youthful spirits and vivacity, getting, for a time, the better of his sad thoughts, he no sooner formed this resolution than he saluted Miss Squeers and the friend, with great gallantry, and drawing a chair to the tea-table, began to make himself more at home than in all probability an usher has ever done in his employer's house since ushers were first invented.

The ladies were in the full delight of this altered behaviour on the part of Mr Nickleby, when the expected swain arrived, with his hair very damp from recent washing, and a clean shirt, whereof the collar might have belonged to some giant ancestor, forming, together with a white waistcoat of similar dimensions, the chief ornament of his person.

'Well, John,' said Miss Matilda Price (which, by-the-bye, was the name of the miller's daughter).

'Weel,' said John with a grin that even the collar could not conceal.

'I beg your pardon,' interposed Miss Squeers, hastening to do the honours, 'Mr Nickleby—Mr John Browdie.'

'Servant, sir,' said John, who was something over six feet high, with a face and body rather above the due proportion than below it.

'Yours to command, sir,' replied Nicholas, making fearful ravages on the bread and butter.

Mr Browdie was not a gentleman of great conversational powers, so he grinned twice more, and having now bestowed his customary mark of recognition on every person in company, grinned at nothing particular, and helped himself to food.

'Old wooman awa', bean't she?' said Mr Browdie, with his mouth full.

Miss Squeers nodded assent.

Mr Browdie gave a grin of special width, as if he thought that really was something to laugh at, and went to work at the bread and butter with increased vigour. It was quite a sight to behold how he and Nicholas emptied the plate between them.

'Ye wean't get bread and butter ev'ery neight, I expect, mun,' said Mr Browdie, after he had sat staring at Nicholas a long time over the empty plate.

Nicholas bit his lip, and coloured, but affected not to hear the remark.

'Ecod,' said Mr Browdie, laughing boisterously, 'they dean't put too much intiv'em. Ye'll be nowt but skeen and boans if you stop here long eneaf. Ho! ho! ho!'

'You are facetious, sir,' said Nicholas, scornfully.

'Na; I dean't know,' replied Mr Browdie, 'but t'oother teacher, 'cod he wur a lean 'un, he wur.' The recollection of the last teacher's leanness seemed to afford Mr Browdie the most exquisite delight, for he laughed until he found it necessary to apply his coat-cuffs to his eyes.

'I don't know whether your perceptions are quite keen enough, Mr Browdie, to enable you to understand that your remarks are offensive,' said Nicholas in a towering passion, 'but if they are, have the goodness to—'

'If you say another word, John,' shrieked Miss Price, stopping her admirer's mouth as he was about to interrupt, 'only half a word, I'll never forgive you, or speak to you again.'

'Weel, my lass, I dean't care aboot 'un,' said the corn-factor, bestowing a hearty kiss on Miss Matilda; 'let 'un gang on, let 'un gang on.'

It now became Miss Squeers's turn to intercede with Nicholas, which she did with many symptoms of alarm and horror; the effect of the double intercession was, that he and John Browdie shook hands across the table with much gravity; and such was the imposing nature of the ceremonial, that Miss Squeers was overcome and shed tears.

'What's the matters, Fanny?' said Miss Price.

'Nothing, 'Tilda,' replied Miss Squeers, sobbing.

'There never was any danger,' said Miss Price, 'was there, Mr Nickleby?'

'None at all,' replied Nicholas. 'Absurd.'

'That's right,' whispered Miss Price, 'say something kind to her, and she'll soon come round. Here! Shall John and I go into the little kitchen, and come back presently?'

'Not on any account,' rejoined Nicholas, quite alarmed at the proposition. 'What on earth should you do that for?'

'Well,' said Miss Price, beckoning him aside, and speaking with some degree of contempt—'you *are* a one to keep company.'

'What do you mean?' said Nicholas; 'I am not a one to keep company at all—here at all events. I can't make this out.'

'No, nor I neither,' rejoined Miss Price; 'but men are always fickle, and always were, and always will be; that I can make out, very easily.'

'Fickle!' cried Nicholas; 'what do you suppose? You don't mean to say that you think—'

'Oh no, I think nothing at all,' retorted Miss Price, pettishly. 'Look at her, dressed so beautiful and looking so well—really *almost* handsome. I am ashamed at you.'

'My dear girl, what have I got to do with her dressing beautifully or looking well?' inquired Nicholas.

'Come, don't call me a dear girl,' said Miss Price—smiling a little though, for she was pretty, and a coquette too in her small way, and Nicholas was good-looking, and she supposed him the property of somebody else, which were all reasons why she should be gratified to think she had made an impression on him,—'Fanny will be saying it's my fault. Come; we're going to have a game at cards.' Pronouncing these last words aloud, she tripped away and rejoined the big Yorkshireman.

This was wholly unintelligible to Nicholas, who had no other distinct impression on his mind at the moment, than that Miss Squeers was an ordinary-looking girl, and her friend Miss Price a pretty one; but he had not time to enlighten himself by reflection, for the hearth being by this time swept up, and the candle snuffed, they sat down to play speculation.

'There are only four of us, 'Tilda,' said Miss Squeers, looking slyly at Nicholas; 'so we had better go partners, two against two.'

'What do you say, Mr Nickleby?' inquired Miss Price.

'With all the pleasure in life,' replied Nicholas. And so saying, quite unconscious of his heinous offence, he amalgamated into one common heap those portions of a Dotheboys Hall card of terms, which represented his own counters, and those allotted to Miss Price, respectively.

'Mr Browdie,' said Miss Squeers hysterically, 'shall we make a bank against them?'

The Yorkshireman assented—apparently quite overwhelmed by the new usher's impudence—and Miss Squeers darted a spiteful look at her friend, and giggled convulsively.

The deal fell to Nicholas, and the hand prospered.

'We intend to win everything,' said he.

' 'Tilda *has* won something she didn't expect, I think, haven't you, dear?' said Miss Squeers, maliciously.

'Only a dozen and eight, love,' replied Miss Price, affecting to take the question in a literal sense.

'How dull you are to-night!' sneered Miss Squeers.

'No, indeed,' replied Miss Price, 'I am in excellent spirits. I was thinking *you* seemed out of sorts.'

'Me!' cried Miss Squeers, biting her lips, and trembling with very jealousy; 'Oh no!'

'That's well,' remarked Miss Price. 'Your hair's coming out of curl, dear.'

'Never mind me,' tittered Miss Squeers; 'you had better attend to your partner.'

'Thank you for reminding her,' said Nicholas. 'So she had.'

The Yorkshireman flattened his nose, once or twice, with his clenched fist, as if to keep his hand in till he had an opportunity of exercising it upon the features of some other gentleman; and Miss Squeers tossed her head with such indignation, that the gust of wind raised by the multitudinous curls in motion nearly blew the candle out.

'I never had such luck, really,' exclaimed coquettish Miss Price, after another hand or two. 'It's all along of you, Mr Nickleby, I think. I should like to have you for a partner always.'

'I wish you had.'

'You'll have a bad wife, though, if you always win at cards,' said Miss Price.

'Not if your wish is gratified,' replied Nicholas. 'I am sure I shall have a good one in that case.'

To see how Miss Squeers tossed her head, and the corn-factor flattened his nose, while this conversation was carrying on! It would have been worth a small annuity to have beheld that; let alone Miss Price's evident joy at making them jealous, and Nicholas Nickleby's happy unconsciousness of making anybody uncomfortable.

'We have all the talking to ourselves, it seems,' said Nicholas, looking good-humouredly round the table as he took up the cards for a fresh deal.

'You do it so well,' tittered Miss Squeers, 'that it would be a pity to interrupt, wouldn't it, Mr Browdie! He! he! he!'

'Nay,' said Nicholas, 'we do it in default of having anybody else to talk to.'

'We'll talk to you, you know, if you'll say anything,' said Miss Price.

'Thank you, 'Tilda, dear,' retorted Miss Squeers, majestically.

'Or you can talk to each other, if you don't choose to talk to us,' said Miss Price, rallying her dear friend. 'John, why don't you say something?'

'Say summat?' repeated the Yorshireman.

'Ay, and not sit there so silent and glum.'

'Weel, then!' said the Yorkshireman, striking the table heavily with his fist, 'what I say's this—Dang my boans and boddy, if I stan' this ony longer. Do ye gang whoam wi' me, and do yon loight an' toight young whipster look sharp out for a brokken head next time he cums under my hond.'

'Mercy on us, what's all this?' cried Miss Price, in affected astonishment.

'Cum whoam, tell'e, cum whoam,' replied the Yorkshireman, sternly. And as he delivered the reply, Miss Squeers burst into a shower of tears; arising in part from desperate vexation, and in part from an impotent desire to lacerate somebody's countenance with her fair finger-nails.

This state of things had been brought about by divers means and workings. Miss Squeers had brought it about, by aspiring to the high state and condition of being matrimonially engaged, without good grounds for so doing; Miss Price had brought it about by indulging in three motives of action: first, a desire to punish her friend for laying claim to a rivalship in dignity, having no good title: secondly, the gratification of her own vanity, in receiving the compliments of a smart young man: and thirdly, a wish to convince the corn-factor of the great danger he ran in deferring the celebration of their expected nuptials; while Nicholas had brought it about, by half an hour's gaiety and thoughtlessness, and a very sincere desire to avoid the imputation of inclining at all to Miss Squeers. So the means employed, and the end produced, were alike the most natural in the world; for young ladies will look forward to being married, and will jostle each other in the race to the altar, and will avail themselves of all opportunities of displaying their own attractions to the best advantage, down to the very end of time, as they have done from its beginning.

'Why, and here's Fanny in tears now!' exclaimed Miss Price, as if in fresh amazement. 'What can be the matter?'

'Oh! you don't know, Miss, of course you don't know. Pray don't trouble yourself to inquire,' said Miss Squeers, producing that change of countenance which children call, making a face.

'Well, I'm sure!' exclaimed Miss Price.

'And who cares whether you are sure or not, ma'am?' retorted Miss Squeers, making another face.

'You are monstrous polite, ma'am,' said Miss Price.

'I shall not come to you to take lessons in the art, ma'am!' retorted Miss Squeers.

'You needn't take the trouble to make yourself plainer than you are, ma'am, however,' rejoined Miss Price, 'because that's quite unnecessary.'

Miss Squeers, in reply, turned very red, and thanked God that she hadn't got the bold faces of some people. Miss Price, in rejoinder, congratulated herself upon not being possessed of the envious feeling of other people; whereupon Miss Squeers made some general remark touching the danger of associating with low persons; in which Miss Price entirely coincided: observing that it was very true indeed, and she had thought so a long time.

' 'Tilda,' exclaimed Miss Squeers with dignity, 'I hate you.'

'Ah! There's no love lost between us, I assure you,' said Miss Price, tying her bonnet strings with a jerk. 'You'll cry your eyes out when I'm gone; you know you will.'

'I scorn your words, Minx,' said Miss Squeers.

'You pay me a great compliment when you say so,' answered the miller's daughter, curtseying very low. 'Wish you a very good night, ma'am, and pleasant dreams attend your sleep!'

With this parting benediction Miss Price swept from the room, followed by the huge Yorkshireman, who exchanged with Nicholas, at parting, that peculiarly expressive scowl with which the cut-and-thrust counts, in melo-dramatic performances, inform each other they will meet again.

They were no sooner gone, than Miss Squeers fulfilled the prediction of her quondam friend by giving vent to a most copious burst of tears, and uttering various dismal lamentations and incoherent words. Nicholas stood looking on for a few seconds, rather doubtful what to do, but feeling uncertain whether the fit would end in his being embraced, or scratched, and considering that either infliction would be equally disagreeable, he walked off very quietly while Miss Squeers was moaning in her pocket-handkerchief.

'This is one consequence,' thought Nicholas, when he had groped his way to the dark sleeping-room, 'of my cursed readiness to adapt myself to any society in which chance carries me. If I had sat mute and motionless, as I might have done, this would not have happened.'

He listened for a few minutes, but all was quiet.

'I was glad,' he murmured, 'to grasp at any relief from the sight of this dreadful place, or the presence of its vile master. I have set these people by the ears, and made two new enemies, where, Heaven knows, I needed none. Well, it is a just punishment for having forgotten, even for an hour, what is around me now!'

So saying, he felt his way among the throng of weary-hearted sleepers, and crept into his poor bed.

*

It was a fortunate circumstance for Miss Fanny Squeers that when her worthy papa returned home on the night of the small tea-party, he was what the initiated term 'too far gone' to observe the numerous tokens of extreme vexation of spirit which were plainly visible in her countenance. Being, however, of a rather violent and quarrelsome mood in his cups, it is not impossible that he might have fallen out with her, either on this or some imaginary topic, if the young lady had not, with a foresight and prudence highly commendable, kept a boy up, on purpose, to bear the first brunt of the good gentleman's anger; which, having vented itself in a variety of kicks and cuffs, subsided sufficiently to admit of his being persuaded to go to bed. Which he did with his boots on, and an umbrella under his arm.

The hungry servant attended Miss Squeers in her own room according to custom, to curl her hair, perform the other little offices of her toilet, and administer as much flattery as she could get up, for the purpose; for Miss Squeers was quite lazy enough (and sufficiently vain and frivolous withal) to have been a fine lady; and it was only the arbitrary distinctions of rank and station which prevented her from being one.

'How lovely your hair do curl to-night, miss!' said the handmaiden. 'I declare if it isn't a pity and a shame to brush it out!'

'Hold your tongue!' replied Miss Squeers wrathfully.

Some considerable experience prevented the girl from being at all surprised at any outbreak of ill-temper on the part of Miss Squeers. Having a half perception of what had occurred in the course of the evening, she changed her mode of making herself agreeable, and proceeded on the indirect tack.

'Well, I couldn't help saying, miss, if you was to kill me for it,' said the attendant, 'that I never see nobody look so vulgar as Miss Price this night.'

Miss Squeers sighed, and composed herself to listen.

'I know it's very wrong in me to say so, miss,' continued the girl, delighted to see the impression she was making, 'Miss Price being a friend of your'n, and all; but she do dress herself out so, and go on in such a manner to get noticed, that—oh—well, if people only saw themselves!'

'What do you mean, Phib?' asked Miss Squeers, looking in her own little glass, where, like most of us, she saw—not herself, but the reflection of some pleasant image in her own brain. 'How you talk!'

'Talk, miss! It's enough to make a Tom cat talk French grammar, only to see how she tosses her head,' replied the handmaid.

'She *does* toss her head,' observed Miss Squeers, with an air of abstraction.

'So vain, and so very—very plain,' said the girl.

'Poor 'Tilda!' sighed Miss Squeers, compassionately.

'And always laying herself out so, to get to be admired.' pursued the servant. 'Oh, dear! It's positive indelicate.'

'I can't allow you to talk in that way, Phib,' said Miss Squeers. ' 'Tilda's friends are low people, and if she don't know any better, it's their fault, and not hers.'

'Well, but you know, miss,' said Phœbe, for which name 'Phib' was used as a patronising abbreviation, 'if she was only to take copy by a friend—oh! if she only knew how wrong she was, and would but set herself right by you, what a nice young woman she might be in time!'

'Phib,' rejoined Miss Squeers, with a stately air, 'it's not proper for me to hear these comparisons drawn; they make 'Tilda look a coarse improper sort of person, and it seems unfriendly in me to listen to them. I would rather you dropped the subject, Phib; at the same time, I must say, that if 'Tilda Price would take pattern by somebody—not me particularly—'

'Oh yes; you, miss,' interposed Phib.

'Well, me, Phib, if you will have it so,' said Miss Squeers. 'I must say, that if she would, she would be all the better for it.'

'So somebody else thinks, or I am much mistaken,' said the girl mysteriously.

'What do you mean?' demanded Miss Squeers.

'Never mind, miss,' replied the girl; '*I* know what I know; that's all.'

'Phib,' said Miss Squeers dramatically, 'I insist upon your explaining yourself. What is this dark mystery? Speak.'

'Why, if you will have it, miss, it's this,' said the servant girl. 'Mr John Browdie thinks as you think; and if he wasn't too far gone to do it creditable, he'd be very glad to be off with Miss Price, and on with Miss Squeers.'

'Gracious Heavens!' exclaimed Miss Squeers, clasping her hands with great dignity. 'What is this?'

'Truth, ma'am, and nothing but truth,' replied the artful Phib.

'What a situation!' cried Miss Squeers; 'on the brink of unconsciously destroying the peace and happiness of my own 'Tilda. What is the reason that men fall in love with me, whether I like it or not, and desert their chosen intendeds for my sake!'

'Because they can't help it, miss,' replied the girl; 'the reason's plain.' (If Miss Squeers were the reason, it was very plain.)

'Never let me hear of it again,' retorted Miss Squeers. 'Never! Do you hear? 'Tilda Price has faults—many faults—but I wish her well, and above all I wish her married; for I think it highly desirable—most desirable from the very nature of her failings—that she should be married as soon as possible. No, Phib. Let her have Mr Browdie. I may pity *him*, poor fellow; but I have a great regard for 'Tilda, and only hope she may make a better wife than I think she will.'

With this effusion of feelings, Miss Squeers went to bed.

Spite is a little word; but it represents as strange a jumble of feelings, and compound of discords, as any polysyllable in the language. Miss Squeers knew as well in her heart of hearts, that what the miserable serving girl had said was sheer, coarse, lying flattery, as did the girl herself; yet the mere opportunity of venting a little ill-nature against the offending Miss Price, and affecting to compassionate her weaknesses and foibles, though only in the presence of a solitary dependant, was almost as great a relief to her spleen as if the whole had been gospel truth. Nay, more. We have such extraordinary powers of persuasion when they are exerted over ourselves, that Miss Squeers felt quite high-minded and great after her noble renunciation of John Browdie's hand, and looked down upon her rival with a kind of holy calmness and tranquillity, that had a mighty effect in soothing her ruffled feelings.

This happy state of mind had some influence in bringing about a reconciliation; for, when a knock came at the front door next day, and the miller's daughter was announced, Miss Squeers betook herself to the parlour in a Christian frame of spirit, perfectly beautiful to behold.

'Well, Fanny,' said the miller's daughter, 'you see I have come to see you, although we *had* some words last night.'

'I pity your bad passions, 'Tilda,' replied Miss Squeers; 'but I bear no malice. I am above it.'

'Don't be cross, Fanny,' said Miss Price. 'I have come to tell you something that I know will please you.'

'What may that be, 'Tilda?' demanded Miss Squeers; screwing up her lips, and looking as if nothing in earth, air, fire, or water, could afford her the slightest gleam of satisfaction.

'This,' rejoined Miss Price. 'After we left here last night, John and I had a dreadful quarrel.'

'That doesn't please me,' said Miss Squeers—relaxing into a smile though.

'Lor! I wouldn't think so bad of you as to suppose it did,' rejoined her companion. 'That's not it.'

'Oh!' said Miss Squeers, relapsing into melancholy. 'Go on.'

'After a great deal of wrangling, and saying we would never see each other any more,' continued Miss Price, 'we made it up, and this morning John went and wrote our names down to be put up, for the first time, next Sunday, so we shall be married in three weeks, and I give you notice to get your frock made.'

There was mingled gall and honey in this intelligence. The prospect of the friend's being married so soon was the gall, and the certainty of her not entertaining serious designs upon Nicholas was the honey. Upon the whole, the sweet greatly preponderated over the bitter, so Miss Squeers said she would get the frock made, and that she hoped 'Tilda might be happy, though at the same time she didn't know, and would not have her build too much upon it, for men were strange creatures, and a great many married women were very miserable, and wished themselves single again with all their hearts; to which condolences Miss Squeers added others equally calculated to raise her friend's spirits and promote her cheerfulness of mind.

'But come now, Fanny,' said Miss Price, 'I want to have a word or two with you about young Mr Nickleby.'

'He is nothing to me,' interrupted Miss Squeers, with hysterical symptoms. 'I despise him too much!'

'Oh, you don't mean that, I am sure?' replied her friend. 'Confess, Fanny; don't you like him now?'

Without returning any direct reply, Miss Squeers, all at once, fell into a paroxysm of spiteful tears, and exclaimed that she was a wretched, neglected, miserable, castaway.

'I hate everybody,' said Miss Squeers, 'and I wish that everybody was dead—that I do.'

'Dear, dear,' said Miss Price, quite moved by this avowal of misanthropical sentiments. 'You are not serious, I am sure.'

'Yes, I am,' rejoined Miss Squeers, tying tight knots in her pocket-handkerchief, and clenching her teeth. 'And I wish *I* was dead too. There!'

'Oh! you'll think very differently in another five minutes,' said Matilda. 'How much better to take him into favour again, than to hurt yourself by going on in that way. Wouldn't it be much nicer, now, to have him all to yourself on good terms, in a company-keeping, love-making, pleasant sort of manner?'

'I don't know but what it would,' sobbed Miss Squeers. 'Oh! 'Tilda, how could you have acted so mean and dishonourable! I wouldn't have believed it of you, if anybody had told me.'

'Heyday!' exclaimed Miss Price, giggling. 'One would suppose I had been murdering somebody at least.'

'Very nigh as bad,' said Miss Squeers passionately.

'And all this, because I happen to have enough of good looks to make people civil to me,' cried Miss Price. 'Persons don't make their own faces, and it's no more my fault if mine is a good one than it is other people's fault if theirs is a bad one.'

'Hold your tongue,' shrieked Miss Squeers, in her shrillest tone; 'or you'll make me slap you, 'Tilda, and afterwards I should be sorry for it!'

It is needless to say, that, by this time, the temper of each young lady was in some slight degree affected by the tone of her conversation, and that a dash of personality was infused into the altercation, in consequence. Indeed, the quarrel, from slight beginnings, rose to a considerable height, and was assuming a very violent complexion, when both parties, falling into a great passion of tears, exclaimed simultaneously, that they had never thought of being spoken to in that way: which exclamation, leading to a remonstrance, gradually brought on an explanation: and the upshot was, that they fell into each other's arms and vowed eternal friendship; the occasion in question, making the fifty-second time of repeating the same impressive ceremony within a twelve-month.

Perfect amicability being thus restored, a dialogue naturally ensued upon the number and nature of the garments which would be indispensable for Miss Price's entrance into the holy state of matrimony, when Miss Squeers clearly showed that a great many more than the miller could, or would, afford, were absolutely necessary, and could not decently be dispensed with. The young lady then, by an easy digression, led the discourse to her own wardrobe, and after recounting its principal beauties at some length, took her friend up stairs to make inspection thereof. The treasures of two drawers and a closet having been displayed, and all the smaller articles tried on, it was time for Miss Price to return home; and as she had been in raptures with all the frocks, and had been stricken quite dumb with admiration of a new pink scarf, Miss Squeers said in high good humour, that she would walk part of the way with her, for the pleasure of her company; and off they went together: Miss Squeers dilating, as they walked along, upon her father's accomplishments: and multiplying his income by ten, to give her friend some faint notion of the vast importance and superiority of her family.

It happened that that particular time, comprising the short daily interval which was suffered to elapse between what was pleasantly called the dinner, of Mr Squeers's pupils, and their return to the pursuit of useful knowledge, was precisely the hour when Nicholas was accustomed to issue forth for a melancholy walk, and to brood, as he sauntered listlessly through the village, upon his miserable lot. Miss Squeers knew this, perfectly well, but had perhaps forgotten it, for when she caught sight of that young gentleman advancing towards them, she evinced many symptoms of surprise and consternation, and assured her friend that she felt 'fit to drop into the earth.'

'Shall we turn back, or run into a cottage?' asked Miss Price. 'He don't see us yet.'

'No, 'Tilda,' replied Miss Squeers, 'it is my duty to go through with it, and I will!'

As Miss Squeers said this, in the tone of one who has made a high moral resolution, and was, besides, taken with one or two chokes and catchings of breath, indicative of feelings at a high pressure, her friend made no farther remark, and they bore straight down upon Nicholas, who, walking with his eyes bent upon the ground, was not aware of their approach until they were close upon him; otherwise he might, perhaps, have taken shelter himself.

'Good morning,' said Nicholas, bowing and passing by.

'He is going,' murmured Miss Squeers. 'I shall choke, 'Tilda.'

'Come back, Mr Nickleby, do!' cried Miss Price, affecting alarm at her friend's threat, but really actuated by a malicious wish to hear what Nicholas would say; 'come back, Mr Nickleby!'

Mr Nickleby came back, and looked as confused as might be, as he inquired whether the ladies had any commands for him.

'Don't stop to talk,' urged Miss Price, hastily; 'but support her on the other side. How do you feel now, dear?'

'Better,' sighed Miss Squeers, laying a beaver bonnet of a reddish brown with a green veil attached, on Mr Nickleby's shoulder. 'This foolish faintness!'

'Don't call it foolish, dear,' said Miss Price: her bright eye dancing with merriment as she saw the perplexity of Nicholas; 'you have no reason to be ashamed of it. It's those who are too proud to come round again, without all this to-do, that ought to be ashamed.'

'You are resolved to fix it upon me, I see,' said Nicholas, smiling, 'although I told you, last night, it was not my fault.'

'There; he says it was not his fault, my dear,' remarked the wicked Miss Price. 'Perhaps you were too jealous, or too hasty with him? He says it was not his fault. You hear; I think that's apology enough.'

'You will not understand me,' said Nicholas. 'Pray dispense with this jesting, for I have no time, and really no inclination, to be the subject or promoter of mirth just now.'

'What do you mean?' asked Miss Price, affecting amazement.

'Don't ask him, 'Tilda,' cried Miss Squeers; 'I forgive him.'

'Dear me,' said Nicholas, as the brown bonnet went down on his shoulder again, 'this is more serious than I supposed. Allow me! Will you have the goodness to hear me speak?'

Here he raised up the brown bonnet, and regarding with most unfeigned astonishment a look of tender reproach from Miss Squeers, shrunk back a few paces to be out of the reach of the fair burden, and went on to say:

'I am very sorry—truly and sincerely sorry—for having been the cause of any difference among you, last night. I reproach myself, most bitterly, for having been so unfortunate as to cause the dissension that occurred, although I did so, I assure you, most unwittingly and heedlessly.'

'Well; that's not all you have got to say surely,' exclaimed Miss Price as Nicholas paused.

'I fear there is something more,' stammered Nicholas with a half smile, and looking towards Miss Squeers, 'it is a most awkward thing to say—but—the very mention of such a supposition makes one look like a puppy—still—may I ask if that lady supposes that I entertain any—in short, does she think that I am in love with her?'

'Delightful embarrassment,' thought Miss Squeers, 'I have brought him to it, at last. Answer for me, dear,' she whispered to her friend.

'Does she think so?' rejoined Miss Price; 'of course she does.'

'She does!' exclaimed Nicholas with such energy of utterance as might have been, for the moment, mistaken for rapture.

'Certainly,' replied Miss Price.

'If Mr Nickleby has doubted that, 'Tilda,' said the blushing Miss Squeers in soft accents, 'he may set his mind at rest. His sentiments are recipro—'

'Stop,' cried Nicholas hurriedly; 'pray hear me. This is the grossest and wildest delusion, the completest and most signal mistake, that ever human being laboured under, or committed. I have scarcely seen the young lady half a dozen times, but if I had seen her sixty times, or am destined to see her sixty thousand, it would be, and will be, precisely the same. I have not one thought, wish or hope, connected with her, unless it be—and I say this, not to hurt her feelings, but to impress her with the real state of my own—unless it be the one object, dear to my heart as life itself, of being one day able to turn my back upon this accursed place, never to set foot in it again, or think of it—even think of it—but with loathing and disgust.'

With this particularly plain and straight-forward declaration, which he made with all the vehemence that his indignant and excited feelings could bring to bear upon it, Nicholas, waiting to hear no more, retreated.

But poor Miss Squeers! Her anger, rage, and vexation; the rapid succession of bitter and passionate feelings that whirled through her mind; are not to be described. Refused! refused by a teacher, picked up by advertisement, at an annual salary of five pounds payable at indefinite periods, and 'found' in food and lodging like the very boys themselves; and this too in the presence of a little chit of a miller's daughter of eighteen, who was going to be married in three weeks' time, to a man who had gone down on his very knees to ask her! She could have choked in right good earnest, at the thought of being so humbled.

But there was one thing clear in the midst of her mortification; and that was, that she hated and detested Nicholas with all the narrowness of mind and littleness of purpose worthy a descendant of the house of Squeers. And there was one comfort too; and that was, that every hour in every day she could wound his pride, and goad him with the infliction of some slight, or insult, or deprivation, which could not but have some effect on the most insensible person, and must be acutely felt by one so sensitive as Nicholas. With these two reflections uppermost in her mind, Miss Squeers made the best of the matter to her friend, by observing that Mr Nickleby was such an odd creature, and of such a violent temper, that she feared she should be obliged to give him up; and parted from her.

And here it may be remarked, that Miss Squeers, having bestowed her affections (or whatever it might be that, in the absence of anything better, represented them) on Nicholas Nickleby, had never once seriously contemplated the possibility of his being of a different opinion from herself in the business. Miss Squeers reasoned that she was prepossessing and beautiful, and that her father was master, and Nicholas man, and that her father had saved money, and Nicholas had none, all of which seemed to her conclusive arguments why the young man should feel only too much honoured by her preference. She had not failed to recollect, either, how much more agreeable she could render his situation if she were his friend, and how much more disagreeable if she were his enemy; and, doubtless, many less scrupulous young gentlemen than Nicholas would have encouraged her extravagance had it been only for this very obvious and intelligible reason. However, he had thought proper to do otherwise, and Miss Squeers was outrageous.

'Let him see,' said the irritated young lady, when she had regained her own room, and eased her mind by committing an assault on Phib, 'if I don't set mother against him a little more when she comes back!'

It was scarcely necessary to do this, but Miss Squeers was as good as her word; and poor Nicholas, in addition to bad food, dirty lodging, and the being compelled to witness one dull unvarying round of squalid misery, was treated with every special indignity that malice could suggest, or the most grasping cupidity put upon him.

Nor was this all. There was another and deeper system of annoyance which made his heart sink, and nearly drove him wild, by its injustice and cruelty.

The wretched creature, Smike, since the night Nicholas had spoken kindly to him in the school-room, had followed him to and fro, with an ever restless desire to serve or help him; anticipating such little wants as his humble ability could supply, and content only to be near him. He would sit beside him for hours, looking patiently into his face; and a word would brighten up his care-worn visage, and call into it a passing gleam, even of happiness. He was an altered being; he had an object now; and that object was, to show his attachment to the only person—that person a stranger—who had treated him, not to say with kindness, but like a human creature.

Upon this poor being, all the spleen and ill-humour that could not be vented on Nicholas were unceasingly bestowed. Drudgery would have been nothing—Smike was well used to that. Buffetings inflicted without cause, would have been equally a matter of course; for to them also, he had served a long and weary apprenticeship; but it was no sooner observed that he had become attached to Nicholas, than stripes and blows, stripes and blows, morning, noon, and night, were his only portion. Squeers was jealous of the influence which his man had so soon acquired, and his family hated him, and Smike paid for both. Nicholas saw it, and ground his teeth at every repetition of the savage and cowardly attack.

He had arranged a few regular lessons for the boys; and one night as he paced up and down the dismal school-room, his swoln heart almost bursting to think that his protection and countenance should have increased the misery of the wretched being whose peculiar destitution had awakened his pity, he paused mechanically in a dark corner where sat the object of his thoughts.

The poor soul was poring hard over a tattered book, with the traces of recent tears still upon his face; vainly endeavouring to master some task which a child of nine years old, possessed of ordinary powers, could have conquered with ease, but which, to the addled brain of the crushed boy of nineteen, was a sealed and hopeless mystery. Yet there he sat, patiently conning the page again and again, stimulated by no boyish ambition, for he was the common jest and scoff even of the uncouth objects that congregated about him, but inspired by the one eager desire to please his solitary friend.

Nicholas laid his hand upon his shoulder.

'I can't do it,' said the dejected creature, looking up with bitter disappointment in every feature. 'No, no.'

'Do not try,' replied Nicholas.

The boy shook his head, and closing the book with a sigh, looked vacantly round, and laid his head upon his arm. He was weeping.

'Do not for God's sake,' said Nicholas, in an agitated voice; 'I cannot bear to see you.'

'They are more hard with me than ever,' sobbed the boy.

'I know it,' rejoined Nicholas. 'They are.'

'But for you,' said the outcast, 'I should die. They would kill me; they would; I know they would.'

'You will do better, poor fellow,' replied Nicholas, shaking his head mournfully, 'when I am gone.'

'Gone!' cried the other, looking intently in his face.

'Softly!' rejoined Nicholas. 'Yes.'

'Are you going?' demanded the boy, in an earnest whisper.

'I cannot say,' replied Nicholas. 'I was speaking more to my thoughts, than to you.'

'Tell me,' said the boy imploringly, 'Oh do tell me, *will* you go—*will* you?'

'I shall be driven to that at last!' said Nicholas. 'The world is before me, after all.'

'Tell me,' urged Smike, 'is the world as bad and dismal as this place?'

'Heaven forbid,' replied Nicholas, pursuing the train of his own thoughts, 'its hardest, coarsest toil were happiness to this.'

'Should I ever meet you there?' demanded the boy, speaking with unusual wildness and volubility.

'Yes,' replied Nicholas, willing to soothe him.

'No, no!' said the other, clasping him by the hand. 'Should I—should I—tell me that again. Say I should be sure to find you.'

'You would,' replied Nicholas, with the same humane intention, 'and I would help and aid you, and not bring fresh sorrow on you as I have done here.'

The boy caught both the young man's hands passionately in his, and, hugging them to his breast, uttered a few broken sounds which were unintelligible. Squeers entered, at the moment, and he shrunk back into his old corner.

The cold, feeble, dawn of a January morning was stealing in at the windows of the common sleeping-room, when Nicholas, raising himself on his arm, looked among the prostrate forms which on every side surrounded him, as though in search of some particular object.

It needed a quick eye to detect, from among the huddled mass of sleepers, the form of any given individual. As they lay closely packed together, covered, for warmth's sake, with their patched and ragged clothes, little could be distinguished but the sharp outlines of pale faces, over which the sombre light shed the same dull heavy colour; with, here and there, a gaunt arm thrust forth: its thinness hidden by no covering, but fully exposed to view, in all its shrunken ugliness. There were some who, lying on their backs with upturned faces and clenched hands, just visible in the leaden light, bore more the aspect of dead bodies than of living creatures; and there were others coiled up into strange and fantastic postures, such as might have been taken for the uneasy efforts of pain to gain some temporary relief, rather than the freaks of slumber. A few—and these were among the youngest of the children—slept peacefully on, with smiles upon their faces, dreaming perhaps of home; but ever and again a deep and heavy sigh, breaking the stillness of the room, announced that some new sleeper had awakened to the misery of another day; and, as morning took the place of night, the smiles gradually faded away, with the friendly darkness which had given them birth.

Dreams are the bright creatures of poem and legend, who sport on earth in the night season, and melt away in the first beam of the sun, which lights grim care and stern reality on their daily pilgrimage through the world.

Nicholas looked upon the sleepers; at first, with the air of one who gazes upon a scene which, though familiar to him, has lost none of its sorrowful effect in consequence; and, afterwards, with a more intense and searching scrutiny, as a man would, who missed something his eye was accustomed to meet, and had expected to rest upon. He was still occupied in this search, and had half risen from his bed in the eagerness of his quest, when the voice of Squeers was heard,calling from the bottom of the stairs.

'Now then,' cried that gentleman, 'are you going to sleep all day, up there—'

'You lazy hounds?' added Mrs Squeers, finishing the sentence, and producing, at the same time, a sharp sound, like that which is occasioned by the lacing of stays.

'We shall be down directly, sir,' replied Nicholas.

'Down directly! said Squeers. 'Ah! you had better be down directly, or I'll be down upon some of you in less. Where's that Smike?'

Nicholas looked hurriedly round again, but made no answer.

'Smike!' shouted Squeers.

'Do you want your head broke in a fresh place, Smike?' demanded his amiable lady in the same key.

Still there was no reply, and still Nicholas stared about him, as did the greater part of the boys, who were by this time roused.

'Confound his impudence!' muttered Squeers, rapping the stair-rail impatiently with his cane. 'Nickleby!'

'Well, sir.'

'Send that obstinate scoundrel down; don't you hear me calling?'

'He is not here, sir,' replied Nicholas.

'Don't tell me a lie,' retorted the schoolmaster. 'He is.'

'He is not,' retorted Nicholas angrily, 'don't tell me one.'

'We shall soon see that,' said Mr Squeers, rushing upstairs. 'I'll find him, I warrant you.'

With which assurance, Mr Squeers bounced into the dormitory, and, swinging his cane in the air ready for a blow, darted into the corner where the lean body of the drudge was usually stretched at night. The cane descended harmlessly upon the ground. There was nobody there.

'What does this mean?' said Squeers, turning round with a very pale face. 'Where have you hid him?'

'I have seen nothing of him since last night,' replied Nicholas.

'Come,' said Squeers, evidently frightened, though he endeavoured to look otherwise, 'you won't save him this way. Where is he?'

'At the bottom of the nearest pond for aught I know,' rejoined Nicholas in a low voice, and fixing his eyes full on the master's face.

'D—n you, what do you mean by that?' retorted Squeers in great perturbation. Without waiting for a reply, he inquired of the boys whether any one among them knew anything of their missing schoolmate.

There was a general hum of anxious denial, in the midst of which, one shrill voice was heard to say (as, indeed, everybody thought):

'Please, sir, I think Smike's run away, sir.'

'Ha!' cried Squeers, turning sharp round; 'Who said that?'

'Tompkins, please sir,' rejoined a chorus of voices. Mr Squeers made a plunge into the crowd, and at one dive, caught a very little boy, habited still in his night gear, and the perplexed expression of whose countenance as he was brought forward, seemed to intimate that he was as yet uncertain whether he was about to be punished or rewarded for the suggestion. He was not long in doubt.

'You think he has run away, do you, sir?' demanded Squeers.

'Yes, please sir,' replied the little boy.

'And what, sir,' said Squeers, catching the little boy suddenly by the arms and whisking up his drapery in a most dexterous manner, 'what reason have you to suppose that any boy would want to run away from this establishment? Eh, sir?'

The child raised a dismal cry, by way of answer, and Mr Squeers, throwing himself into the most favourable attitude for exercising his strength, beat him until the little urchin in his writhings actually rolled out of his hands, when he mercifully allowed him to roll away, as he best could.

'There,' said Squeers. 'Now if any other boy thinks Smike has run away, I should be glad to have a talk with him.'

There was, of course, a profound silence, during which Nicholas showed his disgust as plainly as looks can show it.

'Well, Nickleby,' said Squeers, eyeing him maliciously. '*You* think he has run away, I suppose?'

'I think it extremely likely,' replied Nicholas, in a quiet manner.

'Oh, you do, do you?' sneered Squeers. 'Maybe you know he has?'

'I know nothing of the kind.'

'He didn't tell you he was going, I suppose, did he?' sneered Squeers.

'He did not,' replied Nicholas; 'I am very glad he did not, for it would then have been my duty to have warned you, in time.'

'Which no doubt you would have been devilish sorry to do,' said Squeers in a taunting fashion.

'I should indeed,' replied Nicholas. 'You interpret my feelings with great accuracy.'

Mrs Squeers had listened to this conversation, from the bottom of the stairs; but, now losing all patience, she hastily assumed her night-jacket, and made her way to the scene of action.

'What's all this here to-do?' said the lady, as the boys fell off right and left, to save her the trouble of clearing a passage with her brawny arms. 'What on earth are you a talking to him for, Squeery!'

'Why, my dear,' said Squeers, 'the fact is, that Smike is not to be found.'

'Well, I know that,' said the lady, 'and where's the wonder? If you get a parcel of proud-stomached teachers that set the young dogs a rebelling, what else can you look for? Now, young man, you just have the kindness to take yourself off to the school-room, and take the boys off with you, and don't you stir out of there 'till you have leave given you, or you and I may fall out in a way that'll spoil your beauty, handsome as you think yourself, and so I tell you.'

'Indeed!' said Nicholas.

'Yes; and indeed and indeed again, Mister Jackanapes,' said the excited lady; 'and I wouldn't keep such as you in the house another hour, if I had my way.'

'Nor would you if I had mine,' replied Nicholas. 'Now, boys!'

'Ah! Now boys,' said Mrs Squeers, mimicking, as nearly as she could, the voice and manner of the usher. 'Follow your leader, boys, and take pattern by Smike if you dare. See what he'll get for himself, when he is brought back; and, mind! I tell you that you shall have as bad, and twice as bad, if you so much as open your mouths about him.'

'If I catch him,' said Squeers, 'I'll only stop short of flaying him alive. I give you notice, boys.'

'*If* you catch him,' retorted Mrs Squeers, contemptuously, 'you are sure to; you can't help it, if you go the right way to work. Come! Away with you!'

With these words, Mrs Squeers dismissed the boys, and after a little light skirmishing with those in the rear who were pressing forward to get out of the way, but were detained for a few moments by the throng in front, succeeded in clearing the room, when she confronted her spouse alone.

'He is off,' said Mrs Squeers. 'The cow-house and stable are locked up, so he can't be there; and he's not down stairs anywhere, for the girl has looked. He must have gone York way, and by a public road too.'

'Why must he?' inquired Squeers.

'Stupid!' said Mrs Squeers angrily. 'He hadn't any money, had he?'

'Never had a penny of his own in his whole life, that I know of,' replied Squeers.

'To be sure,' rejoined Mrs Squeers, 'and he didn't take anything to eat with him; that I'll answer for. Ha! ha! ha!'

'Ha! ha! ha!' laughed Squeers.

'Then, of course,' said Mrs S., 'he must beg his way, and he could do that, nowhere, but on the public road.'

'That's true,' exclaimed Squeers, clapping his hands.

'True! Yes; but you would never have thought of it, for all that, if I hadn't said so,' replied his wife. 'Now, if you take the chaise and go one road, and I borrow Swallow's chaise and go the other, what with keeping our eyes open, and asking questions, one or other of us is pretty certain to lay hold of him.'

The worthy lady's plan was adopted and put in execution without a moment's delay. After a very hasty breakfast, and the prosecution of some inquiries in the village, the result of which seemed to show that he was on the right track, Squeers started forth in the pony-chaise, intent upon discovery and vengeance. Shortly afterwards, Mrs Squeers, arrayed in the white top-coat, and tied up in various shawls and handkerchiefs, issued forth in another chaise and another direction, taking with her a good-sized bludgeon, several odd pieces of strong cord, and a stout labouring man: all provided and carried upon the expedition with the sole object of assisting in the capture, and (once caught) insuring the safe custody of the unfortunate Smike.

Nicholas remained behind, in a tumult of feeling, sensible that whatever might be the upshot of the boy's flight, nothing but painful and deplorable consequences were likely to ensue from it. Death, from want and exposure to the weather, was the best that could be expected from the protracted wandering of so poor and helpless a creature, alone and unfriended, through a country of which he was wholly ignorant. There was little, perhaps, to choose between this fate and a return to the tender mercies of the Yorkshire school; but the unhappy being had established a hold upon his sympathy and compassion, which made his heart ache at the prospect of the suffering he was destined to undergo. He lingered on, in restless anxiety, picturing a thousand possibilities, until the evening of next day, when Squeers returned, alone, and unsuccessful.

'No news of the scamp!' said the schoolmaster, who had evidently been stretching his legs, on the old principle, not a few times during the journey. 'I'll have consolation for this out of somebody, Nickleby, if Mrs Squeers don't hunt him down; so I give you warning.'

'It is not in my power to console you, sir,' said Nicholas. 'It is nothing to me.'

'Isn't it?' said Squeers in a threatening manner. 'We shall see!'

'We shall,' rejoined Nicholas.

'Here's the pony run right off his legs, and me obliged to come home with a hack cob, that'll cost fifteen shillings besides other expenses,' said Squeers; 'who's to pay for that, do you hear?'

Nicholas shrugged his shoulders and remained silent.

'I'll have it out of somebody, I tell you,' said Squeers, his usual harsh crafty manner changed to open bullying. 'None of your whining vapourings here, Mr Puppy, but be off to your kennel, for it's past your bed-time! Come! Get out!'

Nicholas bit his lip and knit his hands involuntarily, for his finger ends tingled to avenge the insult; but remembering that the man was drunk, and that it could come to little but a noisy brawl, he contented himself with darting a contemptuous look at the tyrant, and walked, as majestically as he could, up stairs: not a little nettled, however, to observe that Miss Squeers and Master Squeers, and the servant girl, were enjoying the scene from a snug corner; the two former, indulging in many edifying remarks about the presumption of poor upstarts, which occasioned a vast deal of laughter, in which even the most miserable of all miserable servant girls joined: while Nicholas, stung to the quick, drew over his head such bed-clothes as he had, and sternly resolved that the outstanding account between himself and Mr Squeers should be settled rather more speedily than the latter anticipated.

Another day came, and Nicholas was scarcely awake when he heard the wheels of a chaise approaching the house. It stopped. The voice of Mrs Squeers was heard, and in exultation, ordering a glass of spirits for somebody, which was in itself a sufficient sign that something extraordinary had happened. Nicholas hardly dared to look out of the window; but he did so, and the very first object that met his eyes was the wretched Smike: so bedabbled with mud and rain, so haggard and worn and wild, that, but for his garments being such as no scarecrow was ever seen to wear, he might have been doubtful, even then, of his identity.

'Lift him out,' said Squeers, after he had literally feasted his eyes, in silence, upon the culprit. 'Bring him in; bring him in!'

'Take care,' cried Mrs Squeers, as her husband proffered his assistance. 'We tied his legs under the apron and made 'em fast to the chaise, to prevent his giving us the slip again.'

With hands trembling with delight, Squeers unloosened the cord; and Smike, to all appearance more dead than alive, was brought into the house and securely locked up in a cellar, until such time as Mr Squeers should deem it expedient to operate upon him, in presence of the assembled school.

Upon a hasty consideration of the circumstances, it may be matter of surprise to some persons, that Mr and Mrs Squeers should have taken so much trouble to repossess themselves of an incumbrance of which it was their wont to complain so loudly; but their surprise will cease when they are informed that the manifold services of the drudge, if performed by anybody else, would have cost the establishment some ten or twelve shillings per week in the shape of wages; and furthermore, that all runaways were, as a matter of policy, made severe examples of, at Dotheboys Hall, inasmuch as, in consequence of the limited extent of its attractions, there was but little inducement, beyond the powerful impulse of fear, for any pupil, provided with the usual number of legs and the power of using them, to remain.

The news that Smike had been caught and brought back in triumph, ran like wild-fire through the hungry community, and expectation was on tiptoe all the morning. On tiptoe it was destined to remain, however, until afternoon; when Squeers, having refreshed himself with his dinner, and further strengthened himself by an extra libation or so, made his appearance (accompanied by his amiable partner) with a countenance of portentous import, and a fearful instrument of flagellation, strong, supple, wax-ended, and new—in short, purchased that morning, expressly for the occasion.

'Is every boy here?' asked Squeers, in a tremendous voice.

Every boy was there, but every boy was afraid to speak; so Squeers glared along the lines to assure himself; and every eye drooped, and every head cowered down, as he did so.

'Each boy keep his place,' said Squeers, administering his favourite blow to the desk, and regarding with gloomy satisfaction the universal start which it never failed to occasion. 'Nickleby! to your desk, sir.'

It was remarked by more than one small observer, that there was a very curious and unusual expression in the usher's face; but he took his seat, without opening his lips in reply. Squeers, casting a triumphant glance at his assistant and a look of most comprehensive despotism on the boys, left the room, and shortly afterwards returned, dragging Smike by the collar—or rather by that fragment of his jacket which was nearest the place where his collar would have been, had he boasted such a decoration.

In any other place, the appearance of the wretched, jaded, spiritless object would have occasioned a murmur of compassion and remonstrance. It had some effect, even there; for the lookers-on moved uneasily in their seats; and a few of the boldest ventured to steal looks at each other, expressive of indignation and pity.

They were lost on Squeers, however, whose gaze was fastened on the luckless Smike, as he inquired, according to custom in such cases, whether he had anything to say for himself.

'Nothing, I suppose?' said Squeers, with a diabolical grin.

Smike glanced round, and his eye rested, for an instant, on Nicholas, as if he had expected him to intercede; but his look was riveted on his desk.

'Have you anything to say?' demanded Squeers again: giving his right arm two or three flourishes to try its power and suppleness. 'Stand a little out of the way, Mrs Squeers, my dear; I've hardly got room enough.'

'Spare me, sir!' cried Smike.

'Oh! that's all, is it?' said Squeers. 'Yes, I'll flog you within an inch of your life, and spare you that.'

'Ha, ha, ha,' laughed Mrs Squeers, 'that's a good 'un!'

'I was driven to do it,' said Smike faintly; and casting another imploring look about him.

'Driven to do it, were you?' said Squeers. 'Oh! it wasn't your fault; it was mine, I suppose—eh?'

'A nasty, ungrateful, pig-headed, brutish, obstinate, sneaking dog,' exclaimed Mrs Squeers, taking Smike's head under her arm, and administering a cuff at every epithet; 'what does he mean by that?'

'Stand aside, my dear,' replied Squeers. 'We'll try and find out.'

Mrs Squeers being out of breath with her exertions, complied. Squeers caught the boy firmly in his grip; one desperate cut had fallen on his body—he was wincing from the lash and uttering a scream of pain—it was raised again, and again about to fall—when Nicholas Nickleby suddenly starting up, cried 'Stop!' in a voice that made the rafters ring.

'Who cried stop?' said Squeers, turning savagely round.

'I,' said Nicholas, stepping forward. 'This must not go on.'

'Must not go on!' cried Squeers, almost in a shriek.

'No!' thundered Nicholas.

Aghast and stupefied by the boldness of the interference, Squeers released his hold of Smike, and, falling back a pace or two, gazed upon Nicholas with looks that were positively frightful.

'I say must not,' repeated Nicholas, nothing daunted; 'shall not. I will prevent it.'

Squeers continued to gaze upon him, with his eyes starting out of his head; but astonishment had actually, for the moment, bereft him of speech.

'You have disregarded all my quiet interference in the miserable lad's behalf,' said Nicholas; 'you have returned no answer to the letter in which I begged forgiveness for him, and offered to be responsible that he would remain quietly here. Don't blame me for this public interference. You have brought it upon yourself; not I.'

'Sit down, beggar!' screamed Squeers, almost beside himself with rage, and seizing Smike as he spoke.

'Wretch,' rejoined Nicholas, fiercely, 'touch him at your peril! I will not stand by, and see it done. My blood is up, and I have the strength of ten such men as you. Look to yourself, for by Heaven I will not spare you, if you drive me on!'

'Stand back,' cried Squeers, brandishing his weapon.

'I have a long series of insults to avenge,' said Nicholas, flushed with passion; 'and my indignation is aggravated by the dastardly cruelties practised on helpless infancy in this foul den. Have a care; for if you do raise the devil within me, the consequences shall fall heavily upon your own head!'

He had scarcely spoken, when Squeers, in a violent outbreak of wrath, and with a cry like the howl of a wild beast, spat upon him, and struck him a blow across the face with his instrument of torture, which raised up a bar of livid flesh as it was inflicted. Smarting with the agony of the blow, and concentrating into that one moment all his feelings of rage, scorn, and indignation, Nicholas sprang upon him, wrested the weapon from his hand, and pinning him by the throat, beat the ruffian till he roared for mercy.

The boys—with the exception of Master Squeers, who, coming to his father's assistance, harassed the enemy in the rear—moved not, hand or foot; but Mrs Squeers, with many shrieks for aid, hung on to the tail of her partner's coat, and endeavoured to drag him from his infuriated adversary; while Miss Squeers, who had been peeping through the key-hole in expectation of a very different scene, darted in at the very beginning of the attack, and after launching a shower of ink-stands at the usher's head, beat Nicholas to her heart's content: animating herself, at every blow, with the recollection of his having refused her proffered love, and thus imparting additional strength to an arm which (as she took after her mother in this respect) was, at no time, one of the weakest.

Nicholas, in the full torrent of his violence, felt the blows no more than if they had been dealt with feathers; but, becoming tired of the noise and uproar, and feeling that his arm grew weak besides, he threw all his remaining strength into half-a-dozen finishing cuts, and flung Squeers from him, with all the force he could muster. The violence of his fall precipitated Mrs Squeers completely over an adjacent form; and Squeers striking his head against it in his descent, lay at his full length on the ground, stunned and motionless.

Having brought affairs to this happy termination, and ascertained, to his thorough satisfaction, that Squeers was only stunned, and not dead (upon which point he had had some unpleasant doubts at first), Nicholas left his family to restore him, and retired to consider what course he had better adopt. He looked anxiously round for Smike, as he left the room, but he was nowhere to be seen.

After a brief consideration, he packed up a few clothes in a small leathern valise, and, finding that nobody offered to oppose his progress, marched boldly out by the front door, and shortly afterwards, struck into the road which led to Greta Bridge.

When he had cooled sufficiently to be enabled to give his present circumstances some little reflection, they did not appear in a very encouraging light; he had only four shillings and a few pence in his pocket, and was something more than two hundred and fifty miles from London, whither he resolved to direct his steps, that he might ascertain, among other things, what account of the morning's proceedings Mr Squeers transmitted to his most affectionate uncle.

Lifting up his eyes, as he arrived at the conclusion that there was no remedy for this unfortunate state of things, he beheld a horseman coming towards him, whom, on nearer approach, he discovered, to his infinite chagrin, to be no other than Mr John Browdie, who, clad in cords and leather leggings, was urging his animal forward by means of a thick ash stick, which seemed to have been recently cut from some stout sapling.

'I am in no mood for more noise and riot,' thought Nicholas, 'and yet, do what I will, I shall have an altercation with this honest blockhead, and perhaps a blow or two from yonder staff.'

In truth, there appeared some reason to expect that such a result would follow from the encounter, for John Browdie no sooner saw Nicholas advancing, then he reined in his horse by the footpath, and waited until such time as he should come up; looking meanwhile, very sternly between the horse's ears, at Nicholas as he came on at his leisure.

'Servant, young genelman,' said John.

'Yours,' said Nicholas.

'Weel; we ha' met at last,' observed John, making the stirrup ring under a smart touch of the ash stick.

'Yes,' replied Nicholas, hesitating. 'Come!' he said, frankly, after a moment's pause, 'we parted on no very good terms the last time we met; it was my fault, I believe; but I had no intention of offending you, and no idea that I was doing so. I was very sorry for it, afterwards. Will you shake hands?'

'Shake honds!' cried the good-humoured Yorkshireman; 'ah! that I weel;'at the same time, he bent down from the saddle, and gave Nicholas's fist a huge wrench; 'but wa'at be the matther wi' thy feace, mun? it be all brokken loike.'

'It is a cut,' said Nicholas, turning scarlet as he spoke,—'a blow; but I returned it to the giver, and with good interest too.'

'Noa, did 'ee though?' exclaimed John Browdie. 'Well deane! I loike 'un for thot.'

'The fact is,' said Nicholas, not very well knowing how to make the avowal, 'the fact is, that I have been ill-treated.'

'Noa!' interposed John Browdie, in a tone of compassion; for he was a giant in strength and stature, and Nicholas, very likely, in his eyes, seemed a mere dwarf; 'dean't say thot.'

'Yes, I have,' replied Nicholas, 'by that man Squeers, and I have beaten him soundly, and am leaving this place in consequence.'

'What!' cried John Browdie, with such an ecstatic shout, that the horse quite shied at it. 'Beatten the schoolmeasther! Ho! ho! ho! Beatten the schoolmeasther! who ever heard o' the loike o'that noo! Giv's us thee hond agean, yoongster. Beatten the schoolmeasther! Dang it, I loove thee for't.'

With these expressions of delight, John Browdie laughed and laughed again—so loud that the echoes, far and wide, sent back nothing but jovial peals of merriment—and shook Nicholas by the hand meanwhile, no less heartily. When his mirth had subsided, he inquired what Nicholas meant to do; on his informing him, to go straight to London, he shook his head doubtfully, and inquired if he knew how much the coaches charged, to carry passengers so far.

'No, I do not,' said Nicholas; 'but it is of no great consequence to me, for I intend walking.'

'Gang awa' to Lunnun afoot!' cried John, in amazement.

'Every step of the way,' replied Nicholas. 'I should be many steps further on by this time, and so good bye!'

'Nay noo,' replied the honest countryman, reining in his impatient horse, 'stan' still, tellee. Hoo much cash hast thee gotten?'

'Not much,' said Nicholas, colouring 'but I can make it enough. Where there's a will, there's a way, you know.'

John Browdie made no verbal answer to this remark, but putting his hand in his pocket, pulled out an old purse of soiled leather, and insisted that Nicholas should borrow from him whatever he required for his present necessities.

'Dean't be afeard, mun,' he said; 'tak' eneaf to carry thee whoam. Thee'lt pay me yan day, a' warrant.'

Nicholas could by no means be prevailed upon to borrow more than a sovereign, with which loan Mr Browdie, after many entreaties that he would accept of more (observing, with a touch of Yorkshire caution, that if he didn't spend it all, he could put the surplus by, till he had an opportunity of remitting it carriage free), was fain to content himself.

'Tak' that bit o' timber to help thee on wi', mun,' he added, pressing his stick on Nicholas, and giving his hand another squeeze; 'keep a good heart, and bless thee. Beatten the schoolmeasther! 'Cod it's the best thing a've heerd this twonty year!'

So saying, and indulging, with more delicacy than might have been expected from him, in another series of loud laughs, for the purpose of avoiding the thanks which Nicholas poured forth, John Browdie set spurs to his horse, and went off at a smart canter: looking back, from time to time, as Nicholas stood gazing after him, and waving his hand cheerily, as if to encourage him on his way. Nicholas watched the horse and rider until they disappeared over the brow of a distant hill, and then set forward on his journey.

He did not travel far, that afternoon, for by this time it was nearly dark, and there had been a heavy fall of snow, which not only rendered the way toilsome but the track uncertain and difficult to find, after daylight, save by experienced wayfarers. He lay, that night, at a cottage, where beds were let at a cheap rate to the more humble class of travellers; and, rising betimes next morning, made his way before night to Boroughbridge. Passing through that town in search of some cheap resting-place, he stumbled upon an empty barn within a couple of hundred yards of the road side; in a warm corner of which, he stretched his weary limbs, and soon fell asleep.

When he awoke next morning, and tried to recollect his dreams, which had been all connected with his recent sojourn at Dotheboys Hall, he sat up, rubbed his eyes, and stared—not with the most composed countenance possible—at some motionless object which seemed to be stationed within a few yards in front of him.

'Strange!' cried Nicholas; 'can this be some lingering creation of the visions that have scarcely left me! It cannot be real—and yet I—I am awake! Smike!'

The form moved, rose, advanced, and dropped upon its knees at his feet. It was Smike indeed.

'Why do you kneel to me?' said Nicholas, hastily raising him.

'To go with you—anywhere—everywhere—to the world's end—to the churchyard grave,' replied Smike, clinging to his hand. 'Let me, oh do let me. You are my home—my kind friend—take me with you, pray.'

'I am a friend who can do little for you,' said Nicholas, kindly. 'How came you here?'

He had followed him, it seemed; had never lost sight of him all the way; had watched while he slept, and when he halted for refreshment; and had feared to appear, before, lest he should be sent back. He had not intended to appear now, but Nicholas had awakened more suddenly than he looked for, and he had had no time to conceal himself.

'Poor fellow!' said Nicholas, 'your hard fate denies you any friend but one, and he is nearly as poor and helpless as yourself.'

'May I—may I go with you?' asked Smike, timidly. 'I will be your faithful hard-working servant, I will, indeed. I want no clothes,' added the poor creature, drawing his rags together; 'these will do very well. I only want to be near you.'

'And you shall,' cried Nicholas. 'And the world shall deal by you as it does by me, till one or both of us shall quit it for a better. Come!'

With these words, he strapped his burden on his shoulders, and, taking his stick in one hand, extended the other to his delighted charge; and so they passed out of the old barn, together.

THE OLD CURIOSITY SHOP

Little Nell and her grandfather live in the shop of the title. Nell's grandfather claims to be poor but his grandson, Nell's brother Fred, is certain that he has a secret fortune, a belief shared by the moneylender from whom Nell's grandfather regularly borrows, one Daniel Quilp ...

... an elderly man of remarkably hard features and forbidding aspect, and so low in stature as to be quite a dwarf, though his head and face were large enough for the body of a giant. His black eyes were restless, sly, and cunning; his mouth and chin bristly with the stubble of a coarse hard beard; and his complexion was one of that kind which never looks clean or wholesome. But what added most to the grotesque expression of his face was a ghastly smile, which, appearing to be the mere result of habit, and to have no connection with any mirthful or complacent feeling, constantly revealed the few discoloured fangs that were yet scattered in his mouth, and gave him the aspect of a panting dog. His dress consisted of a large high-crowned hat, a worn dark suit, a pair of capacious shoes, and a dirty white neckerchief, sufficiently limp and crumpled to disclose the greater portion of his wiry throat. Such hair as he had, was of a grizzled black, cut short and straight upon his temples, and hanging in a frowsy fringe about his ears. His hands, which were of a rough, coarse grain, were very dirty; his finger-nails were crooked, long, and yellow.

Mr Quilp could scarcely be said to be of any particular trade or calling, though his pursuits were diversified and his occupations numerous. He collected the rents of whole colonies of filthy streets and alleys by the water-side, advanced money to the seamen and petty officers of merchant vessels, had a share in the ventures of divers mates of East

Indiamen, smoked his smuggled cigars under the very nose of the Custom House, and made appointments on 'Change with men in glazed hats and round jackets pretty well every day. On the Surrey side of the river was a small rat-infested dreary yard called 'Quilp's Wharf,' in which were a little wooden counting-house burrowing all awry in the dust as if it had fallen from the clouds and ploughed into the ground; a few fragments of rusty anchors; several large iron rings; some piles of rotten wood; and two or three heaps of old sheet copper, crumpled, cracked, and battered. On Quilp's Wharf, Daniel Quilp was a ship-breaker, yet to judge from these appearances he must either have been a ship-breaker on a very small scale, or have broken his ships up very small indeed. Neither did the place present any extraordinary aspect of life or activity, as its only human occupant was an amphibious boy in a canvas suit, whose sole change of occupation was from sitting on the head of a pile and throwing stones into the mud when the tide was out, to standing with his hands in his pockets gazing listlessly on the motion and on the bustle of the river at high-water.

The dwarf's lodging on Tower Hill comprised, besides the needful accommodation for himself and Mrs Quilp, a small sleeping-closet for that lady's mother, who resided with the couple and waged perpetual war with Daniel; of whom, notwithstanding, she stood in no slight dread. Indeed, the ugly creature contrived by some means or other—whether by his ugliness or his ferocity or his natural cunning is no great matter—to impress with a wholesome fear of his anger, most of those with whom he was brought into daily contact and communication. Over nobody had he such complete ascendency as Mrs Quilp herself—a pretty little, mild-spoken, blue-eyed woman, who having allied herself in wedlock to the dwarf in one of those strange infatuations of which examples are by no means scarce, performed a sound practical penance for her folly, every day of her life.

It has been said that Mrs Quilp was pining in her bower. In her bower she was, but not alone, for besides the old lady her mother of whom mention has recently been made, there were present some half-dozen ladies of the neighbourhood who had happened by a strange accident (and also by a little understanding among themselves) to drop in one after another, just about tea-time. This being a season favourable to conversation, and the room being a cool, shady, lazy kind of place, with some plants at the open window shutting out the dust, and interposing pleasantly enough between the tea-table within and the old Tower without, it is no wonder that the ladies felt an inclination to talk and linger, especially when there are taken into account the additional inducements of fresh butter, new bread, shrimps, and water-cresses.

Now, the ladies being together under these circumstances, it was extremely natural that the discourse should turn upon the propensity of mankind to tyrannise over the weaker sex, and the duty that devolved upon the weaker sex to resist that tyranny and assert their rights and dignity. It was natural for four reasons: firstly, because Mrs Quilp being a young woman and notoriously under the dominion of her husband ought to be excited to rebel; secondly, because Mrs Quilp's parent was known to be laudably shrewish in her disposition and inclined to resist male authority; thirdly, because each visitor wished to show for herself how superior she was in this respect to the generality of her sex; and fourthly, because the company being accustomed to scandalise each other in pairs, were deprived of their usual subject of conversation now that they were all assembled in close friendship, and had consequently no better employment than to attack the common enemy.

Moved by these considerations, a stout lady opened the proceedings by inquiring, with an air of great concern and sympathy, how Mr Quilp was; whereunto Mr Quilp's wife's mother replied sharply, 'Oh! he was well enough—nothing much was ever the matter with him—and ill weeds were sure to thrive.' All the ladies then sighed in concert, shook their heads gravely, and looked at Mrs Quilp as at a martyr.

'Ah!' said the spokeswoman, 'I wish you'd give her a little of your advice, Mrs Jiniwin'—Mrs Quilp had been a Miss Jiniwin it should be observed—'nobody knows better than you, ma'am, what us women owe to ourselves.'

'Owe indeed, ma'am!' replied Mrs Jiniwin. 'When my poor husband, her dear father, was alive, if he had ever ventur'd a cross word to *me*, I'd have—' the good old lady did not finish the sentence, but she twisted off the head of a shrimp with a vindictiveness which seemed to imply that the action was in some degree a substitute for words. In this light it was clearly understood by the other party, who immediately replied with great approbation, 'You quite enter into my feelings, ma'am, and it's jist what I'd do myself.'

'But you have no call to do it,' said Mrs Jiniwin. 'Luckily for you, you have no more occasion to do it than I had.'

'No woman need have, if she was true to herself,' rejoined the stout lady.

'Do you hear that, Betsy?' said Mrs Jiniwin, in a warning voice. 'How often have I said the very same words to you, and almost gone down on my knees when I spoke 'em!'

Poor Mrs Quilp, who had looked in a state of helplessness from one face of condolence to another, coloured, smiled, and shook her head doubtfully. This was the signal for a general clamour, which beginning in a low murmur gradually swelled into a great noise in which everybody spoke at once, and all said that she being a young woman had no right to set up her opinions against the experiences of those who knew so much better; that it was very wrong of her not to take the advice of people who had nothing at heart but her good; that it was next door to being downright ungrateful to conduct herself in that manner; that if she had no respect for herself she ought to have some for other women, all of whom she compromised by her meekness and that if she had no respect for other women, the time would come when other women would have no respect for her; and she would be very sorry for that, they could tell her. Having dealt out these admonitions, the ladies fell to a more powerful assault than they had yet made upon the mixed tea, new bread, fresh butter, shrimps, and water-cresses, and said that their vexation was so great to see her going on like that, that they could hardly bring themselves to eat a single morsel.

'It's all very fine to talk,' said Mrs Quilp with much simplicity, 'but I know that if I was to die to-morrow, Quilp could marry anybody he pleased—now that he could, I know!'

There was a scream of indignation at this idea. Marry whom he pleased! They would like to see him dare to think of marrying any of them; they would like to see the faintest approach to such a thing. One lady (a widow) was quite certain she should stab him if he hinted at it.

'Very well,' said Mrs Quilp, nodding her head, 'as I said just now, it's very easy to talk, but I say again that I know—that I'm sure—Quilp has such a way with him when he likes, that the best-looking woman here couldn't refuse him if I was dead, and she was free, and he chose to make love to her. Come!'

Everybody bridled up at this remark, as much as to say 'I know you mean me. Let him try—that's all.' And yet for some hidden reason they were all angry with the widow, and each lady whispered in her neighbour's ear that it was very plain the said widow thought herself the person referred to, and what a puss she was!

'Mother knows,' said Mrs Quilp, 'that what I say is quite correct, for she often said so before we were married. Didn't you say so, mother?'

This inquiry involved the respected lady in rather a delicate position, for she certainly had been an active party in making her daughter Mrs Quilp, and, besides, it was not supporting the family credit to encourage the idea that she had married a man whom nobody else would have. On the other hand, to exaggerate the captivating qualities of her son-in-law would be to weaken the cause of revolt, in which all her energies were deeply engaged. Beset by these opposing considerations, Mrs Jiniwin admitted the powers of insinuation, but denied the right to govern, and with a timely compliment to the stout lady, brought back the discussion to the point from which it had strayed.

'Oh! It's a sensible and proper thing indeed, what Mrs George has said!' exclaimed the old lady. 'If women are only true to themselves!— But Betsy isn't, and more's the shame and pity.'

'Before I'd let a man order me about as Quilp orders her,' said Mrs George; 'before I'd consent to stand in awe of a man as she does of him, I'd—I'd kill myself and write a letter first to say he did it!'

This remark being loudly commended and approved of, another lady (from the Minories) put in her word:

'Mr Quilp may be a very nice man,' said this lady, 'and I suppose there's no doubt he is, because Mrs Quilp says he is, and Mrs Jiniwin says he is, and they ought to know, or nobody does. But still he is not quite a—what one calls a handsome man, nor quite a young man neither, which might be a little excuse for him if anything could be; whereas his wife is young, and is good-looking, and is a woman—which is the great thing after all.'

This last clause being delivered with extraordinary pathos, elicited a corresponding murmur from the hearers, stimulated by which the lady went on to remark, that if such a husband was cross and unreasonable with such a wife, then —

'If he is!' interposed the mother, putting down her teacup and brushing the crumbs out of her lap, preparatory to making a solemn declaration. 'If he is! He is the greatest tyrant that ever lived, she daren't call her soul her own, he makes her tremble with a word and even with a look, he frightens her to death, and she hasn't the spirit to give him a word back, no, not a single word.'

Notwithstanding that the fact had been notorious before-hand to all the tea-drinkers, and had been discussed and expatiated on at every tea-drinking in the neighbourhood for the last twelve months, this official communication was no sooner made than they all began to talk at once and to vie with each other in vehemence and volubility. Mrs George remarked that people would talk, that people had often said this to her before, that Mrs Simmons, then and there present had told her so twenty times, that she had always said, 'No, Henrietta Simmons, unless I see it with my own eyes and hear it with my own ears, I never will believe it.' Mrs Simmons corroborated this testimony and added strong evidence of her own. The lady from the Minories recounted a successful course of treatment under which she had placed her own husband, who from manifesting one month after marriage unequivocal symptoms of the tiger, had by this means become subdued into a perfect lamb. Another lady recounted her own personal struggle and final triumph, in the course whereof she had found it necessary to call in her mother and two aunts, and to weep incessantly night and day for six weeks. A third, who in the general confusion could secure no other listener, fastened herself upon a young woman still unmarried who happened to be amongst them, and conjured her as she valued her own peace of mind and happiness to profit by this solemn occasion, to take example from the weakness of Mrs Quilp, and from that time forth to direct her whole thoughts to taming and subduing the rebellious spirit of man. The noise was at its height, and half the company had elevated their voices into a perfect shriek in order to drown the voices of the other half, when Mrs Jiniwin was seen to change colour and shake her fore-finger stealthily, as if exhorting them to silence. Then, and not until then, Daniel Quilp himself, the cause and occasion of all this clamour, was observed to be in the room, looking on and listening with profound attention.

'Go on, ladies, go on,' said Daniel. 'Mrs Quilp, pray ask the ladies to stop to supper, and have a couple of lobsters and something light and palatable.'

'I—I didn't ask them to tea, Quilp,' stammered his wife. 'It's quite an accident.'

'So much the better, Mrs Quilp: these accidental parties are always the pleasantest,' said the dwarf, rubbing his hands so hard that he seemed to be engaged in manufacturing, of the dirt with which they were encrusted, little charges for popguns. 'What! Not going, ladies! You are not going, surely!'

His fair enemies tossed their heads slightly as they sought their respective bonnets and shawls, but left all verbal contention to Mrs Jiniwin, who finding herself in the position of champion, made a faint struggle to sustain the character.

'And why *not* stop to supper, Quilp,' said the old lady, 'if my daughter had a mind?'

'To be sure,' rejoined Daniel. 'Why not?'

'There's nothing dishonest or wrong in a supper, I hope?' said Mrs Jiniwin.

'Surely not,' returned the dwarf. 'Why should there be? Nor anything unwholesome either, unless there's lobster-salad or prawns, which I'm told are not good for digestion.'

'And you wouldn't like *your* wife to be attacked with that, or anything else that would make her uneasy, would you?' said Mrs Jiniwin.

'Not for a score of worlds,' replied the dwarf with a grin. 'Not even to have a score of mothers-in-law at the same time—and what a blessing that would be!'

'My daughter's your wife, Mr Quilp, certainly,' said the old lady with a giggle, meant for satirical and to imply that he needed to be reminded of the fact: 'your wedded wife.'

'So she is, certainly. So she is,' observed the dwarf.

'And she has a right to do as she likes, I hope, Quilp,' said the old lady trembling, partly with anger and partly with a secret fear of her impish son-in-law.

'Hope she has!' he replied. 'Oh! Don't you know she has? Don't you know she has, Mrs Jiniwin?'

'I know she ought to have, Quilp, and would have, if she was of my way of thinking.'

'Why ain't you of your mother's way of thinking, my dear?' said the dwarf, turning round and addressing his wife, 'why don't you always imitate your mother, my dear? She's the ornament of her sex—your father said so every day of his life, I am sure he did.'

'Her father was a blessed creetur, Quilp, and worth twenty thousand of some people,' said Mrs Jiniwin; 'twenty hundred million thousand.'

'I should like to have known him,' remarked the dwarf. 'I dare say he was a blessed creature then; but I'm sure he is now. It was a happy release. I believe he had suffered a long time.'

The old lady gave a gasp, but nothing came of it; Quilp resumed, with the same malice in his eye and the same sarcastic politeness on his tongue.

'You look ill, Mrs Jiniwin; I know you have been exciting yourself too much—talking perhaps, for it is your weakness. Go to bed. Do go to bed.'

'I shall go when I please, Quilp, and not before.'

'But please to go now. Do please to go now,' said the dwarf.

The old woman looked angrily at him, but retreated as he advanced, and falling back before him suffered him to shut the door upon her and bolt her out among the guests, who were by this time crowding down stairs. Being left alone with his wife, who sat trembling in a corner with her eyes fixed upon the ground, the little man planted himself before her, at some distance, and folding his arms looked steadily at her for a long time without speaking.

'Oh you nice creature!' were the words with which he broke silence; smacking his lips as if this were no figure of speech, and she were actually a sweetmeat. 'Oh you precious darling! oh you de-licious charmer!'

Mrs Quilp sobbed; and knowing the nature of her pleasant lord, appeared quite as much alarmed by these compliments, as she would have been by the most extreme demonstrations of violence.

'She's such,' said the dwarf, with a ghastly grin,—'such a jewel, such a diamond, such a pearl, such a ruby, such a golden casket set with gems of all sorts! She's such a treasure! I'm so fond of her!'

The poor little woman shivered from head to foot; and raising her eyes to his face with an imploring look, suffered them to droop again, and sobbed once more.

'The best of her is,' said the dwarf, advancing with a sort of skip, which, what with the crookedness of his legs, the ugliness of his face, and the mockery of his manner, was perfectly goblin-like;—'the best of her is that she's so meek, and she's so mild, and she never has a will of her own, and she has such an insinuating mother!'

Uttering these latter words with a gloating maliciousness, within a hundred degrees of which no one but himself could possibly approach, Mr Quilp planted his two hands on his knees, and straddling his legs out very wide apart, stooped slowly down, and down, and down, until, by screwing his head very much on one side, he came between his wife's eyes and the floor.

'Mrs Quilp!'

'Yes, Quilp.'

'Am I nice to look at? Should I be the handsomest creature in the world if I had but whiskers? Am I quite a lady's man as it is?—am I, Mrs Quilp?'

Mrs Quilp dutifully replied, 'Yes, Quilp;' and fascinated by his gaze, remained looking timidly at him, while he treated her with a succession of such horrible grimaces, as none but himself and nightmares had the power of assuming. During the whole of this performance, which was somewhat of the longest, he preserved a dead silence, except when by an unexpected skip or leap, he made his wife start backward with an irrepressible shriek. Then he chuckled.

'Mrs Quilp,' he said at last.

'Yes, Quilp,' she meekly replied.

Instead of pursuing the theme he had in his mind, Quilp rose, folded his arms again, and looked at her more sternly than before, while she averted her eyes and kept them on the ground.

'Mrs Quilp.'

'Yes, Quilp.'

'If ever you listen to these beldames again, I'll bite you.'

With this laconic threat, which he accompanied with a snarl that gave him the appearance of being particularly in earnest, Mr Quilp bade her clear the teaboard away, and bring the rum. The spirit being set before him in a huge case-bottle, which had originally come out of some ship's locker, he ordered cold water and the box of cigars; and these being supplied, he settled himself in an arm-chair with his large head and face squeezed up against the back, and his little legs planted on the table.

'Now, Mrs Quilp,' he said; 'I feel in a smoking humour, and shall probably blaze away all night. But sit where you are, if you please, in case I want you.'

His wife returned no other reply than the customary 'Yes, Quilp,' and the small lord of the creation took his first cigar and mixed his first glass of grog. The sun went down, and the stars peeped out, the Tower turned from its own proper colours to grey and from grey to black, the room became perfectly dark and the end of the cigar a deep fiery red, but still Mr Quilp went on smoking and drinking in the same position, and staring listlessly out of window with the dog-like smile always on his face, save when Mrs Quilp made some involuntary movement of restlessness or fatigue; and then it expanded into a grin of delight.

Whether Mr Quilp took any sleep by snatches of a few winks at a time, or whether he sat with his eyes wide open all night long, certain it is that he kept his cigar alight, and kindled every fresh one from the ashes of that which was nearly consumed, without requiring the assistance of a candle. Nor did the striking of the clocks, hour after hour, appear to inspire him with any sense of drowsiness or any natural desire to go to rest; but rather to increase his wakefulness, which he showed, at every such indication of the progress of the night, by a suppressed cackling in his throat, and a motion of his shoulders, like one who laughs heartily, but at the same time slily and by stealth.

At length the day broke, and poor Mrs Quilp, shivering with the cold of early morning and harassed by fatigue and want of sleep, was discovered sitting patiently on her chair, raising her eyes at intervals in mute appeal to the compassion and clemency of her lord, and gently reminding him by an occasional cough that she was still unpardoned and that her penance had been of long duration. But her dwarfish spouse still smoked his cigar and drank his rum without heeding her; and it was not until the sun had some time risen, and the activity and noise of city day were rife in the street, that he deigned to recognise her presence by any word or sign. He might not have done so even then, but for certain impatient tappings at the door which seemed to denote that some pretty hard knuckles were actively engaged upon the other side.

'Why dear me!' he said, looking round with a malicious grin, 'it's day! Open the door, sweet Mrs Quilp!'

His obedient wife withdrew the bolt, and her lady mother entered.

Now, Mrs Jiniwin bounced into the room with great impetuosity; for, supposing her son-in-law to be still a-bed, she had come to relieve her feelings by pronouncing a strong opinion upon his general conduct and character. Seeing that he was up and dressed, and that the room appeared to have been occupied ever since she quitted it on the previous evening, she stopped short, in some embarrassment.

Nothing escaped the hawk's eye of the ugly little man, who, perfectly understanding what passed in the old lady's mind, turned uglier still in the fulness of his satisfaction, and bade her good morning, with a leer of triumph.

'Why, Betsy,' said the old woman, 'you haven't been a—you don't mean to say you've been a—'

'Sitting up all night?' said Quilp, supplying the conclusion of the sentence. 'Yes, she has!'

'All night!' cried Mrs Jiniwin.

'Aye, all night. Is the dear old lady deaf?' said Quilp, with a smile of which a frown was part. 'Who says man and wife are bad company? Ha, ha! The time has flown.'

'You're a brute!' exclaimed Mrs Jiniwin.

'Come, come,' said Quilp, wilfully misunderstanding her, of course, 'you musn't call her names. She's married now, you know. And though she *did* beguile the time and keep me from my bed, you must not be so tenderly careful of me as to be out of humour with her. Bless you for a dear old lady. Here's your health!'

'I am *much* obliged to you,' returned the old woman, testifying by a certain restlessness in her hands a vehement desire to shake her matronly fist at her son-in-law. 'Oh! I'm very much obliged to you!'

'Grateful soul!' cried the dwarf. 'Mrs Quilp.'

'Yes, Quilp,' said the timid sufferer.

'Help your mother to get breakfast, Mrs Quilp. I am going to the wharf this morning—the earlier, the better, so be quick.'

Mrs Jiniwin made a faint demonstration of rebellion by sitting down in a chair near the door and folding her arms as if in a resolute determination to do nothing. But a few whispered words from her daughter, and a kind inquiry from her son-in-law whether she felt faint, with a hint that there was abundance of cold water in the next apartment, routed these symptoms effectually, and she applied herself to the prescribed preparations with sullen diligence.

While they were in progress, Mr Quilp withdrew to the adjoining room, and, turning back his coat-collar, proceeded to smear his countenance with a damp towel of very unwholesome appearance, which made his complexion rather more cloudy than it had been before. But, while he was thus engaged, his caution and inquisitiveness did not forsake him. With a face as sharp and cunning as ever, he often stopped, even in this short process, and stood listening for any conversation in the next room, of which he might be the theme.

'Ah!' he said, after a short effort of attention, 'it was not the towel over my ears; I thought it wasn't. I'm a little hunchy villain and a monster, am I, Mrs Jiniwin? Oh!'

The pleasure of this discovery called up the old dog-like smile in full force. When he had quite done with it, he shook himself in a very dog-like manner, and rejoined the ladies.

Mr Quilp now walked up to the front of a looking-glass, and was standing there, putting on his neckerchief, when Mrs Jiniwin, happening to be behind him, could not resist the inclination she felt to shake her fist at her tyrant son-in-law. It was the gesture of an instant, but as she did so and accompanied the action with a menacing look, she met his eye in the glass, catching her in the very act. The same glance at the mirror conveyed to her the reflection of a horribly grotesque and distorted face with the tongue lolling out; and the next instant the dwarf, turning about, with a perfectly bland and placid look, inquired in a tone of great affection,

'How are you now, my dear old darling?'

Slight and ridiculous as the incident was, it made him appear such a little fiend, and withal such a keen and knowing one, that the old woman felt too much afraid of him to utter a single word, and suffered herself to be led with extraordinary politeness to the breakfast-table. Here he by no means diminished the impression he had just produced, for he ate hard eggs, shell and all, devoured gigantic prawns with the heads and tails on, chewed tobacco and water-cresses at the same time and with extraordinary greediness, drank boiling tea without winking, bit his fork and spoon till they bent again, and in short performed so many horrifying and uncommon acts that the women were nearly frightened out of their wits and began to doubt if he were really a human creature. At last, having gone through these proceedings and many others which were equally a part of his system, Mr Quilp left them, reduced to a very obedient and humbled state, and betook himself to the river-side, where he took boat for the wharf on which he had bestowed his name.

BARNABY RUDGE

The year is 1775 and, upon the borders of Epping Forest, a storm batters at the diamond-pane lattices of the ancient Maypole Inn …

The evening with which we have to do, was neither a summer nor an autumn one, but the twilight of a day in March, when the wind howled dismally among the bare branches of the trees, and rumbling in the wide chimneys and driving the rain against the windows of the Maypole Inn, gave such of its frequenters as chanced to be there at the moment an undeniable reason for prolonging their stay, and caused the landlord to prophesy that the night would certainly clear at eleven o'clock precisely,—which by a remarkable coincidence was the hour at which he always closed his house.

The name of him upon whom the spirit of prophecy thus descended was John Willet, a burly, large-headed man with a fat face, which betokened profound obstinacy and slowness of apprehension, combined with a very strong reliance upon his own merits. It was John Willet's ordinary boast in his more placid moods that if he were slow he was sure; which assertion could, in one sense at least, be by no means gainsaid, seeing that he was in everything unquestionably the reverse of fast, and withal one of the most dogged and positive fellows in existence—always sure that what he thought or said or did was right, and holding it as a thing quite settled and ordained by the laws of nature and Providence, that anybody who said or did or thought otherwise must be inevitably and of necessity wrong.

Mr Willet walked slowly up to the window, flattened his fat nose against the cold glass, and shading his eyes that his sight might not be affected by the ruddy glow of the fire, looked abroad. Then he walked slowly back to his old seat in the chimney corner, and, composing himself in it with a slight shiver, such as a man might give way to and so acquire an additional relish for the warm blaze, said, looking round upon his guests:

'It'll clear at eleven o'clock. No sooner and no later. Not before and not afterwards.'

'How do you make out that?' said a little man in the opposite corner. 'The moon is past the full, and she rises at nine.'

John looked sedately and solemnly at his questioner until he had brought his mind to bear upon the whole of his observation, and then made answer, in a tone which seemed to imply that the moon was peculiarly his business and nobody else's:

'Never you mind about the moon. Don't you trouble yourself about her. You let the moon alone, and I'll let you alone.'

'No offence, I hope?' said the little man.

Again John waited leisurely until the observation had thoroughly penetrated to his brain, and then replying, 'No offence *as yet*,' applied a light to his pipe and smoked in placid silence; now and then casting a sidelong look at a man wrapped in a loose riding-coat with huge cuffs ornamented with tarnished silver lace and large metal buttons, who sat apart from the regular frequenters of the house, and wearing a hat flapped over his face, which was still further shaded by the hand on which his forehead rested, looked unsociable enough.

There was another guest, who sat, booted and spurred, at some distance from the fire also, and whose thoughts—to judge from his folded arms and knitted brows, and from the untasted liquor before him—were occupied with other matters than the topics under discussion or the persons who discussed them. This was a young man of about eight-and-twenty, rather above the middle height, and though of a somewhat slight figure, gracefully and strongly made. He wore his own dark hair, and was accoutred in a riding-dress, which together with his large boots (resembling in shape and fashion those worn by our Life Guardsmen at the present day), showed indisputable traces of the bad condition of the roads. But travel-stained though he was, he was well and even richly attired, and without being over-dressed looked a gallant gentleman.

Lying upon the table beside him, as he had carelessly thrown them down, were a heavy riding-whip and a slouched hat, the latter worn no doubt as being best suited to the inclemency of the weather. There, too, were a pair of pistols in a holster-case, and a short riding-cloak. Little of his face was visible, except the long dark lashes which concealed his downcast eyes, but an air of careless ease and natural gracefulness of demeanour pervaded the figure, and seemed to comprehend even those slight accessories, which were all handsome, and in good keeping.

Towards this young gentleman the eyes of Mr Willet wandered but once, and then as if in mute inquiry whether he had observed his silent neighbour. It was plain that John and the young gentleman had often met before. Finding that his look was not returned, or indeed observed by the person to whom it was addressed, John gradually concentrated the whole power of his eyes into one focus, and brought it to bear upon the man in the flapped hat, at whom he came to stare in course of time with an intensity so remarkable, that it affected his fireside cronies, who all, as with one accord, took their pipes from their lips, and stared with open mouths at the stranger likewise.

The sturdy landlord had a large pair of dull fish-like eyes, and the little man who had hazarded the remark about the moon (and who was the parish-clerk and bell-ringer of Chigwell; a village hard by) had little round black shiny eyes like beads; moreover this little man wore at the knees of his rusty black breeches, and on his rusty black coat, and all down his long flapped waistcoat, little queer buttons like nothing except his eyes; but so like them, that as they twinkled and glistened in the light of the fire, which shone too in his bright shoe-buckles, he seemed all eyes from head to foot, and to be gazing with every one of them at the unknown customer. No wonder that a man should grow restless under such an inspection as this, to say nothing of the eyes belonging to short Tom Cobb the general chandler and post-office keeper, and long Phil Parkes the ranger, both of whom, infected by the example of their companions, regarded him of the flapped hat no less attentively.

The stranger became restless; perhaps from being exposed to this raking fire of eyes, perhaps from the nature of his previous meditations—most probably from the latter cause, for as he changed his position and looked hastily round, he started to find himself the object of such keen regard, and darted an angry and suspicious glance at the fireside group. It had the effect of immediately diverting all eyes to the chimney, except those of John Willet, who finding himself, as it were, caught in the fact, and not being (as has been already observed) of a very ready nature, remained staring at his guest in a particularly awkward and disconcerted manner.

'Well?' said the stranger.

Well. There was not much in well. It was not a long speech. 'I thought you gave an order,' said the landlord, after a pause of two or three minutes for consideration.

The stranger took off his hat, and disclosed the hard features of a man of sixty or thereabouts, much weather-beaten and worn by time, and the naturally harsh expression of which was not improved by a dark handkerchief which was bound tightly round his head, and, while it served the purpose of a wig, shaded his forehead, and almost hid his eyebrows. If it were intended to conceal or divert attention from a deep gash, now healed into an ugly seam, which when it was first inflicted must have laid bare his cheekbone, the object was but indifferently attained, for it could scarcely fail to be noted at a glance. His complexion was of a cadaverous hue, and he had a grizzly jagged beard of some three weeks' date. Such was the figure (very meanly and poorly clad) that now rose from the seat, and stalking across the room sat down in a corner of the chimney, which the politeness or fears of the little clerk very readily assigned to him.

'A highwayman!' whispered Tom Cobb to Parkes the ranger.

'Do you suppose highwaymen don't dress handsomer than that?' replied Parkes. 'It's a better business than you think for, Tom, and highwaymen don't need or use to be shabby, take my word for it.'

Meanwhile the subject of their speculations had done due honour to the house by calling for some drink, which was promptly supplied by the landlord's son Joe, a broad-shouldered, strapping young fellow of twenty, whom it pleased his father still to consider a little boy, and to treat accordingly. Stretching out his hands to warm them by the blazing fire, the man turned his head towards the company, and after running his eye sharply over them, said in a voice well suited to his appearance:

'What house is that which stands a mile or so from here?'

'Public-house?' said the landlord, with his usual deliberation.

'Public-house, father!' exclaimed Joe, 'where's the public-house within a mile or so of the Maypole? He means the great house—the Warren—naturally and of course. The old red brick house, sir, that stands in its own grounds—?'

'Aye,' said the stranger.

'And that fifteen or twenty years ago stood in a park five times as broad, which with other and richer property has bit by bit changed hands and dwindled away—more's the pity!' pursued the young man.

'Maybe,' was the reply. 'But my question related to the owner. What it has been I don't care to know, and what it is I can see for myself.'

The heir-apparent to the Maypole pressed his finger on his lips, and glancing at the young gentleman already noticed, who had changed his attitude when the house was first mentioned, replied in a lower tone,

'The owner's name is Haredale, Mr Geoffrey Haredale, and'—again he glanced in the same direction as before—'and a worthy gentleman too—hem!'

Paying as little regard to this admonitory cough, as to the significant gesture that had preceded it, the stranger pursued his questioning.

'I turned out of my way coming here, and took the footpath that crosses the grounds. Who was the young lady that I saw entering a carriage? His daughter?'

'Why, how should I know, honest man?' replied Joe, contriving in the course of some arrangements about the hearth, to advance close to his questioner and pluck him by the sleeve, '*I* didn't see the young lady you know. Whew! There's the wind again—*and* rain—well it *is* a night!'

'Rough weather indeed!' observed the strange man.

'You're used to it?' said Joe, catching at anything which seemed to promise a diversion of the subject.

'Pretty well,' returned the other. 'About the young lady—has Mr Haredale a daughter?'

'No, No,' said the young fellow fretfully, 'he's a single gentleman—he's—be quiet, can't you, man? Don't you see this talk is not relished yonder?'

Regardless of this whispered remonstrance, and affecting not to hear it, his tormentor provokingly continued:

'Single men have had daughters before now. Perhaps she may be his daughter, though he is not married.'

'What do you mean?' said Joe, adding in an under tone as he approached him again, 'You'll come in for it presently, I know you will!'

'I mean no harm,' returned the traveller boldly, 'and have said none that I know of. I ask a few questions—as any stranger may, and not unnaturally—about the inmates of a remarkable house in a neighbourhood which is new to me, and you are as aghast and disturbed as if I were talking treason against King George. Perhaps you can tell me why, sir, for (as I say) I am a stranger, and this is Greek to me?'

The latter observation was addressed to the obvious cause of Joe Willet's discomposure, who had risen and was adjusting his riding-cloak preparatory to sallying abroad. Briefly replying that he could give him no information, the young man beckoned to Joe, and handing him a piece of money in payment of his reckoning, hurried out attended by young Willet himself, who taking up a candle followed to light him to the house door.

While Joe was absent on this errand, the elder Willet and his three companions continued to smoke with profound gravity and in a deep silence, each having his eyes fixed on a huge copper boiler that was suspended over the fire. After some time John Willet slowly shook his head, and thereupon his friends slowly shook theirs; but no man withdrew his eyes from the boiler, or altered the solemn expression of his countenance in the slightest degree.

At length Joe returned—very talkative and conciliatory, as though with a strong presentiment that he was going to be found fault with.

'Such a thing as love is!' he said, drawing a chair near the fire, and looking round for sympathy. 'He has set off to walk to London,—all the way to London. His nag gone lame in riding out here this blessed afternoon, and comfortably littered down in our stables at this minute; and he giving up a good hot supper and our best bed, because Miss Haredale has gone to a masquerade up in town, and he has set his heart upon seeing her! I don't think I could persuade myself to do that, beautiful as she is,—but then I'm not in love, (at least I don't think I am,) and that's the whole difference.'

'He is in love, then?' said the stranger.

'Rather,' replied Joe. 'He'll never be more in love, and may very easily be less.'

'Silence, sir!' cried his father.

'What a chap you are, Joe!' said Long Parkes.

'Such an inconsiderate lad!' murmured Tom Cobb.

'Putting himself forward and wringing the very nose off his own father's face!' exclaimed the parish-clerk, metaphorically.

'What *have* I done?' reasoned poor Joe.

'Silence, sir!' returned his father, 'what do you mean by talking, when you see people that are more than two or three times your age sitting still and silent and not dreaming of saying a word?'

'Why that's the proper time for me to talk, isn't it?' said Joe rebelliously.

'The proper time, sir!' retorted his father, 'the proper time's no time.'

'Ah, to be sure!' muttered Parkes, nodding gravely to the other two who nodded likewise, observing under their breaths that that was the point.

'The proper time's no time, sir,' repeated John Willet; 'when I was your age I never talked, I never wanted to talk. I listened and improved myself, that's what *I* did.'

'And you'd find your father rather a tough customer in argeyment, Joe, if anybody was to try and tackle him,' said Parkes.

'For the matter o' that, Phil!' observed Mr Willet, blowing a long, thin, spiral cloud of smoke out of the corner of his mouth, and staring at it abstractedly as it floated away; 'For the matter o' that, Phil, argeyment is a gift of Natur. If Natur has gifted a man with powers of argeyment, a man has a right to make the best of 'em, and has not a right to stand on false delicacy, and deny that he is so gifted; for that is a turning of his back on Natur, a flouting of her, a slighting of her precious caskets, and a proving of one's self to be a swine that isn't worth her scattering pearls before.'

The landlord pausing here for a very long time, Mr Parkes naturally concluded that he had brought his discourse to an end; and therefore, turning to the young man with some austerity, exclaimed:

'You hear what your father says, Joe? You wouldn't much like to tackle him in argeyment, I'm thinking, sir.'

'IF,' said John Willet, turning his eyes from the ceiling to the face of his interrupter, and uttering the monosyllable in capitals, to apprise him that he had put in his oar, as the vulgar say, with unbecoming and irreverent haste; 'IF, sir, Natur has fixed upon me the gift of argeyment, why should I not own to it, and rather glory in the same? Yes, sir, I *am* a tough customer that way. You are right, sir. My toughness has been proved, sir, in this room many and many a time, as I think you know; and if you don't know,' added John, putting his pipe in his mouth again, 'so much the better, for I an't proud and am not going to tell you.'

A general murmur from his three cronies, and a general shaking of heads at the copper boiler, assured John Willet that they had had good experience of his powers and needed no further evidence to assure them of his superiority. John smoked with a little more dignity and surveyed them in silence.

It's all very fine talking,' muttered Joe, who had been fidgeting in his chair with divers uneasy gestures. 'But if you mean to tell me that I'm never to open my lip—'

'Silence, sir!' roared his father. 'No, you never are. When your opinion's wanted, you give it. When you're spoke to, you speak. When your opinion's not wanted and you're not spoke to, don't give an opinion and don't you speak. The world's undergone a nice alteration since my time, certainly. My belief is that there ain't any boys left—that there isn't such a thing as a boy—that there's nothing now between a male baby and a man—and that all the boys went out with his blessed Majesty King George the Second.'

'That's a very true observation, always excepting the young princes,' said the parish-clerk, who, as the representative of church and state in that company, held himself bound to the nicest loyalty. 'If it's godly and righteous for boys, being of the ages of boys, to behave themselves like boys, then the young princes must be boys and cannot be otherwise.'

'Did you ever hear tell of mermaids, sir?' said Mr Willet.

'Certainly I have,' replied the clerk.

'Very good,' said Mr Willet. 'According to the constitution of mermaids, so much of a mermaid as is not a woman must be a fish. According to the constitution of young princes, so much of a young prince (if anything) as is not actually an angel, must be godly and righteous. Therefore if it's becoming and godly and righteous in the young princes (as it is at their ages) that they should be boys, they are and must be boys, and cannot by possibility be anything else.'

This elucidation of a knotty point being received with such marks of approval as to put John Willet into a good humour, he contented himself with repeating to his son his command of silence, and addressing the stranger, said:

'If you had asked your questions of a grown-up person—of me or any of these gentlemen—you'd have had some satisfaction, and wouldn't have wasted breath. Miss Haredale is Mr Geoffrey Haredale's niece.'

'Is her father alive?' said the man carelessly.

'No,' rejoined the landlord, 'he is not alive, and he is not dead—'

'Not dead!' cried the other.

'Not dead in a common sort of way,' said the landlord.

The cronies nodded to each other, and Mr Parkes remarked in an under tone, shaking his head meanwhile as who should say, 'let no man contradict me, for I won't believe him,' that John Willet was in amazing force to-night, and fit to tackle a Chief Justice.

The stranger suffered a short pause to elapse, and then asked abruptly, 'What do you mean?'

'More than you think for, friend,' returned John Willet. 'Perhaps there's more meaning in them words than you suspect.'

'Perhaps there is,' said the strange man, gruffly; 'but what the devil do you speak in such mysteries for? You tell me, first, that a man is not alive, nor yet dead—then, that he's not dead in a common sort of way—then, that you mean a great deal more than I think for. To tell you the truth, you may do that easily; for so far as I can make out, you mean nothing. What *do* you mean, I ask again?'

'That,' returned the landlord, a little brought down from his dignity by the stranger's surliness, 'is a Maypole story, and has been any time these four-and-twenty years. That story is Solomon Daisy's story. It belongs to the house; and nobody but Solomon Daisy has ever told it under this roof, or ever shall—what's more.'

The man glanced at the parish-clerk, whose air of consciousness and importance plainly betokened him to be the person referred to, and, observing that he had taken his pipe from his lips, after a very long whiff to keep it alight, and was evidently about to tell his story without further solicitation, gathered his large coat about him, and shrinking farther back, was almost lost in the gloom of the spacious chimney corner, except when the flame, struggling from under a great faggot, whose weight almost crushed it for the time, shot upward with a strong and sudden glare, and illumining his figure for a moment, seemed afterwards to cast it into deeper obscurity than before.

By this flickering light, which made the old room, with its heavy timbers and panelled walls, look as if it were built of polished ebony—the wind roaring and howling without, now rattling the latch and creaking the hinges of the stout oaken door, and now driving at the casement as though it would beat it in—by this light, and under circumstances so auspicious, Solomon Daisy began his tale:

'It was Mr Reuben Haredale, Mr Geoffrey's elder brother—'

Here he came to a dead stop, and made so long a pause that even John Willet grew impatient and asked why he did not proceed.

'Cobb,' said Solomon Daisy, dropping his voice and appealing to the post-office keeper; 'what day of the month is this?'

'The nineteenth.'

'Of March,' said the clerk, bending forward, 'the nineteenth of March; that's very strange.'

In a low voice they all acquiesced, and Solomon went on:

'It was Mr Reuben Haredale, Mr Geoffrey's elder brother, that twenty-two years ago was the owner of the Warren, which, as Joe has said—not that you remember it, Joe, for a boy like you can't do that, but because you have often heard me say so—was then a much larger and better place, and a much more valuable property than it is now. His lady was lately dead, and he was left with one child—the Miss Haredale you have been inquiring about—who was then scarcely a year old.'

Although the speaker addressed himself to the man who had shown so much curiosity about this same family, and made a pause here as if expecting some exclamation of surprise or encouragement, the latter made no remark, nor gave any indication that he heard or was interested in what was said. Solomon therefore turned to his old companions, whose noses were brightly illuminated by the deep red glow from the bowls of their pipes; assured, by long experience, of their attention, and resolved to show his sense of such indecent behaviour.

'Mr Haredale,' said Solomon, turning his back upon the strange man, 'left this place when his lady died, feeling it lonely like, and went up to London, where he stopped some months; but finding that place as lonely as this—as I suppose and have always heard say—he suddenly came back again with his little girl to the Warren, bringing with him besides, that day, only two women servants, and his steward, and a gardener.'

Mr Daisy stopped to take a whiff at his pipe, which was going out, and then proceeded—at first in a snuffling tone, occasioned by keen enjoyment of the tobacco and strong pulling at the pipe, and afterwards with increasing distinctness:

'—Bringing with him two women servants, and his steward, and a gardener. The rest stopped behind up in London, and were to follow next day. It happened that that night, an old gentleman who lived at Chigwell-row, and had long been poorly, deceased, and an order came to me at half after twelve o'clock at night to go and toll the passing-bell.'

There was a movement in the little group of listeners, sufficiently indicative of the strong repugnance any one of them would have felt to have turned out at such a time upon such an errand. The clerk felt and understood it, and pursued his theme accordingly.

'It *was* a dreary thing, especially as the grave-digger was laid up in his bed, from long working in a damp soil and sitting to take his dinner on cold tombstones, and I was consequently under obligation to go alone, for it was too late to hope to get any other companion. However, I wasn't unprepared for it; as the old gentleman had often made it a request that the bell should be tolled as soon as possible after the breath was out of his body, and he had been expected to go for some days. I put as good a face upon it as I could, and muffling myself up (for it was mortal cold), started out with a lighted lantern in one hand and the key of the church in the other.'

At this point of the narrative, the dress of the strange man rustled as if he had turned himself to hear more distinctly. Slightly pointing over his shoulder, Solomon elevated his eyebrows and nodded a silent inquiry to Joe whether this was the case. Joe shaded his eyes with his hand and peered into the corner, but could make out nothing, and so shook his head.

'It was just such a night as this; blowing a hurricane, raining heavily, and very dark—I often think now, darker than I ever saw it before or since; that may be my fancy, but the houses were all close shut and the folks in doors, and perhaps there is only one other man who knows how dark it really was. I got into the church, chained the door back so that it should keep ajar—for, to tell the truth, I didn't like to be shut in there alone—and putting my lantern on the stone seat in the little corner where the bell-rope is, sat down beside it to trim the candle.

'I sat down to trim the candle, and when I had done so I could not persuade myself to get up again, and go about my work. I don't know how it was, but I thought of all the ghost stories I had ever heard, even those that I had heard when I was a boy at school, and had forgotten long ago; and they didn't come into my head one after another, but all crowding at once, like. I recollected one story there was in the village, how that on a certain night in the year (it might be that very night for anything I knew), all the dead people came out of the ground and sat at the heads of their own graves till morning. This made me think how many people I had known, were buried between the church door and the churchyard gate, and what a dreadful thing it would be to have to pass among them and know them again, so earthy and unlike themselves. I had known all the niches and arches in the church from a child; still, I couldn't persuade myself that those were their natural shadows which I saw on the pavement, but felt sure there were some ugly figures hiding among 'em and peeping out. Thinking on in this way, I began to think of the old gentleman who was just dead, and I could have sworn, as I looked up the dark chancel, that I saw him in his usual place, wrapping his shroud about him and shivering as if he felt it cold. All this time I sat listening and listening, and hardly dared to breathe. At length I started up and took the bell-rope in my hands. At that minute there rang—not that bell, for I had hardly touched the rope—but another!

'I heard the ringing of another bell, and a deep bell too, plainly. It was only for an instant, and even then the wind carried the sound away, but I heard it. I listened for a long time, but it rang no more. I had heard of corpse candles, and at last I persuaded myself that this must be a corpse bell tolling of itself at midnight for the dead. I tolled my bell—how, or how long, I don't know—and ran home to bed as fast as I could touch the ground.

'I was up early next morning after a restless night, and told the story to my neighbours. Some were serious and some made light of it; I don't think anybody believed it real. But, that morning, Mr Reuben Haredale was found murdered in his bed-chamber; and in his hand was a piece of the cord attached to an alarm-bell outside the roof, which hung in his room and had been cut asunder, no doubt by the murderer, when he seized it.

'That was the bell I heard.

'A bureau was found opened, and a cash-box, which Mr Haredale had brought down that day, and was supposed to contain a large sum of money, was gone. The steward and gardener were both missing and both suspected for a long time, but they were never found, though hunted far and wide. And far enough they might have looked for poor Mr Rudge the steward, whose body—scarcely to be recognised but by his clothes and the watch and ring he wore—was found, months afterwards, at the bottom of a piece of water in the grounds, with a deep gash in the breast where he had been stabbed with a knife. He was only partly dressed; and people all agreed that he had been sitting up reading in his own room, where there were many traces of blood, and was suddenly fallen upon and killed before his master.

'Everybody now knew that the gardener must be the murderer, and though he has never been heard of from that day to this, he will be, mark my words. The crime was committed this day two-and-twenty years—on the nineteenth of March, one thousand seven hundred and fifty-three. On the nineteenth of March in some year—no matter when—I know it, I am sure of it, for we have always, in some strange way or other, been brought back to the subject on that day ever since—on the nineteenth of March, in some year, sooner or later, that man will be discovered.'

MARTIN CHUZZLEWIT

Jonas Chuzzlewit has brought about his father's death through greed and impatience. Mr Pecksniff, his distant relative and future father-in-law, has undertaken to help with the funeral arrangements ...

Mr Pecksniff was in a hackney cabriolet, for Jonas Chuzzlewit had said 'Spare no expense.' Mankind is evil in its thoughts and in its base constructions, and Jonas was resolved it should not have an inch to stretch into an ell against him. It never should be charged upon his father's son that he had grudged the money for his father's funeral. Hence, until the obsequies should be concluded, Jonas had taken for his motto 'Spend, and spare not!'

Mr Pecksniff had been to the undertaker, and was now upon his way to another officer in the train of mourning: a female functionary, a nurse, and watcher, and performer of nameless offices about the persons of the dead: whom he had recommended. Her name, as Mr Pecksniff gathered from a scrap of writing in his hand, was Gamp; her residence in Kingsgate Street, High Holborn. So Mr Pecksniff, in a hackney cab, was rattling over Holborn stones, in quest of Mrs Gamp.

This lady lodged at a bird-fancier's, next door but one to the celebrated mutton-pie shop, and directly opposite to the original cat's-meat warehouse; the renown of which establishments was duly heralded on their respective fronts. It was a little house, and this was the more convenient; for Mrs Gamp being, in her highest walk of art, a monthly nurse, or, as her sign-board boldly had it, 'Midwife', and lodging in the first-floor, was easily assailable at night by pebbles, walking-sticks, and fragments of tobacco-pipe: all much more efficacious than the street-door knocker, which was so constructed as to wake the street with ease, and even spread alarms of fire in Holborn, without màking the smallest impression on the premises to which it was addressed.

It chanced on this particular occasion, that Mrs Gamp had been up all the previous night, in attendance upon a ceremony to which the usage of gossips has given that name which expresses, in two syllables, the curse pronounced on Adam. It chanced that Mrs Gamp had not been regularly engaged, but had been called in at a crisis, in consequence of her great repute, to assist another professional lady with her advice; and thus it happened that, all points of interest in the case being over, Mrs Gamp had come home again to the bird-fancier's, and gone to bed. So, when Mr Pecksniff drove up in the hackney cab, Mrs Gamp's curtains were drawn close, and Mrs Gamp was fast asleep behind them.

If the bird-fancier had been at home, as he ought to have been, there would have been no great harm in this; but he was out, and his shop was closed. The shutters were down certainly; and in every pane of glass there was at least one tiny bird in a tiny bird-cage, twittering and hopping his little ballet of despair, and knocking his head against the roof: while one unhappy goldfinch who lived outside in a red villa with his name on the door, drew the water for his own drinking, and mutely appealed to some good man to drop a farthing's worth of poison in it. Still, the door was shut. Mr Pecksniff tried the latch, and shook it, causing a cracked bell inside to ring most mournfully; but no one came. The bird-fancier was an easy shaver also, and a fashionable hair-dresser also; and perhaps he had been sent for, express, from the court end of the town, to trim a lord, or cut and curl a lady; but however that might be, there, upon his own ground, he was not; nor was there any more distinct trace of him to assist the imagination of an inquirer, than a professional print or emblem of his calling (much favoured in the trade), representing a hair-dresser of easy manners curling a lady of distinguished fashion, in the presence of a patent upright grand pianoforte.

Noting these circumstances, Mr Pecksniff, in the innocence of his heart, applied himself to the knocker; but at the first double knock, every window in the street became alive with female heads; and before he could repeat the performance, whole troops of married ladies (some about to trouble Mrs Gamp themselves, very shortly) came flocking round the steps, all crying out with one accord, and with uncommon interest, 'Knock at the winder, sir, knock at the winder. Lord bless you, don't lose no more time than you can help; knock at the winder!'

Acting upon this suggestion, and borrowing the driver's whip for the purpose, Mr Pecksniff soon made a commotion among the first-floor flower-pots, and roused Mrs Gamp, whose voice—to the great satisfaction of the matrons—was heard to say, 'I'm coming.'

'He's as pale as a muffin,' said one lady, in allusion to Mr Pecksniff.

'So he ought to be, if he's the feelings of a man,' observed another.

A third lady (with her arms folded) said she wished he had chosen any other time for fetching Mrs Gamp, but it always happened so with *her*.

It gave Mr Pecksniff much uneasiness to find, from these remarks, that he was supposed to have come to Mrs Gamp upon an errand touching—not the close of life, but the other end. Mrs Gamp herself was under the same impression, for, throwing open the window, she cried behind the curtains, as she hastily attired herself:

'Is it Mrs Perkins?'

'No!' returned Mr Pecksniff, sharply. 'Nothing of the sort.'

'What, Mr Whilks!' cried Mrs Gamp. 'Don't say it's you, Mr Whilks, and that poor creetur Mrs Whilks with not even a pincushion ready. Don't say it's you, Mr Whilks!'

'It isn't Mr Whilks,' said Pecksniff. 'I don't know the man. Nothing of the kind. A gentleman is dead; and some person being wanted in the house, you have been recommended by Mr Mould the undertaker.'

As she was by this time in a condition to appear, Mrs Gamp, who had a face for all occasions, looked out of the window with her mourning countenance, and said she would be down directly. But the matron took it very ill, that Mr Pecksniff's mission was of so unimportant a kind; and the lady with her arms folded rated him in good round terms, signifying that she would be glad to know what he meant by terrifying delicate females 'with his corpses;' and giving it as her opinion that he was quite ugly enough to know better. The other ladies were not at all behind-hand in expressing similar sentiments; and the children, of whom some scores had now collected, hooted and defied Mr Pecksniff quite savagely. So, when Mrs Gamp appeared, the unoffending gentleman was glad to hustle her with very little ceremony into the cabriolet, and drive off, overwhelmed with popular execration.

Mrs Gamp had a large bundle with her, a pair of pattens, and a species of gig umbrella; the latter article in colour like a faded lead, except where a circular patch of a lively blue had been dexterously let in at the top. She was flurried by the haste she had made, and laboured under the most erroneous views of cabriolets, which she appeared to confound with mail-coaches or stage-waggons, inasmuch as she was constantly endeavouring for the first half mile to force her luggage through the little front window, and clamouring to the driver to 'put in the boot.' When she was disabused of this idea, her whole being resolved itself into an absorbing anxiety about her pattens, with which she played innumerable games at quoits, on Mr Pecksniff's legs. It was not until they were close upon the house of mourning that she had enough composure to observe:

'And so the gentleman's dead, sir! Ah! The more's the pity.' She didn't even know his name. 'But it's what we must all come to. It's as certain as being born, except that we can't make our calculations as exact. Ah! Poor dear!'

She was a fat old woman, this Mrs Gamp, with a husky voice and a moist eye, which she had a remarkable power of turning up, and only showing the white of it. Having very little neck, it cost her some trouble to look over herself, if one may say so, at those to whom she talked. She wore a very rusty black gown, rather the worse for snuff, and a shawl and bonnet to correspond. In these dilapidated articles of dress she had, on principle, arrayed herself, time out of mind, on such occasions as the present; for this at once expressed a decent amount of veneration for the deceased, and invited the next of kin to present her with a fresher suit of weeds: an appeal so frequently successful, that the very fetch and ghost of Mrs Gamp, bonnet and all, might be seen hanging up, any hour in the day, in at least a dozen of the second-hand clothes shops about Holborn. The face of Mrs Gamp—the nose in particular—was somewhat red and swollen, and it was difficult to enjoy her society without becoming conscious of a smell of spirits. Like most persons who have attained to great eminence in their profession, she took to hers very kindly; insomuch, that setting aside her natural predilections as a woman, she went to a lying-in or a laying-out with equal zest and relish.

'Ah!' repeated Mrs Gamp; for it was always a safe sentiment in cases of mourning. 'Ah, dear! When Gamp was summoned to his long home, and I see him a lying in Guy's Hospital with a penny-piece on each eye, and his wooden leg under his left arm, I thought I should have fainted away. But I bore up.'

If certain whispers current in the Kingsgate Street circles had any truth in them, she had indeed borne up surprisingly; and had exerted such uncommon fortitude, as to dispose of Mr Gamp's remains for the benefit of science. But it should be added, in fairness, that this had happened twenty years before; and that Mr and Mrs Gamp had long been separated, on the ground of incompatibility of temper in their drink.

'You have become indifferent since then, I suppose?' said Mr Pecksniff. 'Use is second nature, Mrs Gamp.'

'You may well say second nater, sir,' returned that lady. 'One's first ways is to find sich things a trial to the feelings, and so is one's lasting custom. If it wasn't for the nerve a little sip of liquor gives me (I never was able to do more than taste it), I never could go through with what I sometimes has to do. "Mrs Harris," I says, at the very last case as ever I acted in, which it was but a young person, "Mrs Harris," I says, "leave the bottle on the chimley-piece, and don't ask me to take none, but let me put my lips to it when I am so dispoged, and then I will do what I'm engaged to do, according to the best of my ability." "Mrs Gamp," she says, in answer, "if ever there was a sober creetur to be got at eighteen pence a day for working people, and three and six for gentlefolks—night watching," ' said Mrs Gamp, with emphasis, ' "being a extra charge—you are that inwallable person." "Mrs Harris," I says to her, "don't name the charge, for if I could afford to lay all my feller creeturs out for nothink, I would gladly do it, sich is the love I bears 'em. But what I always says to them as has the management of matters, Mrs Harris" '—here she kept her eye on Mr Pecksniff—' "be they gents or be they ladies, is, don't ask me whether I won't take none, or whether I will, but leave the bottle on the chimley-piece, and let me put my lips to it when I am so dispoged." '

The conclusion of this affecting narrative brought them to the house. In the passage they encountered Mr Mould the undertaker: a little elderly gentleman, bald, and in a suit of black; with a note-book in his hand, a massive gold watch-chain dangling from his fob, and a face in which a queer attempt at melancholy was at odds with a smirk of satisfaction; so that he looked as a man might, who, in the very act of smacking his lips over choice old wine, tried to make believe it was physic.

'Well, Mrs Gamp, and how are *you*, Mrs Gamp?' said this gentleman, in a voice as soft as his step.

'Pretty well, I thank you, sir,' dropping a curtsey.

'You'll be very particular here, Mrs Gamp. This is not a common case, Mrs Gamp. Let everything be very nice and comfortable, Mrs Gamp, if you please,' said the undertaker, shaking his head with a solemn air.

'It shall be, sir,' she replied, curtseying again. 'You knows me of old, sir, I hope.'

'I hope so, too, Mrs Gamp,' said the undertaker; 'and I think so, also.' Mrs Gamp curtseyed again. 'This is one of the most impressive cases, sir,' he continued, addressing Mr Pecksniff, 'that I have seen in the whole course of my professional experience.'

'Indeed, Mr Mould!' cried that gentleman.

'Such affectionate regret, sir, I never saw. There is no limitation, there is positively NO limitation:' opening his eyes wide, and standing on tiptoe: 'in point of expense! I have orders, sir! to put on my whole establishment of mutes; and mutes come very dear, Mr Pecksniff; not to mention their drink. To provide silver-plated handles of the very best description, ornamented with angels' heads from the most expensive dies. To be perfectly profuse in feathers. In short, sir, to turn out something absolutely gorgeous.'

'My friend Mr Jonas is an excellent man,' said Mr Pecksniff.

'I have seen a good deal of what is filial in my time, sir,' retorted Mould, 'and what is unfilial too. It is our lot. We come into the knowledge of those secrets. But anything so filial as this; anything so honourable to human nature; so calculated to reconcile all of us to the world we live in; never yet came under my observation. It only proves, sir, what was so forcibly observed by the lamented theatrical poet—buried at Stratford—that there is good in everything.'

'It is very pleasant to hear you say so, Mr Mould,' observed Pecksniff.

'You are very kind, sir. And what a man Mr Chuzzlewit was, sir! Ah! what a man he was. You may talk of your lord mayors,' said Mould, waving his hand at the public in general, 'your sheriffs, your common councilmen, your trumpery; but show me a man in this city who is worthy to walk in the shoes of the departed Mr Chuzzlewit. No, no,' cried Mould, with bitter sarcasm. 'Hang 'em up, hang 'em up; sole 'em and heel 'em, and have 'em ready for his son against he's old enough to wear 'em; but don't try 'em on yourselves, for they won't fit you. We knew him,' said Mould, in the same biting vein, as he pocketed his note-book; 'we knew him, and are not to be caught with chaff. Mr Pecksniff, sir, good morning.'

Mr Pecksniff returned the compliment; and Mould, sensible of having distinguished himself, was going away with a brisk smile, when he fortunately remembered the occasion. Quickly becoming depressed again, he sighed; looked into the crown of his hat, as if for comfort; put it on without finding any; and slowly departed.

Mrs Gamp and Mr Pecksniff then ascended the staircase; and the former, having been shown to the chamber in which all that remained of Anthony Chuzzlewit lay covered up, with but one loving heart, and that a halting one, to mourn it, left the latter free to enter the darkened room below, and rejoin Mr Jonas, from whom he had now been absent nearly two hours.

He found that example to bereaved sons and pattern in the eyes of all performers of funerals, musing over a fragment of writing-paper on the desk, and scratching figures on it with a pen. The old man's chair, and hat, and walking-stick, were removed from their accustomed places, and put out of sight; the window-blinds, as yellow as November fogs, were drawn down close; Jonas himself was so subdued, that he could scarcely be heard to speak, and only seen to walk across the room.

'Pecksniff,' he said, in a whisper, 'you shall have the regulation of it all, mind! You shall be able to tell anybody who talks about it that everything was correctly and freely done. There isn't any one you'd like to ask to the funeral, is there?'

'No, Mr Jonas, I think not.'

'Because if there is, you know,' said Jonas, 'ask him. We don't want to make a secret of it.'

'No,' repeated Mr Pecksniff, after a little reflection. 'I am not the less obliged to you on that account, Mr Jonas, for your liberal hospitality; but there really is no one.'

'Very well,' said Jonas; 'then you, and I, Chuffey, and the doctor, will be just a coachful. We'll have the doctor, Pecksniff, because he knows what was the matter with him, and that it couldn't be helped.'

'Where *is* our dear friend, Mr Chuffey?' asked Pecksniff, looking round the chamber, and winking both his eyes at once. For he was overcome by his feelings.

But here he was interrupted by Mrs Gamp, who, divested of her bonnet and shawl, came sidling and bridling into the room; and, with some sharpness, demanded a conference outside the door with Mr Pecksniff.

'You may say whatever you wish to say here, Mrs Gamp,' said that gentleman, shaking his head with a melancholy expression.

'It is not much as I have to say, when people is a mourning for the dead and gone,' said Mrs Gamp; 'but what I have to say is *to* the pint and purpose, and no offence intended, must be so considered. I have been at a many places in my time, gentlemen, and I hope I knows what my duties is, and how the same should be performed: in course, if I did not, it would be very strange, and very wrong in sich a gentleman as Mr Mould, which has undertook the highest families in this land, and given every satisfaction, so to recommend me as he does. I have seen a deal of trouble my own self,' said Mrs Gamp, laying greater and greater stress upon her words, 'and I can feel for them as has their feelings tried, but I am not a Rooshan or a Prooshan, and consequently cannot suffer spies to be set over me.'

Before it was possible that an answer could be returned, Mrs Gamp, growing redder in the face, went on to say:

'It is not a easy matter, gentlemen, to live when you are left a widder woman; particular when your feelings works upon you to that extent that you often find yourself a going out, on terms which is a certain loss, and never can repay. But, in whatever way you earns your bread, you may have rules and regulations of your own, which cannot be broke through. Some people,' said Mrs Gamp, again entrenching herself behind her strong point, as if it were not assailable by human ingenuity, 'may be Rooshans, and others may be Prooshans; they are born so, and will please themselves. Them which is of other naturs think different.'

'If I understand this good lady,' said Mr Pecksniff, turning to Jonas, 'Mr Chuffey is troublesome to her. Shall I fetch him down?'

'Do,' said Jonas. 'I was going to tell you he was up there, when she came in. I'd go myself and bring him down, only—only I'd rather you went, if you don't mind.'

Mr Pecksniff promptly departed, followed by Mrs Gamp, who, seeing that he took a bottle and glass from the cupboard, and carried it in his hand, was much softened.

'I am sure,' she said, 'that if it wasn't for his own happiness, I should no more mind his being there, poor dear, than if he was a fly. But them as isn't used to these things, thinks so much of 'em afterwards, that it's a kindness to 'em not to let 'em have their wish. And even,' said Mrs Gamp, probably in reference to some flowers of speech she had already strewn on Mr Chuffey, 'even if one calls 'em names, it's only done to rouse 'em.'

Whatever epithets she had bestowed on the old clerk, they had not roused *him*. He sat beside the bed, in the chair he had occupied all the previous night, with his hands folded before him, and his head bowed down; and neither looked up, on their entrance, nor gave any sign of consciousness, until Mr Pecksniff took him by the arm, when he meekly rose.

'Three score and ten,' said Chuffey, 'ought and carry seven. Some men are so strong that they live to four score—four times ought's an ought, four times two's an eight—eighty. Oh! why—why—why—didn't he live to four times ought's an ought, and four times two's an eight, eighty?'

'Ah! what a wale of grief!' cried Mrs Gamp, possessing herself of the bottle and glass.

'Why did he die before his poor old crazy servant?' said Chuffey, clasping his hands and looking up in anguish. 'Take him from me, and what remains?'

'Mr Jonas,' returned Pecksniff, 'Mr Jonas, my good friend.'

'I loved him,' cried the old man, weeping. 'He was good to me. We learnt Tare and Tret together, at school. I took him down once, six boys in the arithmetic class. God forgive me! Had I the heart to take him down!'

'Come, Mr Chuffey,' said Pecksniff, 'come with me. Summon up your fortitude, Mr Chuffey.'

'Yes, I will,' returned the old clerk. 'Yes. I'll sum up my forty—How many times forty—Oh, Chuzzlewit and Son—Your own son, Mr Chuzzlewit; your own son, sir!'

He yielded to the hand that guided him as he lapsed into this familiar expression, and submitted to be led away. Mrs Gamp, with the bottle on one knee, and the glass in the other, sat upon a stool, shaking her head for a long time, until, in a moment of abstraction, she poured out a dram of spirits, and raised it to her lips. It was succeeded by a second, and by a third, and then her eyes—either in the sadness of her reflections upon life and death, or in her admiration of the liquor—were so turned up, as to be quite invisible. But she shook her head still.

Poor Chuffey was conducted to his accustomed corner, and there he remained, silent and quiet, save at long intervals, when he would rise, and walk about the room, and wring his hands, or raise some strange and sudden cry. For a whole week they all three sat about the hearth and never stirred abroad. Mr Pecksniff would have walked out in the evening time, but Mr Jonas was so averse to his being absent for a minute, that he abandoned the idea, and so, from morning until night, they brooded together in the dark room, without relief or occupation.

The weight of that which was stretched out, stiff and stark, in the awful chamber above-stairs, so crushed and bore down Jonas, that he bent beneath the load. During the whole long seven days and nights, he was always oppressed and haunted by a dreadful sense of its presence in the house. Did the door move, he looked towards it with a livid face and starting eye, as if he fully believed that ghostly fingers clutched the handle. Did the fire flicker in a draught of air, he glanced over his shoulder, as almost dreading to behold some shrouded figure fanning and flapping at it with its fearful dress. The lightest noise disturbed him; and once, in the night, at the sound of a footstep overhead, he cried out that the dead man was walking, tramp, tramp, tramp, about his coffin.

He lay at night upon a mattress on the floor of the sitting-room; his own chamber having been assigned to Mrs Gamp; and Mr Pecksniff was similarly accommodated. The howling of a dog before the house, filled him with a terror he could not disguise. He avoided the reflection in the opposite windows of the light that burned above, as though it had been an angry eye. He often, in every night, rose up from his fitful sleep, and looked and longed for dawn; all directions and arrangements, even to the ordering of their daily meals, he abandoned to Mr Pecksniff. That excellent gentleman, deeming that the mourner wanted comfort, and that high feeding was likely to do him infinite service, availed himself of these opportunities to such good purpose, that they kept quite a dainty table during this melancholy season; with sweetbreads, stewed kidneys, oysters, and other such light viands for supper every night; over which, and sundry jorums of hot punch, Mr Pecksniff delivered such moral reflections and spiritual consolation as might have converted a Heathen—especially if he had but an imperfect acquaintance with the English tongue.

Nor did Mr Pecksniff alone indulge in the creature comforts during this sad time. Mrs Gamp proved to be very choice in her eating, and repudiated hashed mutton with scorn. In her drinking too, she was very punctual and particular, requiring a pint of mild porter at lunch, a pint at dinner, half-a-pint as a species of stay or holdfast between dinner and tea, and a pint of the celebrated staggering ale, or Real Old Brighton Tipper, at supper; besides the bottle on the chimney-piece, and such casual invitations to refresh herself with wine as the good breeding of her employers might prompt them to offer. In like manner, Mr Mould's men found it necessary to drown their grief, like a young kitten in the morning of its existence; for which reason they generally fuddled themselves before they began to do anything, lest it should make head and get the better of them. In short, the whole of that strange week was a round of dismal joviality and grim enjoyment; and every one, except poor Chuffey, who came within the shadow of Anthony Chuzzlewit's grave, feasted like a Ghoul.

At length the day of the funeral, pious and truthful ceremony that it was, arrived. Mr Mould, with a glass of generous port between his eye and the light, leaned against the desk in the little glass office with his gold watch in his unoccupied hand, and conversed with Mrs Gamp; two mutes were at the house-door, looking as mournful as could be reasonably expected of men with such a thriving job in hand; the whole of Mr Mould's establishment were on duty within the house or without; feathers waved, horses snorted, silks and velvets fluttered; in a word, as Mr Mould emphatically said, 'everything that money could do was done.'

'And what can do more, Mrs Gamp?' exclaimed the undertaker, as he emptied his glass and smacked his lips.

'Nothing in the world, sir.'

'Nothing in the world,' repeated Mr Mould. 'You are right, Mrs Gamp. Why do people spend more money:' here he filled his glass again: 'upon a death, Mrs Gamp, than upon a birth? Come, that's in your way; you ought to know. How do you account for that now?'

'Perhaps it is because an undertaker's charges comes dearer than a nurse's charges, sir,' said Mrs Gamp, tittering, and smoothing down her new black dress with her hands.

'Ha, ha!' laughed Mr Mould. 'You've been break-fasting at somebody's expense this morning, Mrs Gamp.' But seeing, by the aid of a little shaving-glass which hung opposite, that he looked merry, he composed his features and became sorrowful.

'Many's the time that I've not breakfasted at my own expense along of your kind recommending, sir; and many's the time I hope to do the same in time to come,' said Mrs Gamp, with an apologetic curtsey.

'So be it,' replied Mr Mould, 'please Providence. No, Mrs Gamp; I'll tell you why it is. It's because the laying out of money with a well-conducted establishment, where the thing is performed upon the very best scale, binds the broken heart, and sheds balm upon the wounded spirit. Hearts want binding, and spirits want balming when people die; not when people are born. Look at this gentleman to-day; look at him.'

'An open-handed gentleman?' cried Mrs Gamp, with enthusiasm.

'No, no,' said the undertaker; 'not an open-handed gentleman in general, by any means. There you mistake him: but an afflicted gentleman, an affectionate gentleman, who knows what it is in the power of money to do, in giving him relief, and in testifying his love and veneration for the departed. It can give him,' said Mr Mould, waving his watch-chain slowly round and round, so that he described one circle after every item; 'it can give him four horses to each vehicle; it can give him velvet trappings; it can give him drivers in cloth cloaks and top-boots; it can give him the plumage of the ostrich, dyed black; it can give him any number of walking attendants, dressed in the first style of funeral fashion, carrying batons tipped with brass; it can give him a handsome tomb; it can give him a place in Westminster Abbey itself, if he choose to invest it in such a purchase. Oh! do not let us say that gold is dross, when it can buy such things as these, Mrs Gamp.'

'But what a blessing, sir,' said Mrs Gamp, 'that there are such as you to sell or let 'em out on hire!'

'Ay, Mrs Gamp, you are right,' rejoined the undertaker. 'We should be an honoured calling. We do good by stealth, and blush to have it mentioned in our little bills. How much consolation may I, even I,' cried Mr Mould, 'have diffused among my fellow-creatures by means of my four long-tailed prancers, never harnessed under ten pund ten!'

Mrs Gamp had begun to make a suitable reply, when she was interrupted by the appearance of one of Mr Mould's assistants—his chief mourner in fact—an obese person, with his waistcoat in closer connection with his legs than is quite reconcilable with the established ideas of grace; with that cast of feature which is figuratively called a bottle-nose; and with a face covered all over with pimples. He had been a tender plant once upon a time, but from constant blowing in the fat atmosphere of funeral, had run to seed.

'Well, Tacker,' said Mr Mould, 'is all ready below?'

'A beautiful show, sir,' rejoined Tacker. 'The horses are prouder and fresher than ever I see 'em; and toss their heads, they do, as if they knowed how much their plumes cost. One, two, three, four,' said Mr Tacker, heaping that number of black cloaks upon his left arm.

'Is Tom there with the cake and wine?' asked Mr Mould.

'Ready to come in at a moment's notice, sir,' said Tacker.

'Then,' rejoined Mr Mould, putting up his watch, and glancing at himself in the little shaving-glass, that he might be sure his face had the right expression on it: 'then I think we may proceed to business. Give me the paper of gloves, Tacker. Ah, what a man he was! Ah Tacker, Tacker, what a man he was!'

Mr Tacker, who from his great experience in the performance of funerals, would have made an excellent pantomime actor, winked at Mrs Gamp without at all disturbing the gravity of his countenance, and followed his master into the next room.

It was a great point with Mr Mould, and a part of his professional tact, not to seem to know the doctor; though in reality they were near neighbours, and very often, as in the present instance, worked together. So he advanced to fit on his black kid gloves as if he had never seen him in all his life; while the doctor, on his part, looked as distant and unconscious as if he had heard and read of undertakers, and had passed their shops, but had never before been brought into communication with one.

'Gloves, eh?' said the doctor. 'Mr Pecksniff, after you.'

'I couldn't think of it,' returned Mr Pecksniff.

'You are very good,' said the doctor, taking a pair. 'Well, sir, as I was saying, I was called up to attend that case at about half-past one o'clock. Cake and wine, eh? Which is port? Thank you.'

Mr Pecksniff took some also.

'At about half-past one o'clock in the morning, sir,' resumed the doctor, 'I was called up to attend that case. At the first pull of the night-bell I turned out, threw up the window, and put out my head. Cloak, eh? Don't tie it too tight. That'll do.'

Mr Pecksniff having been likewise inducted into a similar garment, the doctor resumed.

'And put out my head. Hat, eh? My good friend, that is not mine. Mr Pecksniff, I beg your pardon, but I think we have unintentionally made an exchange. Thank you. Well, sir, I was going to tell you—'

'We are quite ready,' interrupted Mould in a low voice.

'Ready, eh?' said the doctor. 'Very good. Mr Pecksniff, I'll take an opportunity of relating the rest in the coach. It's rather curious. Ready, eh? No rain, I hope?'

'Quite fair, sir,' returned Mould.

'I was afraid the ground would have been wet,' said the doctor, 'for my glass fell yesterday. We may congratulate ourselves upon our good fortune.' But seeing by this time that Mr Jonas and Chuffey were going out at the door, he put a white pocket-handkerchief to his face as if a violent burst of grief had suddenly come upon him, and walked down side by side with Mr Pecksniff.

Mr Mould and his men had not exaggerated the grandeur of the arrangements. They were splendid. The four hearse-horses, especially, reared and pranced, and showed their highest action, as if they knew a man was dead, and triumphed in it. 'They break us, drive us, ride us; ill-treat, abuse, and maim us for their pleasure—But they die; Hurrah, they die!'

So through the narrow streets and winding city ways, went Anthony Chuzzlewit's funeral; Mr Jonas glancing stealthily out of the coach-window now and then, to observe its effect upon the crowd; Mr Mould as he walked along, listening with a sober pride to the exclamations of the bystanders; the doctor whispering his story to Mr Pecksniff, without appearing to come any nearer the end of it; and poor old Chuffey sobbing unregarded in a corner. But he had greatly scandalised Mr Mould at an early stage of the ceremony by carrying his handkerchief in his hat in a perfectly informal manner, and wiping his eyes with his knuckles. And as Mr Mould himself had said already, his behaviour was indecent, and quite unworthy of such an occasion; and he never ought to have been there.

There he was, however; and in the churchyard there he was, also, conducting himself in a no less unbecoming manner, and leaning for support on Tacker, who plainly told him that he was fit for nothing better than a walking funeral. But Chuffey, Heaven help him! heard no sound but the echoes, lingering in his own heart, of a voice for ever silent.

'I loved him,' cried the old man, sinking down upon the grave when all was done. 'He was very good to me. Oh, my dear old friend and master!'

'Come, come, Mr Chuffey,' said the doctor, 'this won't do; it's a clayey soil, Mr Chuffey. You mustn't, really.'

'If it had been the commonest thing we do, and Mr Chuffey had been a Bearer, gentlemen,' said Mould, casting an imploring glance upon them as he helped to raise him, 'he couldn't have gone on worse than this.'

'Be a man, Mr Chuffey,' said Pecksniff.

'Be a gentleman, Mr Chuffey,' said Mould.

'Upon my word, my good friend,' murmured the doctor, in a tone of stately reproof, as he stepped up to the old man's side, 'this is worse than weakness. This is bad, selfish, very wrong, Mr Chuffey. You should take example from others, my good sir. You forget that you were not connected by ties of blood with our deceased friend; and that he had a very near and very dear relation, Mr Chuffey.'

'Ay, his own son!' cried the old man, clasping his hands with remarkable passion. 'His own, own, only son!'

'He's not right in his head, you know,' said Jonas, turning pale. 'You're not to mind anything he says. I shouldn't wonder if he was to talk some precious nonsense. But don't you mind him, any of you. I don't. My father left him to my charge; and whatever he says or does, that's enough. *I*'ll take care of him.'

A hum of admiration rose from the mourners (including Mr Mould and his merry men) at this new instance of magnanimity and kind-feeling on the part of Jonas. But Chuffey put it to the test no farther. He said not a word more, and being left to himself for a little while, crept back again to the coach.

It has been said that Mr Jonas turned pale when the behaviour of the old clerk attracted general attention; his discomposure, however, was but momentary, and he soon recovered. But these were not the only changes he had exhibited that day. The curious eyes of Mr Pecksniff had observed that as soon as they left the house upon their mournful errand, he began to mend; that as the ceremonies proceeded he gradually, by little and little, recovered his old condition, his old looks, his old bearing, his old agreeable characteristics of speech and manner, and became, in all respects, his old pleasant self. And now that they were seated in the coach on their return home; and more when they got there, and found the windows open, the light and air admitted, and all traces of the late event removed; he felt so well convinced that Jonas was again the Jonas he had known a week ago, and not the Jonas of the intervening time, that he voluntarily gave up his recently-acquired power without one faint attempt to exercise it, and at once fell back into his former position of mild and deferential guest.

Mrs Gamp went home to the bird-fancier's, and was knocked up again that very night for a birth of twins; Mr Mould dined gaily in the bosom of his family, and passed the evening facetiously at his club; the hearse, after standing for a long time at the door of a roistering public-house, repaired to its stables with the feathers inside and twelve red-nosed undertakers on the roof, each holding on by a dingy peg, to which, in times of state, a waving plume was fitted; the various trappings of sorrow were carefully laid by in presses for the next hirer; the fiery steeds were quenched and quiet in their stalls; the doctor got merry with wine at a wedding-dinner, and forgot the middle of the story which had no end to it; the pageant of a few short hours ago was written nowhere half so legibly as in the undertaker's books.

Not in the churchyard? Not even there. The gates were closed; the night was dark and wet; and the rain fell silently, among the stagnant weeds and nettles. One new mound was there which had not been there last night. Time, burrowing like a mole below the ground, had marked his track by throwing up another heap of earth. And that was all.

DOMBEY AND SON

Paul Dombey is a wealthy businessman, arrogant and cold, with little affection for his daughter Florence. He becomes the proud father of an heir, but his wife dies in childbirth. His son Paul, upon whom he focuses all his hopes and ambitions, is a delicate and dreamy child, and his father sends him to Mrs Pipchin's establishment to improve his health. When he is six years old and a little stronger, his father sends him to Dr Blimber's school to catch up on his education ...

Whenever a young gentleman was taken in hand by Doctor Blimber, he might consider himself sure of a pretty tight squeeze. The Doctor only undertook the charge of ten young gentlemen, but he had, always ready, a supply of learning for a hundred, on the lowest estimate; and it was at once the business and delight of his life to gorge the unhappy ten with it.

In fact, Doctor Blimber's establishment was a great hot-house, in which there was a forcing apparatus incessantly at work. All the boys blew before their time. Mental green peas were produced at Christmas, and intellectual asparagus all the year round. Mathematical gooseberries (very sour ones too) were common at untimely seasons, and from mere sprouts of bushes, under Doctor Blimber's cultivation. Every description of Greek and Latin vegetable was got off the driest twigs of boys, under the frostiest circumstances. Nature was of no consequence at all. No matter what a young gentleman was intended to bear, Doctor Blimber made him bear to pattern, somehow or other.

This was all very pleasant and ingenious, but the system of forcing was attended with its usual disadvantages. There was not the right taste about the premature productions, and they didn't keep well. Moreover, one young gentleman, with a swollen nose and an excessively large head (the oldest of the ten who had 'gone through' everything), suddenly left off blowing one day, and remained in the establishment a mere stalk. And people did say that the Doctor had rather overdone it with young Toots, and that when he began to have whiskers he left off having brains.

There young Toots was, at any rate; possessed of the gruffest of voices and the shrillest of minds; sticking ornamental pins into his shirt, and keeping a ring in his waistcoat pocket to put on his little finger by stealth, when the pupils went out walking; constantly falling in love by sight with nurserymaids, who had no idea of his existence; and looking at the gas-lighted world over the little iron bars in the left-hand corner window of the front three pairs of stairs, after bed-time, like a greatly overgrown cherub who had sat up aloft much too long.

The Doctor was a portly gentleman in a suit of black, with strings at his knees, and stockings below them. He had a bald head, highly polished; a deep voice; and a chin so very double, that it was a wonder how he ever managed to shave into the creases. He had likewise a pair of little eyes that were always half shut up, and a mouth that was always half expanded into a grin, as if he had, that moment, posed a boy, and were waiting to convict him from his own lips. Insomuch, that when the Doctor put his right hand into the breast of his coat, and with his other hand behind him, and a scarcely perceptible wag of his head, made the commonest observation to a nervous stranger, it was like a sentiment from the sphynx, and settled his business.

The Doctor's was a mighty fine house, fronting the sea. Not a joyful style of house within, but quite the contrary. Sad-coloured curtains, whose proportions were spare and lean, hid themselves despondently behind the windows. The tables and chairs were put away in rows, like figures in a sum; fires were so rarely lighted in the rooms of ceremony, that they felt like wells, and a visitor represented the bucket; the dining-room seemed the last place in the world where any eating or drinking was likely to occur; there was no sound through all the house but the ticking of a great clock in the hall, which made itself audible in the very garrets: and sometimes a dull crying of young gentlemen at their lessons, like the murmurings of an assemblage of melancholy pigeons.

Miss Blimber, too, although a slim and graceful maid, did no soft violence to the gravity of the house. There was no light nonsense about Miss Blimber. She kept her hair short and crisp, and wore spectacles. She was dry and sandy with working in the graves of deceased languages. None of your live languages for Miss Blimber. They must be dead—stone dead—and then Miss Blimber dug them up like a Ghoul.

Mrs Blimber, her mamma, was not learned herself, but she pretended to be, and that did quite as well. She said at evening parties, that if she could have known Cicero, she thought she could have died contented. It was the steady joy of her life to see the Doctor's young gentlemen go out walking, unlike all other young gentlemen, in the largest possible shirt-collars, and the stiffest possible cravats. It was so classical, she said.

As to Mr Feeder, B.A., Doctor Blimber's assistant, he was a kind of human barrel-organ, with a little list of tunes at which he was continually working, over and over again, without any variation. He might have been fitted up with a change of barrels, perhaps, in early life, if his destiny had been favourable; but it had not been; and he had only one, with which, in a monotonous round, it was his occupation to bewilder the young ideas of Doctor Blimber's young gentlemen. The young gentlemen were prematurely full of carking anxieties. They knew no rest from the pursuit of stony-hearted verbs, savage noun-substantives, inflexible syntactic passages, and ghosts of exercises that appeared to them in their dreams. Under the forcing system, a young gentleman usually took leave of his spirits in three weeks. He had all the cares of the world on his head in three months. He conceived bitter sentiments against his parents or guardians in four; he was an old misanthrope in five; envied Curtius that blessed refuge in the earth, in six; and at the end of the first twelvemonth had arrived at the conclusion, from which he never afterwards departed, that all the fancies of the poets, and lessons of the sages, were a mere collection of words and grammar, and had no other meaning in the world.

But he went on blow, blow, blowing, in the Doctor's hot-house, all the time; and the Doctor's glory and reputation were great, when he took his wintry growth home to his relations and friends.

Upon the Doctor's door-steps one day, Paul stood with a fluttering heart, and with his small right hand in his father's. His other hand was locked in that of Florence. How tight the tiny pressure of that one; and how loose and cold the other!

Mrs Pipchin hovered behind the victim, with her sable plumage and her hooked beak, like a bird of ill omen. She was out of breath—for Mr Dombey, full of great thoughts, had walked fast—and she croaked hoarsely as she waited for the opening of the door.

'Now, Paul,' said Mr Dombey, exultingly. 'This is the way indeed to be Dombey and Son, and have money. You are almost a man already.'

'Almost,' returned the child.

Even his childish agitation could not master the sly and quaint yet touching look, with which he accompanied the reply.

It brought a vague expression of dissatisfaction into Mr Dombey's face; but the door being opened, it was quickly gone.

'Doctor Blimber is at home, I believe?' said Mr Dombey.

The man said yes; and, as they passed in, looked at Paul as if he were a little mouse, and the house were a trap. He was a weak-eyed young man, with the first faint streak or early dawn of a grin on his countenance. It was mere imbecility; but Mrs Pipchin took it into her head that it was impudence, and made a snap at him directly.

'How dare you laugh behind the gentleman's back?' said Mrs Pipchin. 'And what do you take me for?'

'I ain't a laughing at nobody, and I'm sure I don't take you for nothing, Ma'am,' returned the young man, in consternation.

'A pack of idle dogs!' said Mrs Pipchin, 'only fit to be turnspits. Go and tell your master that Mr Dombey's here, or it'll be worse for you!'

The weak-eyed young man went, very meekly, to discharge himself of this commission; and soon came back to invite them to the Doctor's study.

'You're laughing again, sir,' said Mrs Pipchin, when it came to her turn, bringing up the rear, to pass him in the hall.

'I *ain't*,' returned the young man, grievously oppressed. 'I never see such a thing as this!'

'What is the matter, Mrs Pipchin?' said Mr Dombey, looking round. 'Softly! Pray!'

Mrs Pipchin, in her deference, merely muttered at the young man as she passed on, and said, 'Oh! he was a precious fellow'—leaving the young man, who was all meekness and incapacity, affected even to tears by the incident. But Mrs Pipchin had a way of falling foul of all meek people; and her friends said who could wonder at it, after the Peruvian mines!

The Doctor was sitting in his portentous study, with a globe at each knee, books all round him, Homer over the door, and Minerva on the mantel-shelf. 'And how do you, Sir?' he said to Mr Dombey; 'and how is my little friend?' Grave as an organ was the Doctor's speech; and when he ceased, the great clock in the hall seemed (to Paul at least) to take him up, and to go on saying, 'how, is, my, lit, tle, friend? how, is, my, lit, tle, friend?' over and over and over again.

The little friend being something too small to be seen at all from where the Doctor sat, over the books on his table, the Doctor made several futile attempts to get a view of him round the legs; which Mr

Dombey perceiving, relieved the Doctor from his embarrassment by taking Paul up in his arms, and sitting him on another little table, over against the Doctor, in the middle of the room.

'Ha!' said the Doctor, leaning back in his chair with his hand in his breast. 'Now I see my little friend. How do you do, my little friend?'

The clock in the hall wouldn't subscribe to this alteration in the form of words, but continued to repeat, 'how, is, my, lit, tle, friend? how, is, my, lit, tle, friend?'

'Very well, I thank you, Sir,' returned Paul, answering the clock quite as much as the Doctor.

'Ha!' said Doctor Blimber. 'Shall we make a man of him?'

'Do you hear, Paul?' added Mr Dombey; Paul being silent.

'Shall we make a man of him?' repeated the Doctor.

'I had rather be a child,' replied Paul.

'Indeed!' said the Doctor. 'Why?'

The child sat on the table looking at him, with a curious expression of suppressed emotion in his face, and beating one hand proudly on his knee as if he had the rising tears beneath it, and crushed them. But his other hand strayed a little way the while, a little farther—farther from him yet—until it lighted on the neck of Florence. 'This is why,' it seemed to say, and then the steady look was broken up and gone; the working lip was loosened; and the tears came streaming forth.

'Mrs Pipchin,' said his father, in a querulous manner, 'I am really very sorry to see this.'

'Come away from him, do, Miss Dombey,' quoth the matron.

'Never mind,' said the Doctor, blandly nodding his head, to keep Mrs Pipchin back. 'Ne-ver mind; we shall substitute new cares and new impressions, Mr Dombey, very shortly. You would still wish my little friend to acquire—'

'Everything, if you please, Doctor,' returned Mr Dombey, firmly.

'Yes,' said the Doctor, who, with his half-shut eyes, and his usual smile, seemed to survey Paul with the sort of interest that might attach to some choice little animal he was going to stuff. 'Yes, exactly. Ha! We shall impart a great variety of information to our little friend, and bring him quickly forward, I dare say. I dare say. Quite a virgin soil, I believe you said, Mr Dombey?'

'Except some ordinary preparation at home, and from this lady,' replied Mr Dombey, introducing Mrs Pipchin, who instantly communicated a rigidity to her whole muscular system, and snorted defiance beforehand, in case the Doctor should disparage her; 'except so far, Paul has, as yet, applied himself to no studies at all.'

Doctor Blimber inclined his head, in gentle tolerance of such insignificant poaching as Mrs Pipchin's, and said he was glad to hear it. It was much more satisfactory, he observed, rubbing his hands, to begin at the foundation. And again he leered at Paul, as if he would have liked to tackle him with the Greek alphabet on the spot.

'That circumstance, indeed, Doctor Blimber,' pursued Mr Dombey, glancing at his little son, 'and the interview I have already had the pleasure of holding with you, renders any further explanation, and consequently any further instrusion on your valuable time, so unnecessary, that—'

'Now, Miss Dombey!' said the acid Pipchin.

'Permit me,' said the Doctor, 'one moment. Allow me to present Mrs Blimber and my daughter, who will be associated with the domestic life of our young Pilgrim to Parnassus. Mrs Blimber,' for the lady, who had perhaps been in waiting, opportunely entered, followed by her daughter, that fair Sexton in spectacles, 'Mr Dombey. My daughter Cornelia, Mr Dombey. Mr Dombey, my love,' pursued the Doctor, turning to his wife, 'is so confiding as to—do you see our little friend?'

Mrs Blimber, in an excess of politeness, of which Mr Dombey was the object, apparently did not, for she was backing against the little friend, and very much endangering his position on the table. But, on this hint, she turned to admire his classical and intellectual lineaments, and turning again to Mr Dombey, said, with a sigh, that she envied his dear son.

'Like a bee, Sir,' said Mrs Blimber, with uplifted eyes, 'about to plunge into a garden of the choicest flowers, and sip the sweets for the first time. Virgil, Horace, Ovid, Terence, Plautus, Cicero. What a world of honey have we here. It may appear remarkable, Mr Dombey, in one who is a wife—the wife of such a husband—'

'Hush, hush,' said Doctor Blimber. 'Fie for shame.'

'Mr Dombey will forgive the partiality of a wife,' said Mrs Blimber, with an engaging smile.

Mr Dombey answered, 'Not at all;' applying those words, it is to be presumed, to the partiality, and not to the forgiveness.

'—And it may seem remarkable in one who is a mother also,' resumed Mrs Blimber.

'And such a mother,' observed Mr Dombey, bowing with some confused idea of being complimentary to Cornelia.

'But really,' pursued Mrs Blimber, 'I think if I could have known Cicero, and been his friend, and talked with him in his retirement at Tusculum (beautiful Tusculum!), I could have died contented.'

A learned enthusiasm is so very contagious, that Mr Dombey half believed that this was exactly his case; and even Mrs Pipchin, who was not, as we have seen, of an accommodating disposition generally, gave utterance to a little sound between a groan and a sigh, as if she would have said that nobody but Cicero could have proved a lasting consolation under that failure of the Peruvian mines, but that he indeed would have been a very Davy-lamp of refuge.

Cornelia looked at Mr Dombey through her spectacles, as if she would have liked to crack a few quotations with him from the authority in question. But this design, if she entertained it, was frustrated by a knock at the room-door.

'Who is that?' said the Doctor. 'Oh! Come in, Toots: come in. Mr Dombey, Sir.' Toots bowed. 'Quite a coincidence!' said Doctor Blimber. 'Here we have the beginning and the end. Alpha and Omega. Our head boy, Mr Dombey.'

The Doctor might have called him their head and shoulders boy, for he was at least that much taller that any of the rest. He blushed very much at finding himself among strangers, and chuckled aloud.

'An addition to our little Portico, Toots,' said the Doctor; 'Mr Dombey's son.'

Young Toots blushed again; and finding, from a solemn silence which prevailed, that he was expected to say something, said to Paul, 'How are you?' in a voice so deep, and a manner so sheepish, that if a lamb had roared it couldn't have been more surprising.

'Ask Mr Feeder, if you please, Toots,' said the Doctor, 'to prepare a few introductory volumes for Mr Dombey's son, and to allot him a convenient seat for study. My dear, I believe Mr Dombey has not seen the dormitories.'

'If Mr Dombey will walk up stairs,' said Mrs Blimber, 'I shall be more than proud to show him the dominions of the drowsy god.'

With that, Mrs Blimber, who was a lady of great suavity, and a wiry figure, and who wore a cap composed of sky-blue materials, proceeded up stairs with Mr Dombey and Cornelia; Mrs Pipchin following, and looking out sharp for her enemy the footman.

While they were gone, Paul sat upon the table, holding Florence by the hand, and glancing timidly from the Doctor round and round the room, while the Doctor, leaning back in his chair, with his hand in his breast as usual, held a book from him at arm's length, and read. There was something very awful in this manner of reading. It was such a determined, unimpassioned, inflexible, cold-blooded way of going to work. It left the Doctor's countenance exposed to view; and when the Doctor smiled auspiciously at his author, or knit his brows, or shook his head and made wry faces at him, as much as to say 'Don't tell me, Sir; I know better,' it was terrific.

Toots, too, had no business to be outside the door, ostentatiously examining the wheels in his watch, and counting his half-crowns. But that didn't last long; for Doctor Blimber, happening to change the position of his tight plump legs, as if he were going to get up, Toots swiftly vanished, and appeared no more.

Mr Dombey and his conductress were soon heard coming down stairs again, talking all the way; and presently they re-entered the Doctor's study.

'I hope, Mr Dombey,' said the Doctor, laying down his book, 'that the arrangements meet your approval.'

'They are excellent, Sir,' said Mr Dombey.

'Very fair, indeed,' said Mrs Pipchin, in a low voice; never disposed to give too much encouragement.

'Mrs Pipchin,' said Mr Dombey, wheeling round, 'will, with your permission, Doctor and Mrs Blimber, visit Paul now and then.'

'Whenever Mrs Pipchin pleases,' observed the Doctor.

'Always happy to see her,' said Mrs Blimber.

'I think,' said Mr Dombey, 'I have given all the trouble I need, and may take my leave. Paul, my child,' he went close to him, as he sat upon the table. 'Good-bye.'

'Good-bye, Papa.'

The limp and careless little hand that Mr Dombey took in his, was singularly out of keeping with the wistful face. But he had no part in its sorrowful expression. It was not addressed to him. No, no. To Florence—all to Florence.

If Mr Dombey in his insolence of wealth, had ever made an enemy, hard to appease and cruelly vindictive in his hate, even such an enemy might have received the pang that wrung his proud heart then, as compensation for his injury.

He bent down over his boy, and kissed him. If his sight were dimmed as he did so, by something that for a moment blurred the little face, and made it indistinct to him, his mental vision may have been, for that short time, the clearer perhaps.

'I shall see you soon, Paul. You are free on Saturdays and Sundays, you know.'

'Yes, Papa,' returned Paul: looking at his sister. 'On Saturdays and Sundays.'

'And you'll try and learn a great deal here, and be a clever man,' said Mr Dombey; 'won't you?'

'I'll try,' returned the child wearily.

'And you'll soon be grown up now!' said Mr Dombey.

'Oh! very soon!' replied the child. Once more the old, old look passed rapidly across his features like a strange light. It fell on Mrs Pipchin, and extinguished itself in her black dress. That excellent ogress stepped forward to take leave and to bear off Florence, which she had long been thirsting to do. The move on her part roused Mr Dombey, whose eyes were fixed on Paul. After patting him on the head, and pressing his small hand again, he took leave of Doctor Blimber, Mrs Blimber, and Miss Blimber, with his usual polite frigidity, and walked out of the study.

Despite his entreaty that they would not think of stirring, Doctor Blimber, Mrs Blimber, and Miss Blimber all pressed forward to attend him to the hall; and thus Mrs Pipchin got into a state of entanglement with Miss Blimber and the Doctor, and was crowded out of the study before she could clutch Florence. To which happy accident Paul stood afterwards indebted for the dear remembrance, that Florence ran back to throw her arms round his neck, and that hers was the last face in the doorway: turned towards him with a smile of encouragement, the brighter for the tears through which it beamed.

It made his childish bosom heave and swell when it was gone; and sent the globes, the books, blind Homer and Minerva, swimming round the room. But they stopped, all of a sudden; and then he heard the loud clock in the hall still gravely inquiring, 'how, is, my, lit, tle, friend? how, is, my, lit, tle, friend?' as it had done before.

He sat, with folded hands, upon his pedestal, silently listening. But he might have answered, 'weary, weary! very lonely, very sad' And there, with an aching void in his young heart, and all outside so cold, and bare, and strange, Paul sat as if he had taken life unfurnished, and the upholsterer were never coming.

After the lapse of some minutes, which appeared an immense time to little Paul Dombey on the table, Doctor Blimber came back. The Doctor's walk was stately, and calculated to impress the juvenile mind with solemn feelings. It was a sort of march; but when the Doctor put out his right foot, he gravely turned upon his axis, with a semi-circular sweep towards the left; and when he put out his left foot, he turned in the same manner towards the right. So that he seemed, at every stride he took, to look about him as though he were saying, 'Can anybody have the goodness to indicate any subject, in any direction, on which I am uninformed? I rather think not.'

Mrs Blimber and Miss Blimber came back in the Doctor's company; and the Doctor, lifting his new pupil off the table, delivered him over to Miss Blimber.

'Cornelia,' said the Doctor, 'Dombey will be your charge at first. Bring him on, Cornelia, bring him on.'

Miss Blimber received her young ward from the Doctor's hands; and Paul, feeling that the spectacles were surveying him, cast down his eyes.

'How old are you, Dombey?' said Miss Blimber.

'Six,' answered Paul, wondering, as he stole a glance at the young lady, why her hair didn't grow long like Florence's and why she was like a boy.

'How much do you know of your Latin Grammar, Dombey?' said Miss Blimber.

'None of it,' answered Paul. Feeling that the answer was a shock to Miss Blimber's sensibility, he looked up at the three faces that were looking down at him, and said:

'I hav'n't been well. I have been a weak child. I couldn't learn a Latin Grammar when I was out, every day, with old Glubb. I wish you'd tell old Glubb to come and see me, if you please.'

'What a dreadful low name!' said Mrs Blimber. 'Unclassical to a degree! Who is the monster, child?'

'What monster?' inquired Paul.

'Glubb,' said Mrs Blimber, with a great disrelish.

'He's no more a monster than you are,' returned Paul.

'What!' cried the Doctor, in a terrible voice. 'Aye, aye, aye? Aha! What's that?'

Paul was dreadfully frightened; but still he made a stand for the absent Glubb, though he did it trembling.

'He's a very nice old man, Ma'am,' he said. 'He used to draw my couch. He knows all about the deep sea, and the fish that are in it, and the great monsters that come and lie on rocks in the sun, and dive into the water again when they're startled, blowing and splashing so, that they can be heard for miles. There are some creatures,' said Paul, warming with his subject, 'I don't know how many yards long, and I forget their names, but Florence knows, that pretend to be in distress; and when a man goes near them, out of compassion, they open their great jaws, and attack him. But all he has got to do,' said Paul, boldly tendering this information to the very Doctor himself, 'is to keep on turning as he runs away, and then, as they turn slowly, because they are so long, and can't bend, he's sure to beat them. And though old Glubb don't know why the sea should make me think of my Mama that's dead, or what it is that it is always saying—always saying! he knows a great deal about it. And I wish,' the child concluded, with a sudden falling of his countenance, and falling in his animation, as he looked like one forlorn, upon the three strange faces, 'that you'd let old Glubb come here to see me, for I know him very well, and he knows me.'

'Ha!' said the Doctor, shaking his head: 'this is bad, but study will do much.'

Mrs Blimber opined, with something like a shiver, that he was an unaccountable child; and, allowing for the difference of visage, looked at him pretty much as Mrs Pipchin had been used to do.

'Take him round the house, Cornelia,' said the Doctor, 'and familiarise him with his new sphere. Go with that young lady, Dombey.'

Dombey obeyed; giving his hand to the abstruse Cornelia, and looking at her sideways, with timid curiosity, as they went away together. For her spectacles, by reason of the glistening of the glasses, made her so mysterious, that he didn't know where she was looking, and was not indeed quite sure that she had any eyes at all behind them.

Cornelia took him first to the school-room, which was situated at the back of the hall, and was approached through two baize doors, which deadened and muffled the young gentlemen's voices. Here there were eight young gentlemen in various stages of mental prostration, all very hard at work, and very grave indeed. Toots, as an old hand, had a desk to himself in one corner; and a magnificent man, of immense age, he looked, in Paul's young eyes, behind it.

Mr Feeder, B.A., who sat at another little desk, had his Virgil stop on, and was slowly grinding that tune to four young gentlemen. Of the remaining four, two, who grasped their foreheads convulsively, were engaged in solving mathematical problems; one with his face like a dirty window, from much crying, was endeavouring to flounder through a hopeless number of lines before dinner; and one sat looking at his task in stony stupefaction and despair—which it seemed had been his condition ever since breakfast time.

The appearance of a new boy did not create the sensation that might have been expected. Mr Feeder, B.A. (who was in the habit of shaving his head for coolness, and had nothing but little bristles on it), gave him a bony hand, and told him he was glad to see him—which Paul would have been very glad to have told *him*, if he could have done so with the least sincerity. Then Paul, instructed by Cornelia, shook hands with the four young gentlemen at Mr Feeder's desk; then with the two young gentlemen at work on the problems, who were very feverish; then with the young gentleman at work against time, who was very inky; and lastly with the young gentleman in a state of stupefaction, who was flabby and quite cold.

Paul having been already introduced to Toots, that pupil merely chuckled and breathed hard, as his custom was, and pursued the occupation in which he was engaged. It was not a severe one; for on account of his having 'gone through' so much (in more senses than one), and also of his having, as before hinted, left off blowing in his prime, Toots now had licence to pursue his own course of study: which was chiefly to write long letters to himself from persons of distinction, addressed 'P. Toots, Esquire, Brighton, Sussex,' and to preserve them in his desk with great care.

These ceremonies passed, Cornelia led Paul up stairs to the top of the house; which was rather a slow journey, on account of Paul being obliged to land both feet on every stair, before he mounted another. But they reached their journey's end at last; and there, in a front room, looking over the wild sea, Cornelia showed him a nice little bed with white hangings, close to the window, on which there was already beautifully written on a card in round text—down strokes very thick, and up strokes very fine—DOMBEY; while two other little bedsteads in the same room were announced, through like means, as respectively appertaining unto BRIGGS and TOZER.

Just as they got down stairs again into the hall, Paul saw the weak-eyed young man who had given that mortal offence to Mrs Pipchin, suddenly seize a very large drumstick, and fly at a gong that was hanging up, as if he had gone mad, or wanted vengeance. Instead of receiving warning, however, or being instantly taken into custody, the young man left off unchecked, after having made a dreadful noise. Then Cornelia Blimber said to Dombey that dinner would be ready in a quarter of an hour, and perhaps he had better go into the school-room among his 'friends.'

So Dombey, deferentially passing the great clock which was still as anxious as ever to know how he found himself, opened the school-room door a very little way, and strayed in like a lost boy: shutting it after him with some difficulty. His friends were all dispersed about the room except the stony friend, who remained immoveable. Mr Feeder was stretching himself in his gray gown, as if, regardless of expense, he were resolved to pull the sleeves off.

'Heigh ho hum!' cried Mr Feeder, shaking himself like a cart-horse, 'Oh dear me, dear me! Ya-a-a-ah!'

Paul was quite alarmed by Mr Feeder's yawning; it was done on such a great scale, and he was so terribly in earnest. All the boys too (Toots excepted) seemed knocked up, and were getting ready for dinner—some newly tying their neckcloths, which were very stiff indeed; and others washing their hands or brushing their hair, in an adjoining ante-chamber—as if they didn't think they should enjoy it at all.

Young Toots, who was ready beforehand, and had therefore nothing to do, and had leisure to bestow upon Paul, said, with heavy good nature:

'Sit down, Dombey.'

'Thank you, Sir,' said Paul.

His endeavouring to hoist himself on to a very high window-seat, and his slipping down again, appeared to prepare Toots's mind for the reception of a discovery.

'You're a very small chap,' said Mr Toots.

'Yes, Sir, I'm small,' returned Paul. 'Thank you, Sir.'

For Toots had lifted him into the seat, and done it kindly too.

'Who's your tailor?' inquired Toots, after looking at him for some moments.

'It's a woman that has made my clothes as yet,' asid Paul. 'My sister's dressmaker.'

'My tailor's Burgess and Co.,' said Toots. 'Fash'nable. But very dear.'

Paul had wit enough to shake his head, as if he would have said it was easy to see *that*; and indeed he thought so.

'Your father's regularly rich, ain't he?' inquired Mr Toots.

'Yes, Sir,' said Paul. 'He's Dombey and Son.'

'And which?' demanded Toots.

'And Son, Sir,' replied Paul.

Mr Toots made one or two attempts, in a low voice, to fix the firm in his mind; but not quite succeeding, said he would get Paul to mention the name again to-morrow morning, as it was rather important. And indeed he purposed nothing less than writing himself a private and confidential letter from Dombey and Son immediately.

By this time the other pupils (always excepting the stony boy) gathered round. They were polite, but pale; and spoke low; and they were so depressed in their spirits, that in comparison with the general tone of that company, Master Bitherstone was a perfect Miller, or complete Jest Book. And yet he had a sense of injury upon him, too, had Bitherstone.

'You sleep in my room, don't you?' asked a solemn young gentleman, whose shirt-collar curled up the lobes of his ears.

'Master Briggs?' inquired Paul.

'Tozer,' said the young gentleman.

Paul answered yes; and Tozer pointing out the stony pupil, said that was Briggs. Paul had already felt certain that it must be either Briggs or Tozer, though he didn't know why.

'Is yours a strong constitution?' inquired Tozer.

Paul said he thought not. Tozer replied that *he* thought not also judging from Paul's looks, and that it was a pity, for it need be. He then asked Paul if he were going to begin with Cornelia; and on Paul saying 'yes,' all the young gentlemen (Briggs excepted) gave a low groan.

It was drowned in the tintinnabulation of the gong, which sounding again with great fury, there was a general move towards the dining-room; still excepting Briggs the stony boy, who remained where he was, and as he was, and on its way to whom Paul presently encountered a round of bread, genteelly served on a plate and napkin, and with a silver fork lying crosswise on the top of it.

Doctor Blimber was already in his place in the dining-room, at the top of the table, with Miss Blimber and Mrs Blimber on either side of him. Mr Feeder in a black coat was at the bottom. Paul's chair was next to Miss Blimber; but it being found, when he sat in it, that his eyebrows were not much above the level of the table-cloth, some books were brought in from the Doctor's study, on which he was elevated, and on which he always sat from that time—carrying them in and out himself on after occasions, like a little elephant and castle.

Grace having been said by the Doctor, dinner began. There was some nice soup; also roast meat, boiled meat, vegetables, pie, and cheese. Every young gentleman had a massive silver fork, and a napkin; and all the arrangements were stately and handsome. In particular, there was a butler in a blue coat and bright buttons, who gave quite a winey flavour to the table beer; he poured it out so superbly.

Nobody spoke, unless spoken to, except Doctor Blimber, Mrs Blimber, and Miss Blimber, who conversed occasionally. Whenever a young gentleman was not actually engaged with his knife and fork or spoon, his eye, with an irresistible attraction, sought the eye of Doctor Blimber, Mrs Blimber, or Miss Blimber, and modestly rested there. Toots appeared to be the only exception to this rule. He sat next Mr Feeder on Paul's side of the table, and frequently looked behind and before the intervening boys to catch a glimpse of Paul.

Only once during dinner was there any conversation that included the young gentlemen. It happened at the epoch of the cheese, when the Doctor, having taken a glass of port wine, and hemmed twice or thrice, said:

'It is remarkable, Mr Feeder, that the Romans—'

At the mention of this terrible people, their implacable enemies, every young gentleman fastened his gaze upon the Doctor, with an assumption of the deepest interest. One of the number who happened to be drinking, and who caught the Doctor's eye glaring at him through the side of his tumbler, left off so hastily that he was convulsed for some moments, and in the sequel ruined Doctor Blimber's point.

'It is remarkable, Mr Feeder,' said the Doctor, beginning again slowly, 'that the Romans, in those gorgeous and profuse entertainments of which we read in the days of the Emperors, when luxury had attained a height unknown before or since, and when whole provinces were ravaged to supply the splendid means of one Imperial Banquet—'

Here the offender, who had been swelling and straining, and waiting in vain for a full stop, broke out violently.

'Johnson,' said Mr Feeder, in a low reproachful voice, 'take some water.'

The Doctor, looking very stern, made a pause until the water was brought, and then resumed:

'And when, Mr Feeder—'

But Mr Feeder, who saw that Johnson must break out again, and who knew that the Doctor would never come to a period before the young gentlemen until he had finished all he meant to say, couldn't keep his eye off Johnson; and thus was caught in the fact of not looking at the Doctor, who consequently stopped.

'I beg your pardon, Sir,' said Mr Feeder, reddening. 'I beg your pardon, Doctor Blimber.'

'And when,' said the Doctor, raising, his voice, 'when, Sir, as we read, and have no reason to doubt—incredible as it may appear to the vulgar of our time—the brother of Vitellius prepared for him a feast, in which were served, of fish, two thousand dishes—'

'Take some water, Johnson—dishes, Sir,' said Mr Feeder.

'Of various sorts of fowl, five thousand dishes.'

'Or try a crust of bread,' said Mr Feeder.

'And one dish,' pursued Doctor Blimber, raising his voice still higher as he looked all round the table, 'called, from its enormous dimensions, the Shield of Minerva, and made, among other costly ingredients, of the brains of pheasants—'

'Ow, ow, ow!' (from Johnson).

'Woodcocks—'

'Ow, ow, ow!'

'The sounds of the fish called scari—'

'You'll burst some vessel in your head,' said Mr Feeder. 'You had better let it come.'

'And the spawn of the lamprey, brought from the Carpathian Sea,' pursued the Doctor, in his severest voice; 'when we read of costly entertainments such as these, and still remember, that we have a Titus—'

'What would be your mother's feelings if you died of apoplexy!' said Mr Feeder.

'A Domitian—'

'And you're blue, you know,' said Mr Feeder.

'A Nero, a Tiberius, a Caligula, a Heliogabalus, and many more,' pursued the Doctor; 'it is, Mr Feeder—if you are doing me the honour to attend—remarkable: VERY—remarkable, Sir—'

But Johnson, unable to suppress it any longer, burst at that moment into such an overwhelming fit of coughing, that although both his immediate neighbours thumped him on the back, and Mr Feeder himself held a glass of water to his lips, and the butler walked him up and down several times between his own chair and the sideboard, like a sentry, it was full five minutes before he was moderately composed, and then there was a profound silence.

'Gentlemen,' said Doctor Blimber, 'rise for Grace! Cornelia, lift Dombey down'—nothing of whom but his scalp was accordingly seen above the table-cloth. 'Johnson will repeat to me to-morrow morning before breakfast, without book, and from the Greek Testament, the first chapter of the Epistle of Saint Paul to the Ephesians. We will resume our studies, Mr Feeder, in half-an-hour.'

The young gentlemen bowed and withdrew. Mr Feeder did likewise. During the half-hour the young gentlemen, broken into pairs, loitered arm-in-arm up and down a small piece of ground behind the house, or endeavoured to kindle a spark of animation in the breast of Briggs. But nothing happened so vulgar as play. Punctually at the appointed time, the gong was sounded, and the studies, under the joint auspices of Doctor Blimber and Mr Feeder, were resumed.

As the Olympic game of lounging up and down had been cut shorter than usual that day, on Johnson's account, they all went out for a walk before tea. Even Briggs (though he hadn't begun yet) partook of this dissipation; in the enjoyment of which he looked over the cliff two or three times darkly. Doctor Blimber accompanied them; and Paul had the honour of being taken in tow by the Doctor himself: a distinguished state of things, in which he looked very little and feeble.

Tea was served in a style no less polite than the dinner; and after tea the young gentlemen rising and bowing as before, withdrew to fetch up the unfinished tasks of that day, or to get up the already looming tasks of to-morrow. In the meantime, Mr Feeder withdrew to his own room; and Paul sat in a corner wondering whether Florence was thinking of him, and what they were all about at Mrs Pipchin's.

Mr Toots, who had been detained by an important letter from the Duke of Wellington, found Paul out after a time; and having looked at him for a long while, as before, inquired if he was fond of waistcoats.

Paul said, 'Yes, Sir.'

'So am I,' said Toots.

No word more spake Toots that night; but he stood looking at Paul as if he liked him; and as there was company in that, and Paul was not inclined to talk, it answered his purpose better than conversation.

At eight o'clock or so, the gong sounded again for prayers in the dining-room, where the butler afterwards presided over a side-table, on which bread and cheese and beer were spread for such young gentlemen as desired to partake of those refreshments. The ceremonies concluded by the Doctor's saying, 'Gentlemen, we will resume our studies at seven to-morrow;' and then, for the first time, Paul saw Cornelia Blimber's eye, and saw that it was upon him. When the Doctor had said these words, 'Gentlemen, we will resume our studies at seven to-morrow,' the pupils bowed again, and went to bed.

In the confidence of their own room up stairs, Briggs said his head ached ready to split, and that he should wish himself dead if it wasn't for his mother, and a blackbird he had at home. Tozer didn't say much, but he sighed a good deal, and told Paul to look out, for his turn would come to-morrow. After uttering those prophetic words, he undressed himself moodily, and got into bed. Briggs was in his bed too, and Paul in his bed too, before the weak-eyed young man appeared to take away the candle, when he wished them good night and pleasant dreams. But his benevolent wishes were in vain, as far as Briggs and Tozer were concerned; for Paul, who lay awake for a long while, and often woke afterwards, found that Briggs was ridden by his lesson as a nightmare: and that Tozer, whose mind was affected in his sleep by similar causes, in a minor degree, talked unknown tongues, or scraps of Greek and Latin—it was all one to Paul—which, in the silence of night, had an inexpressibly wicked and guilty effect.

Paul had sunk into a sweet sleep, and dreamed that he was walking hand in hand with Florence through beautiful gardens, when they came to a large sunflower which suddenly expanded itself into a gong, and began to sound. Opening his eyes, he found that it was a dark, windy morning, with a drizzling rain, and that the real gong was giving dreadful note of preparation, down in the hall.

So he got up directly, and found Briggs with hardly any eyes, for nightmare and grief had made his face puffy, putting his boots on: while Tozer stood shivering and rubbing his shoulders in a very bad humour. Poor Paul couldn't dress himself easily, not being used to it, and asked them if they would have the goodness to tie some strings for him; but as Briggs merely said 'Bother!' and Tozer, 'Oh yes!' he went down when he was otherwise ready, to the next story, where he saw a pretty young woman in leather gloves, cleaning a stove. The young woman seemed surprised at his appearance, and asked him where his mother was. When Paul told her she was dead, she took her gloves off, and did what he wanted; and furthermore rubbed his hands to warm them; and gave him a kiss; and told him whenever he wanted anything of that sort—meaning in the dressing way—to ask for 'Melia; which Paul, thanking her very much, said he certainly would. He then proceeded softly on his journey down stairs, towards the room in which the young gentlemen resumed their studies, when, passing by a door that stood ajar, a voice from within cried, 'Is that Dombey?' On Paul replying, 'Yes, Ma'am:' for he knew the voice to be Miss Blimber's: Miss Blimber said, 'Come in, Dombey.' And in he went.

Miss Blimber presented exactly the appearance she had presented yesterday, except that she wore a shawl. Her little light curls were as crisp as ever, and she had already her spectacles on, which made Paul wonder whether she went to bed in them. She had a cool little sitting-room of her own up there, with some books in it, and no fire. But Miss Blimber was never cold, and never sleepy.

'Now, Dombey,' said Miss Blimber, 'I am going out for a constitutional.'

Paul wondered what that was, and why she didn't send the footman out to get it in such unfavourable weather. But he made no observation on the subject: his attention being devoted to a little pile of new books on which Miss Blimber appeared to have been recently engaged.

'These are yours, Dombey,' said Miss Blimber.

'All of 'em, Ma'am?' said Paul.

'Yes,' returned Miss Blimber; 'and Mr Feeder will look you out some more very soon, if you are as studious as I expect you will be, Dombey.'

'Thank you, Ma'am,' said Paul.

'I am going out for a constitutional,' resumed Miss Blimber; 'and while I am gone, that is to say in the interval between this and breakfast, Dombey, I wish you to read over what I have marked in these books, and to tell me if you quite understand what you have got to learn. Don't lose time, Dombey, for you have none to spare, but take them down stairs, and begin directly.'

'Yes, Ma'am,' answered Paul.

There were so many of them, that although Paul put one hand under the bottom book and his other hand and his chin on the top book, and hugged them all closely, the middle book slipped out before he reached the door, and then they all tumbled down on the floor. Miss Blimber said, 'Oh, Dombey, Dombey, this is really very careless!' and piled them up afresh for him; and this time, by dint of balancing them with great nicety, Paul got out of the room, and down a few stairs before two of them escaped again. But he held the rest so tight, that he only left one more on the first floor, and one in the passage; and when he had got the main body down into the school-room, he set off up stairs again to collect the stragglers. Having at last amassed the whole library, and climbed into his place, he fell to work, encouraged by a remark from Tozer to the effect that he 'was in for it now;' which was the only interruption he received till breakfast time. At that meal, for which he had no appetite, everything was quite as solemn and genteel as at the others; and when it was finished, he followed Miss Blimber up stairs.

'Now, Dombey,' said Miss Blimber, 'How have you got on with those books?'

They comprised a little English, and a deal of Latin—names of things, declensions of articles and substantives, exercises thereon, and preliminary rules—a trifle of orthography, a glance at ancient history, a wink or two at modern ditto, a few tables, two or three weights and measures, and a little general information. When poor Paul had spelt out number two, he found he had no idea of number one; fragments whereof afterwards obtruded themselves into number three, which slided into number four, which grafted itself on to number two. So that whether twenty Romuluses made a Remus, or hic hæc hoc was troy weight, or a verb always agreed with an ancient Briton, or three times four was Taurus a bull, were open questions with him.

'Oh, Dombey, Dombey!' said Miss Blimber, 'this is very shocking.'

'If you please,' said Paul, 'I think if I might sometimes talk a little to old Glubb, I should be able to do better.'

'Nonsense, Dombey,' said Miss Blimber. 'I couldn't hear of it. This is not the place for Glubbs of any kind. You must take the books down, I suppose, Dombey, one by one, and perfect yourself in the day's instalment of subject A, before you turn at all to subject B. And now take away the top book, if you please, Dombey, and return when you are master of the theme.'

Miss Blimber expressed her opinions on the subject of Paul's uninstructed state with a gloomy delight, as if she had expected this result, and were glad to find that they must be in constant communication. Paul withdrew with the top task, as he was told, and laboured away at it, down below; sometimes remembering every word of it, and sometimes forgetting it all, and everything else besides: until at last he ventured up stairs again to repeat the lesson, when it was nearly all driven out of his head before he began, by Miss Blimber's shutting up the book, and saying, 'Go on, Dombey!' a proceeding so suggestive of the knowledge inside of her, that Paul looked upon the young lady with consternation, as a kind of learned Guy Faux, or artificial Bogle, stuffed full of scholastic straw.

He acquitted himself very well, nevertheless; and Miss Blimber, commending him as giving promise of getting on fast, immediately provided him with subject B; from which he passed to C, and even D before dinner. It was hard work, resuming his studies, soon after dinner; and he felt giddy and confused and drowsy and dull. But all the other young gentlemen had similar sensations, and were obliged to resume their studies too, if there were any comfort in that. It was a wonder that the great clock in the hall, instead of being constant to its first inquiry, never said, 'Gentlemen, we will now resume our studies,' for that phrase was often enough repeated in its neighbourhood. The studies went round like a mighty wheel, and the young gentlemen were always stretched upon it.

After tea there were exercises again, and preparations for next day by candle-light. And in due course there was bed; where, but for that resumption of the studies which took place in dreams, were rest and sweet forgetfulness.

Oh Saturdays! Oh happy Saturdays, when Florence always came at noon, and never would, in any weather, stay away, though Mrs Pipchin snarled and growled, and worried her bitterly. Those Saturdays were Sabbaths for at least two little Christians among all the Jews, and did the holy Sabbath work of strengthening and knitting up a brother's and a sister's love.

Not even Sunday nights—the heavy Sunday nights, whose shadow darkened the first waking burst of light on Sunday mornings—could mar those precious Saturdays. Whether it was the great sea-shore, where they sat, and strolled together; or whether it was only Mrs Pipchin's dull back room, in which she sang to him so softly, with his drowsy head upon her arm; Paul never cared. It was Florence. That was all he thought of. So, on Sunday nights, when the Doctor's dark door stood agape to swallow him up for another week, the time was come for taking leave of Florence; no one else.

Mrs Wickam had been drafted home to the house in town, and Miss Nipper, now a smart young woman, had come down. To many a single combat with Mrs Pipchin, did Miss Nipper gallantly devote herself; and if ever Mrs Pipchin in all her life had found her match, she had found it now. Miss Nipper threw away the scabbard the first morning she arose in Mrs Pipchin's house. She asked and gave no quarter. She said it must be war, and war it was; and Mrs Pipchin lived from that time in the midst of surprises, harassings, and defiances, and skirmishing attacks that came bouncing in upon her from the passage, even in unguarded moments of chops, and carried desolation to her very toast.

Miss Nipper had returned one Sunday night with Florence, from walking back with Paul to the Doctor's, when Florence took from her bosom a little piece of paper, on which she had pencilled down some words.

'See here, Susan,' she said. 'These are the names of the little books that Paul brings home to do those long exercises with, when he is so tired. I copied them last night while he was writing.'

'Don't shew 'em to me, Miss Floy, if you please,' returned Nipper, 'I'd as soon see Mrs Pipchin.'

'I want you to buy them for me, Susan, if you will, to-morrow morning. I have money enough,' said Florence.

'Why, goodness gracious me, Miss Floy,' returned Miss Nipper, 'how can you talk like that, when you have books upon books already, and masterses and missesses a teaching of you everything continual, though my belief is that your Pa, Miss Dombey, never would have learnt you nothing, never would have thought of it, unless you'd asked him—when he couldn't well refuse; but giving consent when asked, and offering when unasked, Miss, is quite two things; I may not have any objections to a young man's keeping company with me, and when he puts the question, may say "yes," but that's not saying "would you be so kind as like me." '

'But you can buy me the books, Susan; and you will, when you know I want them.'

'Well, Miss, and why do you want 'em?' replied Nipper; adding, in a lower voice, 'If it was to fling at Mrs Pipchin's head, I'd buy a cart-load.'

'I think I could perhaps give Paul some help, Susan, if I had these books,' said Florence, 'and make the coming week a little easier to him. At least I want to try. So buy them for me, dear, and I will never forget how kind it was of you to do it!'

It must have been a harder heart than Susan Nipper's that could have rejected the little purse Florence held out with these words, or the gentle look of entreaty with which she seconded her petition. Susan put the purse in her pocket without reply, and trotted out at once upon her errand.

The books were not easy to procure: and the answer at several shops was, either that they were just out of them, or that they never kept them, or that they had had a great many last month, or that they expected a great many next week. But Susan was not easily baffled in such an enterprise; and having entrapped a white-haired youth, in a black calico apron, from a library where she was known, to accompany her in her quest, she led him such a life in going up and down, that he exerted himself to the utmost, if it were only to get rid of her; and finally enabled her to return home in triumph.

With these treasures then, after her own daily lessons were over, Florence sat down at night to track Paul's footsteps through the thorny ways of learning; and being possessed of a naturally quick and sound capacity, and taught by that most wonderful of masters, love, it was not long before she gained upon Paul's heels, and caught and passed him.

Not a word of this was breathed to Mrs Pipchin; but many a night when they were all in bed, and when Miss Nipper, with her hair in papers and herself asleep in some uncomfortable attitude, reposed unconscious by her side; and when the chinking ashes in the grate were cold and grey; and when the candles were burnt down and guttering out; Florence tried so hard to be a substitute for one small Dombey, that her fortitude and perseverance might have almost won her a free right to bear the name herself.

And high was her reward, when one Saturday evening, as little Paul was sitting down as usual to 'resume his studies,' she sat down by his side, and showed him all that was so rough, made smooth, and all that was so dark, made clear and plain, before him. It was nothing but a startled look in Paul's wan face—a flush—a smile—and then a close embrace—but God knows how her heart leaped up at this rich payment for her trouble.

'Oh, Floy!' cried her brother, 'how I love you! How I love you, Floy!'

'And I you, dear!'

'Oh! I am sure of that, Floy.'

He said no more about it, but all that evening sat close by her, very quiet; and in the night he called out from his little room within hers, three or four times, that he loved her.

Regularly, after that, Florence was prepared to sit down with Paul on Saturday night, and patiently assist him through so much as they could anticipate together, of his next week's work. The cheering thought that he was labouring on where Florence had just toiled before him, would, of itself, have been a stimulant to Paul in the perpetual resumption of his studies; but coupled with the actual lightening of his load, consequent on this assistance, it saved him, possibly, from sinking underneath the burden which the fair Cornelia Blimber piled upon his back.

It was not that Miss Blimber meant to be too hard upon him, or that Doctor Blimber meant to bear too heavily on the young gentlemen in general. Cornelia merely held the faith in which she had been bred; and the Doctor, in some partial confusion of his ideas, regarded the young gentlemen as if they were all Doctors, and were born grown up. Comforted by the applause of the young gentlemen's nearest relations, and urged on by their blind vanity and ill-considered haste, it would have been strange if Doctor Blimber had discovered his mistake, or trimmed his swelling sails to any other tack.

Thus in the case of Paul. When Doctor Blimber said he made great progress, and was naturally clever, Mr Dombey was more bent than ever on his being forced and crammed. In the case of Briggs, when Doctor Blimber reported that he did not make great progress yet, and was not naturally clever, Briggs senior was inexorable in the same purpose. In short, however high and false the temperature at which the Doctor kept his hothouse, the owners of the plants were always ready to lend a helping hand at the bellows, and to stir the fire.

Such spirits as he had in the outset, Paul soon lost of course. But he retained all that was strange, and old, and thoughtful in his character: and under circumstances so favourable to the development of those tendencies, became even more strange, and old, and thoughtful, than before.

The only difference was that he kept his character to himself. He grew more thoughtful and reserved, every day; and had no such curiosity in any living member of the Doctor's household, as he had had in Mrs Pipchin. He loved to be alone; and in those short intervals when he was not occupied with his books, liked nothing so well as wandering about the house by himself, or sitting on the stairs listening to the great clock in the hall. He was intimate with all the paper-hanging in the house; saw things that no one else saw in the patterns; found out miniature tigers and lions running up the bedroom walls, and squinting faces leering in the squares and diamonds of the floor-cloth.

The solitary child lived on, surrounded by this arabesque work of his musing fancy, and no one understood him. Mrs Blimber thought him 'odd,' and sometimes the servants said among themselves that little Dombey 'moped;' but that was all.

Unless young Toots had some idea on the subject, to the expression of which he was wholly unequal. Ideas, like ghosts (according to the common notion of ghosts), must be spoken to a little before they will explain themselves; and Toots had long left off asking any questions of his own mind. Some mist there may have been, issuing from that leaden casket, his cranium, which, if it could have taken shape and form, would have become a genie; but it could not; and it only so far followed the example of the smoke in the Arabian story, as to roll out in a thick cloud, and there hang and hover. But it left a little figure visible upon a lonely shore, and Toots was always staring at it.

'How are you?' he would say to Paul, fifty times a day.

'Quite well, Sir, thank you,' Paul would answer.

'Shake hands,' would be Toots's next advance.

Which Paul, of course, would immediately do. Mr Toots generally said again, after a long interval of staring and hard breathing, 'How are you?' To which Paul again replied, 'Quite well, Sir, thank you.'

One evening Mr Toots was sitting at his desk, oppressed by correspondence, when a great purpose seemed to flash upon him. He laid down his pen, and went off to seek Paul, whom he found at last, after a long search, looking through the window of his little bedroom.

'I say!' cried Toots, speaking the moment he entered the room, lest he should forget it; 'what do you think about?'

'Oh! I think about a great many things,' replied Paul.

'Do you, though?' said Toots, appearing to consider that fact in itself surprising.

'If you had to die,' said Paul, looking up into his face —

Mr Toots started, and seemed much disturbed.

'—Don't you think you would rather die on a moonlight night when the sky was quite clear, and the wind blowing, as it did last night?'

Mr Toots said, looking doubtfully at Paul, and shaking his head, that he didn't know about that.

'Not blowing, at least,' said Paul, 'but sounding in the air like the sea sounds in the shells. It was a beautiful night. When I had listened to the water for a long time, I got up and looked out. There was a boat over there, in the full light of the moon; a boat with a sail.'

The child looked at him so steadfastly, and spoke so earnestly, that Mr Toots, feeling himself called upon to say something about this boat, said, 'Smugglers.' But with an impartial remembrance of there being two sides to every question, he added, 'or Preventive.'

'A boat with a sail,' repeated Paul, 'in the full light of the moon. The sail like an arm, all silver. It went away into the distance, and what do you think it seemed to do as it moved with the waves?'

'Pitch,' said Mr Toots.

'It seemed to beckon,' said the child, 'to beckon me to come!—There she is! There she is!'

Toots was almost beside himself with dismay at this sudden exclamation, after what had gone before, and cried, 'Who?'

'My sister Florence!' cried Paul, 'looking up here, and waving her hand. She sees me—she sees me! Good night, dear, good night, good night.'

His quick transition to a state of unbounded pleasure, as he stood at his window, kissing and clapping his hands: and the way in which the light retreated from his features as she passed out of his view, and left a patient melancholy on the little face: were too remarkable wholly to escape even Toots's notice. Their interview being interrupted at this moment by a visit from Mrs Pipchin, who usually brought her black skirts to bear upon Paul just before dusk, once or twice a week, Toots had no opportunity of improving the occasion; but it left so marked an impression on his mind that he twice returned, after having exchanged the usual salutations, to ask Mrs Pipchin how she did. This the irascible old lady conceived to be a deeply-devised and long-meditated insult, originating in the diabolical invention of the weak-eyed young man down stairs, against whom she accordingly lodged a formal complaint with Doctor Blimber that very night; who mentioned to the young man that if he ever did it again, he should be obliged to part with him.

The evenings being longer now, Paul stole up to his window every evening to look out for Florence. She always passed and repassed at a certain time, until she saw him; and their mutual recognition was a gleam of sunshine in Paul's daily life. Often after dark, one other figure walked alone before the Doctor's house. He rarely joined them on the Saturday now. He could not bear it. He would rather come unrecognised, and look up at the windows where his son was qualifying for a man; and wait, and watch, and plan, and hope.

Oh! could he but have seen, or seen as others did, the slight spare boy above, watching the waves and clouds at twilight, with his earnest eyes, and breasting the window of his solitary cage when birds flew by, as if he would have emulated them, and soared away!

When the Midsummer vacation approached, no indecent manifestations of joy were exhibited by the leaden-eyed young gentlemen assembled at Doctor Blimber's. Any such violent expression as 'breaking up' would have been quite inapplicable to that polite establishment. The young gentlemen oozed away, semi-annually, to their own homes; but they never broke up. They would have scorned the action.

Tozer, who was constantly galled and tormented by a starched white cambric neckerchief, which he wore at the express desire of Mrs Tozer, his parent, who, designing him for the Church, was of opinion that he couldn't be in that forward state of preparation too soon—Tozer said, indeed, that choosing between two evils, he thought he would rather stay where he was than go home. However inconsistent this declaration might appear with that passage in Tozer's Essay on the subject, wherein he had observed 'that the thoughts of home and all its recollections, awakened in his mind the most pleasing emotions of anticipation and delight,' and had also likened himself to a Roman General, flushed with a recent victory over the Iceni, or laden with Carthaginian spoil, advancing within a few hours' march of the Capitol, presupposed, for the purposes of the simile, to be the dwelling-place of Mrs Tozer, still it was very sincerely made. For it seemed that Tozer had a dreadful uncle, who not only volunteered examinations of him, in the holidays, on abstruse points, but twisted innocent events and things, and wrenched them to the same fell purpose. So that if this uncle took him to the Play, or, on a similar pretence of kindness, carried him to see a Giant, or a Dwarf, or a Conjurer, or anything, Tozer knew he had read up some classical allusion to the subject beforehand, and was thrown into a state of mortal apprehension: not foreseeing where he might break out, or what authority he might not quote against him.

As to Briggs, *his* father made no show of artifice about it. He never would leave him alone. So numerous and severe were the mental trials of that unfortunate youth in vacation time, that the friends of the family (then resident near Bayswater, London) seldom approached the ornamental piece of water in Kensington Gardens, without a vague expectation of seeing Master Briggs's hat floating on the surface, and an unfinished exercise lying on the bank. Briggs, therefore, was not at all sanguine on the subject of holidays; and these two sharers of little Paul's bedroom were so fair a sample of the young gentlemen in general, that the most elastic among them contemplated the arrival of those festive periods with genteel resignation.

It was far otherwise with little Paul. The end of these first holidays was to witness his separation from Florence, but who ever looked forward to the end of holidays whose beginning was not yet come! Not Paul, assuredly. As the happy time drew near, the lions and tigers climbing up the bedroom walls, became quite tame and frolicsome. The grim sly faces in the squares and diamonds of the floor-cloth relaxed and peeped out at him with less wicked eyes. The grave old clock had more of personal interest in the tone of its formal inquiry; and the restless sea went rolling on all night, to the sounding of a melancholy strain—yet it was pleasant too—that rose and fell with the waves, and rocked him, as it were, to sleep.

Mr Feeder, B.A., seemed to think that he, too, would enjoy the holidays very much. Mr Toots projected a life of holidays from that time forth; for, as he regularly informed Paul every day, it was his 'last half' at Doctor Blimber's, and he was going to begin to come into his property directly.

It was perfectly understood between Paul and Mr Toots, that they were intimate friends, notwithstanding their distance in point of years and station. As the vacation approached, and Mr Toots breathed harder and stared oftener in Paul's society, than he had done before, Paul knew that he meant he was sorry they were going to lose sight of each other, and felt very much obliged to him for his patronage and good opinion.

It was even understood by Doctor Blimber, Mrs Blimber, and Miss Blimber, as well as by the young gentlemen in general, that Toots had somehow constituted himself protector and guardian of Dombey, and the circumstance became so notorious, even to Mrs Pipchin, that the good old creature cherished feelings of bitterness and jealousy against Toots; and, in the sanctuary of her own home, repeatedly denounced him as a 'chuckle-headed noodle.' Whereas the innocent Toots had no more idea of awakening Mrs Pipchin's wrath, than he had of any other definite possibility or proposition. On the contrary, he was disposed to consider her rather a remarkable character, with many points of interest about her. For this reason he smiled on her with so much urbanity, and asked her how she did, so often, in the course of her visits to little Paul, that at last she one night told him plainly she wasn't used to it, whatever he might think; and she could not, and she would not bear it, either from himself or any other puppy then existing: at which unexpected acknowledgment of his civilities, Mr Toots was so alarmed that he secreted himself in a retired spot until she had gone. Nor did he ever again face the doughty Mrs Pipchin, under Doctor Blimber's roof.

They were within two or three weeks of the holidays, when, one day, Cornelia Blimber called Paul into her room, and said, 'Dombey, I am going to send home your analysis.'

'Thank you, Ma'am,' returned Paul.

'You know what I mean, do you, Dombey?' inquired Miss Blimber, looking hard at him through the spectacles.

'No, Ma'am,' said Paul.

'Dombey, Dombey,' said Miss Blimber, 'I begin to be afraid you are a sad boy. When you don't know the meaning of an expression, why don't you seek for information?'

'Mrs Pipchin told me I wasn't to ask questions,' returned Paul.

'I must beg you not to mention Mrs Pipchin to me, on any account, Dombey,' returned Miss Blimber. 'I couldn't think of allowing it. The course of study here is very far removed from anything of that sort. A repetition of such allusions would make it necessary for me to request to hear, without a mistake, before breakfast-time to-morrow morning, from *Verbun personale* down to *simillima cygno*.'

'I didn't mean, Ma'am—' began little Paul.

'I must trouble you not to tell me that you didn't mean, if you please, Dombey,' said Miss Blimber, who preserved an awful politeness in her admonitions. 'That is a line of argument I couldn't dream of permitting.'

Paul felt it safest to say nothing at all, so he only looked at Miss Blimber's spectacles. Miss Blimber having shaken her head at him gravely, referred to a paper lying before her.

' "Analysis of the character of P. Dombey." If my recollection serves me,' said Miss Blimber, breaking off, 'the word analysis, as opposed to synthesis, is thus defined by Walker. "The resolution of an object, whether of the senses or of the intellect, into its first elements." As opposed to synthesis, you observe. *Now* you know what analysis is, Dombey.'

Dombey didn't seem to be absolutely blinded by the light let in upon his intellect, but he made Miss Blimber a little bow.

' "Analysis," ' resumed Miss Blimber, casting her eye over the paper, ' "of the character of P. Dombey." I find that the natural capacity of Dombey is extremely good; and that his general disposition to study may be stated in an equal ratio. Thus, taking eight as our standard and highest number, I find these qualities in Dombey stated each at six three-fourths!'

Miss Blimber paused to see how Paul received this news. Being undecided whether six three-fourths meant six pounds fifteen, or sixpence three farthings, or six foot three, or three quarters past six, or six somethings that he hadn't learnt yet, with three unknown something elses over, Paul rubbed his hands and looked straight at Miss Blimber. It happened to answer as well as anything else he could have done; and Cornelia proceeded.

' "Violence two. Selfishness two. Inclination to low company, as evinced in the case of a person named Glubb, originally seven, but since reduced. Gentlemanly demeanour four, and improving with advancing years." Now what I particularly wish to call your attention to, Dombey, is the general observation at the close of this analysis.'

Paul set himself to follow it with great care.

' "It may be generally observed of Dombey," ' said Miss Blimber, reading in a loud voice, and at every second word directing her spectacles towards the little figure before her, ' "that his abilities and inclinations are good, and that he has made as much progress as under the circumstances could have been expected. But it is to be lamented of this young gentleman that he is singular (what is usually termed old-fashioned) in his character and conduct, and that, without presenting anything in either which distinctly calls for reprobation, he is often very unlike other young gentlemen of his age and social position." Now, Dombey,' said Miss Blimber, laying down the paper, 'do you understand that?'

'I think I do, Ma'am,' said Paul.

'This analysis, you see, Dombey,' Miss Blimber continued, 'is going to be sent home to your respected parent. It will naturally be very painful to him to find that you are singular in your character and conduct. It is naturally painful to us; for we can't like you, you know, Dombey, as well as we could wish.'

She touched the child upon a tender point. He had secretly become more and more solicitous from day to day, as the time of his departure drew more near, that all the house should like him. For some hidden reason, very imperfectly understood by himself—if understood at all—he felt a gradually increasing impulse of affection, towards almost everything and everybody in the place. He could not bear to think that they would be quite indifferent to him when he was gone. He wanted them to remember him kindly; and he had made it his business even to conciliate a great hoarse shaggy dog, chained up at the back of the house, who had previously been the terror of his life: that even he might miss him when he was no longer there.

Little thinking that in this, he only showed again the difference between himself and his compeers, poor tiny Paul set it forth to Miss Blimber as well as he could, and begged her, in despite of the official analysis, to have the goodness to try and like him. To Mrs Blimber, who had joined them, he preferred the same petition; and when that lady could not forbear, even in his presence, from giving utterance to her often-repeated opinion, that he was an odd child, Paul told her that he was sure she was quite right; that he thought it must be his bones, but he didn't know; and that he hoped she would overlook it, for he was fond of them all.

'Not so fond,' said Paul, with a mixture of timidity and perfect frankness, which was one of the most peculiar and most engaging qualities of the child, 'not so fond as I am of Florence, of course; that could never be. You couldn't expect that, could you, Ma'am?'

'Oh! the old-fashioned little soul!' cried Mrs Blimber, in a whisper.

'But I like everybody here very much,' pursued Paul, 'and I should grieve to go away, and think that any one was glad that I was gone, or didn't care.'

Mrs Blimber was now quite sure that Paul was the oddest child in the world; and when she told the Doctor what had passed, the Doctor did not controvert his wife's opinion. But he said, as he had said before, when Paul first came, that study would do much; and he also said, as he had said on that occasion, 'Bring him on, Cornelia! Bring him on!'

Cornelia had always brought him on as vigorously as she could; and Paul had had a hard life of it. But over and above the getting through his tasks, he had long had another purpose always present to him, and to which he still held fast. It was, to be a gentle, useful, quiet little fellow, always striving to secure the love and attachment of the rest; and though he was yet often to be seen at his old post on the stairs, or watching the waves and clouds from his solitary window, he was oftener found, too, among the other boys, modestly rendering them some little voluntary service. Thus it came to pass, that even among those rigid and absorbed young anchorites, who mortified themselves beneath the roof of Doctor Blimber, Paul was an object of general interest; a fragile little plaything that they all liked, and that no one would have thought of treating roughly. But he could not change his nature, or re-write the analysis; and so they all agreed that Dombey was old-fashioned.

There were some immunities, however, attaching to the character enjoyed by no one else. They could have better spared a newer-fashioned child, and that alone was much. When the others only bowed to Doctor Blimber and family on retiring for the night, Paul would stretch out his morsel of a hand, and boldly shake the Doctor's; also Mrs Blimber's; also Cornelia's. If anybody was to be begged off from impending punishment, Paul was always the delegate. The weak-eyed young man himself had once consulted him, in reference to a little breakage of glass and china. And it was darkly rumoured that the butler, regarding him with favour such as that stern man had never shown before to mortal boy, had sometimes mingled porter with his table-beer to make him strong.

Over and above these extensive privileges, Paul had free right of entry to Mr Feeder's room, from which apartment he had twice led Mr Toots into the open air in a state of faintness, consequent on an unsuccessful attempt to smoke a very blunt cigar: one of a bundle which that young gentleman had covertly purchased on the shingle from a most desperate smuggler, who had acknowledged, in confidence, that two hundred pounds was the price set upon his head, dead or alive, by the Custom House. It was a snug room, Mr Feeder's, with his bed in another little room inside of it; and a flute, which Mr Feeder couldn't play yet, but was going to make a point of learning, he said, hanging up over the fireplace. There were some books in it, too, and a fishing-rod; for Mr Feeder said he should certainly make a point of learning to fish, when he could find time. Mr Feeder had amassed, with similar intentions, a beautiful little curly second-hand key-bugle, a chess-board and men, a Spanish Grammar, a set of sketching materials, and a pair of boxing-gloves. The art of self-defence Mr Feeder said he should undoubtedly make a point of learning, as he considered it the duty of every man to do; for it might lead to the protection of a female in distress.

But Mr Feeder's great possession was a large green jar of snuff, which Mr Toots had brought down as a present, at the close of the last vacation; and for which he had paid a high price, as having been the genuine property of the Prince Regent. Neither Mr Toots nor Mr Feeder could partake of this or any other snuff, even in the most stinted and moderate degree, without being seized with convulsions of sneezing. Nevertheless it was their great delight to moisten a box-full with cold tea, stir it up on a piece of parchment with a paper-knife, and devote themselves to its consumption then and there. In the course of which cramming of their noses, they endured surprising torments with the constancy of martyrs; and, drinking table-beer at intervals, felt all the glories of dissipation.

To little Paul sitting silent in their company, and by the side of his chief patron, Mr Toots, there was a dread charm in these reckless occasions: and when Mr Feeder spoke of the dark mysteries of London, and told Mr Toots that he was going to observe it himself closely in all its ramifications in the approaching holidays, and for that purpose had made arrangements to board with two old maiden ladies at Peckham, Paul regarded him as if he were the hero of some book of travels or wild adventure, and was almost afraid of such a slashing person.

Going into this room one evening, when the holidays were very near, Paul found Mr Feeder filling up the blanks in some printed letters, while some others, already filled up and strewn before him, were being folded and sealed by Mr Toots. Mr Feeder said, 'Aha, Dombey, there you are, are you?'—for they were always kind to him, and glad to see him—and then said, tossing one of the letters towards him, 'And *there* you are, too, Dombey. That's yours.'

'Mine, Sir?' said Paul.

'Your invitation,' returned Mr Feeder.

Paul, looking at it, found, in copper-plate print, with the exception of his own name and the date, which were in Mr Feeder's Penmanship, that Doctor and Mrs Blimber requested the pleasure of Mr P. Dombey's company at an early party on Wednesday Evening, the Seventeenth Instant; and that the hour was half-past seven o'clock; and that the object was Quadrilles. Mr Toots also showed him, by holding up a companion sheet of paper, that Doctor and Mrs Blimber requested the pleasure of Mr Toots's company at an early party on Wednesday Evening, the Seventeenth Instant, when the hour was half-past seven o'clock, and when the object was Quadrilles. He also found, on glancing at the table where Mr Feeder sat, that the pleasure of Mr Briggs's company, and of Mr Tozer's company, and of every young gentleman's company, was requested by Doctor and Mrs Blimber on the same genteel occasion.

Mr Feeder then told him, to his great joy, that his sister was invited, and that it was a half-yearly event, and that, as the holidays began that day, he could go away with his sister after the party, if he liked, which Paul interrupted him to say he *would* like, very much. Mr Feeder then gave him to understand that he would be expected to inform Doctor and Mrs Blimber, in superfine small-hand, that Mr P. Dombey would be happy to have the honour of waiting on them, in accordance with their polite invitation. Lastly, Mr Feeder said, he had better not refer to the festive occasion, in the hearing of Doctor and Mrs Blimber; as these preliminaries, and the whole of the arrangements, were conducted on principles of classicality and high breeding; and that Doctor and Mrs Blimber on the one hand, and the young gentlemen on the other, were supposed, in their scholastic capacities, not to have the least idea of what was in the wind.

Paul thanked Mr Feeder for these hints, and pocketing his invitation, sat down on a stool by the side of Mr Toots as usual. But Paul's head, which had long been ailing more or less, and was sometimes very heavy and painful, felt so uneasy that night that he was obliged to support it on his hand. And yet it dropped so, that by little and little it sank on Mr Toots's knee, and rested there, as if it had no care to be ever lifted up again.

That was no reason why he should be deaf; but he must have been, he thought, for, by and by, he heard Mr Feeder calling in his ear, and gently shaking him to rouse his attention. And when he raised his head, quite scared, and looked about him, he found that Doctor Blimber had come into the room; and that the window was open, and that his forehead was wet with sprinkled water; though how all this had been done without his knowledge, was very curious indeed.

'Ah! Come, come! That's well! How is my little friend now?' said Doctor Blimber, encouragingly.

'Oh, quite well, thank you, Sir,' said Paul.

But there seemed to be something the matter with the floor, for he couldn't stand upon it steadily; and with the walls too, for they were inclined to turn round and round, and could only be stopped by being looked at very hard indeed. Mr Toots's head had the appearance of being at once bigger and farther off than was quite natural: and when he took Paul in his arms, to carry him up stairs, Paul observed with astonishment that the door was in quite a different place from that in which he had expected to find it, and almost thought, at first, that Mr Toots was going to walk straight up the chimney.

It was very kind of Mr Toots to carry him to the top of the house so tenderly; and Paul told him that it was. But Mr Toots said he would do a great deal more than that, if he could; and indeed he did more as it was: for he helped Paul to undress, and helped him to bed, in the kindest manner possible, and then sat down by the bedside and chuckled very much; while Mr Feeder, B.A., leaning over the bottom of the bedstead, set all the little bristles on his head bolt upright with his bony hands, and then made believe to spar at Paul with great science, on account of his being all right again, which was so uncommonly facetious, and kind too in Mr Feeder, that Paul, not being able to make up his mind whether it was best to laugh or cry at him, did both at once.

How Mr Toots melted away, and Mr Feeder changed into Mrs Pipchin, Paul never thought of asking; neither was he at all curious to know; but when he saw Mrs Pipchin standing at the bottom of the bed, instead of Mr Feeder, he cried out, 'Mrs Pipchin, don't tell Florence!'

'Don't tell Florence what, my little Paul?' said Mrs Pipchin, coming round to the bedside, and sitting down in the chair.

'About me,' said Paul.

'No, no,' said Mrs Pipchin.

'What do you think I mean to do when I grow up, Mrs Pipchin?' inquired Paul, turning his face towards her on his pillow, and resting his chin wistfully on his folded hands.

Mrs Pipchin couldn't guess.

'I mean,' said Paul, 'to put my money all together in one Bank, never try to get any more, go away into the country with my darling Florence, have a beautiful garden, fields, and woods, and live there with her all my life!'

'Indeed!' cried Mrs Pipchin.

'Yes,' said Paul. 'That's what I mean to do, when I—' He stopped, and pondered for a moment.

Mrs Pipchin's grey eye scanned his thoughtful face.

'If I grow up,' said Paul. Then he went on immediately to tell Mrs Pipchin all about the party, about Florence's invitation, about the pride he would have in the admiration that would be felt for her by all the boys, about their being so kind to him and fond of him, about his being so fond of them, and about his being so glad of it. Then he told Mrs Pipchin about the analysis, and about his being certainly old-fashioned, and took Mrs Pipchin's opinion on that point, and whether she knew why it was, and what it meant. Mrs Pipchin denied the fact altogether, as the shortest way of getting out of the difficulty; but Paul was far from satisfied with that reply, and looked so searchingly at Mrs Pipchin for a truer answer, that she was obliged to get up and look out of the window to avoid his eyes.

There was a certain calm Apothecary, who attended at the establishment when any of the young gentlemen were ill, and somehow *he* got into the room and appeared at the bedside, with Mrs Blimber. How they came there, or how long they had been there, Paul didn't know; but when he saw them, he sat up in bed, and answered all the Apothecary's questions at full length, and whispered to him that Florence was not to know anything about it, if he pleased, and that he had set his mind upon her coming to the party. He was very chatty with the Apothecary, and they parted excellent friends. Lying down again with his eyes shut, he heard the Apothecary say, out of the room and quite a long way off—or he dreamed it—that there was a want of vital power (what was that, Paul wondered!) and great constitutional weakness. That, as the little fellow had set his heart on parting with his school-mates on the seventeenth, it would be better to indulge the fancy if he grew no worse. That he was glad to hear from Mrs Pipchin, that the little fellow would go to his friends in London on the eighteenth. That he would write to Mr Dombey, when he should have gained a better knowledge of the case, and before that day. That there was no immediate cause for—what? Paul lost that word. And that the little fellow had a fine mind, but was an old-fashioned boy.

What old fashion could that be, Paul wondered with a palpitating heart, that was so visibly expressed in him; so plainly seen by so many people!

He could neither make it out, nor trouble himself long with the effort. Mrs Pipchin was again beside him, if she had ever been away (he thought she had gone out with the Doctor, but it was all a dream perhaps), and presently a bottle and glass got into her hands magically, and she poured out the contents for him. After that, he had some real good jelly, which Mrs Blimber brought to him herself; and then he was so well, that Mrs Pipchin went home, at his urgent solicitation, and Briggs and Tozer came to bed. Poor Briggs grumbled terribly about his own analysis, which could hardly have discomposed him more if it had been a chemical process; but he was very good to Paul, and so was Tozer, and so were all the rest, for they every one looked in before going to bed, and said, 'How are you now, Dombey?' 'Cheer up, little Dombey!' and so forth. After Briggs had got into bed, he lay awake for a long time, still bemoaning his analysis, and saying he knew it was all wrong, and they couldn't have analysed a murderer worse, and how would Doctor Blimber like it if his pocket-money depended on it? It was very easy, Briggs said, to make a galley-slave of a boy all the half-year, and then score him up idle; and to crib two dinners a-week out of his board, and then score him up greedy: but that wasn't going to be submitted to, he believed, was it? Oh! Ah!

Before the weak-eyed young man performed on the gong next morning, he came up stairs to Paul and told him he was to lie still, which Paul very gladly did. Mrs Pipchin reappeared a little before the Apothecary, and a little after the good young woman whom Paul had seen cleaning the stove on that first morning (how long ago it seemed now!) had brought him his breakfast. There was another consultation a long way off, or else Paul dreamed it again; and then the Apothecary, coming back with Doctor and Mrs Blimber, said:

'Yes, I think, Doctor Blimber, we may release this young gentleman from his books just now; the vacation being so very near at hand.'

'By all means,' said Doctor Blimber. 'My love, you will inform Cornelia, if you please.'

'Assuredly,' said Mrs Blimber.

The Apothecary bending down, looked closely into Paul's eyes, and felt his head, and his pulse, and his heart, with so much interest and care, that Paul said, 'Thank you, Sir.'

'Our little friend,' observed Doctor Blimber, 'has never complained.'

'Oh no!' replied the Apothecary. 'He was not likely to complain.'

'You find him greatly better?' said Doctor Blimber.

'Oh! he is greatly better, Sir,' returned the Apothecary.

Paul had begun to speculate, in his own odd way, on the subject that might occupy the Apothecary's mind just at that moment; so musingly had he answered the two questions of Doctor Blimber. But the Apothecary happening to meet his little patient's eyes, as the latter set off on that mental expedition, and coming instantly out of his abstraction with a cheerful smile, Paul smiled in return and abandoned it.

He lay in bed all that day, dozing and dreaming, and looking at Mr Toots; but got up on the next, and went down stairs. Lo and behold, there was something the matter with the great clock; and a workman on a pair of steps had taken its face off, and was poking instruments into the works by the light of a candle! This was a great event for Paul, who sat down on the bottom stair, and watched the operation attentively; now and then glancing at the clock face, leaning all askew, against the wall hard by, and feeling a little confused by a suspicion that it was ogling him.

The workman on the steps was very civil; and as he said, when he observed Paul, 'How do you do, Sir?' Paul got into conversation with him, and told him he hadn't been quite well lately. The ice being thus broken, Paul asked him a multitude of questions about chimes and clocks; as, whether people watched up in the lonely church steeples by night to make them strike, and how the bells were rung when people died, and whether those were different bells from wedding bells, or only sounded dismal in the fancies of the living. Finding that his new acquaintance was not very well informed on the subject of the Curfew Bell of ancient days, Paul gave him an account of that institution; and also asked him, as a practical man, what he thought about King Alfred's idea of measuring time by the burning of candles; to which the workman replied, that he thought it would be the ruin of the clock trade if it was to come up again. In fine, Paul looked on, until the clock had quite recovered its familiar aspect, and resumed its sedate inquiry; when the workman, putting away his tools in a long basket, bade him good day, and went away. Though not before he had whispered something, on the door-mat, to the footman, in which there was the phrase 'old-fashioned'—for Paul heard it.

What could that old fashion be, that seemed to make the people sorry! What could it be!

Having nothing to learn now, he thought of this frequently; though not so often as he might have done, if he had had fewer things to think of. But he had a great many; and was always thinking, all day long.

First, there was Florence coming to the party. Florence would see that the boys were fond of him; and that would make her happy. This was his great theme. Let Florence once be sure that they were gentle and good to him, and that he had become a little favourite among them, and then she would always think of the time he had passed there, without being very sorry. Florence might be all the happier too for that, perhaps, when he came back.

When he came back! Fifty times a day his noiseless little feet went up the stairs to his own room, as he collected every book and scrap, and trifle that belonged to him, and put them all together there, down to the minutest thing, for taking home! There was no shade of coming back on little Paul; no preparation, for it, or other reference to it, grew out of anything he thought or did, except this slight one in connection with his sister. On the contrary, he had to think of everything familiar to him, in his contemplative moods and in his wanderings about the house, as being to be parted with; and hence the many things he had to think of, all day long.

He had to peep into those rooms up stairs, and think how solitary they would be when he was gone, and wonder through how many silent days, weeks, months, and years, they would continue just as grave and undisturbed. He had to think—would any other child (old-fashioned, like himself) stray there at any time, to whom the same grotesque distortions of pattern and furniture would manifest themselves; and would anybody tell that boy of little Dombey, who had been there once?

He had to think of a portrait on the stairs, which always looked earnestly after him as he went away, eyeing it over his shoulder: and which, when he passed it in the company of any one, still seemed to gaze at him, and not at his companion. He had much to think of, in association with a print that hung up in another place, where, in the centre of a wondering group, one figure that he knew, a figure with a light about its head—benignant, mild, and merciful—stood pointing upward.

At his own bedroom window there were crowds of thoughts that mixed with these, and came on, one upon another, like the rolling waves. Where those wild birds lived, that were always hovering out at sea in troubled weather; where the clouds rose and first began; whence the wind issued on its rushing flight, and where it stopped; whether the spot where he and Florence had so often sat, and watched, and talked about these things, could ever be exactly as it used to be without them; whether it could ever be the same to Florence, if he were in some distant place, and she were sitting there alone.

He had to think, too, of Mr Toots, and Mr Feeder, B.A.; of all the boys; and of Doctor Blimber, Mrs Blimber, and Miss Blimber; of home, and of his aunt and Miss Tox; of his father, Dombey and Son, Walter with the poor old uncle who had got the money he wanted, and that gruff-voiced Captain with the iron hand. Besides all this, he had a number of little visits to pay, in the course of the day; to the schoolroom, to Doctor Blimber's study, to Mrs Blimber's private apartment, to Miss Blimber's, and to the dog. For he was free of the whole house now, to range it as he chose; and, in his desire to part with everybody on affectionate terms, he attended, in his way, to them all. Sometimes he found places in books for Briggs, who was always losing them; sometimes he looked up words in dictionaries for other young gentlemen who were in extremity; sometimes he held skeins of silk for Mrs Blimber to wind; sometimes he put Cornelia's desk to rights; sometimes he would even creep into the Doctor's study, and, sitting on the carpet near his learned feet, turn the globes softly, and go round the world, or take a flight among the far-off stars.

In those days immediately before the holidays, in short, when the other young gentlemen were labouring for dear life through a general resumption of the studies of the whole half-year, Paul was such a privileged pupil as had never been seen in that house before. He could hardly believe it himself; but his liberty lasted from hour to hour, and from day to day; and little Dombey was caressed by every one. Doctor Blimber was so particular about him, that he requested Johnson to retire from the dinner-table one day, for having thoughtlessly spoken to him as 'poor little Dombey;' which Paul thought rather hard and severe, though he had flushed at the moment, and wondered why Johnson should pity him. It was the more questionable justice, Paul thought, in the Doctor, from his having certainly overheard that great authority give his assent on the previous evening, to the proposition (stated by Mrs Blimber) that poor dear little Dombey was more old-fashioned than ever. And now it was that Paul began to think it must surely be old-fashioned to be very thin, and light, and easily tired, and soon disposed to lie down anywhere and rest; for he couldn't help feeling that these were more and more his habits every day.

At last the party-day arrived; and Doctor Blimber said at breakfast, 'Gentlemen, we will resume our studies on the twenty-fifth of next month.' Mr Toots immediately threw off his allegiance, and put on his ring: and mentioning the Doctor in casual conversation shortly afterwards, spoke of him as 'Blimber!' This act of freedom inspired the older pupils with admiration and envy; but the younger spirits were appalled, and seemed to marvel that no beam fell down and crushed him.

Not the least allusion was made to the ceremonies of the evening, either at breakfast or at dinner; but there was a bustle in the house all day, and in the course of his perambulations, Paul made acquaintance with various strange benches and candlesticks, and met a harp in a green great-coat standing on the landing outside the drawing-room door. There was something queer, too, about Mrs Blimber's head at dinner-time, as if she had screwed her hair up too tight; and though Miss Blimber showed a graceful bunch of plaited hair on each temple, she seemed to have her own little curls in paper underneath, and in a play-bill too: for Paul read 'Theatre Royal' over one of her sparkling spectacles, and 'Brighton' over the other.

There was a grand array of white waistcoats and cravats in the young gentlemen's bedrooms as evening approached; and such a smell of singed hair, that Doctor Blimber sent up the footman with his compliments, and wished to know if the house was on fire. But it was only the hair-dresser curling the young gentlemen, and over-heating his tongs in the ardour of business.

When Paul was dressed—which was very soon done, for he felt unwell and drowsy, and was not able to stand about it very long—he went down into the drawing-room; where he found Doctor Blimber pacing up and down the room full dressed, but with a dignified and unconcerned demeanour, as if he thought it barely possible that one or two people might drop in by and by. Shortly afterwards, Mrs Blimber appeared looking lovely, Paul thought; and attired in such a number of skirts that it was quite an excursion to walk round her. Miss Blimber came down soon after her mama; a little squeezed in appearance, but very charming.

Mr Toots and Mr Feeder were the next arrivals. Each of these gentlemen brought his hat in his hand, as if he lived somewhere else; and when they were announced by the butler, Doctor Blimber said, 'Aye, aye, aye! God bless my soul!' and seemed extremely glad to see them. Mr Toots was one blaze of jewellery and buttons: and he felt the circumstance so strongly, that when he had shaken hands with the Doctor, and had bowed to Mrs Blimber and Miss Blimber, he took Paul aside, and said, 'What do you think of this, Dombey!'

But notwithstanding this modest confidence in himself, Mr Toots appeared to be involved in a good deal of uncertainty whether, on the whole, it was judicious to button the bottom button of his waistcoat, and whether, on a calm revision of all the circumstances, it was best to wear his wristbands turned up or turned down. Observing that Mr Feeder's were turned up, Mr Toots turned his up; but the wristbands of the next arrival being turned down, Mr Toots turned his down. The differences in point of waistcoat buttoning, not only at the bottom, but at the top too, became so numerous and complicated as the arrivals thickened, that Mr Toots was continually fingering that article of dress, as if he were performing on some instrument; and appeared to find the incessant execution it demanded quite bewildering.

All the young gentlemen, tightly cravatted, curled, and pumped, and with their best hats in their hands, having been at different times announced and introduced, Mr Baps, the dancing-master, came, accompanied by Mrs Baps, to whom Mrs Blimber was extremely kind and condescending. Mr Baps was a very grave gentleman, with a slow and measured manner of speaking; and before he had stood under the lamp five minutes, he began to talk to Toots (who had been silently comparing pumps with him) about what you were to do with your raw materials when they came into your ports in return for your drain of gold. Mr Toots, to whom the question seemed perplexing, suggested 'Cook 'em.' But Mr Baps did not appear to think that would do.

Paul now slipped away from the cushioned corner of a sofa, which had been his post of observation, and went down stairs into the tea-room to be ready for Florence, whom he had not seen for nearly a fortnight, as he had remained at Doctor Blimber's on the previous Saturday and Sunday, lest he should take cold. Presently she came: looking so beautiful in her simple ball dress, with her fresh flowers in her hand, that when she knelt down on the ground to take Paul round the neck and kiss him (for there was no one there, but his friend and another young woman waiting to serve out the tea), he could hardly make up his mind to let her go again, or to take away her bright, and loving eyes from his face.

'But what is the matter, Floy?' asked Paul, almost sure that he saw a tear there.

'Nothing, darling; nothing,' returned Florence.

Paul touched her cheek gently with his finger—and it *was* a tear! 'Why, Floy!' said he.

'We'll go home together, and I'll nurse you, love,' said Florence.

'Nurse me!' echoed Paul.

Paul couldn't understand what that had to do with it, nor why the two young women looked on so seriously, nor why Florence turned away her face for a moment, and then turned it back, lighted up again with smiles.

'Floy,' said Paul, holding a ringlet of her dark hair in his hand. 'Tell me, dear. Do *you* think I have grown old-fashioned?'

His sister laughed, and fondled him, and told him 'No.'

'Because I know they say so,' returned Paul, 'and I want to know what they mean, Floy.'

But a loud double knock coming at the door, and Florence hurrying to the table, there was no more said between them. Paul wondered again when he saw his friend whisper to Florence, as if she were comforting her; but a new arrival put that out of his head speedily.

It was Sir Barnet Skettles, Lady Skettles, and Master Skettles. Master Skettles was to be a new boy after the vacation, and Fame had been busy, in Mr Feeder's room, with his father, who was in the House of Commons, and of whom Mr Feeder had said that when he *did* catch the Speaker's eye (which he had been expected to do for three or four years), it was anticipated that he would rather touch up the Radicals.

'And what room is this now, for instance?' said Lady Skettles to Paul's friend, 'Melia.

'Doctor Blimber's study, Ma'am,' was the reply.

Lady Skettles took a panoramic survey of it through her glass, and said to Sir Barnet Skettles, with a nod of approval, 'Very good.' Sir Barnet assented, but Master Skettles looked suspicious and doubtful.

'And this little creature, now,' said Lady Skettles, turning to Paul. 'Is he one of the—'

'Young gentlemen, Ma'am; yes, Ma'am,' said Paul's friend.

'And what is your name, my pale child?' said Lady Skettles.

'Dombey,' answered Paul.

Sir Barnet Skettles immediately interposed, and said that he had had the honour of meeting Paul's father at a public dinner, and that he hoped he was very well. Then Paul heard him say to Lady Skettles, 'City—very rich—most respectable—Doctor mentioned it.' And then he said to Paul, 'Will you tell your good Papa that Sir Barnet Skettles rejoiced to hear that he was very well, and sent him his best compliments?'

'Yes, Sir,' answered Paul.

'That is my brave boy,' said Sir Barnet Skettles. 'Barnet,' to Master Skettles, who was revenging himself for the studies to come, on the plum-cake, 'this is a young gentleman you ought to know. This is a young gentleman you *may* know, Barnet,' said Sir Barnet Skettles, with an emphasis on the permission.

'What eyes! What hair! What a lovely face!' exclaimed Lady Skettles softly, as she looked at Florence through her glass.

'My sister,' said Paul, presenting her.

The satisfaction of the Skettleses was now complete. And as Lady Skettles had conceived, at first sight, a liking for Paul, they all went up stairs together: Sir Barnet Skettles taking care of Florence, and young Barnet following.

Young Barnet did not remain long in the background after they had reached the drawing-room, for Doctor Blimber had him out in no time, dancing with Florence. He did not appear to Paul to be particularly happy, or particularly anything but sulky, or to care much what he was about; but as Paul heard Lady Skettles say to Mrs Blimber, while she beat time with her fan, that her dear boy was evidently smitten to death by that angel of a child, Miss Dombey, it would seem that Skettles Junior was in a state of bliss, without showing it.

Little Paul thought it a singular coincidence that nobody had occupied his place among the pillows; and that when he came into the room again, they should all make way for him to go back to it, remembering it was his. Nobody stood before him either, when they observed that he liked to see Florence dancing, but they left the space in front quite clear, so that he might follow her with his eyes. They were so kind, too, even the strangers, of whom there were soon a great many, that they came and spoke to him every now and then, and asked him how he was, and if his head ached, and whether he was tired. He was very much obliged to them for all their kindness and attention, and reclining propped up in his corner, with Mrs Blimber and Lady Skettles on the same sofa, Florence coming and sitting by his side as soon as every dance was ended, he looked on very happily indeed.

Florence would have sat by him all night, and would not have danced at all of her own accord, but Paul made her, by telling her how much it pleased him. And he told her the truth, too; for his small heart swelled, and his face glowed, when he saw how much they all admired her, and how she was the beautiful little rosebud of the room.

From his nest among the pillows, Paul could see and hear almost everything that passed, as if the whole were being done for his amusement. Among other little incidents that he observed, he observed Mr Baps the dancing-master get into conversation with Sir Barnet Skettles, and very soon ask him, as he had asked Mr Toots, what you were to do with your raw materials, when they came into your ports in return for your drain of gold—which was such a mystery to Paul that he was quite desirous to know what ought to be done with them. Sir Barnet Skettles had much to say upon the question, and said it; but it did not appear to solve the question, for Mr Baps retorted, Yes, but supposing Russia stepped in with her tallows; which struck Sir Barnet almost dumb, for he could only shake his head after that, and say, why then you must fall back upon your cottons, he supposed.

Sir Barnet Skettles looked after Mr Baps when he went to cheer up Mrs Baps (who, being quite deserted, was pretending to look over the music-book of the gentleman who played the harp), as if he thought him a remarkable kind of man; and shortly afterwards he said so in those words to Doctor Blimber, and inquired if he might take the liberty of asking who he was, and whether he had ever been in the Board of Trade. Doctor Blimber answered no, he believed not; and that in fact he was a Professor of —

'Of something connected with statistics, I'll swear?' observed Sir Barnet Skettles.

'Why no, Sir Barnet,' replied Doctor Blimber, rubbing his chin. 'No, not exactly.'

'Figures of some sort, I would venture a bet,' said Sir Barnet Skettles.

'Why yes,' said Doctor Blimber, 'yes, but not of that sort. Mr Baps is a very worthy sort of man, Sir Barnet, and—in fact he's our professor of dancing.'

Paul was amazed to see that this piece of information quite altered Sir Barnet Skettles' opinion of Mr Baps, and that Sir Barnet flew into a perfect rage, and glowered at Mr Baps over on the other side of the room. He even went so far as to D Mr Baps to Lady Skettles, in telling her what had happened, and to say that it was like his most con-summate and con-foun-ded impudence.

There was another thing that Paul observed. Mr Feeder, after imbibing several custard-cups of negus, began to enjoy himself. The dancing in general was ceremonious, and the music rather solemn—a little like church music in fact—but after the custard-cups, Mr Feeder told Mr Toots that he was going to throw a little spirit into the thing. After that, Mr Feeder not only began to dance as if he meant dancing and nothing else, but secretly to stimulate the music to perform wild tunes. Further, he became particular in his attentions to the ladies; and dancing with Miss Blimber, whispered to her—whispered to her!—though not so softly but that Paul heard him say this remarkable poetry,

'Had I a heart for falsehood framed,
I ne'er could injure YOU!'

This, Paul heard him repeat to four young ladies in succession. Well might Mr Feeder say to Mr Toots, that he was afraid he should be the worse for it to-morrow!

Mrs Blimber was a little alarmed by this—comparatively speaking—profligate behaviour; and especially by the alteration in the character of the music, which, beginning to comprehend low melodies that were popular in the streets, might not unnaturally be supposed to give offence to Lady Skettles. But Lady Skettles was so very kind as to beg Mrs Blimber not to mention it; and to receive her explanation that Mr Feeder's spirits sometimes betrayed him into excesses on these occasions, with the greatest courtesy and politeness; observing, that he seemed a very nice sort of person for his situation, and that she particularly liked the unassuming style of his hair—which (as already hinted) was about a quarter of an inch long.

Once, when there was a pause in the dancing, Lady Skettles told Paul that he seemed very fond of music. Paul replied that he was; and if she was too, she ought to hear his sister, Florence, sing. Lady Skettles presently discovered that she was dying with anxiety to have that gratification; and though Florence was at first very much frightened at being asked to sing before so many people, and begged earnestly to be excused, yet, on Paul calling her to him, and saying, 'Do, Floy! Please! For me, my dear!' she went straight to the piano, and began. When they all drew a little away, that Paul might see her; and when he saw her sitting there all alone, so young, and good, and beautiful, and kind to him; and heard her thrilling voice, so natural and sweet, and such a golden link between him and all his life's love and happiness, rising out of the silence; he turned his face away, and hid his tears. Not, as he told them when they spoke to him, not that the music was too plaintive or too sorrowful, but it was so dear to him.

They all loved Florence! How could they help it! Paul had known beforehand that they must and would; and sitting in his cushioned corner, with calmly folded hands, and one leg loosely doubled under him, few would have thought what triumph and delight expanded his childish bosom while he watched her, or what a sweet tranquillity he felt. Lavish encomiums on 'Dombey's sister' reached his ears from all the boys: admiration of the self-possessed and modest little beauty was on every lip: reports of her intelligence and accomplishments floated past him, constantly; and, as if borne in upon the air of the summer night, there was a half-intelligible sentiment diffused around, referring to Florence and himself, and breathing sympathy for both, that soothed and touched him.

He did not know why. For all that the child observed, and felt, and thought, that night—the present and the absent; what was then and what had been—were blended like the colours in the rainbow, or in the plumage of rich birds when the sun is shining on them, or in the softening sky when the same sun is setting. The many things he had had to think of lately, passed before him in the music; not as claiming his attention over again, or as likely evermore to occupy it, but as peacefully disposed of and gone. A solitary window, gazed through years ago, looked out upon an ocean, miles and miles away; upon its waters, fancies, busy with him only yesterday, were hushed and lulled to rest like broken waves. The same mysterious murmur he had wondered at, when lying on his couch upon the beach, he thought he still heard sounding through his sister's song, and through the hum of voices, and the tread of feet, and having some part in the faces flitting by, and even in the heavy gentleness of Mr Toots, who frequently came up to shake him by the hand. Through the universal kindness he still thought he heard it speaking to him; and even his old-fashioned reputation seemed to be allied to it, he knew not how. Thus little Paul sat musing, listening, looking on, and dreaming; and was very happy.

Until the time arrived for taking leave: and then, indeed, there was a sensation in the party. Sir Barnet Skettles brought up Skettles Junior to shake hands with him, and asked him if he would remember to tell his good Papa, with his best compliments, that he, Sir Barnet Skettles, had said he hoped the two young gentlemen would become intimately acquainted. Lady Skettles kissed him, and parted his hair upon his brow, and held him in her arms; and even Mrs Baps—poor Mrs Baps! Paul was glad of that—came over from beside the music-book of the gentleman who played the harp, and took leave of him quite as heartily as anybody in the room.

'Good-bye, Doctor Blimber,' said Paul, stretching out his hand.

'Good-bye, my little friend,' returned the Doctor.

'I'm very much obliged to you, Sir,' said Paul, looking innocently up into his awful face. 'Ask them to take care of Diogenes, if you please.'

Diogenes was the dog; who had never in his life received a friend into his confidence, before Paul. The Doctor promised that every attention should be paid to Diogenes in Paul's absence, and Paul having again thanked him, and shaken hands with him, bade adieu to Mrs Blimber and Cornelia with such heartfelt earnestness that Mrs Blimber forgot from that moment to mention Cicero to Lady Skettles, though she had fully intended it all the evening. Cornelia, taking both Paul's hands in hers, said, 'Dombey, Dombey, you have always been my favourite pupil. God bless you!' And it showed, Paul thought, how easily one might do injustice to a person; for Miss Blimber meant it—though she *was* a Forcer.

A buzz then went round among the young gentlemen, of 'Dombey's going!' 'Little Dombey's going!' and there was a general move after Paul and Florence down the staircase and into the hall, in which the whole Blimber family were included. Such a circumstance, Mr Feeder said aloud, as had never happened in the case of any former young gentleman within his experience; but it would be difficult to say if this were sober fact or custard-cups. The servants, with the butler at their head, had all an interest in seeing Little Dombey go; and even the weak-eyed young man, taking out his books and trunks to the coach that was to carry him and Florence to Mrs Pipchin's for the night, melted visibly.

Not even the influence of the softer passion on the young gentlemen—and they all, to a boy, doated on Florence—could restrain them from taking quite a noisy leave of Paul; waving hats after him, pressing down stairs to shake hands with him, crying individually 'Dombey, don't forget me!' and indulging in many such ebullitions of feeling, uncommon among those young Chesterfields. Paul whispered Florence, as she wrapped him up before the door was opened. Did she hear them? Would she ever forget it? Was she glad to know it? And a lively delight was in his eyes as he spoke to her.

Once, for a last look, he turned and gazed upon the faces thus addressed to him, surprised to see how shining and how bright, and numerous they were, and how they were all piled and heaped up, as faces are at crowded theatres. They swam before him as he looked, like faces in an agitated glass; and next moment he was in the dark coach outside, holding close to Florence. From that time, whenever he thought of Doctor Blimber's, it came back as he had seen it in this last view; and it never seemed to be a real place again, but always a dream full of eyes.

DAVID COPPERFIELD

David Copperfield is very young when his widowed mother, an inexperienced and gentle creature, is courted by Mr Murdstone, a gentleman to whom the young boy takes an instant dislike. David is packed off to Yarmouth with Peggotty, his mother's devoted servant, and passes there a happy fortnight in the company of Peggotty's bachelor brother, Mr Peggotty, and her orphaned niece and nephew, Little Em'ly and Ham, and Mrs Gummidge, the widow of Mr Peggotty's partner. He returns home to find his bedroom moved, a huge, angry dog installed in the yard—and his mother and Mr Murdstone married ...

If the room to which my bed was removed were a sentient thing that could give evidence, I might appeal to it at this day—who sleeps there now, I wonder!—to bear witness for me what a heavy heart I carried to it. I went up there, hearing the dog in the yard bark after me all the way while I climbed the stairs; and, looking as blank and strange upon the room as the room looked upon me, sat down with my small hands crossed, and thought.

I thought of the oddest things. Of the shape of the room, of the cracks in the ceiling, of the paper on the wall, of the flaws in the window-glass making ripples and dimples on the prospect, of the washing-stand being ricketty on its three legs, and having a discontented something about it, which reminded me of Mrs Gummidge under the influence of the old one. I was crying all the time, but, except that I was conscious of being cold and dejected, I am sure I never thought why I cried. At last in my desolation I began to consider that I was dreadfully in love with little Em'ly, and had been torn away from her to come here where no one seemed to want me, or to care about me, half as much as she did. This made such a very miserable piece of business of it, that I rolled myself up in a corner of the counterpane, and cried myself to sleep.

I was awakened by somebody saying 'Here he is!' and uncovering my hot head. My mother and Peggotty had come to look for me, and it was one of them who had done it.

'Davy,' said my mother. 'What's the matter?'

I thought it was very strange that she should ask me, and answered, 'Nothing.' I turned over on my face, I recollect, to hide my trembling lip, which answered her with greater truth.

'Davy,' said my mother. 'Davy, my child!'

I dare say no words she could have uttered would have affected me so much, then, as her calling me her child. I hid my tears in the bedclothes, and pressed her from me with my hand, when she would have raised me up.

'This is your doing, Peggotty, you cruel thing!' said my mother. 'I have no doubt at all about it. How can you reconcile it to your conscience, I wonder, to prejudice my own boy against me, or against anybody, who is dear to me? What do you mean by it, Peggotty?'

Poor Peggotty lifted up her hands and eyes, and only answered, in a sort of paraphrase of the grace I usually repeated after dinner, 'Lord forgive you, Mrs Copperfield, and for what you have said this minute, may you never be truly sorry!'

'It's enough to distract me,' cried my mother. 'In my honeymoon, too, when my most inveterate enemy might relent, one would think, and not envy me a little peace of mind and happiness. Davy, you naughty boy! Peggotty, you savage creature! Oh, dear me!' cried my mother, turning from one of us to the other, in her pettish, wilful manner. 'What a troublesome world this is, when one has the most right to expect it to be as agreeable as possible!'

I felt the touch of a hand that I knew was neither hers nor Peggotty's, and slipped to my feet at the bed-side. It was Mr Murdstone's hand, and he kept it on my arm as he said:

'What's this? Clara, my love, have you forgotten?—Firmness, my dear!'

'I am very sorry, Edward,' said my mother. 'I meant to be very good, but I am so uncomfortable.'

'Indeed!' he answered. 'That's a bad hearing, so soon, Clara.'

'I say it's very hard I should be made so now,' returned my mother, pouting; 'and it is—very hard—isn't it?'

He drew her to him, whispered in her ear, and kissed her. I knew as well, when I saw my mother's head lean down upon his shoulder, and her arm touch his neck—I knew as well that he could mould her pliant nature into any form he chose, as I know, now, that he did it.

'Go you below, my love,' said Mr Murdstone. 'David and I will come down, together. My friend,' turning a darkening face on Peggotty, when he had watched my mother out, and dismissed her with a nod and a smile; 'do you know your mistress's name?'

'She has been my mistress a long time, sir,' answered Peggotty, 'I ought to know it.'

'That's true,' he answered. 'But I thought I heard you, as I came up-stairs, address her by a name that is not hers. She has taken mine, you know. Will you remember that?'

Peggotty, with some uneasy glances at me, curtseyed herself out of the room without replying: seeing, I suppose, that she was expected to go, and had no excuse for remaining. When we two were left alone, he shut the door, and sitting on a chair, and holding me standing before him, looked steadily into my eyes. I felt my own attracted, no less steadily, to his. As I recall our being opposed thus, face to face, I seem again to hear my heart beat fast and high.

'David,' he said, making his lips thin, by pressing them together, 'if I have an obstinate horse or dog to deal with, what do you think I do?'

'I don't know.'

'I beat him.'

I had answered in a kind of breathless whisper, but I felt, in my silence, that my breath was shorter now.

'I make him wince, and smart. I say to myself, "I'll conquer that fellow;" and if it were to cost him all the blood he had, I should do it. What is that upon your face?'

'Dirt,' I said.

He knew it was the mark of tears as well as I. But if he had asked the question twenty times, each time with twenty blows, I believe my baby heart would have burst before I would have told him so.

'You have a good deal of intelligence for a little fellow,' he said, with a grave smile that belonged to him, 'and you understood me very well, I see. Wash that face, sir, and come down with me.'

He pointed to the washing-stand, which I had made out to be like Mrs Gummidge, and motioned me with his head to obey him directly. I had little doubt then, and I have less doubt now, that he would have knocked me down without the least compunction, if I had hesitated.

'Clara, my dear,' he said, when I had done his bidding, and he walked me into the parlour, with his hand still on my arm; 'you will not be made uncomfortable any more, I hope. We shall soon improve our youthful humours.'

God help me, I might have been improved for my whole life, I might have been made another creature perhaps, for life, by a kind word at that season. A word of encouragement and explanation, of pity for my childish ignorance, of welcome home, of reassurance to me that it *was* home, might have made me dutiful to him in my heart henceforth, instead of in my hypocritical outside, and might have made me respect instead of hate him. I thought my mother was sorry to see me standing in the room so sacred and strange, and that, presently, when I stole to a chair, she followed me with her eyes more sorrowfully still—missing, perhaps, some freedom in my childish tread—but the word was not spoken, and the time for it was gone.

We dined alone, we three together. He seemed to be very fond of my mother—I am afraid I liked him none the better for that—and she was very fond of him. I gathered from what they said, that an elder sister of his was coming to stay with them, and that she was expected that evening. I am not certain whether I found out then or afterwards, that, without being actively concerned in any business, he had some share in, or some annual charge upon the profits of, a wine-merchant's house in London, with which his family had been connected from his great-grandfather's time, and in which his sister had a similar interest; but I may mention it in this place, whether or no.

After dinner, when we were sitting by the fire, and I was meditating an escape to Peggotty without having the hardihood to slip away, lest it should offend the master of the house, a coach drove up to the garden-gate, and he went out to receive the visitor. My mother followed him. I was timidly following her, when she turned round at the parlour-door, in the dusk, and taking me in her embrace as she had been used to do, whispered me to love my new father and be obedient to him. She did this hurriedly and secretly, as if it were wrong, but tenderly; and, putting out her hand behind her, held mine in it, until we came near to where he was standing in the garden, where she let mine go, and drew hers through his arm.

It was Miss Murdstone who was arrived, and a gloomy-looking lady she was; dark, like her brother, whom she greatly resembled in face and voice; and with very heavy eyebrows, nearly meeting over her large nose, as if, being disabled by the wrongs of her sex from wearing whiskers, she had carried them to that account. She brought with her two uncompromising hard black boxes, with her initials on the lids in hard brass nails. When she paid the coachman she took her money out of a hard steel purse, and she kept the purse in a very jail of a bag which hung upon her arm by a heavy chain, and shut up like a bite. I had never, at that time, seen such a metallic lady altogether as Miss Murdstone was.

She was brought into the parlour with many tokens of welcome, and there formally recognised my mother as a new and near relation. Then she looked at me, and said:

'Is that your boy, sister-in-law?'

My mother acknowledged me.

'Generally speaking,' said Miss Murdstone, 'I don't like boys. How d'ye do, boy?'

Under these encouraging circumstances, I replied that I was very well, and that I hoped she was the same; with such an indifferent grace, that Miss Murdstone disposed of me in two words:

'Wants manner!'

Having uttered which with great distinctness, she begged the favour of being shown to her room, which became to me from that time forth a place of awe and dread, wherein the two black boxes were never seen open or known to be left unlocked, and where (for I peeped in once or twice when she was out) numerous little steel fetters and rivets, with which Miss Murdstone embellished herself when she was dressed, generally hung upon the looking-glass in formidable array.

As well as I could make out, she had come for good, and had no intention of ever going again. She began to 'help' my mother next morning, and was in and out of the store-closet all day, putting things to rights, and making havoc in the old arrangements. Almost the first remarkable thing I observed in Miss Murdstone was, her being constantly haunted by a suspicion that the servants had a man secreted somewhere on the premises. Under the influence of this delusion, she dived into the coal-cellar at the most untimely hours, and scarcely ever opened the door of a dark cupboard without clapping it to again, in the belief that she had got him.

Though there was nothing very airy about Miss Murdstone, she was a perfect lark in point of getting up. She was up (and, as I believe to this hour, looking for that man) before anybody in the house was stirring. Peggotty gave it as her opinion that she even slept with one eye open; but I could not concur in this idea; for I tried it myself after hearing the suggestion thrown out, and found it couldn't be done.

On the very first morning after her arrival she was up and ringing her bell at cock-crow. When my mother came down to breakfast and was going to make the tea, Miss Murdstone gave her a kind of peck on the cheek, which was her nearest approach to a kiss, and said:

'Now, Clara, my dear, I am come here, you know, to relieve you of all the trouble I can. You're much too pretty and thoughtless'—my mother blushed but laughed, and seemed not to dislike this character—'to have any duties imposed upon you that can be undertaken by me. If you'll be so good as give me your keys, my dear, I'll attend to all this sort of thing in future.'

From that time, Miss Murdstone kept the keys in her own little jail all day, and under her pillow all night, and my mother had no more to do with them than I had.

My mother did not suffer her authority to pass from her without a shadow of protest. One night when Miss Murdstone had been developing certain household plans to her brother, of which he signified his approbation, my mother suddenly began to cry, and said she thought she might have been consulted.

'Clara!' said Mr Murdstone sternly. 'Clara! I wonder at you.'

'Oh, it's very well to say you wonder, Edward!' cried my mother, 'and it's very well for you to talk about firmness, but you wouldn't like it yourself.'

Firmness, I may observe, was the grand quality on which both Mr and Miss Murdstone took their stand. However I might have expressed my comprehension of it at that time, if I had been called upon, I nevertheless did clearly comprehend in my own way, that it was another name for tyranny; and for a certain gloomy, arrogant, devil's humour, that was in them both. The creed, as I should state it now, was this. Mr Murdstone was firm; nobody in his world was to be so firm as Mr Murdstone; nobody else in his world was to be firm at all, for everybody was to be bent to his firmness. Miss Murdstone was an exception. She might be firm, but only by relationship, and in an inferior and tributary degree. My mother was another exception. She might be firm, and must be; but only in bearing their firmness, and firmly believing there was no other firmness upon earth.

'It's very hard,' said my mother, 'that in my own house—'

'*My* own house?' repeated Mr Murdstone. 'Clara!'

'*Our* own house, I mean,' faltered my mother, evidently frightened—'I hope you must know what I mean, Edward—it's very hard that in *your* own house I may not have a word to say about domestic matters. I am sure I managed very well before we were married. There's evidence,' said my mother sobbing; 'ask Peggotty if I didn't do very well when I wasn't interfered with!'

'Edward,' said Miss Murdstone, 'let there be an end of this. I go to-morrow.'

'Jane Murdstone,' said her brother, 'be silent! How dare you to insinuate that you don't know my character better than your words imply?'

'I am sure,' my poor mother went on at a grievous disadvantage, and with many tears, 'I don't want anybody to go. I should be very miserable and unhappy if anybody was to go. I don't ask much. I am not unreasonable. I only want to be consulted sometimes. I am very much obliged to anybody who assists me, and I only want to be consulted as a mere form, sometimes. I thought you were pleased, once, with my being a little inexperienced and girlish, Edward—I am sure you said so—but you seem to hate me for it now, you are so severe.'

'Edward,' said Miss Murdstone, again, 'let there be an end of this. I go to-morrow.'

'Jane Murdstone,' thundered Mr Murdstone. 'Will you be silent? How dare you?'

Miss Murdstone made a jail-delivery of her pocket-handkerchief, and held it before her eyes.

'Clara,' he continued, looking at my mother, 'you surprise me! You astound me! Yes, I had a satisfaction in the thought of marrying an inexperienced and artless person, and forming her character, and infusing into it some amount of that firmness and decision of which it stood in need. But when Jane Murdstone is kind enough to come to my assistance in this endeavour, and to assume, for my sake, a condition something like a housekeeper's, and when she meets with a base return—'

'Oh, pray, pray, Edward,' cried my mother, 'don't accuse me of being ungrateful. I am sure I am not ungrateful. No one ever said I was before. I have many faults, but not that. Oh, don't, my dear!'

'When Jane Murdstone meets, I say,' he went on, after waiting until my mother was silent, 'with a base return, that feeling of mine is chilled and altered.'

'Don't, my love, say that!' implored my mother very piteously. 'Oh, don't, Edward! I can't bear to hear it. Whatever I am, I am affectionate. I know I am affectionate. I wouldn't say it, if I wasn't sure that I am. Ask Peggotty. I am sure she'll tell you I'm affectionate.'

'There is no extent of mere weakness, Clara,' said Mr Murdstone in reply, 'that can have the least weight with me. You lose breath.'

'Pray let us be friends,' said my mother, 'I couldn't live under coldness or unkindness. I am so sorry. I have a great many defects, I know, and it's very good of you, Edward, with your strength of mind, to endeavour to correct them for me. Jane, I don't object to anything.

I should be quite broken-hearted if you thought of leaving—' My mother was too much overcome to go on.

'Jane Murdstone,' said Mr Murdstone to his sister, 'any harsh words between us are, I hope, uncommon. It is not my fault that so unusual an occurrence has taken place tonight. I was betrayed into it by another. Nor is it your fault. You were betrayed into it by another. Let us both try to forget it. And as this,' he added, after these magnanimous words, 'is not a fit scene for the boy—David, go to bed!'

I could hardly find the door, through the tears that stood in my eyes. I was so sorry for my mother's distress; but I groped my way out, and groped my way up to my room in the dark, without even having the heart to say good night to Peggotty, or to get a candle from her. When her coming up to look for me, an hour or so afterwards, awoke me, she said that my mother had gone to bed poorly, and that Mr and Miss Murdstone were sitting alone.

Going down next morning rather earlier than usual, I paused outside the parlour-door, on hearing my mother's voice. She was very earnestly and humbly entreating Miss Murdstone's pardon, which that lady granted, and a perfect reconciliation took place. I never knew my mother afterwards to give an opinion on any matter, without first appealing to Miss Murdstone, or without having first ascertained by some sure means, what Miss Murdstone's opinion was; and I never saw Miss Murdstone, when out of temper (she was infirm that way), move her hand towards her bag as if she were going to take out the keys and offer to resign them to my mother, without seeing that my mother was in a terrible fright.

The gloomy taint that was in the Murdstone blood, darkened the Murdstone religion, which was austere and wrathful. I have thought, since, that its assuming that character was a necessary consequence of Mr Murdstone's firmness, which wouldn't allow him to let anybody off from the utmost weight of the severest penalties he could find any excuse for. Be this as it may, I well remember the tremendous visages with which we used to go to church, and the changed air of the place. Again the dreaded Sunday comes round, and I file into the old pew first, like a guarded captive brought to a condemned service. Again, Miss Murdstone, in a black velvet gown, that looks as if it had been made out of a pall, follows close upon me; then my mother; then her husband. There is no Peggotty now, as in the old time. Again, I listen to Miss Murdstone mumbling the responses, and emphasising all the dread words with cruel relish. Again, I see her dark eyes roll round the church when she says 'miserable sinners,' as if she were calling all the congregation names.

Again, I catch rare glimpses of my mother, moving her lips timidly between the two, with one of them muttering at each ear like low thunder. Again, I wonder with a sudden fear whether it is likely that our good old clergyman can be wrong, and Mr and Miss Murdstone right, and that all the angels in Heaven can be destroying angels. Again, if I move a finger or relax a muscle of my face, Miss Murdstone pokes me with her prayer-book, and makes my side ache.

Yes, and again, as we walk home, I note some neighbours looking at my mother and at me, and whispering. Again, as the three go on arm-in-arm, and I linger behind alone, I follow some of those looks, and wonder if my mother's step be really not so light as I have seen it, and if the gaiety of her beauty be really almost worried away. Again, I wonder whether any of the neighbours call to mind, as I do, how we used to walk home together, she and I; and I wonder stupidly about that, all the dreary, dismal day.

There had been some talk on occasions of my going to boarding-school. Mr and Miss Murdstone had originated it, and my mother had of course agreed with them. Nothing, however, was concluded on the subject yet. In the meantime, I learnt lessons at home.

Shall I ever forget those lessons! They were presided over nominally by my mother, but really by Mr Murdstone and his sister, who were always present, and found them a favourable occasion for giving my mother lessons in that miscalled firmness, which was the bane of both our lives. I believe I was kept at home for that purpose. I had been apt enough to learn, and willing enough, when my mother and I had lived alone together. I can faintly remember learning the alphabet at her knee. To this day, when I look upon the fat black letters in the primer, the puzzling novelty of their shapes, and the easy good-nature of O and Q and S, seem to present themselves again before me as they used to do. But they recall no feeling of disgust or reluctance. On the contrary, I seem to have walked along a path of flowers as far as the crocodile-book, and to have been cheered by the gentleness of my mother's voice and manner all the way. But these solemn lessons which succeeded those, I remember as the death-blow at my peace, and a grievous daily drudgery and misery. They were very long, very numerous, very hard—perfectly unintelligible, some of them, to me—and I was generally as much bewildered by them as I believe my poor mother was herself.

Let me remember how it used to be, and bring one morning back again.

I come into the second-best parlour after breakfast, with my books, and an exercise-book, and a slate. My mother is ready for me at her writing-desk, but not half so ready as Mr Murdstone in his easy-chair by the window (though he pretends to be reading a book), or as Miss Murdstone, sitting near my mother stringing steel beads. The very sight of those two has such an influence over me, that I begin to feel the words I have been at infinite pains to get into my head, all sliding away, and going I don't know where. I wonder where they *do* go, by-the-bye?

I hand the first book to my mother. Perhaps it is a grammar, perhaps a history or geography. I take a last drowning look at the page as I give it into her hand, and start off aloud at a racing pace while I have got it fresh. I trip over a word. Mr Murdstone looks up. I trip over another word. Miss Murdstone looks up. I redden, tumble over half-a-dozen words, and stop. I think my mother would show me the book if she dared, but she does not dare, and she says softly:

'Oh, Davy, Davy!'

'Now, Clara,' says Mr Murdstone, 'be firm with the boy. Don't say, "Oh, Davy, Davy!" That's childish. He knows his lesson, or he does not know it.'

'He does *not* know it,' Miss Murdstone interposes awfully.

'I am really afraid he does not,' says my mother.

'Then you see, Clara,' returns Miss Murdstone, 'you should just give him the book back, and make him know it.'

'Yes, certainly,' says my mother; 'that is what I intend to do, my dear Jane. Now, Davy, try once more, and don't be stupid.'

I obey the first clause of the injunction by trying once more, but am not so successful with the second, for I am very stupid. I tumble down before I get to the old place, at a point where I was all right before, and stop to think. But I can't think about the lesson. I think of the number of yards of net in Miss Murdstone's cap, or of the price of Mr Murdstone's dressing-gown, or any such ridiculous problem that I have no business with, and don't want to have anything at all to do with. Mr Murdstone makes a movement of impatience which I have been expecting for a long time. Miss Murdstone does the same. My mother glances submissively at them, shuts the book, and lays it by as an arrear to be worked out when my other tasks are done.

There is a pile of these arrears very soon, and it swells like a rolling snowball. The bigger it gets, the more stupid *I* get. The case is so hopeless, and I feel that I am wallowing in such a bog of nonsense, that I give up all idea of getting out, and abandon myself to my fate. The despairing way in which my mother and I look at each other, as I blunder on, is truly melancholy. But the greatest effect in these miserable lessons is when my mother (thinking nobody is observing her) tries to give me the cue by the motion of her lips. At that instant, Miss Murdstone, who has been lying in wait for nothing else all along, says in a deep warning voice:

'Clara!'

My mother starts, colours, and smiles faintly. Mr Murdstone comes out of his chair, takes the book, throws it at me or boxes my ears with it, and turns me out of the room by the shoulders.

Even when the lessons are done, the worst is yet to happen, in the shape of an appalling sum. This is invented for me, and delivered to me orally by Mr Murdstone, and begins, 'If I go into a cheesemonger's shop, and buy five thousand double-Gloucester cheeses at fourpence-halfpenny each, present payment'—at which I see Miss Murdstone secretly overjoyed. I pore over these cheeses without any result or enlightenment until dinner-time, when, having made a Mulatto of myself by getting the dirt of the slate into the pores of my skin, I have a slice of bread to help me out with the cheeses, and am considered in disgrace for the rest of the evening.

It seems to me, at this distance of time, as if my unfortunate studies generally took this course. I could have done very well if I had been without the Murdstones; but the influence of the Murdstones upon me was like the fascination of two snakes on a wretched young bird. Even when I did get through the morning with tolerable credit, there was not much gained but dinner; for Miss Murdstone never could endure to see me untasked, and if I rashly made any show of being unemployed, called her brother's attention to me by saying, 'Clara, my dear, there's nothing like work—give your boy an exercise;' which caused me to be clapped down to some new labour there and then. As to any recreation with other children of my age, I had very little of that; for the gloomy theology of the Murdstones made all children out to be a swarm of little vipers (though there *was* a child once set in the midst of the Disciples), and held that they contaminated one another.

The natural result of this treatment, continued, I suppose, for some six months or more, was to make me sullen, dull, and dogged. I was not made the less so, by my sense of being daily more and more shut out and alienated from my mother. I believe I should have been almost stupefied but for one circumstance.

It was this. My father had left a small collection of books in a little room up-stairs, to which I had access (for it adjoined my own) and which nobody else in our house ever troubled. From that blessed little room, Roderick Random, Peregrine Pickle, Humphry Clinker, Tom Jones, The Vicar of Wakefield, Don Quixote, Gil Blas, and Robinson

Crusoe, came out, a glorious host, to keep me company. They kept alive my fancy, and my hope of something beyond that place and time,—they, and the Arabian Nights, and the Tales of the Genii,—and did me no harm; for whatever harm was in some of them was not there for me; *I* knew nothing of it. It is astonishing to me now, how I found time, in the midst of my porings and blunderings over heavier themes, to read those books as I did. It is curious to me how I could ever have consoled myself under my small troubles (which were great troubles to me), by impersonating my favourite characters in them—as I did—and by putting Mr and Miss Murdstone into all the bad ones—which I did too. I have been Tom Jones (a child's Tom Jones, a harmless creature) for a week together. I have sustained my own idea of Roderick Random for a month at a stretch, I verily believe. I had a greedy relish for a few volumes of Voyages and Travels—I forget what, now—that were on those shelves; and for days and days I can remember to have gone about my region of our house, armed with the centre-piece out of an old set of boot-trees—the perfect realisation of Captain Somebody, of the Royal British Navy, in danger of being beset by savages, and resolved to sell his life at a great price. The Captain never lost dignity, from having his ears boxed with the Latin Grammar. I did; but the Captain was a Captain and a hero, in despite of all the grammars of all the languages in the world, dead or alive.

This was my only and my constant comfort. When I think of it, the picture always rises in my mind, of a summer evening, the boys at play in the churchyard, and I sitting on my bed, reading as if for life. Every barn in the neighbourhood, every stone in the church, and every foot of the churchyard, had some association of its own, in my mind, connected with these books, and stood for some locality made famous in them. I have seen Tom Pipes go climbing up the church-steeple; I have watched Strap, with the knapsack on his back, stopping to rest himself upon the wicket-gate; and I *know* that Commodore Trunnion held that club with Mr Pickle, in the parlour of our little village alehouse.

The reader now understands, as well as I do, what I was when I came to that point of my youthful history to which I am now coming again.

One morning when I went into the parlour with my books, I found my mother looking anxious, Miss Murdstone looking firm, and Mr Murdstone binding something round the bottom of a cane—a lithe and limber cane, which he left off binding when I came in, and poised and switched in the air.

'I tell you, Clara,' said Mr Murdstone, 'I have been often flogged myself.'

'To be sure; of course,' said Miss Murdstone.

'Certainly, my dear Jane,' faltered my mother, meekly. 'But—but do you think it did Edward good?'

'Do you think it did Edward harm, Clara?' asked Mr Murdstone, gravely.

'That's the point,' said his sister.

To this my mother returned, 'Certainly, my dear Jane,' and said no more.

I felt apprehensive that I was personally interested in this dialogue, and sought Mr Murdstone's eye as it lighted on mine.

'Now, David,' he said—and I saw that cast again as he said it—'you must be far more careful to-day than usual.' He gave the cane another poise, and another switch; and having finished his preparation of it, laid it down beside him, with an impressive look, and took up his book.

This was a good freshener to my presence of mind, as a beginning. I felt the words of my lessons slipping off, not one by one, or line by line, but by the entire page; I tried to lay hold of them; but they seemed, if I may so express it, to have put skates on, and to skim away from me with a smoothness there was no checking.

We began badly, and went on worse. I had come in with an idea of distinguishing myself rather, conceiving that I was very well prepared; but it turned out to be quite a mistake. Book after book was added to the heap of failures, Miss Murdstone being firmly watchful of us all the time. And when we came at last to the five thousand cheeses (canes he made it that day, I remember), my mother burst out crying.

'Clara!' said Miss Murdstone, in her warning voice.

'I am not quite well, my dear Jane, I think,' said my mother.

I saw him wink, solemnly, at his sister, as he rose and said, taking up the cane:

'Why, Jane, we can hardly expect Clara to bear, with perfect firmness, the worry and torment that David has occasioned her to-day. That would be stoical. Clara is greatly strengthened and improved, but we can hardly expect so much from her. David, you and I will go up-stairs, boy.'

As he took me out at the door, my mother ran towards us. Miss Murdstone said, 'Clara! are you a perfect fool?' and interfered. I saw my mother stop her ears then, and I heard her crying.

He walked me up to my room slowly and gravely—I am certain he had a delight in that formal parade of executing justice—and when we got there, suddenly twisted my head under his arm.

'Mr Murdstone! Sir!' I cried to him. 'Don't! Pray don't beat me! I have tried to learn, sir, but I can't learn while you and Miss Murdstone are by. I can't indeed!'

'Can't you, indeed, David?' he said. 'We'll try that.'

He had my head as in a vice, but I twined round him somehow, and stopped him for a moment, entreating him not to beat me. It was only for a moment that I stopped him, for he cut me heavily an instant afterwards, and in the same instant I caught the hand with which he held me in my mouth, between my teeth, and bit it through. It sets my teeth on edge to think of it.

He beat me then as if he would have beaten me to death. Above all the noise we made, I heard them running up the stairs and crying out—I heard my mother crying out—and Peggotty. Then he was gone; and the door was locked outside; and I was lying, fevered and hot, and torn, and sore, and raging in my puny way, upon the floor.

How well I recollect, when I became quiet, what an unnatural stillness seemed to reign through the whole house! How well I remember, when my smart and passion began to cool, how wicked I began to feel!

I sat listening for a long while, but there was not a sound. I crawled up from the floor, and saw my face in the glass, so swollen, red, and ugly that it almost frightened me. My stripes were sore and stiff, and made me cry afresh, when I moved; but they were nothing to the guilt I felt. It lay heavier on my breast than if I had been a most atrocious criminal, I dare say.

It had begun to grow dark, and I had shut the window (I had been lying, for the most part, with my head upon the sill, by turns crying, dozing, and looking listlessly out), when the key was turned, and Miss Murdstone came in with some bread and meat, and milk. These she put down upon the table without a word, glaring at me the while with exemplary firmness, and then retired, locking the door after her.

Long after it was dark I sat there, wondering whether anybody else would come. When this appeared improbable for that night, I undressed, and went to bed; and there, I began to wonder fearfully what would be done to me. Whether it was a criminal act that I had committed? Whether I should be taken into custody, and sent to prison? Whether I was at all in danger of being hanged?

I never shall forget the waking next morning; the being cheerful and fresh for the first moment, and then the being weighed down by the stale and dismal oppression of remembrance. Miss Murdstone reappeared before I was out of bed; told me, in so many words, that I was free to walk in the garden for half an hour and no longer; and retired, leaving the door open, that I might avail myself of that permission.

I did so, and did so every morning of my imprisonment, which lasted five days. If I could have seen my mother alone, I should have gone down on my knees to her and besought her forgiveness; but I saw no one, Miss Murdstone excepted, during the whole time—except at evening prayers in the parlour; to which I was escorted by Miss Murdstone after everybody else was placed; where I was stationed, a young outlaw, all alone by myself near the door; and whence I was solemnly conducted by my jailer, before any one arose from the devotional posture. I only observed that my mother was as far off from me as she could be, and kept her face another way, so that I never saw it; and that Mr Murdstone's hand was bound up in a large linen wrapper.

The length of those five days I can convey no idea of to any one. They occupy the place of years in my remembrance. The way in which I listened to all the incidents of the house that made themselves audible to me; the ringing of bells, the opening and shutting of doors, the murmuring of voices, the footsteps on the stairs; to any laughing, whistling, or singing, outside, which seemed more dismal than anything else to me in my solitude and disgrace—the uncertain pace of the hours, especially at night, when I would wake thinking it was morning, and find that the family were not yet gone to bed, and that all the length of night had yet to come—the depressed dreams and nightmares I had—the return of day, noon, afternoon, evening, when the boys played in the churchyard, and I watched them from a distance within the room, being ashamed to show myself at the window lest they should know I was a prisoner—the strange sensation of never hearing myself speak—the fleeting intervals of something like cheerfulness, which came with eating and drinking, and went away with it—the setting in of rain one evening, with a fresh smell, and its coming down faster and faster between me and the church, until it and gathering night seemed to quench me in gloom, and fear, and remorse—all this appears to have gone round and round for years instead of days, it is so vividly and strongly stamped on my remembrance.

On the last night of my restraint, I was awakened by hearing my own name spoken in a whisper. I started up in bed, and putting out my arms in the dark, said:

'Is that you, Peggotty?'

There was no immediate answer, but presently I heard my name again, in a tone so very mysterious and awful, that I think I should have gone into a fit, if it had not occurred to me that it must have come through the keyhole.

I groped my way to the door and putting my own lips to the keyhole whispered:

'Is that you Peggotty dear?'

'Yes, my own precious Davy' she replied. 'Be as soft as a mouse, or the Cat'll hear us.'

I understood this to mean Miss Murdstone, and was sensible of the urgency of the case; her room being close by.

'How's mama, dear Peggotty? Is she very angry with me?'

I could hear Peggotty crying softly on her side of the keyhole as I was doing on mine, before she answered. 'No. Not very.'

'What is going to be done with me, Peggotty dear? Do you know?'

'School. Near London,' was Peggotty's answer. I was obliged to get her to repeat it, for she spoke it the first time quite down my throat, in consequence of my having forgotten to take my mouth away from the keyhole and put my ear there; and though her words tickled me a good deal, I didn't hear them.

'When, Peggotty?'

'To-morrow.'

'Is that the reason why Miss Murdstone took the clothes out of my drawers?' which she had done, though I have forgotten to mention it.

'Yes' said Peggotty. 'Box.'

'Shan't I see mama?'

'Yes' said Peggotty. 'Morning.'

Then Peggotty fitted her mouth close to the keyhole, and delivered these words through it with as much feeling and earnestness as a keyhole has ever been the medium of communicating, I will venture to assert: shooting in each broken little sentence in a convulsive little burst of its own.

'Davy, dear. If I ain't been azackly as intimate with you. Lately, as I used to be. It ain't because I don't love you. Just as well and more, my pretty poppet. It's because I thought it better for you. And for some one else besides. Davy, my darling, are you listening? Can you hear?'

'Ye-ye-ye-yes, Peggotty!' I sobbed.

'My own!' said Peggotty, with infinite compassion. 'What I want to say, is. That you must never forget me. For I'll never forget you. And I'll take as much care of your mama, Davy. As ever I took of you. And I won't leave her. The day may come when she'll be glad to lay her poor head. On her stupid, cross, old Peggotty's arm again. And I'll write to you, my dear. Though I ain't no scholar. And I'll—I'll' Peggotty fell to kissing the keyhole, as she couldn't kiss me.

'Thank you, dear Peggotty!' said I. 'Oh, thank you! Thank you! Will you promise me one thing, Peggotty? Will you write and tell Mr Peggotty and little Em'ly, and Mrs Gummidge and Ham, that I am not so bad as they might suppose, and that I sent 'em all my love—especially to little Em'ly? Will you, if you please, Peggotty?'

The kind soul promised, and we both of us kissed the keyhole with the greatest affection—I patted it with my hand, I recollect, as if it had been her honest face—and parted. From that night there grew up in my breast a feeling for Peggotty which I cannot very well define. She did not replace my mother; no one could do that; but she came into a vacancy in my heart, which closed upon her, and I felt towards her something I have never felt for any other human being. It was a sort of comical affection, too; and yet if she had died, I cannot think what I should have done, or how I should have acted out the tragedy it would have been to me.

In the morning Miss Murdstone appeared as usual, and told me I was going to school; which was not altogether such news to me as she supposed. She also informed me that when I was dressed, I was to come down-stairs into the parlour, and have my breakfast. There I found my mother, very pale and with red eyes: into whose arms I ran, and begged her pardon from my suffering soul.

'Oh, Davy!' she said. 'That you could hurt any one I love! Try to be better, pray to be better! I forgive you; but I am so grieved, Davy, that you should have such bad passions in your heart.'

They had persuaded her that I was a wicked fellow, and she was more sorry for that than for my going away. I felt it sorely. I tried to eat my parting breakfast, but my tears dropped upon my bread-and-butter, and trickled into my tea. I saw my mother look at me sometimes, and then glance at the watchful Miss Murdstone, and then look down, or look away.

'Master Copperfield's box there!' said Miss Murdstone, when wheels were heard at the gate.

I looked for Peggotty, but it was not she; neither she nor Mr Murdstone appeared. My former acquaintance, the carrier, was at the door; the box was taken out to his cart, and lifted in.

'Clara!' said Miss Murdstone, in her warning note.

'Ready, my dear Jane,' returned my mother. 'Good-bye, Davy. You are going for your own good. Good-bye, my child. You will come home in the holidays, and be a better boy.'

'Clara!' Miss Murdstone repeated.

'Certainly, my dear Jane,' replied my mother, who was holding me. 'I forgive you, my dear boy. God bless you!'

'Clara!' Miss Murdstone repeated.

Miss Murdstone was good enough to take me out to the cart, and to say on the way that she hoped I would repent, before I came to a bad end; and then I got into the cart, and the lazy horse walked off with it.

BLEAK HOUSE

Lady Dedlock is one of the claimants in the case of Jarndyce and Jarndyce. One day, in the presence of the lawyer Tulkinghorn, she is startled by the sight of some handwriting on a legal document, copied by a nameless scrivener. Tulkinghorn, legal adviser to her husband, Sir Leicester, scents a mystery and his enquiries lead him to a ragged, half-starved orphan, Jo the crossing-sweeper. Jo remembers a poor, penniless scrivener who was kind to him while he lived. Lady Dedlock, meanwhile, has been pursuing her own enquiries and they also lead to Jo ...

My Lady Dedlock is restless, very restless. The astonished fashionable intelligence hardly knows where to have her. To-day, she is at Chesney Wold; yesterday she was at her house in town; to-morrow, she may be abroad, for anything the fashionable intelligence can with confidence predict. Even Sir Leicester's gallantry has some trouble to keep pace with her. It would have more, but that his other faithful ally, for better and for worse—the gout—darts into the old oak bedchamber at Chesney Wold, and grips him by both legs.

Sir Leicester receives the gout as a troublesome demon, but still a demon of the patrician order. All the Dedlocks, in the direct male line, through a course of time during and beyond which the memory of man goeth not to the contrary, have had the gout. It can be proved, sir. Other men's fathers may have died of the rheumatism, or may have taken base contagion from the tainted blood of the sick vulgar, but the Dedlock family have communicated something exclusive, even to the levelling process of dying, by dying of their own family gout. It has come down, through the illustrious line, like the plate, or the pictures, or the place in Lincolnshire. It is among their dignities. Sir Leicester is, perhaps, not wholly without an impression, though he has never resolved it into words, that the angel of death in the discharge of his necessary duties may observe to the shades of the aristocracy, 'My lords and gentlemen, I have the honour to present to you another Dedlock certified to have arrived per the family gout.'

Hence, Sir Leicester yields up his family legs to the family disorder, as if he held his name and fortune on that feudal tenure. He feels, that for a Dedlock to be laid upon his back and spasmodically twitched and stabbed in his extremities, is a liberty taken somewhere; but, he thinks, 'We have all yielded to this; it belongs to us; it has, for some hundreds of years, been understood that we are not to make the vaults in the park interesting on more ignoble terms; and I submit myself to the compromise.'

And a goodly show he makes, lying in a flush of crimson and gold, in the midst of the great drawing-room, before his favourite picture of my Lady, with broad strips of sunlight shining in, down the long perspective, through the long line of windows, and alternating with soft reliefs of shadow. Outside, the stately oaks, rooted for ages in the green ground which has never known ploughshare, but was still a Chase when kings rode to battle with sword and shield, and rode a-hunting with bow and arrow; bear witness to his greatness. Inside, his forefathers, looking on him from the walls, say, 'Each of us was a passing reality here, and left this coloured shadow of himself, and melted into remembrance as dreamy as the distant voices of the rooks now lulling you to rest;' and bear their testimony to his greatness, too. And he is very great, this day. And woe to Boythorn, or other daring wight, who shall presumptuously contest an inch with him!

My Lady is at present represented, near Sir Leicester, by her portrait. She has flitted away to town, with no intention of remaining there, and will soon flit hither again, to the confusion of the fashionable intelligence. The house in town is not prepared for her reception. It is muffled and dreary. Only one Mercury in powder, gapes disconsolate at the hall-window; and he mentioned last night to another Mercury of his acquaintance, also accustomed to good society, that if that sort of thing was to last—which it couldn't, for a man of his spirits couldn't bear it, and a man of his figure couldn't be expected to bear it—there would be no resource for him, upon his honour, but to cut his throat!

What connexion can there be, between the place in Lincolnshire, the house in town, the Mercury in powder, and the whereabout of Jo the outlaw with the broom, who had that distant ray of light upon him when he swept the churchyard-step? What connexion can there have been between many people in the innumerable histories of this world, who, from opposite sides of great gulfs, have, nevertheless, been very curiously brought together!

Jo sweeps his crossing all day long, unconscious of the link, if any link there be. He sums up his mental condition, when asked a question, by replying that he 'don't know nothink.' He knows that it's hard to keep the mud off the crossing in dirty weather, and harder still to live by doing it. Nobody taught him, even that much; he found it out.

Jo lives—that is to say, Jo has not yet died—in a ruinous place, known to the like of him by the name of Tom-all-Alone's. It is a black, dilapidated street, avoided by all decent people; where the crazy houses were seized upon, when their decay was far advanced, by some bold vagrants, who, after establishing their own possession, took to letting them out in lodgings. Now, these tumbling tenements contain, by night, a swarm of misery. As, on the ruined human wretch, vermin parasites appear, so, these ruined shelters have bred a crowd of foul existence that crawls in and out of gaps in walls and boards; and coils itself to sleep, in maggot numbers, where the rain drips in; and comes and goes, fetching and carrying fever, and sowing more evil in its every footprint than Lord Coodle, and Sir Thomas Doodle, and the Duke of Foodle, and all the fine gentlemen in office, down to Zoodle, shall set right in five hundred years—though born expressly to do it.

Twice, lately, there has been a crash and a cloud of dust, like the springing of a mine, in Tom-all-Alone's; and, each time, a house has fallen. These accidents have made a paragraph in the newspapers, and have filled a bed or two in the nearest hospital. The gaps remain, and there are not unpopular lodgings among the rubbish. As several more houses are nearly ready to go, the next crash in Tom-all-Alone's may be expected to be a good one.

This desirable property is in Chancery, of course. It would be an insult to the discernment of any man with half an eye, to tell him so. Whether 'Tom' is the popular representative of the original plaintiff or defendant in Jarndyce and Jarndyce; or, whether Tom lived here when the suit had laid the street waste, all alone, until other settlers came to join him; or, whether the traditional title is a comprehensive name for a retreat cut off from honest company and put out of the pale of hope; perhaps nobody knows. Certainly, Jo don't know.

'For *I* don't,' says Jo; '*I* don't know nothink.'

It must be a strange state to be like Jo! To shuffle through the streets, unfamiliar with the shapes, and in utter darkness as to the meaning, of those mysterious symbols, so abundant over the shops, and at the corners of streets, and on the doors, and in the windows! To see people read, and to see people write, and to see the postman deliver letters, and not to have the least idea of all that language—to be, to every scrap of it, stone blind and dumb! It must be very puzzling to see the good company going to the churches on Sundays, with their books in their hands, and to think (for perhaps Jo *does* think, at odd times) what does it all mean, and if it means anything to anybody, how comes it that it means nothing to me? To be hustled, and jostled, and moved on; and really to feel that it would appear to be perfectly true that I have no business, here, or there, or anywhere; and yet to be perplexed by the consideration that I *am* here somehow, too, and everybody overlooked me until I became the creature that I am! It must be a strange state, not merely to be told that I am scarcely human (as in the case of my offering myself for a witness), but to feel it of my own knowledge all my life! To see the horses, dogs, and cattle, go by me, and to know that in ignorance I belong to them, and not to the superior beings in my shape, whose delicacy I offend! Jo's ideas of a Criminal Trial, or a Judge, or a Bishop, or a Government, or that inestimable jewel to him (if he only knew) the Constitution, should be strange! His whole material and immaterial life is wonderfully strange; his death, the strangest thing of all.

Jo comes out of Tom-all-Alone's, meeting the tardy morning which is always late in getting down there, and munches his dirty bit of bread as he comes along. His way lying through many streets, and the houses not yet being open, he sits down to breakfast on the door-step of the Society for the Propagation of the Gospel in Foreign Parts, and gives it a brush when he has finished, as an acknowledgment of the accommodation. He admires the size of the edifice, and wonders what it's all about. He has no idea, poor wretch, of the spiritual destitution of a coral reef in the Pacific, or what it costs to look up the precious souls among the cocoa-nuts and bread-fruit.

He goes to his crossing, and begins to lay it out for the day. The town awakes; the great tee-totum is set up for its daily spin and whirl; all that unaccountable reading and writing, which has been suspended for a few hours, recommences. Jo, and the other lower animals, get on in the unintelligible mess as they can. It is market-day. The blinded oxen, over-goaded, over-driven, never guided, run into wrong places and are beaten out; and plunge, red-eyed and foaming, at stone walls; and often sorely hurt the innocent, and often sorely hurt themselves. Very like Jo and his order; very, very like!

A band of music comes and plays. Jo listens to it. So does a dog—a drover's dog, waiting for his master outside a butcher's shop, and evidently thinking about those sheep he has had upon his mind for some hours, and is happily rid of. He seems perplexed respecting three or four; can't remember where he left them; looks up and down the street, as half expecting to see them astray; suddenly pricks up his ears and remembers all about it. A thoroughly vagabond dog, accustomed to low company and public-houses; a terrific dog to sheep; ready at a whistle to scamper over their backs, and tear out mouthfuls of their wool; but an educated, improved, developed dog, who has been taught his duties and knows how to discharge them. He and Jo listen to the music, probably with much the same amount of animal satisfaction; likewise, as to awakened association, aspiration or regret, melancholy or joyful reference to things beyond the senses, they are probably upon a par. But, otherwise, how far above the human listener is the brute!

Turn that dog's descendants wild, like Jo, and in a very few years they will so degenerate that they will lose even their bark—but not their bite.

The day changes as it wears itself away, and becomes dark and drizzly. Jo fights it out, at his crossing, among the mud and wheels, the horses, whips, and umbrellas, and gets but a scanty sum to pay for the unsavoury shelter of Tom-all-Alone's. Twilight comes on; gas begins to start up in the shops; the lamplighter, with his ladder, runs along the margin of the pavement. A wretched evening is beginning to close in.

In his chambers, Mr Tulkinghorn sits meditating an application to the nearest magistrate to-morrow morning for a warrant. Gridley, a disappointed suitor, has been here to-day, and has been alarming. We are not to be put in bodily fear, and that ill-conditioned fellow shall be held to bail again. From the ceiling, foreshortened Allegory, in the person of one impossible Roman upside down, points with the arm of Samson (out of joint, and an odd one) obtrusively toward the window. Why should Mr Tulkinghorn, for such no reason, look out of window? Is the hand not always pointing there? So he does not look out of window.

And if he did, what would it be to see a woman going by? There are women enough in the world, Mr Tulkinghorn thinks—too many; they are at the bottom of all that goes wrong in it, though, for the matter of that, they create business for lawyers. What would it be to see a woman going by, even though she were going secretly? They are all secret. Mr Tulkinghorn knows that, very well.

But they are not all like the woman who now leaves him and his house behind; between whose plain dress, and her refined manner, there is something exceedingly inconsistent. She should be an upper servant by her attire, yet, in her air and step, though both are hurried and assumed—as far as she can assume in the muddy streets, which she treads with an unaccustomed foot—she is a lady. Her face is veiled, and still she sufficiently betrays herself to make more than one of those who pass her look round sharply.

She never turns her head. Lady or servant, she has a purpose in her, and can follow it. She never turns her head, until she comes to the crossing where Jo plies with his broom. He crosses with her, and begs. Still, she does not turn her head until she has landed on the other side. Then, she slightly beckons to him, and says 'Come here!'

Jo follows her, a pace or two, into a quiet court.

'Are you the boy I've read of in the papers?' she asks behind her veil.

'I don't know,' says Jo, staring moodily at the veil, 'nothink about no papers. I don't know nothink about nothink at all.'

'Were you examined at an Inquest?'

'I don't know nothink about no—where I was took by the beadle, do you mean?' says Jo. 'Was the boy's name at the Inkwhich, Jo?'

'Yes.'

'That's me!' says Jo.

'Come farther up.'

'You mean about the man?' says Jo, following. 'Him as wos dead?'

'Hush! Speak in a whisper! Yes. Did he look, when he was living, so very ill and poor?'

'Oh, jist!' says Jo.

'Did he look like—not like *you*?' says the woman, with abhorrence.

'Oh, not so bad as me,' says Jo. 'I'm a reg'lar one *I* am! You didn't know him, did you?'

'How dare you ask me if I knew him?'

'No offence, my lady,' says Jo, with much humility; for even he has got at the suspicion of her being a lady.

'I am not a lady. I am a servant.'

'You are a jolly servant!' says Jo, without the least idea of saying anything offensive; merely as a tribute of admiration.

'Listen and be silent. Don't talk to me, and stand farther from me! Can you show me all those places that were spoken of in the account I read? The place he wrote for, the place he died at, the place where you were taken to, and the place where he was buried? Do you know the place where he was buried?'

Jo answers with a nod; having also nodded as each other place was mentioned.

'Go before me, and show me all those dreadful places. Stop opposite to each, and don't speak to me unless I speak to you. Don't look back. Do what I want, and I will pay you well.'

Jo attends closely while the words are being spoken; tells them off on his broom-handle, finding them rather hard; pauses to consider their meaning; considers it satisfactory, and nods his ragged head.

'I'm fly,' says Jo. 'But fen larks, you know. Stow hooking it!'

'What does the horrible creature mean?' exclaims the servant, recoiling from him.

'Stow cutting away, you know!' says Jo.

'I don't understand you. Go on before! I will give you more money than you ever had in your life.'

Jo screws up his mouth into a whistle, gives his ragged head a rub, takes his broom under his arm, and leads the way; passing deftly, with his bare feet, over the hard stones, and through the mud and mire.

Cook's Court. Jo stops. A pause.

'Who lives here?'

'Him wot give him his writing, and give me half a bull,' says Jo, in a whisper, without looking over his shoulder.

'Go on to the next.'

Krook's house. Jo stops again. A longer pause.

'Who lives here?'

'*He* lived here,' Jo answers, as before.

After a silence he is asked 'In which room?'

'In the back room up there. You can see the winder from this corner. Up there! That's where I see him stritched out. This is the public 'ouse where I was took to.'

'Go on to the next!'

It is a longer walk to the next; but Jo, relieved of his first suspicions, sticks to the terms imposed upon him, and does not look round. By many devious ways, reeking with offence of many kinds, they come to the little tunnel of a court, and to the gas-lamp (lighted now), and to the iron gate.

'He was put there,' says Jo, holding to the bars and looking in.

'Where? O, what a scene of horror!'

'There!' says Jo, pointing. 'Over yinder. Among them piles of bones, and close to that there kitchin winder! They put him wery nigh the top. They was obliged to stamp upon it to git it in. I could unkiver it for you with my broom, if the gate was open. That's why they locks it, I s'pose,' giving it a shake. 'It's always locked. Look at the rat!' cries Jo, excited. 'Hi! Look! There he goes! Ho! Into the ground!'

The servant shrinks into a corner—into a corner of that hideous archway, with its deadly stains contaminating her dress; and putting out her two hands, and passionately telling him to keep away from her, for he is loathsome to her, so remains for some moments. Jo stands staring, and is still staring when she recovers herself.

'Is this place of abomination, consecrated ground?'

'I don't know nothink of consequential ground,' says Jo, still staring.

'Is it blessed?'

'WHICH?' says Jo, in the last degree amazed.

'Is it blessed?'

'I'm blest if I know,' says Jo, staring more than ever; 'but I shouldn't think it warn't. Blest?' repeats Jo, something troubled in his mind. 'It ain't done it much good if it is. Blest? I should think it was t'othered myself. But I don't know nothink!'

The servant takes as little heed of what he says, as she seems to take of what she has said herself. She draws off her glove, to get some money from her purse. Jo silently notices how white and small her hand is, and what a jolly servant she must be to wear such sparkling rings.

She drops a piece of money in his hand, without touching it, and shuddering as their hands approach. 'Now,' she adds, 'show me the spot again!'

Joe thrusts the handle of his broom between the bars of the gate, and, with his utmost power of elaboration, points it out. At length, looking aside to see if he has made himself intelligible, he finds that he is alone.

His first proceeding, is, to hold the piece of money to the gas-light, and to be overpowered at finding that it is yellow—gold. His next, is, to give it a one-sided bite at the edge, as a test of its quality. His next, to put it in his mouth for safety, and to sweep the step and passage with great care. His job done, he sets off for Tom-all-Alone's; stopping in the light of innumerable gas-lamps to produce the piece of gold, and give it another one-sided bite, as a reassurance of its being genuine.

HARD TIMES

Coketown is a dirty, unlovely mill town, undistinguished in the uniformity of its public buildings and the drudgery of its common people ...

I entertain a weak idea that the English people are as hard-worked as any people upon whom the sun shines. I acknowledge to this ridiculous idiosyncrasy, as a reason why I would give them a little more play.

In the hardest working part of Coketown; in the innermost fortifications of that ugly citadel, where Nature was as strongly bricked out as killing airs and gases were bricked in; at the heart of the labyrinth of narrow courts upon courts, and close streets upon streets, which had come into existence piecemeal, every piece in a violent hurry for some one man's purpose, and the whole an unnatural family, shouldering, and trampling, and pressing one another to death; in the last close nook of this great exhausted receiver, where the chimneys, for want of air to make a draught, were built in an immense variety of stunted and crooked shapes, as though every house put out a sign of the kind of people who might be expected to be born in it; among the multitude of Coketown, generically called 'the Hands,'—a race who would have found more favour with some people, if Providence had seen fit to make them only hands, or, like the lower creatures of the seashore, only hands and stomachs—lived a certain Stephen Blackpool, forty years of age.

Stephen looked older, but he had had a hard life. It is said that every life has its roses and thorns; there seemed, however, to have been a misadventure or mistake in Stephen's case, whereby somebody else had become possessed of his roses, and he had become possessed of the same somebody else's thorns in addition to his own. He had known, to use his words, a peck of trouble. He was usually called Old Stephen, in a kind of rough homage to the fact.

A rather stooping man, with a knitted brow, a pondering expression of face, and a hard-looking head sufficiently capacious, on which his iron-grey hair lay long and thin, Old Stephen might have passed for a particularly intelligent man in his condition. Yet he was not. He took no place among those remarkable 'Hands,' who, piecing together their broken intervals of leisure through many years, had mastered difficult sciences, and acquired a knowledge of most unlikely things. He held no station among the Hands who could make speeches and carry on debates. Thousands of his compeers could talk much better than he, at any time. He was a good power-loom weaver, and a man of perfect integrity. What more he was, or what else he had in him, if anything, let him show for himself.

The lights in the great factories, which looked, when they were illuminated, like Fairy palaces—or the travellers by express-train said so—were all extinguished; and the bells had rung for knocking off for the night, and had ceased again; and the Hands, men and women, boy and girl, were clattering home. Old Stephen was standing in the street, with the odd sensation upon him which the stoppage of the machinery always produced—the sensation of its having worked and stopped in his own head.

'Yet I don't see Rachael, still!' said he.

It was a wet night, and many groups of young women passed him, with their shawls drawn over their bare heads and held close under their chins to keep the rain out. He knew Rachael well, for a glance at any one of these groups was sufficient to show him that she was not there. At last, there were no more to come; and then he turned away, saying in a tone of disappointment, 'Why, then, I ha' missed her!'

But, he had not gone the length of three streets, when he saw another of the shawled figures in advance of him, at which he looked so keenly that perhaps its mere shadow indistinctly reflected on the wet pavement—if he could have seen it without the figure itself moving along from lamp to lamp, brightening and fading as it went—would have been enough to tell him who was there. Making his pace at once much quicker and much softer, he darted on until he was very near this figure, then fell into his former walk, and called, 'Rachael!'

She turned, being then in the brightness of a lamp; and raising her hood a little, showed a quiet oval face, dark and rather delicate, irradiated by a pair of very gentle eyes, and further set off by the perfect order of her shining black hair. It was not a face in its first bloom; she was a woman five and thirty years of age.

'Ah, lad! 'Tis thou?' When she had said this, with a smile which would have been quite expressed, though nothing of her had been seen but her pleasant eyes, she replaced her hood again, and they went on together.

'I thought thou wast ahind me, Rachael?'

'No.'

'Early t'night, lass?'

' 'Times I'm a little early, Stephen; 'times a little late. I'm never to be counted on, going home.'

'Nor going t'other way, neither, 't seems to me, Rachael?'

'No, Stephen.'

He looked at her with some disappointment in his face, but with a respectful and patient conviction that she must be right in whatever she did. The expression was not lost upon her; she laid her hand lightly on his arm a moment, as if to thank him for it.

'We are such true friends, lad, and such old friends, and getting to be such old folk, now.'

'No, Rachael, thou'rt as young as ever thou wast.'

'One of us would be puzzled how to get old, Stephen, without t'other getting so too, both being alive,' she answered, laughing; 'but, anyways, we're such old friends, that t'hide a word of honest truth fro' one another would be a sin and a pity. 'Tis better not to walk too much together. 'Times, yes! 'Twould be hard, indeed, if 'twas not to be at all,' she said, with a cheerfulness she sought to communicate to him.

' 'Tis hard, anyways, Rachael.'

'Try to think not, and 'twill seem better.'

'I've tried a long time, and 'ta'nt got better. But thou'rt right; 'tmight mak folk talk, even of thee. Thou hast been that to me, Rachael, through so many year: thou hast done me so much good, and heartened of me in that cheering way, that thy word is a law to me. Ah, lass, and a bright good law! Better than some real ones.'

'Never fret about them, Stephen,' she answered quickly, and not without an anxious glance at his face. 'Let the laws be.'

'Yes,' he said, with a slow nod or two. 'Let 'em be. Let everything be. Let all sorts alone. 'Tis a muddle, and that's aw.'

'Always a muddle?' said Rachael, with another gentle touch upon his arm, as if to recall him out of the thoughtfulness, in which he was biting the long ends of his loose neckerchief as he walked along. The touch had its instantaneous effect. He let them fall, turning a smiling face upon her, and said, as he broke into a good-humoured laugh, 'Ay, Rachael, lass, awlus a muddle. That's where I stick. I come to the muddle many times and agen, and I never get beyond it.'

They had walked some distance, and were near their own homes. The woman's was the first reached. It was in one of the many small streets for which the favourite undertaker (who turned a handsome sum out of the one poor ghastly pomp of the neighbourhood) kept a black ladder, in order that those who had done their daily groping up and down the narrow stairs might slide out of this working world by the windows. She stopped at the corner, and putting her hand in his, wished him good night.

'Good night, dear lass; good night!'

She went, with her neat figure and her sober womanly step, down the dark street, and he stood looking after her until she turned into one of the small houses. There was not a flutter of her coarse shawl, perhaps, but had its interest in this man's eyes; not a tone of her voice but had its echo in his innermost heart.

When she was lost to his view, he pursued his homeward way, glancing up sometimes at the sky, where the clouds were sailing fast and wildly. But, they were broken now, and the rain had ceased, and the moon shone—looking down the high chimneys of Coketown on the deep furnaces below, and casting Titantic shadows of the steam-engines at rest, upon the walls where they were lodged. The man seemed to have brightened with the night, as he went on.

His home, in such another street as the first, saving that it was narrower, was over a little shop. How it came to pass that any people found it worth their while to sell or buy the wretched little toys, mixed up in its window with cheap newspapers and pork (there was a leg to be raffled for to-morrow-night), matters not here. He took his end of candle from a shelf, lighted it at another end of candle on the counter, without disturbing the mistress of the shop who was asleep in her little room, and went upstairs into his lodging.

It was a room, not unacquainted with the black ladder under various tenants; but as neat, at present, as such a room could be. A few books and writings were on an old bureau in a corner, the furniture was decent and sufficient, and, though the atmosphere was tainted, the room was clean.

Going to the hearth to set the candle down upon a round three-legged table standing there, he stumbled against something. As he recoiled, looking down at it, it raised itself up into the form of a woman in a sitting attitude.

'Heaven's mercy, woman!' he cried, falling farther off from the figure. 'Hast thou come back again!'

Such a woman! A disabled, drunken creature, barely able to preserve her sitting posture by steadying herself with one begrimed hand on the floor, while the other was so purposeless in trying to push away her tangled hair from her face, that it only blinded her the more with the dirt upon it. A creature so foul to look at, in her tatters, stains and splashes, but so much fouler than that in her moral infamy, that it was a shameful thing even to see her.

After an impatient oath or two, and some stupid clawing of herself with the hand not necessary to her support, she got her hair away from her eyes sufficiently to obtain a sight of him. Then she sat swaying her body to and fro, and making gestures with her unnerved arm, which seemed intended as the accompaniment to a fit of laughter, though her face was stolid and drowsy.

'Eigh lad? What, yo'r there?' Some hoarse sounds meant for this, came mockingly out of her at last; and her head dropped forward on her breast.

'Back agen?' she screeched, after some minutes, as if he had that moment said it. 'Yes! And back agen. Back agen ever and ever so often. Back? Yes, back. Why not?'

Roused by the unmeaning violence with which she cried it out, she scrambled up, and stood supporting herself with her shoulders against the wall; dangling in one hand, by the string, a dunghill-fragment of a bonnet, and trying to look scornfully at him.

'I'll sell thee off again, and I'll sell thee off again, and I'll sell thee off a score of times!' she cried, with something between a furious menace and an effort at a defiant dance. 'Come awa' from th' bed!' He was sitting on the side of it, with his face hidden in his hands. 'Come awa' from't. 'Tis mine, and I've a right to't!'

As she staggered to it, he avoided her with a shudder, and passed—his face still hidden—to the opposite end of the room. She threw herself upon the bed heavily, and soon was snoring hard. He sank into a chair, and moved but once all that night. It was to throw a covering over her; as if his hands were not enough to hide her, even in the darkness.

The Fairy palaces burst into illumination, before pale morning showed the monstrous serpents of smoke trailing themselves over Coketown. A clattering of clogs upon the pavement; a rapid ringing of bells; and all the melancholy mad elephants, polished and oiled up for the day's monotony, were at their heavy exercise again.

Stephen bent over his loom, quiet, watchful, and steady. A special contrast, as every man was in the forest of looms where Stephen worked, to the crashing, smashing, tearing piece of mechanism at which he laboured. Never fear, good people of an anxious turn of mind, that Art will consign Nature to oblivion. Set anywhere, side by side, the work of GOD and the work of man; and the former, even though it be a troop of Hands of very small account, will gain in dignity from the comparison.

So many hundred Hands in this mill; so many hundred horse Steam Power. It is known, to the force of a single pound weight, what the engine will do; but, not all the calculators of the National Debt can tell me the capacity for good or evil, for love or hatred, for patriotism or discontent, for the decomposition of virtue into vice, or the reverse, at any single moment in the soul of one of these its quiet servants, with the composed faces and the regulated actions. There is no mystery in it: there is an unfathomable mystery in the meanest of them, for ever.—Supposing we were to reserve our arithmetic for material objects, and to govern these awful unknown quantities by other means!

The day grew strong, and showed itself outside, even against the flaming lights within. The lights were turned out, and the work went on. The rain fell, and the Smoke-serpents, submissive to the curse of all that tribe, trailed themselves upon the earth. In the waste-yard outside, the steam from the escape pipe, the litter of barrels and old iron, the shining heaps of coals, the ashes everywhere, were shrouded in a veil of mist and rain.

The work went on, until the noon-bell rang. More clattering upon the pavements. The looms, and wheels, and Hands, all out of gear for an hour.

Stephen came out of the hot mill into the damp wind and cold wet streets, haggard and worn. He turned from his own class and his own quarter, taking nothing but a little bread as he walked along, towards the hill on which his principal employer lived, in a red house with black outside shutters, green inside blinds, a black street door, up two white steps, BOUNDERBY (in letters very like himself) upon a brazen plate, and a round brazen door-handle underneath it like a brazen full-stop.

Mr Bounderby was at his lunch. So Stephen had expected. Would his servant say that one of the Hands begged leave to speak to him? Message in return, requiring name of such Hand. Stephen Blackpool. There was nothing troublesome against Stephen Blackpool; yes, he might come in.

Stephen Blackpool in the parlour. Mr Bounderby (whom he just knew by sight) at lunch on chop and sherry. Mrs Sparsit netting at the fireside, in a side-saddle attitude, with one foot in a cotton stirrup. It was a part, at one of Mrs Sparsit's dignity and service, not to lunch. She supervised the meal officially, but implied that in her own stately person she considered lunch a weakness.

'Now, Stephen,' said Mr Bounderby, 'what's the matter with *you*?'

Stephen made a bow. Not a servile one—these Hands will never do that! Lord bless you, sir, you'll never catch them at that, if they have been with you twenty years!—and, as a complimentary toilet for Mrs Sparsit, tucked his neckerchief ends into his waistcoat.

'Now, you know,' said Mr Bounderby, taking some sherry, 'we have never had any difficulty with you, and you have never been one of the unreasonable ones. You don't expect to be set up in a coach and six, and to be fed on turtle soup and venison, with a gold spoon, as a good many of 'em do!'—Mr Bounderby always represented this to be the sole, immediate, and direct object of any Hand who was not entirely satisfied—'and therefore I know already that you have not come here to make a complaint. Now, you know, I am certain of that, beforehand.'

'No, sir, sure I ha' not coom for nowt o' th' kind.'

Mr Bounderby seemed agreeably surprised, notwithstanding his previous strong conviction. 'Very well,' he returned. 'You're a steady Hand, and I was not mistaken. Now, let me hear what it's all about. As it's not that, let me hear what it is. What have you got to say? Out with it, lad!'

Stephen happened to glance towards Mrs Sparsit. 'I can go, Mr Bounderby, if you wish it,' said that self-sacrificing lady, making a feint of taking her foot out of the stirrup.

Mr Bounderby stayed her, by holding a mouthful of chop in suspension before swallowing it, and putting out his left hand. Then, withdrawing his hand and swallowing his mouthful of chop, he said to Stephen:

'Now, you know, this good lady is a born lady, a high lady. You are not to suppose because she keeps my house for me, that she hasn't been very high up the tree—ah, up at the top of the tree! Now, if you have got anything to say that can't be said before a born lady, this lady will leave the room. If what you have got to say *can* be said before a born lady, this lady will stay where she is.'

'Sir, I hope I never had nowt to say, not fitten for a born lady to year, sin' I were born mysen',' was the reply, accompanied with a slight flush.

'Very well,' said Mr Bounderby, pushing away his plate, and leaning back. 'Fire away!'

'I ha' coom,' Stephen began, raising his eyes from the floor, after a moment's consideration, 'to ask yo yor advice. I need't overmuch. I were married on Eas'r Monday nineteen year sin', long and dree. She were a young lass—pretty enow—wi' good accounts of herseln. Well! She went bad—soon. Not along of me. Gonnows I were not a unkind husband to her.'

'I have heard all this before,' said Mr Bounderby. 'She took to drinking, left off working, sold the furniture, pawned the clothes, and played old Gooseberry.'

'I were patient wi' her.'

('The more fool you, I think,' said Mr Bounderby, in confidence to his wine-glass.)

'I were very patient wi' her. I tried to wean her fra't, ower and ower agen. I tried this, I tried that, I tried t'other. I ha' gone home, many's the time, and found all vanished as I had in the world, and her without a sense left to bless herseln lying on bare ground. I ha' dun't not once, not twice—twenty time!'

Every line in his face deepened as he said it, and put in its affecting evidence of the suffering he had undergone.

'From bad to worse, from worse to worsen. She left me. She disgraced herseln everyways, bitter and bad. She coom back, she coom back, she coom back. What could I do t'hinder her? I ha' walked the streets nights long, ere ever I'd go home. I ha' gone t' th' brigg, minded to fling myseln ower, and ha' no more on't. I ha' bore that much, that I were owd when I were young.'

Mrs Sparsit, easily ambling along with her netting-needles, raised the Coriolanian eyebrows and shook her head, as much as to say, 'The great know trouble as well as the small. Please to turn your humble eye in My direction.'

'I ha' paid her to keep awa' fra' me. These five year I ha' paid her. I ha' gotten decent fewtrils about me agen. I ha' lived hard and sad, but not ashamed and fearfo' a' the minnits o' my life. Last night, I went home. There she lay upon my har-stone! There she is!'

In the strength of his misfortune, and the energy of his distress, he fired for the moment like a proud man. In another moment, he stood as he had stood all the time—his usual stoop upon him; his pondering face addressed to Mr Bounderby, with a curious expression on it, half shrewd, half perplexed, as if his mind were set upon unravelling something very difficult; his hat held tight in his left hand, which rested on his hip; his right arm, with a rugged propriety and force of action, very earnestly emphasising what he said; not least so when it always paused, a little bent, but not withdrawn, as he paused.

'I was acquainted with all this, you know,' said Mr Bounderby, 'except the last clause, long ago. It's a bad job; that's what it is. You had better have been satisfied as you were, and not have got married. However, it's too late to say that.'

'Was it an unequal marriage, sir, in point of years?' asked Mrs Sparsit.

'You hear what this lady asks. Was it an unequal marriage in point of years, this unlucky job of yours?' said Mr Bounderby.

'Not e'en so. I were one-and-twenty myseln; she were twenty nighbut.'

'Indeed, sir?' said Mrs Sparsit to her chief, with great placidity. 'I inferred, from its being so miserable a marriage, that it was probably an unequal one in point of years.'

Mr Bounderby looked very hard at the good lady in a side-long way that had an odd sheepishness about it. He fortified himself with a little more sherry.

'Well? Why don't you go on?' he then asked, turning rather irritably on Stephen Blackpool.

'I ha' coom to ask yo, sir, how I am to be ridded o' this woman.' Stephen infused a yet deeper gravity into the mixed expression of his attentive face. Mrs Sparsit uttered a gentle ejaculation, as having received a moral shock.

'What do you mean?' said Bounderby, getting up to lean his back against the chimney-piece. 'What are you talking about? You took her for better for worse.'

'I mun' be ridden o' her. I cannot bear 't nommore. I ha' lived under 't so long, for that I ha' had'n the pity and comforting words o' th' best lass living or dead. Haply, but for her, I should ha' gone hottering mad.'

'He wishes to be free, to marry the female of whom he speaks, I fear, sir,' observed Mrs Sparsit in an undertone, and much dejected by the immorality of the people.

'I do. The lady says what's right. I do. I were acoming to 't. I ha' read i' th' papers that great fok (fair faw 'em a'! I wishes 'em no hurt!) are not bonded together for better for worse so fast, but that they can be set free fro' *their* misfortnet marriages, an' marry ower agen. When they dunnot agree, for that their tempers is ill-sorted, they has rooms o' one kind an another in their houses, above a bit, and they can live asunders. We fok ha' only one room and we can't. When that won't do, they ha' gowd an' other cash, an' they can say "This for yo and that for me," an' they can go their separate ways. We can't. Spite o' all that, they can be set free for smaller wrongs than mine. So, I mun be ridden o' this woman, an' I want t' know how?'

'No how,' returned Mr Bounderby.

'If I do her any hurt, sir, there's a law to punish me?'

'Of course there is.'

'If I flee from her, there's a law to punish me?'

'Of course there is.'

'If I marry t'oother dear lass, there's a law to punish me?'

'Of course there is.'

'If I was to live wi' her and not marry her—saying such a thing could be, which it never could or would, an' her so good—there's a law to punish me, in every innocent child belonging to me?'

'Of course there is.'

'Now, a' God's name,' said Stephen Blackpool, 'show me the law to help me!'

'Hem! There's a sanctity in this relation of life,' said Mr Bounderby, 'and—and—it must be kept up.'

'No, no, dunnot say that, sir. 'Tain't kep' up that way. Not that way. 'Tis kep' down that way. I'm a weaver, I were in a fact'ry when a chilt, but I ha' gotten een to see wi' and eern to year wi'. I read in th' papers every 'Sizes, every Sessions—and you read too—I know it!—with dismay—how th' supposed unpossibility o' ever getting unchained from one another, at any price, on any terms, brings blood upon this land, and brings many common married fok to battle, murder, and sudden death. Let us ha' this right understood. Mine's a grievous case, an' I want—if yo will be so good—t'know the law that helps me.'

'Now, I tell you what!' said Mr Bounderby, putting his hands in his pockets. 'There *is* such a law.'

Stephen, subsiding into his quiet manner, and never wandering in his attention, gave a nod.

'But it's not for you at all. It costs money. It costs a mint of money.'

'How much might that be?' Stephen calmly asked.

'Why, you'd have to go to Doctors' Commons with a suit, and you'd have to go to a court of Common Law with a suit, and you'd have to go to the House of Lords with a suit, and you'd have to get an Act of Parliament to enable you to marry again, and it would cost you (if it was a case of very plain-sailing), I suppose from a thousand to fifteen hundred pound,' said Mr Bounderby. 'Perhaps twice the money.'

'There's no other law?'

'Certainly not.'

'Why, then, sir,' said Stephen, turning white, and motioning with that right hand of his, as if he gave everything to the four winds, ' '*tis* a muddle. 'Tis just a muddle a'toogether, and the sooner I am dead, the better.'

(Mrs Sparsit again dejected by the impiety of the people.)

'Pooh, pooh! Don't you talk nonsense, my good fellow,' said Mr Bounderby, 'about things you don't understand; and don't you call the Institutions of your country a muddle, or you'll get yourself into a real muddle one of these fine mornings. The institutions of your country are not your piece-work, and the only thing you have got to do is, to mind your piece-work. You didn't take your wife for fast and for loose; but for better for worse. If she has turned out worse—why, all we have got to say is, she might have turned out better.'

' 'Tis a muddle,' said Stephen, shaking his head as he moved to the door. ' 'Tis a' a muddle!'

'Now, I'll tell you what!' Mr Bounderby resumed, as a valedictory address. 'With what I shall call your unhallowed opinions, you have been quite shocking this lady, who, as I have already told you, is a born lady, and who, as I have not already told you, has had her own marriage misfortunes to the tune of tens of thousands of pounds—tens of Thousands of Pounds!' (he repeated it with great relish). 'Now, you have always been a steady Hand hitherto; but my opinion is, and so I tell you plainly, that you are turning into the wrong road. You have been listening to some mischievous stranger or other—they're always about—and the best thing you can do is, to come out of that. Now you know'—here his countenance expressed marvellous acuteness—'I can see as far into a grindstone as another man; farther than a good many, perhaps, because I had my nose well kept to it when I was young. I see traces of the turtle soup, and venison, and gold spoon in this. Yes, I do!' cried Mr Bounderby, shaking his head with obstinate cunning. 'By the Lord Harry, I do!'

With a very different shake of the head and a deep sigh, Stephen said, 'Thank you, sir, I wish you good day.' So he left Mr Bounderby swelling at his own portrait on the wall, as if he were going to explode himself into it; and Mrs Sparsit still ambling on with her foot in her stirrup, looking quite cast down by the popular vices.

LITTLE DORRIT

William Dorrit and his children Edward, Fanny and Amy (Little Dorrit) live in the Marshalsea debtors' prison. Little Dorrit was born in the prison and has known no other life than to attend there to her father's needs and to go forth each day to work. The family is befriended by Arthur Clennam for whose mother Little Dorrit does sewing, but Edward and Fanny take a dislike to him after a misunderstanding about money. Little Dorrit loves Arthur but, knowing him to be in love with Minnie Meagles who has married Henry Gowan and gone to Italy, she remains silent about her feelings for him.

After many years in the Marshalsea, William Dorrit inherits a fortune and is suddenly rich. He and his children are finally able to leave the prison, and his brother Frederick goes with them ...

And now the day arrived, when Mr Dorrit and his family were to leave the prison for ever, and the stones of its much-trodden pavement were to know them no more.

The interval had been short, but he had greatly complained of its length, and had been imperious with Mr Rugg touching the delay. He had been high with Mr Rugg, and had threatened to employ some one else. He had requested Mr Rugg not to presume upon the place in which he found him, but to do his duty, sir, and to do it with promptitude. He had told Mr Rugg that he knew what lawyers and agents were, and that he would not submit to imposition. On that gentleman's humbly representing that he exerted himself to the utmost, Miss Fanny was very short with him; desiring to know what less he could do, when he had been told a dozen times that money was no object, and expressing her suspicion that he forgot whom he talked to.

Towards the Marshal, who was a Marshal of many years' standing, and with whom he had never had any previous difference, Mr Dorrit comported himself with severity. That officer, on personally tendering his congratulations, offered the free use of two rooms in his house for

Mr Dorrit's occupation until his departure. Mr Dorrit thanked him at the moment, and replied that he would think of it; but the Marshal was no sooner gone than he sat down and wrote him a cutting note, in which he remarked that he had never on any former occasion had the honour of receiving his congratulations (which was true, though indeed there had not been anything particular to congratulate him upon), and that he begged, on behalf of himself and family, to repudiate the Marshal's offer, with all those thanks which its disinterested character and its perfect independence of all worldly considerations demanded.

Although his brother showed so dim a glimmering of interest in their altered fortunes, that it was very doubtful whether he understood them, Mr Dorrit caused him to be measured for new raiment by the hosiers, tailors, hatters, and bootmakers whom he called in for himself; and ordered that his old clothes should be taken from him and burned. Miss Fanny and Mr Tip required no direction in making an appearance of great fashion and elegance; and the three passed this interval together at the best hotel in the neighbourhood—though truly, as Miss Fanny said, the best was very indifferent. In connection with that establishment, Mr Tip hired a cabriolet, horse, and groom, a very neat turnout, which was usually to be observed for two or three hours at a time, gracing the Borough High Street, outside the Marshalsea court-yard. A modest little hired chariot and pair was also frequently to be seen there; in alighting from and entering which vehicle, Miss Fanny fluttered the Marshal's daughters by the display of inaccessible bonnets.

A great deal of business was transacted in this short period. Among other items, Messrs Peddle and Pool, solicitors, of Monument Yard, were instructed by their client Edward Dorrit, Esquire, to address a letter to Mr Arthur Clennam, enclosing the sum of twenty-four pounds nine shillings and eightpence, being the amount of principal and interest computed at the rate of five per cent. per annum, in which their client believed himself to be indebted to Mr Clennam. In making this communication and remittance, Messrs Peddle and Pool were further instructed by their client to remind Mr Clennam, that the favour of the advance now repaid (including gate-fees) had not been asked of him, and to inform him that it would not have been accepted if it had been openly proffered in his name. With which they requested a stamped receipt, and remained his obedient servants. A great deal of business had likewise to be done, within the so-soon-to-be-orphaned Marshalsea, by Mr Dorrit so long its Father, chiefly arising out of applications made to him by Collegians for small sums of money. To these he responded with the greatest liberality, and with no lack of formality; always first writing to appoint a time at which the applicant might wait upon him in his room, and then receiving him in the midst of a vast accumulation of documents, and accompanying his donation (for he said in every such case, 'it is a donation, not a loan') with a great deal of good counsel: to the effect that he, the expiring Father of the Marshalsea, hoped to be long remembered, as an example that a man might preserve his own and the general respect even there.

The Collegians were not envious. Besides that they had a personal and traditional regard for a Collegian of so many years' standing, the event was creditable to the College, and made it famous in the newspapers. Perhaps more of them thought, too, than were quite aware of it, that the thing might in the lottery of chances have happened to themselves, or that something of the sort might yet happen to themselves, some day or other. They took it very well. A few were low at the thought of being left behind, and being left poor; but even these did not grudge the family their brilliant reverse. There might have been much more envy in politer places. It seems probable that mediocrity of fortune would have been disposed to be less magnanimous than the Collegians, who lived from hand to mouth—from the pawnbroker's hand to the day's dinner.

They got up an address to him, which they presented in a neat frame and glass (though it was not afterwards displayed in the family mansion or preserved among the family papers); and to which he returned a gracious answer. In that document he assured them, in a Royal manner, that he received the profession of their attachment with a full conviction of its sincerity; and again generally exhorted them to follow his example—which, at least in so far as coming into a great property was concerned, there is no doubt they would have gladly imitated. He took the same occasion of inviting them to a comprehensive entertainment, to be given to the whole College in the yard, and at which he signified he would have the honour of taking a parting glass to the health and happiness of all those whom he was about to leave behind.

He did not in person dine at this public repast (it took place at two in the afternoon, and his dinners now came in from the hotel at six), but his son was so good as to take the head of the principal table, and to be very free and engaging. He himself went about among the company, and took notice of individuals, and saw that the viands were of the quality he had ordered, and that all were served. On the whole, he was like a baron of the olden time, in a rare good humour. At the conclusion of the repast, he pledged his guests in a bumper of old

Madeira; and told them that he hoped they had enjoyed themselves, and what was more, that they would enjoy themselves for the rest of the evening; that he wished them well; and that he bade them welcome. His health being drunk with acclamations, he was not so baronial after all but that in trying to return thanks he broke down, in the manner of a mere serf with a heart in his breast, and wept before them all. After this great success, which he supposed to be a failure, he gave them 'Mr Chivery and his brother officers;' whom he had beforehand presented with ten pounds each, and who were all in attendance. Mr Chivery spoke to the toast, saying, What you undertake to lock up, lock up; but remember that you are, in the words of the fettered African, a man and a brother ever. The list of toasts disposed of, Mr Dorrit urbanely went through the motions of playing a game at skittles with the Collegian who was the next oldest inhabitant to himself; and left the tenantry to their diversions.

But all these occurrences preceded the final day. And now the day arrived when he and his family were to leave the prison for ever, and when the stones of its much-trodden pavement were to know them no more.

Noon was the hour appointed for the departure. As it approached, there was not a Collegian within doors, nor a turnkey absent. The latter class of gentlemen appeared in their Sunday clothes, and the greater part of the Collegians were brightened up as much as circumstances allowed. Two or three flags were even displayed, and the children put on odds and ends of ribbon. Mr Dorrit himself, at this trying time, preserved a serious but graceful dignity. Much of his attention was given to his brother, as to whose bearing on the great occasion he felt anxious.

'My dear Frederick,' said he, 'if you will give me your arm, we will pass among our friends together. I think it is right that we should go out arm-in-arm, my dear Frederick.'

'Hah!' said Frederick. 'Yes, yes, yes, yes.'

'And if, my dear Frederick—if you could, without putting any great constraint upon yourself, throw a little (pray excuse me, Frederick), a little polish into your usual demeanour—'

'William, William,' said the other, shaking his head, 'it's for you to do all that. I don't know how. All forgotten, forgotten!'

'But, my dear fellow,' returned William, 'for that very reason, if for no other, you must positively try to rouse yourself. What you have forgotten you must now begin to recall, my dear Frederick. Your position—'

'Eh?' said Frederick.

'Your position, my dear Frederick.'

'Mine?' He looked first at his own figure, and then at his brother's, and then, drawing a long breath, cried, 'Hah, to be sure! Yes, yes, yes.'

'Your position, my dear Frederick, is now a fine one. Your position, as my brother, is a very fine one. And I know that it belongs to your conscientious nature, to try to become worthy of it, my dear Frederick, and to try to adorn it. To be no discredit to it, but to adorn it.'

'William,' said the other weakly, and with a sigh, 'I will do anything you wish, my brother, provided it lies in my power. Pray be so kind as to recollect what a limited power mine is. What would you wish me to do to-day, brother? Say what it is, only say what it is.'

'My dearest Frederick, nothing. It is not worth troubling so good a heart as yours with.'

'Pray trouble it,' returned the other. 'It finds it no trouble, William, to do anything it can for you.'

William passed his hands across his eyes, and murmured with august satisfaction, 'Blessings on your attachment, my poor dear fellow!' Then he said aloud, 'Well, my dear Frederick, if you will only try, as we walk out, to show that you are alive to the occasion—that you think about it—'

'What would you advise me to think about it?' returned his submissive brother.

'Oh! my dear Frederick, how can I answer you? I can only say what, in leaving these good people, I think myself.'

'That's it!' cried his brother. 'That will help me.'

'I find that I think, my dear Frederick, and with mixed emotions in which a softened compassion predominates, What will they do without me!'

'True,' returned his brother. 'Yes, yes, yes, yes. I'll think that as we go, What will they do without my brother! Poor things! What will they do without him!'

Twelve o'clock having just struck, and the carriage being reported ready in the outer court-yard, the brothers proceeded down-stairs arm-in-arm. Edward Dorrit, Esquire (once Tip), and his sister Fanny followed, also arm-in-arm; Mr Plornish and Maggy, to whom had been entrusted the removal of such of the family effects as were considered worth removing, followed, bearing bundles and burdens to be packed in a cart.

In the yard, were the Collegians and turnkeys. In the yard, were Mr Pancks and Mr Rugg, come to see the last touch given to their work.

In the yard, was Young John making a new epitaph for himself, on the occasion of his dying of a broken heart. In the yard, was the Patriarchal Casby, looking so tremendously benevolent that many enthusiastic Collegians grasped him fervently by the hand, and the wives and female relatives of many more Collegians kissed his hand, nothing doubting that he had done it all. In the yard, was the usual chorus of people proper to such a place. In the yard, was the man with the shadowy grievance respecting the Fund which the Marshal embezzled, who had got up at five in the morning to complete the copying of a perfectly unintelligible history of that transaction, which he had committed to Mr Dorrit's care, as a document of the last importance, calculated to stun the Government and effect the Marshal's downfall. In the yard, was the insolvent whose utmost energies were always set on getting into debt, who broke into prison with as much pains as other men have broken out of it, and who was always being cleared and complimented; while the insolvent at his elbow—a mere little, snivelling, striving tradesman, half dead of anxious efforts to keep out of debt—found it a hard matter, indeed, to get a Commissioner to release him with much reproof and reproach. In the yard, was the man of many children and many burdens, whose failure astonished everybody; in the yard, was the man of no children and large resources, whose failure astonished nobody. There, were the people who were always going out to-morrow, and always putting it off; there, were the people who had come in yesterday, and who were much more jealous and resentful of this freak of fortune than the seasoned birds. There, were some who, in pure meanness of spirit, cringed and bowed before the enriched Collegian and his family; there, were others who did so really because their eyes, accustomed to the gloom of their imprisonment and poverty, could not support the light of such bright sunshine. There, were many whose shillings had gone into his pocket to buy him meat and drink; but none who were now obtrusively Hail fellow well met! with him, on the strength of that assistance. It was rather to be remarked of the caged birds, that they were a little shy of the bird about to be so grandly free, and that they had a tendency to withdraw themselves towards the bars, and seem a little fluttered as he passed.

Through these spectators, the little procession, headed by the two brothers, moved slowly to the gate. Mr Dorrit, yielding to the vast speculation how the poor creatures were to get on without him, was great, and sad, but not absorbed. He patted children on the head like Sir Roger de Coverley going to church, he spoke to people in the background by their Christian names, he condescended to all present, and seemed for their consolation to walk encircled by the legend in golden characters, 'Be comforted, my people! Bear it!'

At last three honest cheers announced that he had passed the gate, and that the Marshalsea was an orphan. Before they had ceased to ring in the echoes of the prison walls, the family had got into their carriage, and the attendant had the steps in his hand.

Then, and not before, 'Good Gracious!' cried Miss Fanny all at once, 'Where's Amy!'

Her father had thought she was with her sister. Her sister had thought she was 'somewhere or other.' They had all trusted to finding her, as they had always done, quietly in the right place at the right moment. This going away was perhaps the very first action of their joint lives that they had got through without her.

A minute might have been consumed in the ascertaining of these points, when Miss Fanny, who, from her seat in the carriage, commanded the long narrow passage leading to the Lodge, flushed indignantly.

'Now I do say, Pa,' cried she, 'that this is disgraceful!'

'What is disgraceful, Fanny?'

'I do say,' she repeated, 'this is perfectly infamous! Really almost enough, even at such a time as this, to make one wish one was dead! Here is that child Amy, in her ugly old shabby dress, which she was so obstinate about, Pa, which I over and over again begged and prayed her to change, and which she over and over again objected to, and promised to change to-day, saying she wished to wear it as long as ever she remained in there with you—which was absolutely romantic nonsense of the lowest kind—here is that child Amy disgracing us, to the last moment and at the last moment, by being carried out in that dress after all. And by that Mr Clennam too!'

The offence was proved, as she delivered the indictment. Clennam appeared at the carriage-door, bearing the little insensible figure in his arms.

'She has been forgotten,' he said, in a tone of pity not free from reproach. 'I ran up to her room (which Mr Chivery showed me) and found the door open, and that she had fainted on the floor, dear child. She appeared to have gone to change her dress, and to have sunk down overpowered. It may have been the cheering, or it may have happened sooner. Take care of this poor cold hand, Miss Dorrit. Don't let it fall.'

'Thank you, sir,' returned Miss Dorrit, bursting into tears. 'I believe I know what to do, if you will give me leave. Dear Amy, open your eyes, that's a love! Oh, Amy, Amy, I really am so vexed and ashamed! Do rouse yourself, darling! Oh, why are they not driving on! Pray, Pa, do drive on!'

The attendant, getting between Clennam and the carriage-door, with a sharp 'By your leave, sir!' bundled up the steps, and they drove away.

In the autumn of the year, Darkness and Night were creeping up to the highest ridges of the Alps.

It was vintage time in the valleys on the Swiss side of the Pass of the Great Saint Bernard, and along the banks of the Lake of Geneva. The air there was charged with the scent of gathered grapes. Baskets, troughs, and tubs of grapes, stood in the dim village door-ways, stopped the steep and narrow village streets, and had been carrying all day along the roads and lanes. Grapes, spilt and crushed under foot, lay about everywhere. The child carried in a sling by the laden peasant woman toiling home, was quieted with picked-up grapes; the idiot sunning his big goître under the eaves of the wooden châlet by the way to the waterfall, sat munching grapes; the breath of the cows and goats was redolent of leaves and stalks of grapes; the company in every little cabaret were eating, drinking, talking grapes. A pity that no ripe touch of this generous abundance could be given to the thin, hard, stony wine, which after all was made from the grapes!

The air had been warm and transparent through the whole of the bright day. Shining metal spires and church-roofs, distant and rarely seen, had sparkled in the view; and the snowy mountain-tops had been so clear that unaccustomed eyes, cancelling the intervening country, and slighting their rugged height for something fabulous, would have measured them as within a few hours' easy reach. Mountain-peaks of great celebrity in the valleys, whence no trace of their existence was visible sometimes for months together, had been since morning plain and near, in the blue sky. And now, when it was dark below, though they seemed solemnly to recede, like spectres who were going to vanish, as the red dye of the sunset faded out of them and left them coldly white, they were yet distinctly defined in their loneliness, above the mists and shadows.

Seen from those solitudes, and from the Pass of the Great Saint Bernard, which was one of them, the ascending Night came up the mountain like a rising water. When it at last rose to the walls of the convent of the Great Saint Bernard, it was as if that weather-beaten structure were another Ark, and floated on the shadowy waves.

Darkness, outstripping some visitors on mules, had risen thus to the rough convent walls, when those travellers were yet climbing the mountain. As the heat of the glowing day, when they had stopped to drink at the streams of melted ice and snow, was changed to the searching cold of the frosty rarefied night air at a great height, so the fresh beauty of the lower journey had yielded to barrenness and desolation. A craggy track, up which the mules in single file, scrambled and turned from block to block, as though they were ascending the broken staircase of a gigantic ruin, was their way now. No trees were to be seen, nor any vegetable growth, save a poor brown scrubby moss, freezing in the chinks of rock. Blackened skeleton arms of wood by the wayside pointed upward to the convent, as if the ghosts of former travellers overwhelmed by the snow haunted the scene of their distress. Icicle-hung caves and cellars built for refuges from sudden storms, were like so many whispers of the perils of the place; never-resting wreaths and mazes of mist wandered about, hunted by a moaning wind; and snow, the besetting danger of the mountain, against which all its defences were taken, drifted sharply down.

The file of mules, jaded by their day's work, turned and wound slowly up the steep ascent; the foremost led by a guide on foot, in his broad-brimmed hat and round jacket, carrying a mountain staff or two upon his shoulder, with whom another guide conversed. There was no speaking among the string of riders. The sharp cold, the fatigue of the journey, and a new sensation of a catching in the breath, partly as if they had just emerged from very clear crisp water, and partly as if they had been sobbing, kept them silent.

At length, a light on the summit of the rocky staircase gleamed through the snow and mist. The guides called to the mules, the mules pricked up their drooping heads, the travellers' tongues were loosened, and in a sudden burst of slipping, climbing, jingling, clinking, and talking, they arrived at the convent door.

Other mules had arrived not long before, some with peasant riders and some with goods, and had trodden the snow about the door into a pool of mud. Riding-saddles and bridles, pack-saddles and strings of bells, mules and men, lanterns, torches, sacks, provender, barrels, cheeses, kegs of honey and butter, straw bundles and packages of many shapes, were crowded confusedly together in this thawed quagmire, and about the steps. Up here in the clouds, everything was seen through cloud, and seemed dissolving into cloud. The breath of the men was cloud, the breath of the mules was cloud, the lights were encircled by cloud, speakers close at hand were not seen for cloud, though their voices and all other sounds were surprisingly clear. Of the cloudy line of mules hastily tied to rings in the wall, one would bite another, or kick another, and then the whole mist would be disturbed: with men diving into it, and cries of men and beasts coming out of it, and no bystander discerning what was wrong. In the midst of this, the great stable of the convent, occupying the basement story, and entered by the basement door, outside which all the disorder was, poured forth its contribution of cloud, as if the whole rugged edifice were filled with nothing else, and would collapse as soon as it had emptied itself, leaving the snow to fall upon the bare mountain summit.

While all this noise and hurry were rife among the living travellers, there, too, silently assembled in a grated house, half-a-dozen paces removed, with the same cloud enfolding them, and the same snow-flakes drifting in upon them, were the dead travellers found upon the mountain. The mother, storm-belated many winters ago, still standing in the corner with her baby at her breast; the man who had frozen with his arm raised to his mouth in fear or hunger, still pressing it with his dry lips after years and years. An awful company, mysteriously come together! A wild destiny for that mother to have foreseen, 'Surrounded by so many and such companions upon whom I never looked, and never shall look, I and my child will dwell together inseparable, on the Great Saint Bernard, outlasting generations who will come to see us, and will never know our name, or one word of our story but the end.'

The living travellers thought little or nothing of the dead just then. They thought much more of alighting at the convent door, and warming themselves at the convent fire. Disengaged from the turmoil, which was already calming down as the crowd of mules began to be bestowed in the stable, they hurried shivering up the steps and into the building. There was a smell within, coming up from the floor, of tethered beasts, like the smell of a menagerie of wild animals. There were strong arched galleries within, huge stone piers, great staircases, and thick walls pierced with small sunken windows—fortifications against the mountain storms, as if they had been human enemies. There were gloomy vaulted sleeping-rooms within, intensely cold, but clean and hospitably prepared for guests. Finally, there was a parlour for guests to sit in and sup in, where a table was already laid, and where a blazing fire shone red and high.

In this room, after having had their quarters for the night allotted to them by two young Fathers, the travellers presently drew round the hearth. They were in three parties; of whom the first, as the most numerous and important, was the slowest, and had been overtaken by one of the others on the way up. It consisted of an elderly lady, two grey-haired gentlemen, two young ladies, and their brother. These were attended (not to mention four guides) by a courier, two footmen, and two waiting-maids: which strong body of inconvenience was accommodated elsewhere under the same roof. The party that had overtaken them, and followed in their train, consisted of only three members: one lady and two gentlemen. The third party, which had ascended from the valley on the Italian side of the Pass, and had arrived first, were four in number; a plethoric, hungry, and silent German tutor in spectacles, on a tour with three young men, his pupils, all plethoric, hungry, and silent, and all in spectacles.

These three groups sat round the fire eyeing each other drily, and waiting for supper. Only one among them, one of the gentlemen belonging to the party of three, made advances towards conversation. Throwing out his lines for the Chief of the important tribe, while addressing himself to his own companions, he remarked, in a tone of voice which included all the company if they chose to be included, that it had been a long day, and that he felt for the ladies. That he feared one of the young ladies was not a strong or accustomed traveller, and had been over-fatigued two or three hours ago. That he had observed, from his station in the rear, that she sat her mule as if she were exhausted. That he had, twice or thrice afterwards, done himself the honour of inquiring of one of the guides, when he fell behind, how the young lady did. That he had been enchanted to learn that she had recovered her spirits, and that it had been but a passing discomfort. That he trusted (by this time he had secured the eyes of the Chief, and addressed him) he might be permitted to express his hope that she was now none the worse, and that she would not regret having made the journey.

'My daughter, I am obliged to you, sir,' returned the Chief, 'is quite restored, and has been greatly interested.'

'New to mountains, perhaps?' said the insinuating traveller.

'New to—ha—to mountains,' said the Chief.

'But you are familiar with them, sir?' the insinuating traveller assumed.

'I am—hum—tolerably familiar. Not of late years. Not of late years,' replied the Chief, with a flourish of his hand.

The insinuating traveller, acknowledging the flourish with an inclination of his head, passed from the Chief to the second young lady, who had not yet been referred to, otherwise than as one of the ladies in whose behalf he felt so sensitive an interest.

He hoped she was not incommoded by the fatigues of the day.

'Incommoded, certainly,' returned the young lady, 'but not tired.'

The insinuating traveller complimented her on the justice of the distinction. It was what he had meant to say. Every lady must doubtless be incommoded, by having to do with that proverbially unaccommodating animal, the mule.

'We have had, of course,' said the young lady, who was rather reserved and haughty, 'to leave the carriages and fourgon at Martigny. And the impossibility of bringing anything that one wants to this inaccessible place, and the necessity of leaving every comfort behind, is not convenient.'

'A savage place, indeed,' said the insinuating traveller.

The elderly lady, who was a model of accurate dressing, and whose manner was perfect, considered as a piece of machinery, here interposed a remark in a low soft voice.

'But, like other inconvenient places,' she observed, 'it must be seen. As a place much spoken of, it is necessary to see it.'

'Oh! I have not the least objection to seeing it, I assure you, Mrs General,' returned the other, carelessly.

'You, madam,' said the insinuating traveller, 'have visited this spot before?'

'Yes,' returned Mrs General. 'I have been here before. Let me recommend you, my dear,' to the former young lady, 'to shade your face from the hot wood, after exposure to the mountain air and snow. You, too, my dear,' to the other and younger lady, who immediately did so; while the former merely said, 'Thank you, Mrs General, I am perfectly comfortable, and prefer remaining as I am.'

The brother, who had left his chair to open a piano that stood in the room, and who had whistled into it and shut it up again, now came strolling back to the fire with his glass in his eye. He was dressed in the very fullest and completest travelling trim. The world seemed hardly large enough to yield him an amount of travel proportionate to his equipment.

'These fellows are an immense time with supper,' he drawled. 'I wonder what they'll give us! Has anybody any idea?'

'Not roast man, I believe,' replied the voice of the second gentleman of the party of three.

'I suppose not. What d'ye mean?' he inquired.

'That, as you are not to be served for the general supper, perhaps you will do us the favour of not cooking yourself at the general fire,' returned the other.

The young gentleman, who was standing in an easy attitude on the hearth, cocking his glass at the company, with his back to the blaze and his coat tucked under his arms, something as if he were of the poultry species and were trussed for roasting, lost countenance at this reply; he seemed about to demand further explanation, when it was discovered—through all eyes turning on the speaker—that the lady with him, who was young and beautiful, had not heard what had passed, through having fainted with her head upon his shoulder.

'I think,' said the gentleman in a subdued tone, 'I had best carry her straight to her room. Will you call to some one to bring a light?' addressing his companion, 'and to show the way? In this strange rambling place I don't know that I could find it.'

'Pray let me call my maid,' cried the taller of the young ladies.

'Pray let me put this water to her lips,' said the shorter, who had not spoken yet.

Each doing what she suggested, there was no want of assistance. Indeed, when the two maids came in (escorted by the courier, lest any one should strike them dumb by addressing a foreign language to them on the road), there was a prospect of too much assistance. Seeing this, and saying as much in a few words to the slighter and younger of the two ladies, the gentleman put his wife's arm over his shoulder, lifted her up, and carried her away.

His friend, being left alone with the other visitors, walked slowly up and down the room, without coming to the fire again, pulling his black moustache in a contemplative manner, as if he felt himself committed to the late retort. While the subject of it was breathing injury in a corner, the Chief loftily addressed this gentleman.

'Your friend, sir,' said he, 'is—ha—is a little impatient; and, in his impatience, is not perhaps fully sensible of what he owes to—hum—to—but we will waive that, we will waive that. Your friend is a little impatient, sir.'

'It may be so, sir,' returned the other. 'But having had the honour of making that gentleman's acquaintance at the hotel at Geneva, where we and much good company met some time ago, and having had the honour of exchanging company and conversation with that gentleman on several subsequent excursions, I can hear nothing—no, not even from one of your appearance and station, sir—detrimental to that gentleman.'

'You are in no danger, sir, of hearing any such thing from me. In remarking that your friend has shown impatience, I say no such thing. I make that remark, because it is not to be doubted that my son, being by birth and by—ha—by education a—hum—a gentleman, would have readily adapted himself to any obligingly expressed wish on the subject of the fire being equally accessible to the whole of the present circle. Which, in principle, I—ha—for all are—hum—equal on these occasions—I consider right.'

'Good,' was the reply. 'And there it ends! I am your son's obedient servant. I beg your son to receive the assurance of my profound consideration. And now, sir, I may admit, freely admit, that my friend is sometimes of a sarcastic temper.'

'The lady is your friend's wife, sir?'

'The lady is my friend's wife, sir.'

'She is very handsome.'

'Sir, she is peerless. They are still in the first year of their marriage. They are still partly on a marriage, and partly on an artistic tour.'

'Your friend is an artist, sir?'

The gentleman replied by kissing the fingers of his right hand, and wafting the kiss the length of his arm towards Heaven. As who should say, I devote him to the celestial Powers as an immortal artist!

'But he is a man of family,' he added. 'His connexions are of the best. He is more than an artist: he is highly connected. He may, in effect, have repudiated his connexions, proudly, impatiently, sarcastically (I make the concession of both words); but he has them. Sparks that have been struck out during our intercourse have shown me this.'

'Well! I hope,' said the lofty gentleman, with the air of finally disposing of the subject, 'that the lady's indisposition may be only temporary.'

'Sir, I hope so.'

'Mere fatigue, I dare say.'

'Not altogether mere fatigue, sir, for her mule stumbled today, and she fell from the saddle. She fell lightly, and was up again without assistance, and rode from us laughing; but she complained towards evening of a slight bruise in the side. She spoke of it more than once, as we followed your party up the mountain.'

The head of the large retinue, who was gracious but not familiar, appeared by this time to think that he had condescended more than enough. He said no more, and there was silence for some quarter of an hour until supper appeared.

With the supper came one of the young Fathers (there seemed to be no old Fathers) to take the head of the table. It was like the supper of an ordinary Swiss hotel, and good red wine grown by the convent in more genial air was not wanting. The artist traveller calmly came and took his place at table when the rest sat down, with no apparent sense upon him of his late skirmish with the completely dressed traveller.

'Pray,' he inquired of the host, over his soup, 'has your convent many of its famous dogs now?'

'Monsieur, it has three.'

'I saw three in the gallery below. Doubtless the three in question.'

The host, a slender, bright-eyed, dark young man of polite manners, whose garment was a black gown with strips of white crossed over it like braces, and who no more resembled the conventional breed of Saint Bernard monks than he resembled the conventional breed of Saint Bernard dogs, replied, doubtless those were the three in question.

'And I think,' said the artist traveller, 'I have seen one of them before.'

It was possible. He was a dog sufficiently well known. Monsieur might have easily seen him in the valley or somewhere on the lake, when he (the dog) had gone down with one of the order to solicit aid for the convent.

'Which is done in its regular season of the year, I think?'

Monsieur was right.

'And never without the dog. The dog is very important.'

Again Monsieur was right. The dog was very important. People were justly interested in the dog. As one of the dogs celebrated everywhere, Ma'amselle would observe.

Ma'amselle was a little slow to observe it, as though she were not yet well accustomed to the French tongue. Mrs General, however, observed it for her.

'Ask him if he has saved many lives?' said, in his native English, the young man who had been put out of countenance.

The host needed no translation of the question. He promptly replied in French, 'No. Not this one.'

'Why not?' the same gentleman asked.

'Pardon,' returned the host, composedly, 'give him the opportunity and he will do it without doubt. For example, I am well convinced,' smiling sedately, as he cut up the dish of veal to be handed round, on the young man who had been put out of countenance, 'that if you, Monsieur, would give him the opportunity, he would hasten with great ardour to fulfil his duty.'

The artist traveller laughed. The insinuating traveller (who evinced a provident anxiety to get his full share of the supper), wiping some drops of wine from his moustache with a piece of bread, joined the conversation.

'It is becoming late in the year, my Father,' said he, 'for tourist-travellers, is it not?'

'Yes, it is late. Yet two or three weeks, at most, and we shall be left to the winter snows.'

'And then,' said the insinuating traveller, 'for the scratching dogs and the buried children, according to the pictures!'

'Pardon,' said the host, not quite understanding the allusion. 'How, then the scratching dogs and the buried children according to the pictures?'

The artist traveller struck in again, before an answer could be given.

'Don't you know,' he coldly inquired across the table of his companion, 'that none but smugglers come this way in the winter or can have any possible business this way?'

'Holy blue! No; never heard of it.'

'So it is, I believe. And as they know the signs of the weather tolerably well, they don't give much employment to the dogs—who have consequently died out rather—though this house of entertainment is conveniently situated for themselves. Their young families, I am told, they usually leave at home. But it's a grand idea!' cried the artist traveller, unexpectedly rising into a tone of enthusiasm. 'It's a sublime idea. It's the finest idea in the world, and brings tears into a man's eyes, by Jupiter!' He then went on eating his veal with great composure.

There was enough of mocking inconsistency at the bottom of this speech to make it rather discordant, though the manner was refined and the person well-favoured, and though the depreciatory part of it was so skilfully thrown off, as to be very difficult for one not perfectly acquainted with the English language to understand, or, even understanding, to take offence at: so simple and dispassionate was its tone. After finishing his veal in the midst of silence, the speaker again addressed his friend.

'Look,' said he, in his former tone, 'at this gentleman our host, not yet in the prime of life, who in so graceful a way and with such courtly urbanity and modesty presides over us! Manners fit for a crown! Dine with the Lord Mayor of London (if you can get an invitation) and observe the contrast. This dear fellow, with the finest cut face I ever saw, a face in perfect drawing, leaves some laborious life and comes up here I don't know how many feet above the level of the sea, for no other purpose on earth (except enjoying himself, I hope, in a capital refectory) than to keep an hotel for idle poor devils like you and me, and leave the bill to our consciences! Why, isn't it a beautiful sacrifice? What do you want more to touch us? Because rescued people of interesting appearance are not, for eight or nine months out of every twelve, holding on here round the necks of the most sagacious of dogs carrying wooden bottles, shall we disparage the place? No! Bless the place. It's a great place, a glorious place!'

The chest of the grey-haired gentleman who was the Chief of the important party, had swelled as if with a protest against his being numbered among poor devils. No sooner had the artist traveller ceased speaking than he himself spoke with great dignity, as having it incumbent on him to take the lead in most places, and having deserted that duty for a little while.

He weightily communicated his opinion to their host, that his life must be a very dreary life here in the winter.

The host allowed to Monsieur that it was a little monotonous. The air was difficult to breathe for a length of time consecutively. The cold was very severe. One needed youth and strength to bear it. However, having them and the blessing of Heaven—

Yes, that was very good. 'But the confinement,' said the grey-haired gentleman.

There were many days, even in bad weather, when it was possible to walk about outside. It was the custom to beat a little track, and take exercise there.

'But the space,' urged the grey-haired gentleman. 'So small. So—ha—very limited.'

Monsieur would recall to himself that there were the refuges to visit, and that tracks had to be made to them also.

Monsieur still urged, on the other hand, that the space was so—ha—hum—so very contracted. More than that, it was always the same, always the same.

With a deprecating smile, the host gently raised and gently lowered his shoulders. That was true, he remarked, but permit him to say that almost all objects had their various points of view. Monsieur and he did not see this poor life of his from the same point of view. Monsieur was not used to confinement.

'I—ha—yes, very true,' said the grey-haired gentleman. He seemed to receive quite a shock from the force of the argument.

Monsieur, as an English traveller, surrounded by all means of travelling pleasantly; doubtless possessing fortune, carriages, and servants—

'Perfectly, perfectly. Without doubt,' said the gentleman.

Monsieur could not easily place himself in the position of a person who had not the power to choose, I will go here to-morrow, or there next day; I will pass these barriers, I will enlarge those bounds. Monsieur could not realise, perhaps, how the mind accommodated itself in such things to the force of necessity.

'It is true,' said Monsieur. 'We will—ha—not pursue the subject. You are—hum—quite accurate, I have no doubt. We will say no more.'

The supper having come to a close, he drew his chair away as he spoke, and moved back to his former place by the fire. As it was very cold at the greater part of the table, the other guests also resumed their former seats by the fire, designing to toast themselves well before going to bed. The host, when they rose from table, bowed to all present, wished them good night, and withdrew. But first the insinuating traveller had asked him if they could have some wine made hot; and as he had answered Yes, and had presently afterwards sent it in, that traveller, seated in the centre of the group, and in the full heat of the fire, was soon engaged in serving it out to the rest.

At this time, the younger of the two young ladies, who had been silently attentive in her dark corner (the fire-light was the chief light in the sombre room, the lamp being smoky and dull) to what had been said of the absent lady, glided out. She was at a loss which way to turn, when she had softly closed the door; but, after a little hesitation among the sounding passages and the many ways, came to a room in a corner of the main gallery, where the servants were at their supper. From these she obtained a lamp, and a direction to the lady's room.

It was up the great staircase on the story above. Here and there, the bare white walls were broken by an iron grate, and she thought as she went along that the place was something like a prison. The arched door of the lady's room, or cell, was not quite shut. After knocking at it two or three times without receiving an answer, she pushed it gently open, and looked in.

The lady lay with closed eyes on the outside of the bed, protected from the cold by the blankets and wrappers with which she had been covered when she revived from her fainting fit. A dull light placed in the deep recess of the window, made little impression on the arched room. The visitor timidly stepped to the bed, and said, in a soft whisper, 'Are you better?'

The lady had fallen into a slumber, and the whisper was too low to awake her. Her visitor, standing quite still, looked at her attentively.

'She is very pretty,' she said to herself. 'I never saw so beautiful a face. O how unlike me!'

It was a curious thing to say, but it had some hidden meaning, for it filled her eyes with tears.

'I know I must be right. I know he spoke of her that evening. I could very easily be wrong on any other subject, but not on this, not on this!'

With a quiet and tender hand she put aside a straying fold of the sleeper's hair, and then touched the hand that lay outside the covering.

'I like to look at her,' she breathed to herself. 'I like to see what has affected him so much.'

She had not withdrawn her hand, when the sleeper opened her eyes, and started.

'Pray don't be alarmed. I am only one of the travellers from downstairs. I came to ask if you were better, and if I could do anything for you.'

'I think you have already been so kind as to send your servants to my assistance?'

'No, not I; that was my sister. Are you better?'

'Much better. It is only a slight bruise, and has been well looked to, and is almost easy now. It made me giddy and faint in a moment. It had hurt me before; but at last it overpowered me all at once.'

'May I stay with you until some one comes? Would you like it?'

'I should like it, for it is lonely here; but I am afraid you will feel the cold too much.'

'I don't mind cold. I am not delicate, if I look so.' She quickly moved one of the two rough chairs to the bedside, and sat down. The other as quickly moved a part of some travelling wrapper from herself, and drew it over her, so that her arm, in keeping it about her, rested on her shoulder.

'You have so much the air of a kind nurse,' said the lady, smiling on her, 'that you seem as if you had come to me from home.'

'I am very glad of it.'

'I was dreaming of home when I woke just now. Of my old home, I mean, before I was married.'

'And before you were so far away from it.'

'I have been much farther away from it than this; but then I took the best part of it with me, and missed nothing. I felt solitary as I dropped asleep here, and, missing it a little, wandered back to it.'

There was a sorrowfully affectionate and regretful sound in her voice, which made her visitor refrain from looking at her for the moment.

'It is a curious chance which at last brings us together, under this covering in which you have wrapped me,' said the visitor, after a pause; 'for do you know, I think I have been looking for you, some time.'

'Looking for me?'

'I believe I have a little note here, which I was to give to you whenever I found you. This is it. Unless I greatly mistake, it is addressed to you. Is it not?'

The lady took it, and said yes, and read it. Her visitor watched her as she did so. It was very short. She flushed a little as she put her lips to her visitor's cheek, and pressed her hand.

'The dear young friend to whom he presents me, may be a comfort to me at some time, he says. She is truly a comfort to me, the first time I see her.'

'Perhaps you don't,' said the visitor, hesitating—'perhaps you don't know my story? Perhaps he never told you my story?'

'No.'

'O, no, why should he! I have scarcely the right to tell it myself at present, because I have been entreated not to do so. There is not much in it, but it might account to you for my asking you not to say anything about the letter here. You saw my family with me, perhaps? Some of them—I only say this to you—are a little proud, a little prejudiced.'

'You shall take it back again,' said the other; 'and then my husband is sure not to see it. He might see it and speak of it, otherwise, by some accident. Will you put it in your bosom again, to be certain?'

She did so with great care. Her small, slight hand was still upon the letter, when they heard some one in the gallery outside.

'I promised,' said the visitor, rising, 'that I would write to him after seeing you (I could hardly fail to see you sooner or later), and tell him if you were well and happy. I had better say you were well and happy.'

'Yes, yes, yes! Say I was very well and very happy. And that I thanked him affectionately, and would never forget him.'

'I shall see you in the morning. After that we are sure to meet again before very long. Good night!'

'Good night. Thank you, thank you. Good night, my dear!'

Both of them were hurried and fluttered as they exchanged this parting, and as the visitor came out of the door. She had expected to meet the lady's husband approaching it; but the person in the gallery was not he: it was the traveller who had wiped the wine-drops from his moustache with the piece of bread. When he heard the step behind him, he turned round—for he was walking away in the dark.

His politeness, which was extreme, would not allow of the young lady's lighting herself down-stairs, or going down alone. He took her lamp, held it so as to throw the best light on the stone steps, and followed her all the way to the supper-room. She went down, not easily hiding how much she was inclined to shrink and tremble; for the appearance of this traveller was particularly disagreeable to her. She had sat in her quiet corner before supper, imagining what he would have been in the scenes and places within her experience, until he inspired her with an aversion, that made him little less than terrific.

He followed her down with his smiling politeness, followed her in, and resumed his seat in the best place on the hearth. There, with the wood-fire, which was beginning to burn low, rising and falling upon him in the dark room, he sat with his legs thrust out to warm, drinking the hot wine down to the lees, with a monstrous shadow imitating him on the wall and ceiling.

The tired company had broken up, and all the rest were gone to bed except the young lady's father, who dozed in his chair by the fire. The traveller had been at the pains of going a long way up-stairs to his sleeping room, to fetch his pocket-flask of brandy. He told them so, as he poured its contents into what was left of the wine, and drank with a new relish.

'May I ask, sir, if you are on your way to Italy?'

The grey-haired gentleman had roused himself, and was preparing to withdraw. He answered in the affirmative.

'I also!' said the traveller. 'I shall hope to have the honour of offering my compliments in fairer scenes, and under softer circumstances, than on this dismal mountain.'

The gentleman bowed, distantly enough, and said he was obliged to him.

'We poor gentlemen, sir,' said the traveller, pulling his moustache dry with his hand, for he had dipped it in the wine and brandy; 'we poor gentlemen do not travel like princes, but the courtesies and graces of life are precious to us. To your health, sir!'

'Sir, I thank you.'

'To the health of your distinguished family—of the fair ladies, your daughters!'

'Sir, I thank you again. I wish you good night. My dear, are our—ha—our people in attendance?'

'They are close by, father.'

'Permit me!' said the traveller, rising and holding the door open, as the gentleman crossed the room towards it with his arm drawn through his daughter's. 'Good repose! To the pleasure of seeing you once more! To to-morrow!'

As he kissed his hand, with his best manner and his daintiest smile, the young lady drew a little nearer to her father, and passed him with a dread of touching him.

'Humph!' said the insinuating traveller, whose manner shrunk, and whose voice dropped when he was left alone. 'If they all go to bed, why I must go. They are in a devil of a hurry. One would think the night would be long enough, in this freezing silence and solitude, if one went to bed two hours hence.'

Throwing back his head in emptying his glass, he cast his eyes upon the travellers' book, which lay on the piano, open, with pens and ink beside it, as if the night's names had been registered when he was absent. Taking it in his hand, he read these entries.

William Dorrit, Esquire	
Frederick Dorrit, Esquire	And suite.
Edward Dorrit, Esquire	From
Miss Dorrit	France
Miss Amy Dorrit	to Italy.
Mrs General	

Mr and Mrs Henry Gowan. From France to Italy.

To which he added, in a small complicated hand, ending with a long lean flourish, not unlike a lasso thrown at all the rest of the names:

Blandois. Paris. From France to Italy.

And then, with his nose coming down over his moustache, and his moustache going up under his nose, repaired to his allotted cell.

It is indispensable to present the accomplished lady, who was of sufficient importance in the suite of the Dorrit Family to have a line to herself in the Travellers' Book.

Mrs General was the daughter of a clerical dignitary in a cathedral town, where she had led the fashion until she was as near forty-five as a single lady can be. A stiff commissariat officer of sixty, famous as a martinet, had then become enamoured of the gravity with which she drove the proprieties four-in-hand through the cathedral town society, and had solicited to be taken beside her on the box of the cool coach of ceremony to which that team was harnessed. His proposal of marriage being accepted by the lady, the commissary took his seat behind the proprieties with great decorum, and Mrs General drove until the commissary died. In the course of their united journey, they ran over several people who came in the way of the proprieties; but always in a high style, and with composure.

The commissary having been buried with all the decorations suitable to the service (the whole team of proprieties were harnessed to his hearse, and they all had feathers and black velvet housings, with his coat of arms in the corner), Mrs General began to inquire what quantity of dust and ashes was deposited at the bankers'. It then transpired that the commissary had so far stolen a march on Mrs General as to have bought himself an annuity some years before his marriage, and to have reserved that circumstance, in mentioning, at the period of his proposal, that his income was derived from the interest of his money. Mrs General consequently found her means so much diminished, that, but for the perfect regulation of her mind, she might have felt disposed to question the accuracy of that portion of the late service which had declared that the commissary could take nothing away with him.

In this state of affairs it occurred to Mrs General, that she might 'form the mind,' and eke the manners of some young lady of distinction. Or, that she might harness the proprieties to the carriage of some rich young heiress or widow, and become at once the driver and guard of such vehicle through the social mazes. Mrs General's communication of this idea to her clerical and commissariat connection was so warmly applauded that, but for the lady's undoubted merit, it might have appeared as though they wanted to get rid of her. Testimonials representing Mrs General as a prodigy of piety, learning, virtue, and gentility, were lavishly contributed from influential quarters; and one venerable archdeacon even shed tears in recording his testimony to her perfections (described to him by persons on whom he could rely), though he had never had the honour and moral gratification of setting eyes on Mrs General in all his life.

Thus delegated on her mission, as it were by Church and State, Mrs General, who had always occupied high ground, felt in a condition to keep it, and began by putting herself up at a very high figure. An interval of some duration elapsed, in which there was no bid for Mrs General. At length a county-widower, with a daughter of fourteen, opened negotiations with the lady; and as it was a part either of the native dignity or of the artificial policy of Mrs General (but certainly one or the other) to comport herself as if she were much more sought than seeking, the widower pursued Mrs General until he prevailed upon her to form his daughter's mind and manners.

The execution of this trust occupied Mrs General about seven years, in the course of which time she made the tour of Europe, and saw most of that extensive miscellany of objects which it is essential that all persons of polite cultivation should see with other people's eyes, and never with their own. When her charge was at length formed, the marriage, not only of the young lady, but likewise of her father the widower, was resolved on. The widower then finding Mrs General both inconvenient and expensive, became of a sudden almost as much affected by her merits as the archdeacon had been, and circulated such praises of her surpassing worth, in all quarters where he thought an opportunity might arise of transferring the blessing to somebody else, that Mrs General was a name more honourable than ever.

The phoenix was to let, on this elevated perch, when Mr Dorrit, who had lately succeeded to his property, mentioned to his bankers that he wished to discover a lady, well bred, accomplished, well connected, well accustomed to good society, who was qualified at once to complete the education of his daughters, and to be their matron or chaperon. Mr Dorrit's bankers, as the bankers of the county-widower, instantly said, 'Mrs General.'

Pursuing the light so fortunately hit upon, and finding the concurrent testimony of the whole of Mrs General's acquaintance to be of the pathetic nature already recorded, Mr Dorrit took the trouble of going down to the county of the county-widower, to see Mrs General. In whom he found a lady of a quality superior to his highest expectations.

'Might I be excused,' said Mr Dorrit, 'if I inquired—ha—what remune—'

'Why, indeed,' returned Mrs General, stopping the word, 'it is a subject on which I prefer to avoid entering. I have never entered on it with my friends here; and I cannot overcome the delicacy, Mr Dorrit, with which I have always regarded it. I am not, as I hope you are aware, a governess—'

'O dear no!' said Mr Dorrit. 'Pray, madam, do not imagine for a moment that I think so.' He really blushed to be suspected of it.

Mrs General gravely inclined her head. 'I cannot, therefore, put a price upon services which it is a pleasure to me to render, if I can render them spontaneously, but which I could not render in mere return for any consideration. Neither do I know how, or where, to find a case parallel to my own. It is peculiar.'

No doubt. But how then (Mr Dorrit not unnaturally hinted) could the subject be approached?

'I cannot object,' said Mrs General—'though even that is disagreeable to me—to Mr Dorrit's inquiring, in confidence of my friends here, what amount they have been accustomed, at quarterly intervals, to pay to my credit at my bankers'.'

Mr Dorrit bowed his acknowledgments.

'Permit me to add,' said Mrs General, 'that beyond this, I can never resume the topic. Also that I can accept no second or inferior position. If the honour were proposed to me of becoming known to Mr Dorrit's family—I think two daughters were mentioned?—'

'Two daughters.'

'I could only accept it on terms of perfect equality, as a companion, protector, Mentor, and friend.'

Mr Dorrit, in spite of his sense of his importance, felt as if it would be quite a kindness in her to accept it on any conditions. He almost said as much.

'I think,' repeated Mrs General, 'two daughters were mentioned?'

'Two daughters,' said Mr Dorrit again.

'It would therefore,' said Mrs General, 'be necessary to add a third more to the payment (whatever its amount may prove to be), which my friends here have been accustomed to make to my bankers.'

Mr Dorrit lost no time in referring the delicate question to the county-widower, and, finding that he had been accustomed to pay three hundred pounds a-year to the credit of Mrs General, arrived, without any severe strain on his arithmetic, at the conclusion that he himself must pay four. Mrs General being an article of that lustrous surface which suggests that it is worth any money, he made a formal proposal to be allowed to have the honour and pleasure of regarding her as a member of his family. Mrs General conceded that high privilege, and here she was.

In person, Mrs General, including her skirts which had much to do with it, was of a dignified and imposing appearance; ample, rustling, gravely voluminous; always upright behind the properties. She might have been taken—had been taken—to the top of the Alps and the bottom of Herculaneum, without disarranging a fold in her dress, or displacing a pin. If her countenance and hair had rather a floury appearance, as though from living in some transcendently genteel Mill, it was rather because she was a chalky creation altogether, than because she mended her complexion with violet powder, or had turned grey. If her eyes had no expression, it was probably because they had nothing to express. If she had few wrinkles, it was because her mind had never traced its name or any other inscription on her face. A cool, waxy, blown-out woman, who had never lighted well.

Mrs General had no opinions. Her way of forming a mind was to prevent it from forming opinions. She had a little circular set of mental grooves or rails on which she started little trains of other people's opinions, which never overtook one another, and never got anywhere. Even her propriety could not dispute that there was impropriety in the world; but Mrs General's way of getting rid of it was to put it out of sight, and make believe that there was no such thing. This was another of her ways of forming a mind—to cram all articles of difficulty into cupboards, lock them up, and say they had no existence. It was the easiest way, and, beyond all comparison, the properest.

Mrs General was not to be told of anything shocking. Accidents, miseries, and offences, were never to be mentioned before her. Passion was to go to sleep in the presence of Mrs General, and blood was to change to milk and water. The little that was left in the world, when all these deductions were made, it was Mrs General's province to varnish. In that formation process of hers, she dipped the smallest of brushes into the largest of pots, and varnished the surface of every object that came under consideration. The more cracked it was, the more Mrs General varnished it.

There was varnish in Mrs General's voice, varnish in Mrs General's touch, an atmosphere of varnish round Mrs General's figure. Mrs General's dreams ought to have been varnished—if she had any—lying asleep in the arms of the good Saint Bernard, with the feathery snow falling on his house-top.

The bright morning sun dazzled the eyes, the snow had ceased, the mists had vanished, the mountain air was so clear and light that the new sensation of breathing it was like the having entered on a new existence. To help the delusion, the solid ground itself seemed gone, and the mountain, a shining waste of immense white heaps and masses, to be a region of cloud floating between the blue sky above and the earth far below.

Some dark specks in the snow, like knots upon a little thread, beginning at the convent door and winding away down the descent in broken lengths which were not yet pieced together, showed where the Brethren were at work in several places clearing the track. Already the snow had begun to be foot-thawed again about the door. Mules were busily brought out, tied to the rings in the wall, and laden; strings of bells were buckled on, burdens were adjusted, the voices of drivers and riders sounded musically. Some of the earliest had even already resumed their journey; and, both on the level summit by the dark water near the convent, and on the downward way of yesterday's ascent, little moving figures of men and mules, reduced to miniatures by the immensity around, went with a clear tinkling of bells and a pleasant harmony of tongues.

In the supper-room of last night, a new fire piled upon the feathery ashes of the old one, shone upon a homely breakfast of loaves, butter, and milk. It also shone on the courier of the Dorrit family, making tea for his party from a supply he had brought up with him, together with several other small stores which were chiefly laid in for the use of the strong body of inconvenience. Mr Gowan, and Blandois of Paris, had already breakfasted, and were walking up and down by the lake, smoking their cigars.

'Gowan, eh?' muttered Tip, otherwise Edward Dorrit, Esquire, turning over the leaves of the book, when the courier had left them to breakfast. 'Then Gowan is the name of a puppy, that's all I have got to say! If it was worth my while, I'd pull his nose. But it isn't worth my while—fortunately for him. How's his wife, Amy? I suppose you know. You generally know things of that sort.'

'She is better, Edward. But they are not going to-day.'

'Oh! They are not going to-day! Fortunately for that fellow too,' said Tip, 'or he and I might have come into collision.'

'It is thought better here that she should lie quiet to-day, and not be fatigued and shaken by the ride down until to-morrow.'

'With all my heart. But you talk as if you had been nursing her. You haven't been relapsing into (Mrs General is not here) into old habits, have you, Amy?'

He asked her the question with a sly glance of observation at Miss Fanny, and at his father too.

'I have only been in to ask her if I could do anything for her, Tip,' said Little Dorrit.

'You needn't call me Tip, Amy child,' returned that young gentleman with a frown; 'because that's an old habit, and one you may as well lay aside.'

'I didn't mean to say so, Edward dear. I forgot. It was so natural once, that it seemed at the moment the right word.'

'Oh yes!' Miss Fanny struck in. 'Natural, and right word, and once, and all the rest of it! Nonsense, you little thing! I know perfectly well why you have been taking such an interest in this Mrs Gowan. You can't blind *me*.'

'I will not try to, Fanny. Don't be angry.'

'Oh! angry!' returned that young lady with a flounce. 'I have no patience' (which indeed was the truth).

'Pray, Fanny,' said Mr Dorrit, raising his eyebrows, 'what do you mean? Explain yourself.'

'Oh! Never mind, Pa,' replied Miss Fanny, 'it's no great matter. Amy will understand me. She knew, or knew of, this Mrs Gowan before yesterday, and she may as well admit that she did.'

'My child,' said Mr Dorrit, turning to his younger daughter, 'has your sister—any—ha—authority for this curious statement?'

'However meek we are,' Miss Fanny struck in before she could answer, 'we don't go creeping into people's rooms on the tops of cold mountains, and sitting perishing in the frost with people, unless we know something about them beforehand. It's not very hard to divine whose friend Mrs Gowan is.'

'Whose friend?' inquired her father.

'Pa, I am sorry to say,' returned Miss Fanny, who had by this time succeeded in goading herself into a state of much ill-usage and grievance, which she was often at great pains to do: 'that I believe her to be a friend of that very objectionable and unpleasant person, who, with a total absence of all delicacy, which our experience might have led us to expect from him, insulted us and outraged our feelings in so public and wilful a manner, on an occasion to which it is understood among us that we will not more pointedly allude.'

'Amy, my child,' said Mr Dorrit, tempering a bland severity with a dignified affection, 'is this the case?'

Little Dorrit mildly answered, yes it was.

'Yes it is!' cried Miss Fanny. 'Of course! I said so! And now, Pa, I do declare once for all,' this young lady was in the habit of declaring the same thing once for all every day of her life, and even several times in a day, 'that this is shameful! I do declare once for all that it ought to be put a stop to. Is it not enough that we have gone through what is only known to ourselves, but are we to have it thrown in our faces, perseveringly and systematically, by the very person who should spare our feelings most? Are we to be exposed to this unnatural conduct every moment of our lives? Are we never to be permitted to forget? I say again, it is absolutely infamous!'

'Well, Amy,' observed her brother, shaking his head, 'you know I stand by you whenever I can, and on most occasions. But I must say, that upon my soul I do consider it rather an unaccountable mode of showing your sisterly affection, that you should back up a man who treated me in the most ungentlemanly way in which one man can treat another. And who,' he added convincingly, 'must be a low-minded thief, you know, or he never could have conducted himself as he did.'

'And see,' said Miss Fanny, 'see what is involved in this! Can we ever hope to be respected by our servants? Never. Here are our two women, and Pa's valet, and a footman, and a courier, and all sorts of dependants, and yet in the midst of these, we are to have one of ourselves rushing about with tumblers of cold water, like a menial! Why, a policeman,' said Miss Fanny, 'if a beggar had a fit in the street, could but go plunging about with tumblers, as this very Amy did in this very room before our very eyes last night!'

'I don't so much mind that, once in a way,' remarked Mr Edward; 'but your Clennam, as he thinks proper to call himself, is another thing.'

'He is a part of the same thing,' returned Miss Fanny, 'and of a piece with all the rest. He obtruded himself upon us in the first instance. We never wanted him. I always showed him, for one, that I could have dispensed with his company with the greatest pleasure. He then commits that gross outrage upon our feelings, which he never could or would have committed but for the delight he took in exposing us; and then we are to be demeaned for the service of his friends! Why, I don't wonder at this Mr Gowan's conduct towards you. What else was to be expected when he was enjoying our past misfortunes—gloating over them at the moment!'

'Father—Edward—no indeed!' pleaded Little Dorrit. 'Neither Mr nor Mrs Gowan had ever heard our name. They were, and they are, quite ignorant of our history.'

'So much the worse,' retorted Fanny, determined not to admit anything in extenuation, 'for then you have *no* excuse. If they had known about us, you might have felt yourself called upon to conciliate them. That would have been a weak and ridiculous mistake, but I can respect a mistake, whereas I can't respect a wilful and deliberate abasing of those who should be nearest and dearest to us. No. I can't respect that. I can do nothing but denounce that.'

'I never offend you wilfully, Fanny,' said Little Dorrit, 'though you are so hard with me.'

'Then you should be more careful, Amy,' returned her sister. 'If you do such things by accident, you should be more careful. If I happened to have been born in a peculiar place, and under peculiar circumstances that blunted my knowledge of propriety, I fancy I should think myself bound to consider at every step, "Am I going, ignorantly, to compromise any near and dear relations?" That is what I fancy *I* should do, if it was *my* case.'

Mr Dorrit now interposed, at once to stop these painful subjects by his authority, and to point their moral by his wisdom.

'My dear,' said he to his younger daughter, 'I beg you to—ha—to say no more. Your sister Fanny expresses herself strongly, but not without considerable reason. You have now a—hum—a great position to support. That great position is not occupied by yourself alone, but by—ha—by me, and—ha hum—by us. Us. Now, it is incumbent upon all people in an exalted position, but it is particularly so on this family, for reasons which I—ha—will not dwell upon, to make themselves respected. To be vigilant in making themselves respected. Dependants, to respect us, must be—ha—kept at a distance and—hum—kept down. Down. Therefore, your not exposing yourself to the remarks of our attendants, by appearing to have at any time dispensed with their services and performed them for yourself, is—ha—highly important.'

'Why, who can doubt it?' cried Miss Fanny. 'It's the essence of everything.'

'Fanny,' returned her father, grandiloquently, 'give me leave, my dear. We then come to—ha—to Mr Clennam. I am free to say that I do not, Amy, share your sister's sentiments—that is to say altogether—hum—altogether—in reference to Mr Clennam. I am content to regard that individual in the light of—ha—generally—a well-behaved person. Hum. A well-behaved person. Nor will I inquire whether Mr Clennam did, at any time, obtrude himself on—ha—my society. He knew my society to be—hum—sought, and his plea might be that he regarded me in the light of a public character. But there were circumstances attending my—ha—slight knowledge of Mr Clennam (it was very slight), which,' here Mr Dorrit became extremely grave and impressive, 'would render it highly indelicate in Mr Clennam to—ha—to seek to renew communication with me or with any member of my family under existing circumstances. If Mr Clennam has sufficient delicacy to perceive the impropriety of any such attempt, I am bound as a responsible gentleman to—ha—defer to that delicacy on his part. If, on the other hand, Mr Clennam has not that delicacy, I cannot for a moment—ha—hold any correspondence with so—hum—coarse a mind. In either case, it would appear that Mr Clennam is put altogether out of the question, and that we have nothing to do with him or he with us. Ha—Mrs General!'

The entrance of the lady whom he announced, to take her place at the breakfast-table, terminated the discussion. Shortly afterwards, the courier announced that the valet, and the footman, and the two maids, and the four guides, and the fourteen mules, were in readiness; so the breakfast party went out to the convent door to join the cavalcade.

Mr Gowan stood aloof with his cigar and pencil, but Mr Blandois was on the spot to pay his respects to the ladies. When he gallantly pulled off his slouched hat to Little Dorrit, she thought he had even a more sinister look, standing swart and cloaked in the snow, than he had in the fire-light over-night. But, as both her father and her sister received his homage with some favour, she refrained from expressing any distrust of him, lest it should prove to be a new blemish derived from her prison birth.

Nevertheless, as they wound down the rugged way while the convent was yet in sight, she more than once looked round, and descried Mr Blandois, backed by the convent smoke which rose straight and high from the chimneys in a golden film, always standing on one jutting point looking down after them. Long after he was a mere black stick in the snow, she felt as though she could yet see that smile of his, that high nose, and those eyes that were too near it. And even after that, when the convent was gone and some light morning clouds veiled the pass below it, the ghastly skeleton arms by the wayside seemed to be all pointing up at him.

More treacherous than snow, perhaps, colder at heart, and harder to melt, Blandois of Paris by degrees passed out of her mind, as they came down into the softer regions. Again the sun was warm, again the streams descending from glaciers and snowy caverns were refreshing to drink at, again they came among the pine-trees, the rocky rivulets, the verdant heights and dales, the wooden châlets and rough zigzag fences of Swiss country. Sometimes, the way so widened that she and her father could ride abreast. And then to look at him, handsomely clothed in his fur and broadcloths, rich, free, numerously served and attended, his eyes roving far away among the glories of the landscape, no miserable screen before them to darken his sight and cast its shadow on him, was enough.

Her uncle was so far rescued from that shadow of old, that he wore the clothes they gave him, and performed some ablutions as a sacrifice to the family credit, and went where he was taken, with a certain patient animal enjoyment, which seemed to express that the air and change did him good. In all other respects, save one, he shone with no light but such as was reflected from his brother. His brother's greatness, wealth, freedom, and grandeur, pleased him without any reference to himself. Silent and retiring, he had no use for speech when he could hear his brother speak; no desire to be waited on, so that the servants devoted themselves to his brother. The only noticeable change he originated in himself, was an alteration in his manner to his younger niece. Every day it refined more and more into a marked respect, very rarely shown by age to youth, and still more rarely susceptible, one would have said, of the fitness with which he invested it. On those occasions when Miss Fanny did declare once for all, he would take the next opportunity of baring his grey head before his younger niece, and of helping her to alight, or handing her to the carriage, or showing her any other attention, with the profoundest deference. Yet it never appeared misplaced or forced, being always heartily simple, spontaneous, and genuine. Neither would he ever consent, even at his brother's request, to be helped to any place before her, or to take precedence of her in anything. So jealous was he of her being respected, that on this very journey down from the Great Saint Bernard, he took sudden and violent umbrage at the footman's being remiss to hold her stirrup, though standing near when she dismounted; and unspeakably astonished the whole retinue by charging at him on a hard-headed mule, riding him into a corner, and threatening to trample him to death.

They were a goodly company, and the Innkeepers all but worshipped them. Wherever they went, their importance preceded them in the person of the courier riding before, to see that the rooms of state were ready. He was the herald of the family procession. The great travelling-carriage came next: containing, inside, Mr Dorrit, Miss Dorrit, Miss Amy Dorrit, and Mrs General; outside, some of the retainers, and (in fine weather) Edward Dorrit, Esquire, for whom the box was reserved. Then came the chariot containing Frederick Dorrit, Esquire, and an empty place occupied by Edward Dorrit, Esquire, in wet weather. Then came the fourgon with the rest of the retainers, the heavy baggage, and as much as it could carry of the mud and dust which the other vehicles left behind.

These equipages adorned the yard of the hotel at Martigny, on the return of the family from their mountain excursion. Other vehicles were there, much company being on the road, from the patched Italian Vettura—like the body of a swing from an English fair put upon a wooden tray on wheels, and having another wooden tray without wheels put atop of it—to the trim English carriage. But there was another adornment of the hotel which Mr Dorrit had not bargained for. Two strange travellers embellished one of his rooms.

The Innkeeper, hat in hand in the yard, swore to the courier that he was blighted, that he was desolated, that he was profoundly afflicted, that he was the most miserable and unfortunate of beasts, that he had the head of a wooden pig. He ought never to have made the concession, he said, but the very genteel lady had so passionately prayed him for the accommodation of that room to dine in, only for a little half-hour, that he had been vanquished. The little half-hour was expired, the lady and gentleman were taking their little dessert and half-cup of coffee, the note was paid, the horses were ordered, they would depart immediately; but, owing to an unhappy destiny and the curse of Heaven, they were not yet gone.

Nothing could exceed Mr Dorrit's indignation, as he turned at the foot of the staircase on hearing these apologies. He felt that the family dignity was struck at, by an assassin's hand. He had a sense of his dignity, which was of the most exquisite nature. He could detect a design upon it when nobody else had any perception of the fact. His life was made an agony by the number of fine scalpels that he felt to be incessantly engaged in dissecting his dignity.

'Is it possible, sir,' said Mr Dorrit, reddening excessively, 'that you have—ha—had the audacity to place one of my rooms at the disposition of any other person?'

Thousands of pardons! It was the host's profound misfortune to have been overcome by that too genteel lady. He besought Monseigneur not to enrage himself. He threw himself on Monseigneur for clemency. If Monseigneur would have the distinguished goodness to occupy the other salon especially reserved for him, for but five minutes, all would go well.

'No, sir,' said Mr Dorrit. 'I will not occupy any salon. I will leave your house without eating or drinking, or setting foot in it. How do you dare to act like this? Who am I that you—ha—separate me from other gentlemen?'

Alas! The host called all the universe to witness that Monseigneur was the most amiable of the whole body of nobility, the most important, the most estimable, the most honoured. If he separated Monseigneur from others, it was only because he was more distinguished, more cherished, more generous, more renowned.

'Don't tell me so, sir,' returned Mr Dorrit, in a mighty heat. 'You have affronted me. You have heaped insults upon me. How dare you? Explain yourself.'

Ah, just Heaven, then, how could the host explain himself when he had nothing more to explain; when he had only to apologise, and confide himself to the so well-known magnanimity of Monseigneur!

'I tell you, sir,' said Mr Dorrit, panting with anger, 'that you separate me—ha—from other gentlemen; that you make distinctions between me, and other gentlemen of fortune and station. I demand of you, why? I wish to know on—ha—what authority, on whose authority. Reply, sir. Explain. Answer why.'

Permit the landlord humbly to submit to Monsieur the Courier then, that Monseigneur, ordinarily so gracious, enraged himself without cause. There was no why. Monsieur the Courier would represent to Monseigneur, that he deceived himself in suspecting that there was any why, but the why his devoted servant had already had the honour to present to him. The very genteel lady—

'Silence!' cried Mr Dorrit. 'Hold your tongue! I will hear no more of the very genteel lady; I will hear no more of you. Look at this family—my family—a family more genteel than any lady. You have treated this family with disrespect; you have been insolent to this family. I'll ruin you. Ha—send for the horses, pack the carriages, I'll not set foot in this man's house again!'

No one had interfered in the dispute, which was beyond the French colloquial powers of Edward Dorrit, Esquire, and scarcely within the province of the ladies. Miss Fanny, however, now supported her father with great bitterness; declaring, in her native tongue, that it was quite clear there was something special in this man's impertinence; and that she considered it important that he should be, by some means, forced to give up his authority for making distinctions between that family and other wealthy families. What the reasons of his presumption could be, she was at a loss to imagine; but reasons he must have, and they ought to be torn from him.

All the guides, mule-drivers, and idlers in the yard, had made themselves parties to the angry conference, and were much impressed by the courier's now bestirring himself to get the carriages out. With the aid of some dozen people to each wheel, this was done at a great cost of noise; and then the loading was proceeded with, pending the arrival of the horses from the post-house.

But, the very genteel lady's English chariot being already horsed and at the inn-door, the landlord had slipped upstairs to represent his hard case. This was notified to the yard by his now coming down the staircase in attendance on the gentleman and the lady, and by his pointing out the offended majesty of Mr Dorrit to them with a significant motion of his hand.

'Beg your pardon,' said the gentleman, detaching himself from the lady, and coming forward. 'I am a man of few words and a bad hand at an explanation—but lady here is extremely anxious that there should be no Row. Lady—a mother of mine, in point of fact—wishes me to say that she hopes no Row.'

Mr Dorrit, still panting under his injury, saluted the gentleman, and saluted the lady, in a distant, final, and invincible manner.

'No, but really—here, old feller; you!' This was the gentleman's way of appealing to Edward Dorrit, Esquire, on whom he pounced as a great and providential relief. 'Let you and I try to make this all right. Lady so very much wishes no Row.'

Edward Dorrit, Esquire, led a little apart by the button, assumed a diplomatic expression of countenance in replying. 'Why you must confess, that when you bespeak a lot of rooms beforehand, and they belong to you, it's not pleasant to find other people in 'em.'

'No,' said the other, 'I know it isn't. I admit it. Still, let you and I try to make it all right, and avoid Row. The fault is not this chap's at all, but my mother's. Being a remarkably fine woman with no bigodd nonsense about her—well educated, too—she was too many for this chap. Regularly pocketed him.'

'If that's the case—' Edward Dorrit, Esquire, began.

'Assure you 'pon my soul 'tis the case. Consequently,' said the other gentleman, retiring on his main position, 'why Row?'

'Edmund,' said the lady from the doorway, 'I hope you have explained, or are explaining, to the satisfaction of this gentleman and his family that the civil landlord is not to blame?'

'Assure you, ma'am,' returned Edmund, 'perfectly paralysing myself with trying it on.' He then looked steadfastly at Edward Dorrit, Esquire, for some seconds, and suddenly added, in a burst of confidence, 'Old feller! *Is* it all right?'

'I don't know, after all,' said the lady, gracefully advancing a step or two towards Mr Dorrit, 'but that I had better say myself, at once, that I assured this good man I took all the consequences on myself of occupying one of a stranger's suite of rooms during his absence, for just as much (or as little) time as I could dine in. I had no idea the rightful owner would come back so soon, nor had I any idea that he had come back, or I should have hastened to make restoration of my ill-gotten chamber, and to have offered my explanation and apology. I trust in saying this—'

For a moment the lady, with a glass at her eye, stood transfixed and speechless before the two Miss Dorrits. At the same moment, Miss Fanny, in the foreground of a grand pictorial composition, formed by the family, the family equipages, and the family servants, held her sister tight under one arm to detain her on the spot, and with the other arm fanned herself with a distinguished air, and negligently surveyed the lady from head to foot.

The lady, recovering herself quickly—for it was Mrs Merdle and she was not easily dashed—went on to add that she trusted, in saying this, she apologised for her boldness, and restored this well-behaved landlord to the favour that was so very valuable to him. Mr Dorrit, on the altar of whose dignity all this was incense, made a gracious reply; and said that his people should—ha—countermand his horses, and he would—hum—overlook what he had at first supposed to be an affront, but now regarded as an honour. Upon this the bosom bent to him; and its owner, with a wonderful command of feature, addressed a winning smile of adieu to the two sisters, as young ladies of fortune in whose favour she was much prepossessed, and whom she had never had the gratification of seeing before.

Not so, however, Mr Sparkler. This gentleman, becoming transfixed at the same moment as his lady-mother, could not by any means unfix himself again, but stood stiffly staring at the whole composition with Miss Fanny in the foreground. On his mother's saying, 'Edmund, we are quite ready; will you give me your arm?' he seemed, by the motion of his lips, to reply with some remark comprehending the form of words in which his shining talents found the most frequent utterance, but he relaxed no muscle. So fixed was his figure, that it would have been matter of some difficulty to bend him sufficiently to get him in the carriage-door, if he had not received the timely assistance of a maternal pull from within. He was no sooner within, than the pad of the little window in the back of the chariot disappeared, and his eye usurped its place. There it remained as long as so small an object was discernible, and probably much longer, staring (as though something inexpressibly surprising should happen to a cod-fish) like an ill-executed eye in a large locket.

This encounter was so highly agreeable to Miss Fanny, and gave her so much to think of with triumph afterwards, that it softened her asperities exceedingly. When the procession was again in motion next day, she occupied her place in it with a new gaiety; and showed such a flow of spirits indeed, that Mrs General looked rather surprised.

Little Dorrit was glad to be found no fault with, and to see that Fanny was pleased; but her part in the procession was a musing part, and a quiet one. Sitting opposite her father in the travelling-carriage, and recalling the old Marshalsea room, her present existence was a dream. All that she saw was new and wonderful, but it was not real; it seemed to her as if those visions of mountains and picturesque countries might melt away at any moment, and the carriage, turning some abrupt corner, bring up with a jolt at the old Marshalsea gate.

To have no work to do was strange, but not half so strange as having glided into a corner where she had no one to think for, nothing to plan and contrive, no cares of others to load herself with. Strange as that was, it was far stranger yet to find a space between herself and her father, where others occupied themselves in taking care of him, and where she was never expected to be. At first, this was so much more unlike her old experience than even the mountains themselves, that she had been unable to resign herself to it, and had tried to retain her old place about him. But he had spoken to her alone, and had said that people—ha—people in an exalted position, my dear, must scrupulously exact respect from their dependants; and that for her, his daughter, Miss Amy Dorrit, of the sole remaining branch of the Dorrits of Dorsetshire, to be known to—hum—to occupy herself in fulfilling the functions of—ha hum—a valet, would be incompatible with that respect. Therefore, my dear, he—ha—he laid his parental injunctions upon her, to remember that she was a lady, who had now to conduct herself with—hum—a proper pride, and to preserve the rank of a lady; and consequently he requested her to abstain from doing what would occasion—ha—unpleasant and derogatory remarks. She had obeyed without a murmur. Thus it had been brought about that she now sat in her corner of the luxurious carriage with her little patient hands folded before her, quite displaced even from the last point of the old standing ground in life on which her feet had lingered.

It was from this position that all she saw appeared unreal; the more surprising the scenes, the more they resembled the unreality of her own inner life as she went through its vacant places all day long. The gorges of the Simplon, its enormous depths and thundering waterfalls, the wonderful road, the points of danger where a loose wheel or a faltering horse would have been destruction, the descent into Italy, the opening of that beautiful land, as the rugged mountain-chasm widened and let them out from a gloomy and dark imprisonment—all a dream—only the old mean Marshalsea a reality. Nay, even the old mean Marshalsea was shaken to its foundations, when she pictured it without her father. She could scarcely believe that the prisoners were still lingering in the close yard, that the mean rooms were still every one tenanted, and that the turnkey still stood in the Lodge letting people in and out, all just as she well knew it to be.

With a remembrance of her father's old life in prison hanging about her like the burden of a sorrowful tune, Little Dorrit would wake from a dream of her birth-place into a whole day's dream. The painted room in which she awoke, often a humbled state-chamber in a dilapidated palace, would begin it; with its wild red autumnal vine-leaves overhanging the glass, its orange-trees on the cracked white terrace outside the window, a group of monks and peasants in the little street below, misery and magnificence wrestling with each other upon every rood of ground in the prospect, no matter how widely diversified, and misery throwing magnificence with the strength of fate. To this would succeed a labyrinth of bare passages and pillared galleries, with the family procession already preparing in the quadrangle below, through the carriages and luggage being brought together by the servants for the day's journey. Then, breakfast in another painted chamber, damp-stained and of desolate proportions; and then the departure, which, to her timidity and sense of not being grand enough for her place in the ceremonies, was always an uneasy thing. For, then the courier (who himself would have been a foreign gentleman of high mark in the Marshalsea) would present himself to report that all was ready; and then her father's valet would pompously induct him into his travelling-cloak; and then Fanny's maid, and her own maid (who was a weight on Little Dorrit's mind—absolutely made her cry at first, she knew so little what to do with her), would be in attendance; and then her brother's man would complete his master's equipment; and then her father would give his arm to Mrs General, and her uncle would give his to her, and, escorted by the landlord and Inn servants, they would swoop downstairs. There, a crowd would be collected to see them enter their carriages, which, amidst much bowing, and begging, and prancing, and lashing, and clattering, they would do; and so they would be driven madly through the narrow unsavoury streets, and jerked out at the town gate.

Among the day's unrealities would be, roads where the bright red vines were looped and garlanded together on trees for many miles; woods of olives; white villages and towns on hillsides, lovely without, but frightful in their dirt and poverty within; crosses by the way; deep blue lakes with fairy islands, and clustering boats with awnings of bright colours and sails of beautiful forms; vast piles of building mouldering to dust; hanging-gardens where the weeds had grown so strong that their stems, like wedges driven home, had split the arch and rent the wall; stone-terraced lanes, with the lizards running into and out of every chink; beggars of all sorts everywhere: pitiful, picturesque, hungry, merry: children beggars and aged beggars. Often at posting-houses, and other halting places, these miserable creatures would appear to her the only realities of the day; and many a time, when the money she had brought to give them was all given away, she would sit with her folded hands, thoughtfully looking after some diminutive girl leading her grey father, as if the sight reminded her of something in the days that were gone.

Again, there would be places where they stayed the week together, in splendid rooms, had banquets every day, rode out among heaps of wonders, walked through miles of palaces, and rested in dark corners of great churches; where there were winking lamps of gold and silver among pillars and arches, kneeling figures dotted about at confessionals and on the pavements; where there was the mist and scent of incense; where there were pictures, fantastic images, gaudy altars, great heights and distances, all softly lighted through stained glass, and the massive curtains that hung in the doorways. From these cities they would go on again, by the roads of vines and olives, through squalid villages where there was not a hovel without a gap in its filthy walls, not a window with a whole inch of glass or paper; where there seemed to be nothing to support life, nothing to eat, nothing to make, nothing to grow, nothing to hope, nothing to do but die.

Again they would come to whole towns of palaces, whose proper inmates were all banished, and which were all changed into barracks; troops of idle soldiers leaning out of the state windows, where their accoutrements hung drying on the marble architecture, and showing to the mind like hosts of rats who were (happily) eating away the props of the edifices that supported them, and must soon, with them, be smashed on the heads of the other swarms of soldiers, and the swarms of priests, and the swarms of spies, who were all the ill-looking population left to be ruined, in the streets below.

Through such scenes, the family procession moved on to Venice. And here it dispersed for a time, as they were to live in Venice some few months, in a palace (itself six times as big as the whole Marshalsea) on the Grand Canal.

In this crowning unreality, where all the streets were paved with water, and where the death-like stillness of the days and nights was broken by no sound but the softened ringing of church-bells, the rippling of the current, and the cry of the gondoliers turning the corners of the flowing streets, Little Dorrit, quite lost by her task being done, sat down to muse. The family began a gay life, went here and there, and turned night into day; but, she was timid of joining in their gaieties, and only asked leave to be left alone.

Sometimes she would step into one of the gondolas that were always kept in waiting, moored to painted posts at the door—when she could escape from the attendance of that oppressive maid, who was her mistress, and a very hard one—and would be taken all over the strange city. Social people in other gondolas began to ask each other who the little solitary girl was whom they passed, sitting in her boat with folded hands, looking so pensively and wonderingly about her. Never thinking that it would be worth anybody's while to notice her or her doings, Little Dorrit, in her quiet, scared, lost manner, went about the city none the less.

But, her favourite station was the balcony of her own room, overhanging the canal, with other balconies below, and none above. It was of massive stone darkened by ages, built in a wild fancy which came from the East to that collection of wild fancies; and Little Dorrit was little indeed, leaning on the broad-cushioned ledge, and looking over. As she liked no place of an evening half so well, she soon began to be watched for, and many eyes in passing gondolas were raised, and many people said, There was the little figure of the English girl who was always alone.

Such people were not realities to the little figure of the English girl; such people were all unknown to her. She would watch the sunset, in its long low lines of purple and red, and its burning flush high up into the sky: so glowing on the buildings, and so lightening their structure, that it made them look as if their strong walls were transparent, and they shone from within. She would watch those glories expire; and then, after looking at the black gondolas underneath, taking guests to music and dancing, would raise her eyes to the shining stars. Was there no party of her own, in other times, on which the stars had shone? To think of that old gate now!

She would think of that old gate, and of herself sitting at it in the dead of the night, pillowing Maggy's head; and of other places and of other scenes associated with those different times. And then she would lean upon her balcony, and look over at the water, as though they all lay underneath it. When she got to that, she would musingly watch its running, as if, in the general vision, it might run dry, and show her the prison again, and herself, and the old room, and the old inmates, and the old visitors: all lasting realities that had never changed.

Dear Mr Clennam,

I write to you from my own room at Venice, thinking you will be glad to hear from me. But I know you cannot be so glad to hear from me, as I am to write to you; for everything about you is as you have been accustomed to see it, and you miss nothing—unless it should be me, which can only be for a very little while together and very seldom—while everything in my life is so strange, and I miss so much.

When we were in Switzerland, which appears to have been years ago, though it was only weeks, I met young Mrs Gowan, who was on a mountain excursion like ourselves. She told me she was very well and very happy. She sent you the message, by me, that she thanked you affectionately and would never forget you. She was quite confiding with me, and I loved her almost as soon as I spoke to her. But there is nothing singular in that; who could help loving so beautiful and winning a creature! I could not wonder at any one loving her. No, indeed.

It will not make you uneasy on Mrs Gowan's account, I hope—for I remember that you said you had the interest of a true friend in her—if I tell you that I wish she could have married some one better suited to her. Mr Gowan seems fond of her, and of course she is very fond of him, but I thought he was not earnest enough—I don't mean in that respect—I mean in anything. I could not keep it out of my mind that if I was Mrs Gowan (what a change that would be, and how I must alter to become like her!) I should feel that I was rather lonely and lost, for the want of some one who was steadfast and firm in purpose. I even thought she felt this want a little, almost without knowing it. But mind you are not made uneasy by this, for she was 'very well and very happy.' And she looked most beautiful.

I expect to meet her again before long, and indeed have been expecting for some days past to see her here. I will ever be as good a friend to her as I can for your sake. Dear Mr Clennam, I dare say you think little of having been a friend to me when I had no other (not that I have any other now, for I have made no new friends), but I think much of it, and I never can forget it.

I wish I knew—but it is best for no one to write to me—how Mr and Mrs Plornish prosper in the business which my dear father bought for them, and that old Mr Nandy lives happily with them and his two grandchildren, and sings all his songs over and over again. I cannot quite keep back the tears from my eyes when I think of my poor Maggy, and of the blank she must have felt at first, however kind they all are to her, without her Little Mother. Will you go and tell her, as a strict secret, with my love, that she never can have regretted our separation more than I have regretted it? And will you tell them all that I have thought of them every day, and that my heart is faithful to them everywhere? O, if you could know how faithful, you would almost pity me for being so far away and being so grand!

You will be glad, I am sure, to know that my dear father is very well in health, and that all these changes are highly beneficial to him, and that he is very different indeed from what he used to be when you used to see him. There is an improvement in my uncle too, I think, though he never complained of old, and never exults now. Fanny is very graceful, quick, and clever. It is natural to her to be a lady; she has adapted herself to our new fortunes, with wonderful ease.

This reminds me that I have not been able to do so, and that I sometimes almost despair of ever being able to do so. I find that I cannot learn. Mrs General is always with us, and we speak French and speak Italian, and she takes pains to form us in many ways. When I say we speak French and Italian, I mean they do. As for me, I am so slow that I scarcely get on at all. As soon as I begin to plan, and think, and try, all my planning, thinking, and trying go in old directions, and I begin to feel careful again about the expenses of the day, and about my dear father, and about my work, and then I remember with a start that there are no such cares left, and that in itself is so new and improbable that it sets me wandering again. I should not have the courage to mention this to any one but you.

It is the same with all these new countries and wonderful sights. They are very beautiful, and they astonish me, but I am not collected enough—not familiar enough with myself, if you can quite understand what I mean—to have all the pleasure in them that I might have. What I knew before them, blends with them, too, so curiously. For instance, when we were among the mountains, I often felt (I hesitate to tell such an idle thing, dear Mr Clennam, even to you) as if the Marshalsea must be behind that great rock; or as if Mrs Clennam's room where I have worked so many days, and where I first saw you, must be just beyond that snow. Do you remember one night when I came with Maggy to your lodging in Covent Garden? That room I have often and often fancied I have seen before me, travelling along for miles by the side of our carriage, when I have looked out of the carriage-window after dark. We were shut out that night, and sat at the iron gate, and walked about till morning. I often look up at the stars, even from the balcony of this room, and believe that I am in the street again, shut out with Maggy. It is the same with people that I left in England.

When I go about here in a gondola, I surprise myself looking into other gondolas as if I hoped to see them. It would overcome me with joy to see them, but I don't think it would surprise me much, at first.

In my fanciful times, I fancy that they might be anywhere; and I almost expect to see their dear faces on the bridges or the quays.

Another difficulty that I have will seem very strange to you. It must seem very strange to any one but me, and does even to me: I often feel the old sad pity for—I need not write the word—for him. Changed as he is, and inexpressibly blest and thankful as I always am to know it, the old sorrowful feeling of compassion comes upon me sometimes with such strength, that I want to put my arms round his neck, tell him how I love him, and cry a little on his breast. I should be glad after that, and proud and happy. But I know that I must not do this; that he would not like it, that Fanny would be angry, that Mrs General would be amazed; and so I quiet myself. Yet in doing so, I struggle with the feeling that I have come to be at a distance from him; and that even in the midst of all the servants and attendants, he is deserted, and in want of me.

Dear Mr Clennam, I have written a great deal about myself, but I must write a little more still, or what I wanted most of all to say in this weak letter would be left out of it. In all these foolish thoughts of mine, which I have been so hardy as to confess to you because I know you will understand me if anybody can, and will make more allowance for me than anybody else would if you cannot—in all these thoughts, there is one thought scarcely ever—never—out of my memory, and that is that I hope you sometimes, in a quiet moment, have a thought for me. I must tell you that as to this, I have felt, ever since I have been away, an anxiety which I am very very anxious to relieve. I have been afraid that you may think of me in a new light, or a new character. Don't do that, I could not bear that—it would make me more unhappy than you can suppose. It would break my heart to believe that you thought of me in any way that would make me stranger to you, than I was when you were so good to me. What I have to pray and entreat of you is, that you will never think of me as the daughter of a rich person; that you will never think of me as dressing any better, or living any better, than when you first knew me. That you will remember me only as the little shabby girl you protected with so much tenderness, from whose threadbare dress you have kept away the rain, and whose wet feet you have dried at your fire. That you will think of me (when you think of me at all), and of my true affection and devoted gratitude, always without change, as of

Your poor child,
LITTLE DORRIT

P.S.—Particularly remember that you are not to be uneasy about

Mrs Gowan. Her words were, 'Very well and very happy.' And she looked most beautiful.

The family had been a month or two at Venice, when Mr Dorrit, who was much among Counts and Marquises, and had but scant leisure, set an hour of one day apart, before-hand, for the purpose of holding some conference with Mrs General.

The time he had reserved in his mind arriving, he sent Mr Tinkler, his valet, to Mrs General's apartment (which would have absorbed about a third of the area of the Marshalsea), to present his compliments to that lady, and represent him as desiring the favour of an interview. It being that period of the forenoon when the various members of the family had coffee in their own chambers, some couple of hours before assembling at breakfast in a faded hall which had once been sumptuous, but was now the prey of watery vapours and a settled melancholy, Mrs General was accessible to the valet. That envoy found her on a little square of carpet, so extremely diminutive in reference to the size of her stone and marble floor, that she looked as if she might have had it spread for the trying on of a ready-made pair of shoes; or as if she had come into possession of the enchanted piece of carpet, bought for forty purses by one of the three princes in the Arabian Nights, and had that moment been transported on it, at a wish, into a palatial saloon with which it had no connection.

Mrs General, replying to the envoy, as she set down her empty coffee-cup, that she was willing at once to proceed to Mr Dorrit's apartment, and spare him the trouble of coming to her (which, in his gallantry, he had proposed), the envoy threw open the door, and escorted Mrs General to the presence. It was quite a walk, by mysterious staircase and corridors, from Mrs General's apartment,—hoodwinked by a narrow side street with a low gloomy bridge in it, and dungeon-like opposite tenements, their walls besmeared with a thousand downward stains and streaks, as if every crazy aperture in them had been weeping tears of rust into the Adriatic for centuries—to Mr Dorrit's apartment: with a whole English house-front of window, a prospect of beautiful church-domes rising into the blue sky sheer out of the water which reflected them, and a hushed murmur of the Grand Canal laving the doorways below, where his gondolas and gondoliers attended his pleasure, drowsily swinging in a little forest of piles.

Mr Dorrit, in a resplendent dressing-gown and cap—the dormant grub that had so long bided its time among the Collegians had burst into a rare butterfly—rose to receive Mrs General. A chair to Mrs General. An easier chair, sir; what are you doing, what are you about, what do you mean? Now, leave us!

'Mrs General,' said Mr Dorrit, 'I took the liberty—'

'By no means,' Mrs General interposed. 'I was quite at your disposition. I had had my coffee.'

'I took the liberty,' said Mr Dorrit again, with the magnificent placidity of one who was above correction, 'to solicit the favour of a little private conversation with you, because I feel rather worried respecting my—ha—my younger daughter. You will have observed a great difference of temperament, madam, between my two daughters?'

Said Mrs General in response, crossing her gloved hands (she was never without gloves, and they never creased and always fitted), 'There is a great difference.'

'May I ask to be favoured with your view of it?' said Mr Dorrit, with a deference not incompatible with majestic serenity.

'Fanny,' returned Mrs General, 'has force of character and self-reliance. Amy, none.'

None? O Mrs General, ask the Marshalsea stones and bars. O Mrs General, ask the milliner who taught her to work, and the dancing-master who taught her sister to dance. O Mrs General, Mrs General, ask me, her father, what I owe to her; and hear my testimony touching the life of this slighted little creature, from her childhood up!

No such adjuration entered Mr Dorrit's head. He looked at Mrs General, seated in her usual erect attitude on her coach-box behind the proprieties, and he said in a thoughtful manner, 'True, madam.'

'I would not,' said Mrs General, 'be understood to say, observe, that there is nothing to improve in Fanny. But there is material there—perhaps, indeed, a little too much.'

'Will you be kind enough, madam,' said Mr Dorrit, 'to be—ha—more explicit? I do not quite understand my elder daughter's having—hum—too much material. What material?'

'Fanny,' returned Mrs General, 'at present forms too many opinions. Perfect breeding forms none, and is never demonstrative.'

Lest he himself should be found deficient in perfect breeding, Mr Dorrit hastened to reply, 'Unquestionably, madam, you are right.' Mrs General returned, in her emotionless and expressionless manner, 'I believe so.'

'But you are aware, my dear madam,' said Mr Dorrit, 'that my daughters had the misfortune to lose their lamented mother when they were very young; and that, in consequence of my not having been until lately the recognised heir to my property, they have lived with me as a comparatively poor, though always proud, gentleman, in—ha hum—retirement!'

'I do not,' said Mrs General, 'lose sight of the circumstance.'

'Madam,' pursued Mr Dorrit, 'of my daughter Fanny, under her present guidance and with such an example constantly before her—'

(Mrs General shut her eyes.)

'—I have no misgivings. There is adaptability of character in Fanny. But my younger daughter, Mrs General, rather worries and vexes my thoughts. I must inform you that she has always been my favourite.'

'There is no accounting,' said Mrs General, 'for these partialities.'

'Ha—no,' assented Mr Dorrit. 'No. Now, madam, I am troubled by noticing that Amy is not, so to speak, one of ourselves. She does not care to go about with us; she is lost in the society we have here; our tastes are evidently not her tastes. Which,' said Mr Dorrit, summing up with judicial gravity, 'is to say, in other words, that there is something wrong in—ha—Amy.'

'May we incline to the supposition,' said Mrs General, with a little touch of varnish, 'that something is referable to the novelty of the position?'

'Excuse me, madam,' observed Mr Dorrit, rather quickly. 'The daughter of a gentleman, though—ha—himself at one time comparatively far from affluent—comparatively—and herself reared in—hum—retirement, need not of necessity find this position so very novel.'

'True,' said Mrs General, 'true.'

'Therefore, madam,' said Mr Dorrit, 'I took the liberty' (he laid an emphasis on the phrase and repeated it, as though he stipulated, with urbane firmness, that he must not be contradicted again), 'I took the liberty of requesting this interview, in order that I might mention the topic to you, and inquire how you would advise me?'

'Mr Dorrit,' returned Mrs General, 'I have conversed with Amy several times since we have been residing here, on the general subject of the formation of a demeanour. She has expressed herself to me as wondering exceedingly at Venice. I have mentioned to her that it is better not to wonder. I have pointed out to her that the celebrated Mr Eustace, the classical tourist, did not think much of it; and that he compared the Rialto, greatly to its disadvantage, with Westminster and Blackfriars Bridges. I need not add, after what you have said, that I have not yet found my arguments successful. You do me the honour to ask me what I advise. It always appears to me (if this should prove to be a baseless assumption, I shall be pardoned), that Mr Dorrit has been accustomed to exercise influence over the minds of others.'

'Hum—madam,' said Mr Dorrit, 'I have been at the head of—ha—of a considerable community. You are right in supposing that I am not unaccustomed to—an influential position.'

'I am happy,' returned Mrs General, 'to be so corroborated. I would therefore the more confidently recommend, that Mr Dorrit should speak to Amy himself, and make his observations and wishes known to her. Being his favourite besides, and no doubt attached to him, she is all the more likely to yield to his influence.'

'I had anticipated your suggestion, madam,' said Mr Dorrit, 'but—ha—was not sure that I might—hum—not encroach on—'

'On my province, Mr Dorrit?' said Mrs General, graciously. 'Do not mention it.'

'Then, with your leave, madam,' resumed Mr Dorrit, ringing his little bell to summon his valet, 'I will send for her at once.'

'Does Mr Dorrit wish me to remain?'

'Perhaps, if you have no other engagement, you would not object for a minute or two—'

'Not at all.'

So, Tinkler the valet was instructed to find Miss Amy's maid, and to request that subordinate to inform Miss Amy that Mr Dorrit wished to see her in his own room. In delivering this charge to Tinkler, Mr Dorrit looked severely at him, and also kept a jealous eye upon him until he went out at the door, mistrusting that he might have something in his mind prejudicial to the family dignity; that he might have even got wind of some Collegiate joke before he came into the service, and might be derisively reviving its remembrance at the present moment. If Tinkler had happened to smile, however faintly and innocently, nothing would have persuaded Mr Dorrit, to the hour of his death, but that this was the case. As Tinkler happened, however, very fortunately for himself, to be of a serious and composed countenance, he escaped the secret danger that threatened him. And as on his return—when Mr Dorrit eyed him again—he announced Miss Amy as if she had come to a funeral, he left a vague impression on Mr Dorrit's mind that he was a well-conducted young fellow, who had been brought up in the study of his Catechism, by a widowed mother.

'Amy,' said Mr Dorrit, 'you have just now been the subject of some conversation between myself and Mrs General. We agree that you scarcely seem at home here. Ha—how is this?'

A pause.

'I think, father, I require a little time.'

'Papa is a preferable mode of address,' observed Mrs General. 'Father is rather vulgar, my dear. The word Papa, besides, gives a pretty form to the lips. Papa, potatoes, poultry, prunes, and prism, are all very good words for the lips: especially prunes and prism. You will find it serviceable, in the formation of a demeanour, if you sometimes say to yourself in company—on entering a room, for instance—Papa, potatoes, poultry, prunes and prism, prunes and prism.'

'Pray, my child,' said Mr Dorrit, 'attend to the—hum—precepts of Mrs General.'

Poor Little Dorrit, with a rather forlorn glance at that eminent varnisher, promised to try.

'You say, Amy,' pursued Mr Dorrit, 'that you think you require time. Time for what?'

Another pause.

'To become accustomed to the novelty of my life, was all I meant,' said Little Dorrit, with her loving eyes upon her father; whom she had very nearly addressed as poultry, if not prunes and prism too, in her desire to submit herself to Mrs General and please him.

Mr Dorrit frowned, and looked anything but pleased. 'Amy,' he returned, 'it appears to me, I must say, that you have had abundance of time for that. Ha—you surprise me. You disappoint me. Fanny has conquered any such little difficulties, and—hum—why not you?'

'I hope I shall do better soon,' said Little Dorrit.

'I hope so,' returned her father. 'I—ha—I most devoutly hope so, Amy. I sent for you, in order that I might say—hum—impressively say, in the presence of Mrs General, to whom we are all so much indebted for obligingly being present among us, on—ha—on this or any other occasion,' Mrs General shut her eyes, 'that I—ha hum—am not pleased with you. You make Mrs General's a thankless task. You—ha—embarrass me very much. You have always (as I have informed Mrs General) been my favourite child; I have always made you a—hum—a friend and companion; in return, I beg—I—ha—I *do* beg, that you accommodate yourself better to—hum—circumstances, and dutifully do what becomes your—your station.'

Mr Dorrit was even a little more fragmentary than usual; being excited on the subject, and anxious to make himself particularly emphatic.

'I do beg,' he repeated, 'that this may be attended to, and that you will seriously take pains and try to conduct yourself in a manner both becoming your position as—ha—Miss Amy Dorrit, and satisfactory to myself and Mrs General.'

That lady shut her eyes again, on being again referred to; then, slowly opening them and rising, added these words:

'If Miss Amy Dorrit will direct her own attention to, and will accept of my poor assistance in, the formation of a surface, Mr Dorrit will have no further cause of anxiety. May I take this opportunity of remarking, as an instance in point, that it is scarcely delicate to look at vagrants with the attention which I have seen bestowed upon them, by a very dear young friend of mine? They should not be looked at. Nothing disagreeable should ever be looked at. Apart from such a habit standing in the way of that graceful equanimity of surface which is so expressive of good breeding, it hardly seems compatible with refinement of mind. A truly refined mind will seem to be ignorant of the existence of anything that is not perfectly proper, placid, and pleasant.' Having delivered this exalted sentiment, Mrs General made a sweeping obedience, and retired with an expression of mouth indicative of Prunes and Prism.

Little Dorrit, whether speaking or silent, had preserved her quiet earnestness and her loving look. It had not been clouded, except for a passing moment, until now. But now that she was left alone with him, the fingers of her lightly folded hands were agitated, and there was repressed emotion in her face.

Not for herself. She might feel a little wounded, but her care was not for herself. Her thoughts still turned, as they always had turned, to him. A faint misgiving, which had hung about her since their accession to fortune, that even now she could never see him as he used to be before the prison days, had gradually begun to assume form in her mind. She felt that, in what he had just now said to her, and in his whole bearing towards her, there was the well-known shadow of the Marshalsea wall. It took a new shape, but it was the old sad shadow. She began with sorrowful unwillingness to acknowledge to herself, that she was not strong enough to keep off the fear that no space in the life of man could overcome that quarter of a century behind the prison bars. She had no blame to bestow upon him, therefore: nothing to reproach him with, no emotions in her faithful heart but great compassion and unbounded tenderness.

This is why it was, that, even as he sat before her on his sofa, in the brilliant light of a bright Italian day, the wonderful city without and the splendours of an old palace within, she saw him at the moment in the long-familiar gloom of his Marshalsea lodging, and wished to take her seat beside him, and comfort him, and be again full of confidence with him, and of usefulness to him. If he divined what was in her thoughts, his own were not in tune with it. After some uneasy moving in his seat, he got up, and walked about, looking very much dissatisfied.

'Is there anything else you wish to say to me, dear father?'

'No, no. Nothing else.'

'I am sorry you have not been pleased with me, dear. I hope you will not think of me with displeasure now. I am going to try, more than ever, to adapt myself as you wish to what surrounds me—for indeed I have tried all along, though I have failed, I know.'

'Amy,' he returned, turning short upon her. 'You—ha—habitually hurt me.'

'Hurt you, father! I!'

'There is a—hum—a topic,' said Mr Dorrit, looking all about the ceiling of the room, and never at the attentive, uncomplainingly shocked face, 'a painful topic, a series of events which I wish—ha—altogether to obliterate. This is understood by your sister, who has already remonstrated with you in my presence; it is understood by your brother; it is understood by—ha hum—by every one of delicacy and sensitiveness, except yourself—ha—I am sorry to say, except yourself. You, Amy—hum—you alone and only you—constantly revive the topic, though not in words.'

She laid her hand on his arm. She did nothing more. She gently touched him. The trembling hand may have said, with some expression, 'Think of me, think how I have worked, think of my many cares!' But, she said not a syllable herself.

There was a reproach in the touch so addressed to him that she had not foreseen, or she would have withheld her hand. He began to justify himself; in a heated, stumbling, angry manner, which made nothing of it.

'I was there all those years. I was—ha—universally acknowledged as the head of the place. I—hum—I caused you to be respected there, Amy. I—ha hum—I gave my family a position there. I deserve a return. I claim a return. I say, sweep it off the face of the earth and begin afresh. Is that much? I ask, is *that* much?'

He did not once look at her, as he rambled on in this way; but gesticulated at, and appealed to, the empty air.

'I have suffered. Probably I know how much I have suffered, better than any one—ha—I say than any one! If *I* can put that aside, if *I* can eradicate the marks of what I have endured, and can emerge before the world a—ha—gentleman unspoiled, unspotted—is it a great deal to expect—I say again, is it a great deal to expect—that my children should—hum—do the same, and sweep that accursed experience off the face of the earth?'

In spite of his flustered state, he made all these exclamations in a carefully suppressed voice, lest the valet should overhear anything.

'Accordingly, they do it. Your sister does it. Your brother does it. You alone, my favourite child, whom I made the friend and companion of my life when you were a mere—hum—Baby, do not do it. You alone say you can't do it. I provide you with valuable assistance to do it. I attach an accomplished and highly bred lady—ha—Mrs General, to you, for the purpose of doing it. Is it surprising that I should be displeased? Is it necessary that I should defend myself for expressing my displeasure? No!'

Notwithstanding which, he continued to defend himself, without any abatement of his flushed mood.

'I am careful to appeal to that lady for confirmation, before I express any displeasure at all. I—hum—I necessarily make that appeal within limited bounds, or I—ha—should render legible, by that lady, what I desire to be blotted out. Am I selfish? Do I complain for my own sake? No. No. Principally for—ha hum—your sake, Amy.'

This last consideration plainly appeared, from his manner of pursuing it, to have just that instant come into his head.

'I said I was hurt. So I am. So I—ha—am determined to be, whatever is advanced to the contrary. I am hurt, that my daughter, seated in the—hum—lap of fortune, should mope and retire, and proclaim herself unequal to her destiny. I am hurt that she should—ha—systematically reproduce what the rest of us blot out; and seem—hum—I had almost said positively anxious—to announce to wealthy and distinguished society, that she was born and bred in—ha hum—a place that I, myself, decline to name. But there is no inconsistency—ha—not the least, in my feeling hurt, and yet complaining principally for your sake, Amy. I do; I say again, I do. It is for your sake, that I wish you, under the auspices of Mrs General, to form a—hum—a surface. It is for your sake, that I wish you to have a—ha—truly refined mind, and (in the striking words of Mrs General) to be ignorant of everything that is not perfectly proper, placid, and pleasant.'

He had been running down by jerks, during his last speech, like a sort of ill-adjusted alarum. The touch was still upon his arm. He felt silent; and after looking about the ceiling again, for a little while, looked down at her. Her head drooped, and he could not see her face; but her touch was tender and quiet, and in the expression of her dejected figure there was no blame—nothing but love. He began to whimper, just as he had done that night in the prison when she afterwards sat at his bedside till morning; exclaimed that he was a poor ruin and a poor wretch in the midst of his wealth; and clasped her in his arms. 'Hush, hush, my own dear! Kiss me!' was all she said to him. His tears were soon dried, much sooner than on the former occasion; and he was presently afterwards very high with his valet, as a way of righting himself for having shed any.

With one remarkable exception, to be recorded in its place, this was the only time, in his life of freedom and fortune, when he spoke to his daughter Amy of the old days.

But, now, the breakfast hour arrived; and with it Miss Fanny from her apartment, and Mr Edward from his apartment. Both these young persons of distinction were something the worse for late hours. As to Miss Fanny, she had become the victim of an insatiate mania for what she called 'going into society;' and would have gone into it head-foremost fifty times between sunset and sunrise, if so many opportunities had been at her disposal. As to Mr Edward, he, too, had a large acquaintance, and was generally engaged (for the most part, in diceing circles, or others of a kindred nature), during the greater part of every night. For, this gentleman, when his fortunes changed, had stood at the great advantage of being already prepared for the highest associates, and having little to learn: so much was he indebted to the happy accidents which had made him acquainted with horse-dealing and billiard-marking.

At breakfast, Mr Frederick Dorrit likewise appeared. As the old gentleman inhabited the highest story of the palace, where he might have practised pistol-shooting without much chance of discovery by the other inmates, his younger niece had taken courage to propose the restoration to him of his clarionet: which Mr Dorrit had ordered to be confiscated, but which she had ventured to preserve. Notwithstanding some objections from Miss Fanny, that it was a low instrument, and that she detested the sound of it, the concession had been made. But, it was then discovered that he had had enough of it, and never played it, now that it was no longer his means of getting bread. He had insensibly acquired a new habit of shuffling into the picture-galleries, always with his twisted paper of snuff in his hand (much to the indignation of Miss Fanny, who had proposed the purchase of a gold box for him that the family might not be discredited, which he had absolutely refused to carry when it was bought); and of passing hours and hours before the portraits of renowned Venetians. It was never made out what his dazed eyes saw in them: whether he had an interest in them merely as pictures, or whether he confusedly identified them with a glory that was departed, like the strength of his own mind. But he paid his court to them with great exactness, and clearly derived pleasure from the pursuit. After the first few days, Little Dorrit happened one morning to assist at these attentions. It so evidently heightened his gratification that she often accompanied him afterwards, and the greatest delight of which the old man had shown himself susceptible since his ruin, arose out of these excursions, when he would carry a chair about for her from picture to picture, and stand behind it, in spite of all her remonstrances, silently presenting her to the noble Venetians.

It fell out that at this family breakfast, he referred to their having seen in a gallery, on the previous day, the lady and gentleman whom they had encountered on the Great Saint Bernard. 'I forget the name,' said he. 'I dare say you remember them, William? I dare say you do, Edward?'

'*I* remember 'em well enough,' said the latter.

'I should think so,' observed Miss Fanny, with a toss of her head, and a glance at her sister. 'But they would not have been recalled to our remembrance, I suspect, if Uncle hadn't tumbled over the subject.'

'My dear, what a curious phrase,' said Mrs General. 'Would not inadvertently lighted upon, or accidentally referred to, be better?'

'Thank you very much, Mrs General,' returned the young lady, 'no, I think not. On the whole I prefer my own expression.'

This was always Miss Fanny's way of receiving a suggestion from Mrs General. But, she always stored it up in her mind, and adopted it at another time.

'I should have mentioned our having met Mr and Mrs Gowan, Fanny,' said Little Dorrit, 'even if Uncle had not. I have scarcely seen you since, you know. I meant to have spoken of it at breakfast; because I should like to pay a visit to Mrs Gowan, and to become better acquainted with her, if Papa and Mrs General do not object.'

'Well, Amy,' said Fanny, 'I am sure I am glad to find you, at last, expressing a wish to become better acquainted with anybody in Venice. Though whether Mr and Mrs Gowan are desirable acquaintances, remains to be determined.'

'Mrs Gowan I spoke of, dear.'

'No doubt,' said Fanny. 'But you can't separate her from her husband, I believe, without an Act of Parliament.'

'Do you think, Papa,' inquired Little Dorrit, with diffidence and hesitation, 'there is any objection to my making this visit?'

'Really,' he replied, 'I—ha—what is Mrs General's view?'

Mrs General's view was, that not having the honour of any acquaintance with the lady and gentleman referred to, she was not in a position to varnish the present article. She could only remark, as a general principle observed in the varnishing trade, that much depended on the quarter from which the lady under consideration was accredited, to a family so conspicuously niched in the social temple as the family of Dorrit.

At this remark the face of Mr Dorrit gloomed considerably. He was about (connecting the accrediting with an obtrusive person of the name of Clennam, whom he imperfectly remembered in some former state of existence) to black-ball the name of Gowan finally, when Edward Dorrit, Esquire, came into the conversation, with his glass in his eye, and the preliminary remark of 'I say—you there! Go out, will you!' Which was addressed to a couple of men who were handing the dishes round, as a courteous intimation that their services could be temporarily dispensed with.

Those menials having obeyed the mandate, Edward Dorrit, Esquire proceeded.

'Perhaps it's a matter of policy to let you all know that these Gowans—in whose favour, or at least the gentleman's, I can't be supposed to be much prepossessed myself—are known to people of importance, if that makes any difference.'

'That, I would say,' observed the fair varnisher, 'makes the greatest difference. The connexion in question, being really people of importance and consideration—'

'As to that,' said Edward Dorrit, Esquire, 'I'll give you the means of judging for yourself. You are acquainted, perhaps, with the famous name of Merdle?'

'The great Merdle!' exclaimed Mrs General.

'*The* Merdle,' said Edward Dorrit, Esquire. 'They are known to him. Mrs Gowan—I mean the dowager, my polite friend's mother—is intimate with Mrs Merdle, and I know these two to be on their visiting list.'

'If so, a more undeniable guarantee could not be given,' said Mrs General to Mr Dorrit, raising her gloves and bowing her head, as if she were doing homage to some visible graven image.

'I beg to ask my son, from motives of—ha—curiosity,' Mr Dorrit observed, with a decided change in his manner, 'how he becomes possessed of this—hum—timely information?'

'It's not a long story, sir,' returned Edward Dorrit, Esquire, 'and you shall have it out of hand. To begin with, Mrs Merdle is the lady you had the parley with, at what's-his-name place.'

'Martigny,' interposed Miss Fanny, with an air of infinite languor.

'Martigny,' assented her brother, with a slight nod and a slight wink; in acknowledgment of which, Miss Fanny looked surprised, and laughed and reddened.

'How can that be, Edward?' said Mr Dorrit. 'You informed me that the name of the gentleman with whom you conferred was—ha—Sparkler. Indeed, you showed me his card. Hum Sparkler.'

'No doubt of it, father; but it doesn't follow that his mother's name must be the same. Mrs Merdle was married before, and he is her son. She is in Rome now; where probably we shall know more of her, as you decide to winter there. Sparkler is just come here. I passed last evening in company with Sparkler. Sparkler is a very good fellow on the whole, though rather a bore on one subject, in consequence of being tremendously smitten with a certain young lady.' Here Edward Dorrit, Esquire, eyed Miss Fanny through his glass across the table. 'We happened last night to compare notes about our travels, and I had the information I have given you from Sparkler himself.' Here he ceased; continuing to eye Miss Fanny through his glass, with a face much twisted, and not ornamentally so, in part by the action of keeping his glass in his eye, and in part by the great subtlety of his smile.

'Under these circumstances,' said Mr Dorrit, 'I believe I express the sentiments of—ha—Mrs General, no less than my own, when I say that there is no objection, but—ha hum—quite the contrary—to your gratifying your desire, Amy. I trust I may—ha—hail—this desire,' said Mr Dorrit, in an encouraging and forgiving manner, 'as an auspicious omen. It is quite right to know these people. It is a very proper thing. Mr Merdle's a name of—ha—world-wide repute. Mr Merdle's undertakings are immense. They bring him in such vast sums of money, that they are regarded as—hum—national benefits. Mr Merdle is the man of this time. The name of Merdle is the name of the age. Pray do everything on my behalf that is civil to Mr and Mrs Gowan, for we will—ha—we will certainly notice them.'

This magnificent accordance of Mr Dorrit's recognition settled the matter. It was not observed that Uncle had pushed away his plate, and forgotten his breakfast; but he was not much observed at any time, except by Little Dorrit. The servants were recalled, and the meal proceeded to its conclusion. Mrs General rose and left the table. Little Dorrit rose and left the table. When Edward and Fanny remained whispering together across it, and when Mr Dorrit remained eating figs and reading a French newspaper, Uncle suddenly fixed the attention of all three, by rising out of his chair, striking his hand upon the table, and saying, 'Brother! I protest against it!'

If he had made a proclamation in an unknown tongue, and given up the ghost immediately afterwards, he could not have astounded his audience more. The paper fell from Mr Dorrit's hand, and he sat petrified, with a fig half-way to his mouth.

'Brother!' said the old man, conveying a surprising energy into his trembling voice, 'I protest against it! I love you; you know I love you dearly. In these many years, I have never been untrue to you in a single thought. Weak as I am, I would at any time have struck any man who spoke ill of you. But, brother, brother, brother, I protest against it!'

It was extraordinary to see of what a burst of earnestness such a decrepit man was capable. His eyes became bright, his grey hair rose on his head, markings of purpose on his brow and face which had faded from them for five-and-twenty years, started out again, and there was an energy in his hand that made its action nervous once more.

'My dear Frederick!' exclaimed Mr Dorrit, faintly. 'What is wrong? What is the matter?'

'How dare you,' said the old man, turning round on Fanny, 'how dare you do it? Have you no memory? Have you no heart?'

'Uncle?' cried Fanny, affrighted and bursting into tears, 'why do you attack me in this cruel manner? What have I done?'

'Done?' returned the old man, pointing to her sister's place, 'where's your affectionate invaluable friend? Where's your devoted guardian? Where's your more than mother? How dare you set up superiorities against all these characters combined in your sister? For shame, you false girl, for shame!'

'I love Amy,' cried Miss Fanny, sobbing and weeping, 'as well as I love my life—better than I love my life. I don't deserve to be so treated. I am as grateful to Amy, and as fond of Amy, as it's possible for any human being to be. I wish I was dead. I never was so wickedly wronged. And only because I am anxious for the family credit.'

'To the winds with the family credit!' cried the old man, with great scorn and indignation. 'Brother, I protest against pride. I protest against ingratitude. I protest against any one of us here who have known what we have known, and have seen what we have seen, setting up any pretension that puts Amy at a moment's disadvantage, or to the cost of a moment's pain. We may know that it's a base pretension by its having that effect. It ought to bring a judgment on us. Brother, I protest against it, in the sight of God!'

As his hand went up above his head and came down on the table, it might have been a blacksmith's. After a few moments' silence, it had relaxed into its usual weak condition. He went round to his brother with his ordinary shuffling step, put the hand on his shoulder, and said, in a softened voice, 'William, my dear, I felt obliged to say it; forgive me, for I felt obliged to say it!' and then went, in his bowed way, out of the palace hall, just as he might have gone out of the Marshalsea room.

All this time Fanny had been sobbing and crying, and still continued to do so. Edward, beyond opening his mouth in amazement, had not opened his lips, and had done nothing but stare. Mr Dorrit also had been utterly discomfited, and quite unable to assert himself in any way. Fanny was now the first to speak.

'I never, never, never, was so used!' she sobbed. 'There never was anything so harsh and unjustifiable, so disgracefully violent and cruel! Dear, kind, quiet little Amy, too, what would she feel if she could know that she had been innocently the means of exposing me to such treatment! But I'll never tell her! No, good darling, I'll never tell her!'

This helped Mr Dorrit to break his silence.

'My dear,' said he, 'I—ha—approve of your resolution. It will be—ha hum—much better not to speak of this to Amy. It might—hum—it might distress her. Ha. No doubt it would distress her greatly. It is considerate and right to avoid doing so. We will—ha—keep this to ourselves.'

'But the cruelty of Uncle!' cried Miss Fanny. 'O, I never can forgive the wanton cruelty of Uncle!'

'My dear,' said Mr Dorrit, recovering his tone, though he remained unusually pale, 'I must request you not to say so. You must remember that your uncle is—ha—not what he formerly was. You must remember that your uncle's state requires—hum—great forbearance from us, great forbearance.'

'I am sure,' cried Fanny, piteously, 'it is only charitable to suppose that there must be something wrong in him somewhere, or he never could have so attacked Me, of all the people in the world.'

'Fanny,' returned Mr Dorrit, in a deeply fraternal tone, 'you know, with his innumerable good points, what a—hum—Wreck your uncle is; and I entreat you by the fondness that I have for him, and by the fidelity that you know I have always shown him, to—ha—to draw your own conclusions, and to spare my brotherly feelings.'

This ended the scene; Edward Dorrit, Esquire, saying nothing throughout, but looking, to the last, perplexed and doubtful. Miss Fanny awakened much affectionate uneasiness in her sister's mind that day, by passing the greater part of it in violent fits of embracing her, and in alternately giving her brooches, and wishing herself dead.

GREAT EXPECTATIONS

Orphan Pip lives in the Kent marshes with his sister and brother-in-law, Mr and Mrs Joe Gargery ...

As I never saw my father or my mother, and never saw any likeness of either of them (for their days were long before the days of photographs), my first fancies regarding what they were like, were unreasonably derived from their tombstones. The shape of the letters on my father's, gave me an odd idea that he was a square, stout, dark man, with curly black hair. From the character and turn of the inscription, '*Also Georgiana Wife of the Above,*' I drew a childish conclusion that my mother was freckled and sickly. To five little stone lozenges, each about a foot and a half long, which were arranged in a neat row beside their grave, and were sacred to the memory of five little brothers of mine—who gave up trying to get a living exceedingly early in that universal struggle—I am indebted for a belief I religiously entertained that they had all been born on their backs with their hands in their trousers-pockets, and had never taken them out in this state of existence.

Ours was the marsh country, down by the river, within, as the river wound, twenty miles of the sea. My first most vivid and broad impression of the identity of things, seems to me to have been gained on a memorable raw afternoon towards evening. At such a time I found out for certain, that this bleak place overgrown with nettles was the churchyard; and that Philip Pirrip, late of this parish, and also Georgiana wife of the above, were dead and buried; and that Alexander, Bartholomew, Abraham, Tobias, and Roger, infant children of the aforesaid, were also dead and buried; and that the dark flat wilderness beyond the churchyard, intersected with dykes and mounds and gates, with scattered cattle feeding on it, was the marshes; and that the low leaden line beyond was the river; and that the distant savage lair from which the wind was rushing, was the sea; and that the small bundle of shivers growing afraid of it all and beginning to cry, was Pip.

'Hold your noise!' cried a terrible voice, as a man started up from among the graves at the side of the church porch. 'Keep still, you little devil, or I'll cut your throat!'

A fearful man, all in coarse gray, with a great iron on his leg. A man with no hat, and with broken shoes, and with an old rag tied round his head. A man who had been soaked in water, and smothered in mud, and lamed by stones, and cut by flints, and stung by nettles, and torn by briars; who limped and shivered, and glared and growled; and whose teeth chattered in his head as he seized me by the chin.

'O! Don't cut my throat, sir,' I pleaded in terror. 'Pray don't do it, sir.'

'Tell us your name!' said the man. 'Quick!'

'Pip, sir.'

'Once more,' said the man, staring at me. 'Give it mouth!'

'Pip. Pip, sir.'

'Show us where you live,' said the man. 'Pint out the place!'

I pointed to where our village lay, on the flat in-shore among the alder-trees and pollards, a mile or more from the church.

The man, after looking at me for a moment, turned me upside down, and emptied my pockets. There was nothing in them but a piece of bread. When the church came to itself—for he was so sudden and strong that he made it go head over heels before me, and I saw the steeple under my feet—when the church came to itself, I say, I was seated on a high tombstone, trembling, while he ate the bread ravenously.

'You young dog,' said the man, licking his lips, 'what fat cheeks you ha' got.'

I believe they were fat, though I was at that time undersized for my years, and not strong.

'Darn me if I couldn't eat 'em,' said the man, with a threatening shake of his head, 'and if I han't half a mind to't!'

I earnestly expressed my hope that he wouldn't, and held tighter to the tombstone on which he had put me; partly, to keep myself upon it; partly, to keep myself from crying.

'Now lookee here!' said the man. 'Where's your mother?'

'There, sir!' said I.

He started, made a short run, and stopped and looked over his shoulder.

'There, sir!' I timidly exclaimed. 'Also Georgiana. That's my mother.'

'Oh!' said he, coming back. 'And is that your father alonger your mother?'

'Yes, sir,' said I; 'him too; late of this parish.'

'Ha!' he muttered then, considering. 'Who d'ye live with—supposin' you're kindly let to live, which I han't made up my mind about?'

'My sister, sir—Mrs Joe Gargery—wife of Joe Gargery, the blacksmith, sir.'

'Blacksmith, eh?' said he. And he looked down at his leg.

After darkly looking at his leg and at me several times, he came closer to my tombstone, took me by both arms, and tilted me back as far as he could hold me; so that his eyes looked most powerfully down into mine, and mine looked most helplessly up into his.

'Now lookee here,' he said, 'the question being whether you're to be let to live. You know what a file is?'

'Yes, sir.'

'And you know what wittles is?'

'Yes, sir.'

After each question he tilted me over a little more, so as to give me a greater sense of helplessness and danger.

'You get me a file,' He tilted me again. 'And you get me wittles.' He tilted me again. 'You bring 'em both to me.' He tilted me again. 'Or I'll have your heart and liver out.' He tilted me again.

I was dreadfully frightened, and so giddy that I clung to him with both hands, and said, 'If you would kindly please to let me keep upright, sir, perhaps I shouldn't be sick, and perhaps I could attend more.'

He gave me a most tremendous dip and roll, so that the church jumped over its own weather-cock. Then, he held me by the arms in an upright position on the top of the stone, and went on in these fearful terms:

'You bring me, to-morrow morning early, that file and them wittles. You bring the lot to me, at that old Battery over yonder. You do it, and you never dare to say a word or dare to make a sign concerning your having seen such a person as me, or any person sumever, and you shall be let to live. You fail, or you go from my words in any partickler, no matter how small it is, and your heart and your liver shall be tore out, roasted and ate. Now, I ain't alone, as you may think I am. There's a young man hid with me, in comparison with which young man I am a Angel. That young man hears the words I speak. That young man has a secret way pecooliar to himself, of getting at a boy, and at his heart, and at his liver. It is in wain for a boy to attempt to hide himself from that young man. A boy may lock his door, may be warm in bed, may tuck himself up, may draw the clothes over his head, may think himself comfortable and safe, but that young man will softly creep and creep his way to him and tear him open. I am a keeping that young man from harming of you at the present moment, with great difficulty. I find it wery hard to hold that young man off of your inside. Now, what do you say?'

I said that I would get him the file, and I would get him what broken bits of food I could, and I would come to him at the Battery, early in the morning.

'Say, Lord strike you dead if you don't!' said the man. I said so, and he took me down.

'Now,' he pursued, 'you remember what you've undertook, and you remember that young man, and you get home!'

'Goo-good night, sir,' I faltered.

'Much of that!' said he, glancing about him over the cold wet flat. 'I wish I was a frog. Or a eel!'

At the same time, he hugged his shuddering body in both his arms—clasping himself, as if to hold himself together—and limped towards the low church wall. As I saw him go, picking his way among the nettles, and among the brambles that bound the green mounds, he looked in my young eyes as if he were eluding the hands of the dead people, stretching up cautiously out of their graves, to get a twist upon his ankle and pull him in.

When he came to the low church wall, he got over it, like a man whose legs were numbed and stiff, and then turned round to look for me. When I saw him turning, I set my face towards home, and made the best use of my legs. But presently I looked over my shoulder, and saw him going on again towards the river, still hugging himself in both arms, and picking his way with his sore feet among the great stones dropped into the marshes here and there, for stepping-places when the rains were heavy, or the tide was in.

The marshes were just a long black horizontal line then, as I stopped to look after him; and the river was just another horizontal line, not nearly so broad nor yet so black; and the sky was just a row of long angry, red lines and dense black lines intermixed. On the edge of the river I could faintly make out the only two black things in all the prospect that seemed to be standing upright; one of these was the beacon by which the sailors steered—like an unhooped cask upon a pole—an ugly thing when you were near it; the other, a gibbet, with some chains hanging to it which had once held a pirate. The man was limping on towards this latter, as if he were the pirate come to life, and come down, and going back to hook himself up again. It gave me a terrible turn when I thought so; and as I saw the cattle lifting their heads to gaze after him, I wondered whether they thought so too. I looked all round for the horrible young man, and could see no signs of him. But now I was frightened again, and ran home without stopping.

My sister, Mrs Joe Gargery, was more than twenty years older than I, and had established a great reputation with herself and the neighbours because she had brought me up 'by hand.' Having at that time to find out for myself what the expression meant, and knowing her to have a hard and heavy hand, and to be much in the habit of laying it upon her husband as well as upon me, I supposed that Joe Gargery and I were both brought up by hand.

She was not a good-looking woman, my sister; and I had a general impression that she must have made Joe Gargery marry her by hand. Joe was a fair man, with curls of flaxen hair on each side of his smooth face, and with eyes of such a very undecided blue that they seemed to have somehow got mixed with their own whites. He was a mild, good-natured, sweet-tempered, easy-going foolish, dear fellow—a sort of Hercules in strength, and also in weakness.

My sister, Mrs Joe, with black hair and eyes, had such a prevailing redness of skin, that I sometimes used to wonder whether it was possible she washed herself with a nutmeg-grater instead of soap. She was tall and bony, and almost always wore a coarse apron, fastened over her figure behind with two loops, and having a square impregnable bib in front, that was stuck full of pins and needles. She made it a powerful merit in herself, and a strong reproach against Joe, that she wore this apron so much. Though I really see no reason why she should have worn it at all: or why if she did wear it at all, she should not have taken it off every day of her life.

Joe's forge adjoined our house, which was a wooden house, as many of the dwellings in our country were—most of them, at that time. When I ran home from the churchyard, the forge was shut up, and Joe was sitting alone in the kitchen. Joe and I being fellow-sufferers, and having confidences as such, Joe imparted a confidence to me, the moment I raised the latch of the door and peeped in at him opposite to it, sitting in the chimney corner.

'Mrs Joe has been out a dozen times, looking for you, Pip. And she's out now, making it a baker's dozen.'

'Is she?'

'Yes, Pip,' said Joe; 'and what's worse, she's got Tickler with her.'

At this dismal intelligence, I twisted the only button on my waistcoat round and round, and looked in great depression at the fire. Tickler was a wax-ended piece of cane, worn smooth by collision with my tickled frame.

'She sot down,' said Joe, 'and she got up, and she made a grab at Tickler, and she Ram-paged out. That's what she did,' said Joe, slowly clearing the fire between the lower bars with the poker, and looking at it; 'she Ram-paged out, Pip.'

'Has she been gone long, Joe?' I always treated him as a larger species of child, and as no more than my equal.

'Well,' said Joe, glancing up at the Dutch clock, 'she's been on the Ram-page, this last spell, about five minutes, Pip. She's a-coming! Get behind the door, old chap, and have the jack-towel betwixt you.'

I took the advice. My sister, Mrs Joe, throwing the door wide open, and finding an obstruction behind it, immediately divined the cause, and applied Tickler to its further investigation. She concluded by throwing me—I often served as a connubial missile—at Joe, who, glad to get hold of me on any terms, passed me on into the chimney and quietly fenced me up there with his great leg.

'Where have you been, you young monkey?' said Mrs Joe, stamping her foot, 'Tell me directly what you've been doing to wear me away with fret and fright and worrit, or I'd have you out of that corner if you was fifty Pips, and he was five hundred Gargerys.'

'I have only been to the churchyard,' said I, from my stool, crying and rubbing myself.

'Churchyard!' repeated my sister. 'If it warn't for me you'd have been to the churchyard long ago, and stayed there. Who brought you up by hand?'

'You did,' said I.

'And why did I do it, I should like to know?' exclaimed my sister.

I whimpered, 'I don't know.'

'*I* don't!' said my sister. 'I'd never do it again! I know that. I may truly say I've never had this apron of mine off, since born you were. It's bad enough to be a blacksmith's wife (and him a Gargery), without being your mother.'

My thoughts strayed from that question as I looked disconsolately at the fire. For, the fugitive out on the marshes with the ironed leg, the mysterious young man, the file, the food, and the dreadful pledge I was under to commit a larceny on those sheltering premises, rose before me in the avenging coals.

'Hah!' said Mrs Joe, restoring Tickler to his station. 'Churchyard, indeed! You may well say churchyard, you two.' One of us, by-the-bye, had not said it at all. 'You'll drive *me* to the churchyard betwixt you, one of these days, and oh, a pr-r-recious pair you'd be without me!'

As she applied herself to set the tea-things, Joe peeped down at me over his leg, as if he were mentally casting me and himself up, and calculating what kind of pair we practically should make, under the grievous circumstances foreshadowed. After that, he sat feeling his right-side flaxen curls and whiskers, and following Mrs Joe about with his blue eyes, as his manner always was at squally times.

My sister had a trenchant way of cutting our bread-and-butter for us, that never varied. First, with her left hand she jammed the loaf hard and fast against her bib—where it sometimes got a pin into it, and sometimes a needle, which we afterwards got into our mouths. Then she took some butter (not too much) on a knife and spread it on the loaf, in an apothecary kind of way, as if she were making a plaister—using both sides of the knife with a slapping dexterity, and trimming and moulding the butter off round the crust. Then, she gave the knife a final smart wipe on the edge of the plaister, and then sawed a very thick round off the loaf: which she finally, before separating from the loaf, hewed into two halves, of which Joe got one, and I the other.

On the present occasion, though I was hungry, I dared not eat my slice. I felt I must have something in reserve for my dreadful acquaintance, and his ally the still more dreadful young man. I knew Mrs Joe's housekeeping to be of the strictest kind, and that my larcenous researches might find nothing available in the safe. Therefore I resolved to put my hunk of bread-and-butter down the leg of my trousers.

The effort of resolution necessary to the achievement of this purpose, I found to be quite awful. It was as if I had to make up my mind to leap from the top of a high house, or plunge into a great depth of water. And it was made the more difficult by the unconscious Joe. In our already-mentioned freemasonry as fellow-sufferers, and in his good-natured companionship with me, it was our evening habit to compare the way we bit through our slices, by silently holding them up to each other's admiration now and then—which stimulated us to new exertions. To-night, Joe several times invited me, by the display of his fast-diminishing slice, to enter upon our usual friendly competition; but he found me, each time, with my yellow mug of tea on one knee, and my untouched bread-and-butter on the other. At last, I desperately considered that the thing I contemplated must be done, and that it had best be done in the least improbable manner consistent with the circumstances. I took advantage of a moment when Joe had just looked at me, and got my bread-and-butter down my leg.

Joe was evidently made uncomfortable by what he supposed to be my loss of appetite, and took a thoughtful bite out of his slice, which he didn't seem to enjoy. He turned it about in his mouth much longer than usual, pondering over it a good deal, and after all gulped it down like a pill. He was about to take another bite, and had just got his head on one side for a good purchase on it, when his eye fell on me, and he saw that my bread-and-butter was gone.

The wonder and consternation with which Joe stopped on the threshold of his bite and stared at me, were too evident to escape my sister's observation.

'What's the matter now?' said she, smartly, as she put down her cup.

'I say, you know!' muttered Joe, shaking his head at me in very serious remonstrance. 'Pip, old chap! You'll do yourself a mischief. It'll stick somewhere. You can't have chawed it, Pip.'

'What's the matter *now*?' repeated my sister, more sharply than before.

'If you can cough any trifle on it up, Pip, I'd recommend you to do it,' said Joe, all aghast. 'Manners is manners, but still your elth's your elth.'

By this time, my sister was quite desperate, so she pounced on Joe, and, taking him by the two whiskers, knocked his head for a little while against the wall behind him: while I sat in the corner, looking guiltily on.

'Now, perhaps you'll mention what's the matter,' said my sister, out of breath, 'you staring great stuck pig.'

Joe looked at her in a helpless way; then took a helpless bite, and looked at me again.

'You know, Pip,' said Joe, solemnly, with his last bite in his cheek, and speaking in a confidential voice, as if we two were quite alone, 'you and me is always friends, and I'd be the last to tell upon you, any time. But such a'—he moved his chair, and looked about the floor between us, and then again at me—'such a most oncommon bolt as that!'

'Been bolting his food, has he?' cried my sister.

'You know, old chap,' said Joe, looking at me, and not at Mrs Joe, with his bite still in his cheek, 'I Bolted, myself, when I was your age—frequent—and as a boy I've been among a many Bolters; but I never seen your bolting equal yet, Pip, and it's a mercy you ain't Bolted dead.'

My sister made a dive at me, and fished me up by the hair: saying nothing more than the awful words, 'You come along and be dosed.'

Some medical beast had revived Tar-water in those days as a fine medicine, and Mrs Joe always kept a supply of it in the cupboard; having a belief in its virtues correspondent to its nastiness. At the best of times, so much of this elixir was administered to me as a choice restorative, that I was conscious of going about, smelling like a new fence. On this particular evening, the urgency of my case demanded a pint of this mixture, which was poured down my throat, for my greater comfort, while Mrs Joe held my head under her arm, as a boot would be held in a boot-jack. Joe got off with half a pint; but was made to swallow that (much to his disturbance, as he sat slowly munching and meditating before the fire), 'because he had had a turn.' Judging from myself, I should say he certainly had a turn afterwards, if he had had none before.

Conscience is a dreadful thing when it accuses man or boy; but when, in the case of a boy, that secret burden co-operates with another secret burden down the leg of his trousers, it is (as I can testify) a great punishment. The guilty knowledge that I was going to rob Mrs Joe—I never thought I was going to rob Joe, for I never thought of any of the housekeeping property as his—united to the necessity of always keeping one hand on my bread-and-butter as I sat, or when I was ordered about the kitchen on any small errand, almost drove me out of my mind. Then, as the marsh winds made the fire glow and flare, I thought I heard the voice outside, of the man with the iron on his leg who had sworn me to secrecy, declaring that he couldn't and wouldn't starve until to-morrow, but must be fed now. At other times, I thought, What if the young man who was with so much difficulty restrained from imbruing his hands in me, should yield to a constitutional impatience, or should mistake the time, and should think himself accredited to my heart and liver to-night, instead of to-morrow! If ever anybody's hair stood on end in terror, mine must have done so then. But, perhaps, nobody's ever did?

It was Christmas Eve, and I had to stir the pudding for next day, with a copper-stick, from seven to eight by the Dutch clock. I tried it with the load upon my leg (and that made me think afresh of the man with the load on *his* leg), and found the tendency of exercise to bring the bread-and-butter out at my ankle, quite unmanageable. Happily I slipped away, and deposited that part of my conscience in my garret bedroom.

'Hark!' said I, when I had done my stirring, and was taking a final warm in the chimney-corner before being sent up to bed; 'was that great guns, Joe?'

'Ah!' said Joe. 'There's another conwict off.'

'What does that mean, Joe?' said I.

Mrs Joe, who always took explanations upon herself said snappishly. 'Escaped. Escaped.' Administering the definition like Tar-water.

While Mrs Joe sat with her head bending over her needlework, I put my mouth into the forms of saying to Joe, 'What's a convict?' Joe put *his* mouth into the forms of returning such a highly elaborate answer, that I could make out nothing of it but the single word, 'Pip.'

'There was a conwict off last night,' said Joe, aloud, 'after sunset-gun. And they fired warning of him. And now it appears they're firing warning of another.'

'*Who*'s firing?' said I.

'Drat that boy,' interposed my sister, frowning at me over her work, 'what a questioner he is. Ask no questions, and you'll be told no lies.'

It was not very polite to herself, I thought, to imply that I should be told lies by her, even if I did ask questions. But she never was polite, unless there was company.

At this point, Joe greatly augmented my curiosity by taking the utmost pains to open his mouth very wide, and to put it into the form of a word that looked to me like 'sulks.' Therefore, I naturally pointed to Mrs Joe, and put my mouth into the form of saying 'her?' But Joe wouldn't hear of that at all, and again opened his mouth very wide, and shook the form of a most emphatic word out of it. But I could make nothing of the word.

'Mrs Joe,' said I, as a last resort, 'I should like to know—if you wouldn't much mind—where the firing comes from?'

'Lord bless the boy!' exclaimed my sister, as if she didn't quite mean that, but rather the contrary, 'From the Hulks!'

'Oh-h!' said I, looking at Joe. 'Hulks!'

Joe gave a reproachful cough, as much as to say, 'Well, I told you so.'

'And please what's Hulks?' said I.

'That's the way with this boy!' exclaimed my sister, pointing me out with her needle and thread, and shaking her head at me. 'Answer him one question, and he'll ask you a dozen directly. Hulks are prison-ships, right 'cross th' meshes.' We always used that name for marshes in our country.

'I wonder who's put into prison-ships, and why they're put there?' said I, in a general way, and with quiet desperation.

It was too much for Mrs Joe, who immediately rose. 'I tell you what, young fellow,' said she, 'I didn't bring you up by hand to badger people's lives out. It would be blame to me, and not praise, if I had. People are put in the Hulks because they do murder, and because they rob, and forge, and do all sorts of bad; and they always begin by asking questions. Now, you get along to bed!'

I was never allowed a candle to light me to bed, and, as I went up-stairs in the dark, with my head tingling—from Mrs Joe's thimble having played the tambourine upon it, to accompany her last words—I felt fearfully sensible of the great convenience that the hulks were handy for me. I was clearly on my way there. I had begun by asking questions, and I was going to rob Mrs Joe.

Since that time, which is far enough away now, I have often thought that few people know what secrecy there is in the young, under terror. No matter how unreasonable the terror, so that it be terror. I was in mortal terror of the young man who wanted my heart and liver; I was in mortal terror of my interlocutor with the ironed leg; I was in mortal terror of myself, from whom an awful promise had been extracted; I had no hope of deliverance through my all-powerful sister, who repulsed me at every turn; I am afraid to think of what I might have done on requirement, in the secrecy of my terror.

If I slept at all that night, it was only to imagine myself drifting down the river on a strong spring-tide, to the Hulks; a ghostly pirate calling out to me through a speaking-trumpet, as I passed the gibbet-station, that I had better come ashore and be hanged there at once, and not put it off. I was afraid to sleep, even if I had been inclined, for I knew that at the first faint dawn of morning I must rob the pantry. There was no doing it in the night, for there was no getting a light by easy friction then; to have got one, I must have struck it out of flint and steel, and have made a noise like the very pirate himself rattling his chains.

As soon as the great black velvet pall outside my little window was shot with grey, I got up and went down-stairs; every board upon the way, and every crack in every board, calling after me, 'Stop thief!' and 'Get up, Mrs Joe!' In the pantry, which was far more abundantly supplied than usual, owing to the season, I was very much alarmed, by a hare hanging up by the heels, whom I rather thought I caught, when my back was half turned, winking. I had no time for verification, no time for selection, no time for anything, for I had no time to spare. I stole some bread, some rind of cheese, about half a jar of mincemeat (which I tied up in my pocket-handkerchief with my last night's slice), some brandy from a stone bottle (which I decanted into a glass bottle I had secretly used for making that intoxicating fluid, Spanish-liquorice-water, up in my room; diluting the stone bottle from a jug in the kitchen cupboard), a meat bone with very little on it, and a beautiful round compact pork pie. I was nearly going away without the pie, but I was tempted to mount upon a shelf, to look what it was that was put away so carefully in a covered earthenware dish in a corner, and I found it was the pie, and I took it, in the hope that it was not intended for early use, and would not be missed for some time.

There was a door in the kitchen communicating with the forge; I unlocked and unbolted that door, and got a file from among Joe's tools. Then I put the fastenings as I had found them, opened the door at which I had entered when I ran home last night, shut it, and ran for the misty marshes.

It was a rimy morning, and very damp. I had seen the damp lying on the outside of my little window, as if some goblin had been crying there all night, and using the window for a pocket-handkerchief. Now I saw the damp lying on the bare hedges and spare grass, like a coarser sort of spiders' webs; hanging itself from twig to twig and blade to blade. On every rail and gate, wet lay clammy, and the marsh-mist was so thick, that the wooden finger on the post directing people to our village—a direction which they never accepted, for they never came there—was invisible to me until I was quite close under it. Then, as I looked up at it, while it dripped, it seemed to my oppressed conscience like a phantom devoting me to the Hulks.

The mist was heavier yet when I got out upon the marshes, so that instead of my running at everything, everything seemed to run at me. This was very disagreeable to a guilty mind. The gates and dykes and banks came bursting at me through the mist, as if they cried as plainly as could be, 'A boy with Somebody-else's pork pie! Stop him!' The cattle came upon me with like suddenness, staring out of their eyes, and steaming out of their nostrils, 'Halloa, young thief!' One black ox, with a white cravat on—who even had to my awakened conscience something of a clerical air—fixed me so obstinately with his eyes, and moved his blunt head round in such an accusatory manner as I moved round, that I blubbered out to him, 'I couldn't help it, sir! It wasn't for myself I took it!' Upon which he put down his head, blew a cloud of smoke out of his nose, and vanished with a kick-up of his hind legs and a flourish of his tail.

All this time I was getting on towards the river; but however fast I went, I couldn't warm my feet, to which the damp cold seemed riveted, as the iron was riveted to the leg of the man I was running to meet. I knew my way to the Battery, pretty straight, for I had been down there on a Sunday with Joe, and Joe, sitting on an old gun, had told me that when I was 'prentice to him, regularly bound, we would have such Larks there! However, in the confusion of the mist, I found myself at last too far to the right, and consequently had to try back along the river-side, on the banks of loose stones above the mud and the stakes that staked the tide out. Making my way along here with all despatch, I had just crossed a ditch which I knew to be very near the Battery, and had just scrambled up the mound beyond the ditch, when I saw a man sitting before me. His back was towards me, and he had his arms folded, and was nodding forward, heavy with sleep.

I thought he would be more glad if I came upon him with his breakfast, in that unexpected manner, so I went forward softly and touched him on the shoulder. He instantly jumped up, and it was not the same man, but another man!

And yet this man was dressed in coarse grey, too, and had a great iron on his leg, and was lame, and hoarse and cold, and was everything that the other man was; except that he had not the same face, and had a flat, broad-brimmed, low-crowned, felt hat on. All this I saw in a moment, for I had only a moment to see it in: he swore an oath at me, made a hit at me—it was a round, weak blow that missed me and almost knocked himself down, for it made him stumble—and then he ran into the mist, stumbling twice as he went, and I lost him.

'It's the young man!' I thought, feeling my heart shoot as I identified him. I daresay I should have felt a pain in my liver, too, if I had known where it was.

I was soon at the Battery, after that, and there was the right man—hugging himself and limping to and fro, as if he had never all night left off hugging and limping—waiting for me. He was awfully cold, to be sure. I half expected to see him drop down before my face and die of deadly cold. His eyes looked so awfully hungry, too, that when I handed him the file and he laid it down on the grass, it occurred to me he would have tried to eat it, if he had not seen my bundle. He did not turn me upside down, this time, to get at what I had, but left me right side upwards while I opened the bundle and emptied my pockets.

'What's in the bottle, boy?' said he.

'Brandy,' said I.

He was already handing mincemeat down his throat in the most curious manner—more like a man who was putting it away somewhere in a violent hurry, than a man who was eating it—but he left off to take some of the liquor. He shivered all the while so violently, that it was quite as much as he could do to keep the neck of the bottle between his teeth, without biting it off.

'I think you have got the ague,' said I.

'I'm much of your opinion, boy,' said he.

'It's bad about here,' I told him. 'You've been lying out on the meshes, and they're dreadful aguish. Rheumatic, too.'

'I'll eat my breakfast afore they're the death of me,' said he. 'I'd do that, if I was going to be strung up to that there gallows as there is over there, directly afterwards. I'll beat the shivers so far, *I*'ll bet you.'

He was gobbling mincemeat, meat bone, bread, cheese, and pork pie, all at once: staring distrustfully while he did so at the mist all round us, and often stopping—even stopping his jaws—to listen. Some real or fancied sound, some clink upon the river or breathing of beast upon the marsh, now gave him a start, and he said, suddenly:

'You're not a deceiving imp? You brought no one with you?'

'No, sir! No!'

'Nor giv' no one the office to follow you?'

'No!'

'Well,' said he, 'I believe you. You'd be but a fierce young hound indeed, if at your time of life you could help to hunt a wretched warmint, hunted as near death and dung-hill as this poor wretched warmint is!'

Something clicked in his throat, as if he had works in him like a clock, and was going to strike. And he smeared his ragged rough sleeve over his eyes.

Pitying his desolation, and watching him as he gradually settled down upon the pie, I made bold to say, 'I am glad you enjoy it.'

'Did you speak?'

'I said I was glad you enjoyed it.'

'Thankee, my boy. I do.'

I had often watched a large dog of ours eating his food, and I now noticed a decided similarity between the dog's way of eating and the man's. The man took strong sharp sudden bites, just like the dog. He swallowed, or rather snapped up, every mouthful, too soon and too fast; and he looked sideways here and there while he ate, as if he thought there was danger in every direction of somebody's coming to take the pie away. He was altogether too unsettled in his mind over it, to appreciate it comfortably, I thought, or to have anybody to dine with him, without making a chop with his jaws at the visitor. In all of which particulars he was very like the dog.

'I am afraid you won't leave any of it for him,' said I, timidly; after a silence during which I had hesitated as to the politeness of making the remark. 'There's no more to be got where that came from.' It was the certainty of this fact that impelled me to offer the hint.

'Leave any for him? Who's him?' said my friend, stopping in his crunching of pie-crust.

'The young man. That you spoke of. That was hid with you.'

'Oh, ah!' he returned, with something like a gruff laugh. 'Him? Yes, yes! *He* don't want no wittles.'

'I thought he looked as if he did,' said I.

The man stopped eating, and regarded me with the keenest scrutiny and the greatest surprise.

'Looked? When?'

'Just now.'

'Where?'

'Yonder,' said I, pointing; 'over there, where I found him nodding asleep, and thought it was you.'

He held me by the collar and stared at me so, that I began to think his first idea about cutting my throat had revived.

'Dressed like you, you know, only with a hat,' I explained, trembling; 'and—and'—I was very anxious to put this delicately—'and with—the same reason for wanting to borrow a file. Didn't you hear the cannon last night?'

'Then, there *was* firing!' he said to himself.

'I wonder you shouldn't have been sure of that,' I returned, 'for we heard it up at home, and that's farther away, and we were shut in besides.'

'Why, see now!' said he. 'When a man's alone on these flats, with a light head and a light stomach, perishing of cold and want, he hears nothin' all night, but guns firing, and voices calling. Hears? He sees the soldiers, with their red coats lighted up by the torches carried afore, closing in round him. Hears his number called, hears himself challenged, hears the rattle of the muskets, hears the orders, 'Make ready! Present! Cover him steady, men!' and is laid hands on—and there's nothin! Why, if I see one pursuing party last night—coming up in order, Damn 'em, with their tramp, tramp—I see a hundred. And as to firing! Why, I see the mist shake with the cannon, arter it was broad day.—But this man;' he had said all the rest, as if he had forgotten my being there: 'did you notice anything in him?'

'He had a badly bruised face,' said I, recalling what I hardly knew I knew.

'Not here?' exclaimed the man, striking his left cheek mercilessly, with the flat of his hand.

'Yes, there!'

'Where is he?' He crammed what little food was left, into the breast of his grey jacket. 'Show me the way he went. I'll pull him down, like a blood-hound. Curse this iron on my sore leg! Give us hold of the file, boy.'

I indicated in what direction the mist had shrouded the other man, and he looked up at it for an instant. But he was down on the rank wet grass, filing at his iron like a madman, and not minding me or minding his own leg, which had an old chafe upon it and was bloody, but which he handled as roughly as if it had no more feeling in it than the file. I was very much afraid of him again, now that he had worked himself into this fierce hurry, and I was likewise very much afraid of keeping away from home any longer. I told him I must go, but he took no notice, so I thought the best thing I could do was to slip off. The last I saw of him, his head was bent over his knee and he was working hard at his fetter, muttering impatient imprecations at it and his leg. The last I heard of him, I stopped in the mist to listen, and the file was still going.

I fully expected to find a Constable in the kitchen, waiting to take me up. But not only was there no Constable there, but no discovery had yet been made of the robbery. Mrs Joe was prodigiously busy in getting the house ready for the festivities of the day, and Joe had been put upon the kitchen door-step to keep him out of the dust-pan—an article into which his destiny always led him, sooner or later, when my sister was vigorously reaping the floors of her establishment.

'And where the deuce ha' *you* been?' was Mrs Joe's Christmas salutation, when I and my conscience showed ourselves.

I said I had been down to hear the Carols. 'Ah! Well!' observed Mrs Joe. 'You might ha' done worse.' Not a doubt of that, I thought.

'Perhaps if I warn't a blacksmith's wife, and (what's the same thing) a slave with her apron never off, *I* should have been to hear the Carols,' said Mrs Joe. 'I'm rather partial to Carols myself, and that's the best of reasons for my never hearing any.'

Joe, who had ventured into the kitchen after me as the dust-pan had retired before us, drew the back of his hand across his nose with a conciliatory air, when Mrs Joe darted a look at him, and, when her eyes were withdrawn, secretly crossed his two forefingers, and exhibited them to me, as our token that Mrs Joe was in a cross temper. This was so much her normal state, that Joe and I would often, for weeks together, be, as to our fingers, like monumental Crusaders as to their legs.

We were to have a superb dinner, consisting of a leg of pickled pork and greens, and a pair of roast stuffed fowls. A handsome mince-pie had been made yesterday morning (which accounted for the mince-meat not being missed), and the pudding was already on the boil. These extensive arrangements occasioned us to be cut off unceremoniously in respect of breakfast: 'for I ain't,' said Mrs Joe, 'I ain't a-goin to have no formal cramming and bursting and washing up now, with what I've got before me, I promise you!'

So, we had our slices served out, as if we were two thousand troops on a forced march instead of a man and boy at home; and we took gulps of milk and water, with apologetic countenances, from a jug on the dresser. In the meantime, Mrs Joe put clean white curtains up, and tacked a new flowered-flounce across the wide chimney to replace the old one, and uncovered the little state parlour across the passage, which was never uncovered at any other time, but passed the rest of the year in a cool haze of silver paper, which even extended to the four little white crockery poodles on the mantelshelf, each with a black nose and a basket of flowers in his mouth, and each the counterpart of the other. Mrs Joe was a very clean housekeeper, but had an exquisite art of making her cleanliness more uncomfortable and unacceptable than dirt itself. Cleanliness is next to Godliness, and some people do the same by their religion.

My sister having so much to do, was going to church vicariously; that is to say, Joe and I were going. In his working clothes, Joe was a well-knit, characteristic-looking blacksmith; in his holiday clothes, he was more like a scarecrow in good circumstances, than anything else. Nothing that he wore then, fitted him or seemed to belong to him; and everything that he wore then, grazed him. On the present festive occasion he emerged from his room, when the blithe bells were going, the picture of misery, in a full suit of Sunday penitentials. As to me, I think my sister must have had some general idea that I was a young offender whom an Accoucheur Policeman had taken up (on my birthday) and delivered over to her, to be dealt with according to the outraged majesty of the law. I was always treated as if I had insisted on being born in opposition to the dictates of reason, religion, and morality, and against the dissuading arguments of my best friends. Even when I was taken to have a new suit of clothes, the tailor had orders to make them like a kind of Reformatory, and on no account to let me have the free use of my limbs.

Joe and I going to church, therefore, must have been a moving spectacle for compassionate minds. Yet, what I suffered outside, was nothing to what I underwent within. The terrors that had assailed me whenever Mrs Joe had gone near the pantry, or out of the room, were only to be equalled by the remorse with which my mind dwelt on what my hands had done. Under the weight of my wicked secret, I pondered whether the Church would be powerful enough to shield me from the vengeance of the terrible young man, if I divulged to that establishment. I conceived the idea that the time when the banns were read and when the clergyman said 'Ye are now to declare it!' would be the time for me to rise and propose a private conference in the vestry. I am far from being sure that I might not have astonished our small congregation by resorting to this extreme measure, but for its being Christmas Day and no Sunday.

Mr Wopsle, the clerk at church, was to dine with us; and Mr Hubble, the wheelwright, and Mrs Hubble; and Uncle Pumblechook (Joe's uncle, but Mrs Joe appropriated him), who was a well-to-do corn-chandler in the nearest town, and drove his own chaise-cart. The dinner hour was half-past one. When Joe and I got home, we found the table laid, and Mrs Joe dressed, and the dinner dressing, and the front door unlocked (it never was at any other time) for the company to enter by, and everything most splendid. And still, not a word of the robbery.

The time came, without bringing with it any relief to my feelings, and the company came. Mr Wopsle, united to a Roman nose and a large shining bald forehead, had a deep voice which he was uncommonly proud of; indeed it was understood among his acquaintance that if you could only give him his head, he would read the clergyman into fits; he himself confessed that if the Church was 'thrown open,' meaning to competition, he would not despair of making his mark in it. The Church not being 'thrown open,' he was, as I have said, our clerk. But he punished the Amens tremendously; and when he gave out the psalm—always giving the whole verse—he looked all round the congregation first, as much as to say, 'You have heard our friend overhead; oblige me with your opinion of this style!'

I opened the door to the company—making believe that it was a habit of ours to open that door—and I opened it first to Mr Wopsle, next to Mr and Mrs Hubble, and last of all to Uncle Pumblechook. N. B., *I* was not allowed to call him uncle, under the severest penalties.

'Mrs Joe,' said Uncle Pumblechook; a large hard-breathing middle-aged slow man, with a mouth like a fish, dull staring eyes, and sandy hair standing upright on his head, so that he looked as if he had just been all but choked, and had that moment come to; 'I have brought you as the compliments of the season—I have brought you, Mum, a bottle of sherry wine—and I have brought you, Mum, a bottle of port wine.'

Every Christmas Day he presented himself, as a profound novelty, with exactly the same words, and carrying the two bottles like dumb-bells. Every Christmas Day, Mrs Joe replied, as she now replied, 'Oh, Un—cle Pum—ble—chook! This is kind!' Every Christmas Day, he retorted, as he now retorted, 'It's no more than your merits. And now are you all bobbish, and how's Sixpennorth of halfpence?' meaning me.

We dined on these occasions in the kitchen, and adjourned, for the nuts and oranges and apples, to the parlour; which was a change very like Joe's change from his working clothes to his Sunday dress. My sister was uncommonly lively on the present occasion, and indeed was generally more gracious in the society of Mrs Hubble than in any other company. I remember Mrs Hubble as a little curly sharp-edged person in sky-blue, who held a conventionally juvenile position, because she had married Mr Hubble—I don't know at what remote period—when she was much younger than he. I remember Mr Hubble as a tough high-shouldered stooping old man, of a saw-dusty fragrance, with his legs extraordinarily wide apart: so that in my short days I always saw some miles of open country between them when I met him coming up the lane.

Among this good company I should have felt myself, even if I hadn't robbed the pantry, in a false position. Not because I was squeezed in at an acute angle of the tablecloth, with the table in my chest, and the Pumblechookian elbow in my eye, nor because I was not allowed to speak (I didn't want to speak), nor because I was regaled with the scaly tips of the drumsticks of the fowls, and with those obscure corners of pork of which the pig, when living, had had the least reason to be vain. No; I should not have minded that, if they would only have left me alone. But they wouldn't leave me alone. They seemed to think the opportunity lost, if they failed to point the conversation at me, every now and then, and stick the point into me. I might have been an unfortunate little bull in a Spanish arena, I got so smartingly touched up by these moral goads.

It began the moment we sat down to dinner. Mr Wopsle said grace with theatrical declamation—as it now appears to me, something like a religious cross of the Ghost in Hamlet with Richard the Third—and ended with the proper aspiration that we might be truly grateful. Upon which my sister fixed me with her eye, and said, in a low, reproachful voice, 'Do you hear that? Be grateful.'

'Especially,' said Mr Pumblechook, 'be grateful, boy, to them which brought you up by hand.'

Mrs Hubble shook her head, and contemplating me with a mournful presentiment that I should come to no good, asked, 'Why is it that the young are never grateful?' This moral mystery seemed too much for the company until Mr Hubble tersely solved it by saying, 'Naterally wicious.' Everybody then murmured, 'True!' and looked at me in a particularly unpleasant and personal manner.

Joe's station and influence were something feebler (if possible) when there was company, then when there was none. But he always aided and comforted me when he could, in some way of his own, and he always did so at dinner-time by giving me gravy, if there were any. There being plenty of gravy to-day, Joe spooned into my plate, at this point, about half a pint.

A little later on in the dinner, Mr Wopsle reviewed the sermon with some severity, and intimated—in the usual hypothetical case of the Church being 'thrown open'—what kind of sermon *he* would have given them. After favouring them with some heads of that discourse, he remarked that he considered the subject of the day's homily ill-chosen; which was the less excusable, he added, when there were so many subjects 'going about.'

'True again,' said Uncle Pumblechook. 'You've hit it, sir! Plenty of subjects going about, for them that know how to put salt upon their tails. That's what's wanted. A man needn't go far to find a subject, if he's ready with his salt-box.' Mr Pumblechook added, after a short interval of reflection, 'Look at Pork alone. There's a subject! If you want a subject, look at Pork!'

'True, sir. Many a moral for the young,' returned Mr Wopsle; and I knew he was going to lug me in, before he said it; 'might be deduced from that text.'

('You listen to this,' said my sister to me, in a severe parenthesis.)

Joe gave me some more gravy.

'Swine,' pursued Mr Wopsle, in his deepest voice, and pointing his fork at my blushes, as if he were mentioning my christian name; 'Swine were the companions of the prodigal. The gluttony of Swine is put before us, as an example to the young.' (I thought this pretty well in him who had been praising up the pork for being so plump and juicy.) 'What is detestable in a pig, is more detestable in a boy.'

'Or girl,' suggested Mr Hubble.

'Of course, or girl, Mr Hubble,' assented Mr Wopsle, rather irritably, 'but there is no girl present.'

'Besides,' said Mr Pumblechook, turning sharp on me, 'think what you've got to be grateful for. If you'd been born a Squeaker—'

'He *was*, if ever a child was,' said my sister most emphatically.

Joe gave me some more gravy.

'Well, but I mean a four-footed Squeaker,' said Mr Pumblechook. 'If you had been born such, would you have been here now. Not you—'

'Unless in that form,' said Mr Wopsle, nodding towards the dish.

'But I don't mean in that form, sir,' returned Mr Pumblechook, who had an objection to being interrupted; 'I mean, enjoying himself with his elders and betters, and improving himself with their conversation, and rolling in the lap of luxury. Would he have been doing that? No, he wouldn't. And what would have been your destination?' turning on me again. 'You would have been disposed of for so many shillings according to the market price of the article, and Dunstable the butcher would have come up to you as you lay in your straw, and he would have whipped you under his left arm, and with his right he would have tucked up his frock to get a penknife from out of his waistcoat pocket, and he would have shed your blood and had your life. No bringing up by hand then. Not a bit of it!'

Joe offered me more gravy, which I was afraid to take.

'He was a world of trouble to you, ma'am,' said Mrs Hubble, commiserating my sister.

'Trouble?' echoes my sister; 'trouble?' And then entered on a fearful catalogue of all the illnesses I had been guilty of, and all the acts of sleeplessness I had committed, and all the high places I had tumbled from, and all the low places I had tumbled into, and all the injuries I had done myself, and all the times she had wished me in my grave, and I had contumaciously refused to go there.

I think the Romans must have aggravated one another very much with their noses. Perhaps, they became the restless people they were, in consequence. Anyhow, Mr Wopsle's Roman nose so aggravated me, during the recital of my misdemeanours, that I should have liked to pull it until he howled. But, all I had endured up to this time, was nothing in comparison with the awful feelings that took possession of me when the pause was broken which ensued upon my sister's recital, and in which pause everybody had looked at me (as I felt painfully conscious) with indignation and abhorrence.

'Yet,' said Mr Pumblechook, leading the company gently back to the theme from which they had strayed, 'Pork—regarded as biled—is rich, too; ain't it?'

'Have a little brandy, uncle,' said my sister.

O Heavens, it had come at last! He would find it was weak, he would say it was weak, and I was lost! I held tight to the leg of the table under the cloth, with both hands, and awaited my fate.

My sister went for the stone bottle, came back with the stone bottle, and poured his brandy out: no one else taking any. The wretched man trifled with his glass—took it up, looked at it through the light, put it down—prolonged my misery. All this time, Mrs Joe and Joe were briskly clearing the table for the pie and pudding.

I couldn't keep my eyes off him. Always holding tight by the leg of the table with my hands and feet, I saw the miserable creature finger his glass playfully, take it up, smile, throw his head back, and drink the brandy off. Instantly afterwards, the company were seized with unspeakable consternation, owing to his springing to his feet, turning round several times in an appalling spasmodic whooping-cough dance, and rushing out at the door; he then became visible through the window, violently plunging and expectorating, making the most hideous faces, and apparently out of his mind.

I held on tight, while Mrs Joe and Joe ran to him. I didn't know how I had done it, but I had no doubt I had murdered him somehow. In my dreadful situation, it was a relief when he was brought back, and, surveying the company all round as if *they* had disagreed with him, sank down into his chair with the one significant gasp, 'Tar!'

I had filled up the bottle from the tar-water jug. I knew he would be worse by-and-by. I moved the table, like a Medium of the present day, by the vigour of my unseen hold upon it.

'Tar!' cried my sister in amazement. 'Why, however could Tar come there?'

But, Uncle Pumblechook, who was omnipotent in that kitchen, wouldn't hear the word, wouldn't hear the subject, imperiously waved it all away with his hand, and asked for hot gin-and-water. My sister, who had begun to be alarmingly meditative, had to employ herself actively in getting the gin, the hot water, the sugar, and the lemon-peel, and mixing them. For the time being at least, I was saved. I still held on to the leg of the table, but clutched it now with the fervour of gratitude.

By degrees, I became calm enough to release my grasp, and partake of pudding. Mr Pumblechook partook of pudding. All partook of pudding. The course terminated, and Mr Pumblechook had begun to beam under the genial influence of gin-and-water. I began to think I should get over the day, when my sister said to Joe, 'Clean plates—cold.'

I clutched the leg of the table again immediately, and pressed it to my bosom as if it had been the companion of my youth and friend of my soul. I foresaw what was coming, and I felt that this time I really was gone.

'You must taste,' said my sister, addressing the guests with her best grace, 'you must taste, to finish with, such a delightful and delicious present of Uncle Pumblechook's!'

Must they! Let them not hope to taste it!

'You must know,' said my sister, rising, 'it's a pie; a savoury pork pie.'

The company murmured their compliments. Uncle Pumblechook, sensible of having deserved well of his fellow-creatures, said—quite vivaciously, all things considered—'Well, Mrs Joe, we'll do our best endeavours; let us have a cut at this same pie.'

My sister went out to get it. I heard her steps proceed to the pantry. I saw Mr Pumblechook balance his knife. I saw re-awakening appetite in the Roman nostrils of Mr Wopsle. I heard Mr Hubble remark that 'a bit of savoury pork pie would lay atop of anything you could mention, and do no harm,' and I heard Joe say, 'You shall have some, Pip.' I have never been absolutely certain whether I uttered a shrill yell of terror, merely in spirit, or in the bodily hearing of the company. I felt that I could bear no more, and that I must run away. I released the leg of the table, and ran for my life.

But I ran no further than the house door, for there I ran head foremost into a party of soldiers with their muskets; one of whom held out a pair of handcuffs to me saying, 'Here you are, look sharp, come on!'

The apparition of a file of soldiers ringing down the buttends of their loaded muskets on our door-step, caused the dinner-party to rise from table in confusion, and caused Mrs Joe, re-entering the kitchen empty-handed, to stop short and stare, in her wondering lament of 'Gracious goodness gracious me, what's gone—with the—pie!'

The sergeant and I were in the kitchen when Mrs Joe stood staring; at which crisis I partially recovered the use of my senses. It was the sergeant who had spoken to me, and he was now looking round at the company, with his handcuffs invitingly extended towards them in his right hand, and his left on my shoulder.

'Excuse me, ladies and gentlemen,' said the sergeant, 'but as I have mentioned at the door to this smart young shaver' (which he hadn't), 'I am on a chase in the name of the king, and I want the blacksmith.'

'And pray what might you want with *him*?' retorted my sister, quick to resent his being wanted at all.

'Missis,' returned the gallant sergeant, 'speaking for myself, I should reply, the honour and pleasure of his fine wife's acquaintance; speaking for the king, I answer, a little job done.'

This was received as rather neat in the sergeant; insomuch that Mr Pumblechook cried audibly, 'Good again!'

'You see, blacksmith,' said the sergeant, who had by this time picked out Joe with his eye, 'we have had an accident with these, and I find the lock of one of 'em goes wrong, and the coupling don't act pretty. As they are wanted for immediate service, will you throw your eye over them?'

Joe threw his eye over them, and pronounced that the job would necessitate the lighting of his forge fire, and would take nearer two hours than one. 'Will it? Then will you set about it at once, blacksmith,' said the off-hand sergeant, 'as it's on his Majesty's service. And if my men can bear a hand anywhere, they'll make themselves useful.' With that he called to his men, who came trooping into the kitchen one after another, and piled their arms in a corner. And then they stood about, as soldiers do; now, with their hands loosely before them; now, resting a knee or a shoulder; now, easing a belt or a pouch; now, opening the door to spit stiffly over their high stocks, out into the yard.

All these things I saw without then knowing that I saw them, for I was in an agony of apprehension. But, beginning to perceive that the handcuffs were not for me, and that the military had so far got the better of the pie as to put it in the background, I collected a little more of my scattered wits.

'Would you give me the Time?' said the sergeant, addressing himself to Mr Pumblechook, as to a man whose appreciative powers justified the inference that he was equal to the time.

'It's just gone half-past two.'

'That's not so bad,' said the sergeant, reflecting; 'even if I was forced to halt here nigh two hours, that'll do. How far might you call yourselves from the marshes, hereabouts? Not above a mile, I reckon?'

'Just a mile,' said Mrs Joe.

'That'll do. We begin to close in upon 'em about dusk. A little before dusk, my orders are. That'll do.'

'Convicts, sergeant?' asked Mr Wopsle, in a matter-of-course way.

'Ay!' returned the sergeant, 'two. They're pretty well known to be out on the marshes still, and they won't try to get clear of 'em before dusk. Anybody here seen anything of such game?'

Everybody, myself excepted, said no, with confidence. Nobody thought of me.

'Well!' said the sergeant, 'they'll find themselves trapped in a circle, I expect, sooner than they count on. Now, blacksmith! If you're ready, his Majesty the King is.'

Joe had got his coat and waistcoat and cravat off, and his leather apron on, and passed into the forge. One of the soldiers opened its wooden windows, another lighted the fire, another turned to at the bellows, the rest stood round the blaze, which was soon roaring. Then Joe began to hammer and clink, hammer and clink, and we all looked on.

The interest of the impending pursuit not only absorbed the general attention, but even made my sister liberal. She drew a pitcher of beer from the cask, for the soldiers, and invited the sergeant to take a glass of brandy. But Mr Pumblechook said, sharply, 'Give him wine, Mum. I'll engage there's no Tar in that:' so, the sergeant thanked him and said that, as he preferred his drink without tar, he would take wine, if it was equally convenient. When it was given him, he drank his Majesty's health and compliments of the season, and took it all at a mouthful and smacked his lips.

'Good stuff, eh, sergeant?' said Mr Pumblechook.

'I'll tell you something,' returned the sergeant: 'I suspect that stuff's of *your* providing.'

Mr Pumblechook, with a fat sort of laugh, said 'Ay, ay? Why?'

'Because,' returned the sergeant, clapping him on the shoulder, 'you're a man that knows what's what.'

'D'ye think so?' said Mr Pumblechook, with his former laugh. 'Have another glass!'

'With you. Hob and nob,' returned the sergeant. 'The top of mine to the foot of yours—the foot of yours to the top of mine—Ring once, ring twice—the best tune on the Musical Glasses! Your health. May you live a thousand years, and never be a worse judge of the right sort than you are at the present moment of your life!'

The sergeant tossed off his glass again, and seemed quite ready for another glass. I noticed that Mr Pumblechook in his hospitality appeared to forget that he had made a present of the wine, but took the bottle from Mrs Joe and had all the credit of handing it about in a gush of joviality. Even I got some. And he was so very free of the wine that he even called for the other bottle, and handed that about with the same liberality, when the first was gone.

As I watched them while they all stood clustering about the forge, enjoying themselves so much, I thought what terrible good sauce for a dinner my fugitive friend on the marshes was. They had not enjoyed themselves a quarter so much, before the entertainment was brightened with the excitement he furnished. And now, when they were all in lively anticipation of 'the two villains' being taken, and when the bellows seemed to roar for the fugitives, the fire to flare for them, the smoke to hurry away in pursuit of them, Joe to hammer and clink for them, and all the murky shadows on the wall to shake at them in menace as the blaze rose and sank and the red-hot sparks dropped and died, the pale afternoon outside almost seemed in my pitying young fancy to have turned pale on their account, poor wretches.

At last, Joe's job was done, and the ringing and roaring stopped. As Joe got on his coat, he mustered courage to propose that some of us should go down with the soldiers and see what came of the hunt. Mr Pumblechook and Mr Hubble declined, on the plea of a pipe and ladies' society; but Mr Wopsle said he would go, if Joe would. Joe said he was agreeable, and would take me, if Mrs Joe approved. We never should have got leave to go, I am sure, but for Mrs Joe's curiosity to know all about it and how it ended. As it was, she merely stipulated, 'If you bring the boy back with his head blown to bits by a musket, don't look to me to put it together again.'

The sergeant took a polite leave of the ladies, and parted from Mr Pumblechook as from a comrade; though I doubt if he were quite as fully sensible of that gentleman's merits under arid conditions, as when something moist was going. His men resumed their muskets and fell in. Mr Wopsle, Joe and I, received strict charge to keep in the rear, and to speak no word after we reached the marshes. When we were all out in the raw air and were steadily moving towards our business, I treasonably whispered to Joe, 'I hope, Joe, we shan't find them.' And Joe whispered to me, 'I'd give a shilling if they had cut and run, Pip.'

We were joined by no stragglers from the village, for the weather was cold and threatening, the way dreary, the footing bad, darkness coming on, and the people had good fires indoors and were keeping the day. A few faces hurried to glowing windows and looked after us, but none came out. We passed the finger-post, and held straight on to the churchyard. There, we were stopped a few minutes by a signal from the sergeant's hand, while two or three of his men dispersed themselves among the graves, and also examined the porch. They came in again without finding anything, and then we struck out on the open marshes, through the gate at the side of the churchyard. A bitter sleet came rattling against us here on the east wind, and Joe took me on his back.

Now that we were out upon the dismal wilderness where they little thought I had been within eight or nine hours, and seen both men hiding, I considered for the first time, with great dread, if we should come upon them, would my particular convict suppose that it was I who had brought the soldiers there? He had asked me if I was a deceiving imp, and he had said I should be a fierce young hound if I joined the hunt against him. Would he believe that I was both imp and hound in treacherous earnest, and had betrayed him?

It was of no use asking myself this question now. There I was, on Joe's back, and there was Joe beneath me, charging at the ditches like a hunter, and stimulating Mr Wopsle not to tumble on his Roman nose, and to keep up with us. The soldiers were in front of us, extended into a pretty wide line with an interval between man and man. We were taking the course I had begun with, and from which I had diverged in the mist. Either the mist was not out again yet, or the wind had dispelled it. Under the low red glare of the sunset, the beacon, and the gibbet, and the mound of the Battery, and the opposite shore of the river, were plain, though all of a watery lead colour.

With my heart thumping like a blacksmith at Joe's broad shoulder, I looked all about for any sign of the convicts. I could see none, I could hear none. Mr Wopsle had greatly alarmed me more than once, by his blowing and hard breathing; but I knew the sound by this time, and could disassociate them from the object of pursuit. I got a dreadful start, when I thought I heard the file still going; but it was only a sheep bell. The sheep stopped in their eating and looked timidly at us; and the cattle, their heads turned from the wind and sleet, stared angrily as if they held us responsible for both annoyances; but, except these things, and the shudder of the dying day in every blade of grass, there was no break in the bleak stillness of the marshes.

The soldiers were moving on in the direction of the old Battery, and we were moving on a little way behind them, when, all of a sudden, we all stopped. For there had reached us, on the wings of the wind and rain, a long shout. It was repeated. It was at a distance towards the east, but it was long and loud. Nay, there seemed to be two or more shouts raised together—if one might judge from a confusion in the sound.

To this effect the sergeant and the nearest men were speaking under their breath, when Joe and I came up. After another moment's listening, Joe (who was a good judge) agreed, and Mr Wopsle (who was a bad judge) agreed. The sergeant, a decisive man, ordered that the sound should not be answered, but that the course should be changed, and that his men should make towards it 'at the double.' So we slanted to the right (where the East was), and Joe pounded away so wonderfully, that I had to hold on tight to keep my seat.

It was a run indeed now, and what Joe called, in the only two words he spoke all the time, 'a Winder.' Down banks and up banks, and over gates, and splashing into dykes, and breaking among coarse rushes; no man cared where he went. As we came nearer to the shouting, it became more and more apparent that it was made by more than one voice. Sometimes, it seemed to stop altogether, and then the soldiers stopped. When it broke out again, the soldiers made for it at a greater rate than ever, and we after them. After a while, we had so run it down, that we could hear one voice calling 'Murder!' and another voice, 'Convicts! Runaways! Guard! This way for the runaway convicts!' Then both voices would seem to be stifled in a struggle, and then would break out again. And when it had come to this, the soldiers ran like deer, and Joe too.

The sergeant ran in first, when we had run the noise quite down, and two of his men ran in close upon him. Their pieces were cocked and levelled when we all ran in.

'Here are both men!' panted the sergeant, struggling at the bottom of a ditch. 'Surrender, you two! and confound you for two wild beasts! Come asunder!'

Water was splashing, and mud was flying, and oaths were being sworn, and blows were being struck, when some more men went down into the ditch to help the sergeant, and dragged out, separately, my convict and the other one. Both were bleeding and panting and execrating and struggling; but of course I knew them both directly.

'Mind!' said my convict, wiping blood from his face with his ragged sleeves, and shaking torn hair from his fingers; '*I* took him! *I* give him up to you! Mind that!'

'It's not much to be particular about,' said the sergeant; 'it'll do you small good, my man, being in the same plight yourself. Handcuffs there!'

'I don't expect it to do me any good. I don't want it to do me more good than it does now,' said my convict, with a greedy laugh. 'I took him. He knows it. That's enough for me.'

The other convict was livid to look at, and, in addition to the old bruised left side of his face, seemed to be bruised and torn all over. He could not so much as get his breath to speak, until they were both separately handcuffed, but leaned upon a soldier to keep himself from falling.

'Take notice, guard—he tried to murder me,' were his first words.

'Tried to murder him?' said my convict, disdainfully. 'Try, and not do it? I took him, and giv' him up; that's what I done. I not only prevented him getting off the marshes, but I dragged him here—dragged him this far on his way back. He's a gentleman, if you please, this villain. Now, the Hulks has got its gentleman again, through me. Murder him? Worth my while, too, to murder him, when I could do worse and drag him back!'

The other one still gasped, 'He tried—he tried—to—murder me. Bear—bear witness.'

'Lookee here!' said my convict to the sergeant. 'Single-handed I got clear of the prison-ship; I made a dash and I done it. I could ha' got clear of these death-cold flats likewise—look at my leg: you won't find much iron on it—if I hadn't made the discovery that *he* was here. Let *him* go free? Let *him* profit by the means as I found out? Let *him* make a tool of me afresh and again? Once more? No, no, no. If I had died at the bottom there;' and he made an emphatic swing at the ditch with his manacled hands; 'I'd have held to him with that grip, that you should have been safe to find him in my hold.'

The other fugitive, who was evidently in extreme horror of his companion, repeated, 'He tried to murder me. I should have been a dead man if you had not come up.'

'He lies!' said my convict, with fierce energy. 'He's a liar born, and he'll die a liar. Look at his face; ain't it written there? Let him turn those eyes of his on me. I defy him to do it.'

The other, with an effort at a scornful smile—which could not, however, collect the nervous working of his mouth into any set expression, looked at the soldiers, and looked about at the marshes, and at the sky, but certainly did not look at the speaker.

'Do you see him?' pursued my convict. 'Do you see what a villain he is? Do you see those grovelling and wandering eyes? That's how he looked when we were tried together. He never looked at me.'

The other, always working and working his dry lips and turning his eyes restlessly about him far and near, did at last turn them for a moment on the speaker, with the words, 'You are not much to look at,' and with a half-taunting glance at the bound hands. At that point, my convict became so frantically exasperated, that he would have rushed upon him but for the interposition of the soldiers. 'Didn't I tell you,' said the other convict then, 'that he would murder me if he could?'

And anyone could see that he shook with fear, and that there broke out upon his lips curious white flakes, like thin snow.

'Enough of this parley,' said the sergeant. 'Light those torches.'

As one of the soldiers, who carried a basket in lieu of a gun, went down on his knee to open it, my convict looked round him for the first time, and saw me. I had alighted from Joe's back on the brink of the ditch when we came up, and had not moved since. I looked at him eagerly when he looked at me, and slightly moved my hands and shook my head. I had been waiting for him to see me, that I might try to assure him of my innocence. It was not at all expressed to me that he even comprehended my intention, for he gave me a look that I did not understand, and it all passed in a moment. But if he had looked at me for an hour or for a day, I could not have remembered his face ever afterwards, as having been more attentive.

The soldier with the basket soon got a light, and lighted three or four torches, and took one himself and distributed the others. It had been almost dark before, but now it seemed quite dark, and soon afterwards very dark. Before we departed from that spot, four soldiers standing in a ring, fired twice into the air. Presently we saw other torches kindled at some distance behind us, and others on the marshes on the opposite bank of the river. 'All right,' said the sergeant. 'March.'

We had not gone far when three cannons were fired ahead of us with a sound that seemed to burst something inside my ear. 'You are expected on board,' said the sergeant to my convict; 'they know you are coming. Don't straggle, my man. Close up here.'

The two were kept apart, and each walked surrounded by a separate guard. I had hold of Joe's hand now, and Joe carried one of the torches. Mr Wopsle had been for going back, but Joe was resolved to see it out, so we went on with the party. There was a reasonably good path now, mostly on the edge of the river, with a divergence here and there where a dyke came, with a miniature windmill on it and a muddy sluice-gate. When I looked round, I could see the other lights coming in after us. The torches we carried, dropped great blotches of fire upon the track, and I could see those, too, lying smoking and flaring. I could see nothing else but black darkness. Our lights warmed the air about us with their pitchy blaze, and the two prisoners seemed rather to like that, as they limped along in the midst of the muskets. We could not go fast, because of their lameness; and they were so spent, that two or three times we had to halt while they rested.

After an hour or so of this travelling, we came to a rough wooden hut, and a landing-place. There was a guard in the hut, and they challenged, and the sergeant answered. Then, we went into the hut, where there was a smell of tobacco and whitewash, and a bright fire, and a lamp, and a stand of muskets, and a drum, and a low wooden bedstead, like an overgrown mangle without the machinery, capable of holding about a dozen soldiers all at once. Three or four soldiers who lay upon it in their great-coats were not much interested in us, but just lifted their heads and took a sleepy stare, and then lay down again. The sergeant made some kind of report, and some entry in a book, and then the convict whom I call the other convict was drafted off with his guard, to go on board first.

My convict never looked at me, except that once. While we stood in the hut, he stood before the fire looking thoughtfully at it, or putting up his feet by turns upon the hob, and looking thoughtfully at them as if he pitied them for their recent adventures. Suddenly, he turned to the sergeant, and remarked:

'I wish to say something respecting this escape. It may prevent some persons laying under suspicion alonger me.'

'You can say what you like,' returned the sergeant, standing coolly looking at him with his arms folded, 'but you have no call to say it here. You'll have opportunity enough to say about it, and hear about it, before it's done with, you know.'

'I know, but this is another pint, a separate matter. A man can't starve; at least *I* can't. I took some wittles, up at the village over yonder—where the church stands a'most out on the marshes.'

'You mean stole,' said the sergeant.

'And I'll tell you where from. From the blacksmith's.'

'Halloa!' said the sergeant, staring at Joe.

'Halloa, Pip!' said Joe, staring at me.

'It was some broken wittles—that's what it was—and a dram of liquor, and a pie.'

'Have you happened to miss such an article as a pie, blacksmith?' asked the sergeant confidentially.

'My wife did, at the very moment when you came in. Don't you know, Pip?'

'So,' said my convict, turning his eyes on Joe in a moody manner, and without the least glance at me; 'so you're the blacksmith, are you? Then I'm sorry to say, I've eat your pie.'

'God knows you're welcome to it—so far as it was ever mine,' returned Joe, with a saving remembrance of Mrs Joe. 'We don't know what you have done, but we wouldn't have you starved to death for it, poor miserable fellow-creatur.—Would us, Pip?'

The something that I had noticed before, clicked in the man's throat again, and he turned his back. The boat had returned, and his guard were ready, so we followed him to the landing-place made of rough stakes and stones, and saw him put into the boat, which was rowed by a crew of convicts like himself. No one seemed surprised to see him, or interested in seeing him, or glad to see him, or sorry to see him, or spoke a word, except that somebody in the boat growled as if to dogs, 'Give way, you!' which was the signal for the dip of the oars. By the light of the torches, we saw the black Hulk lying out a little way from the mud of the shore, like a wicked Noah's ark. Cribbed and barred and moored by massive rusty chains, the prison-ship seemed in my young eyes to be ironed like the prisoners. We saw the boat go alongside, and we saw him taken up the side and disappear. Then, the ends of the torches were flung hissing into the water, and went out, as if it were all over with him.

OUR MUTUAL FRIEND

Silas Wegg is a one-legged pedlar who keeps a street-stall near Cavendish Square, selling a poor collection of fruit, nuts, sweets and halfpenny ballads. He is employed by the illiterate Mr Boffin to read to him in the evenings. For this purpose, Mr Boffin has purchased in a sale the 'Decline-and-Fall-Off-The-Rooshan-Empire' in eight volumes ...

Silas Wegg, being on his road to the Roman Empire, approaches it by way of Clerkenwell. The time is early in the evening; the weather moist and raw. Mr Wegg finds leisure to make a little circuit, by reason that he folds his screen early, now that he combines another source of income with it, and also that he feels it due to himself to be anxiously expected at the Bower. 'Boffin will get all the eagerer for waiting a bit,' says Silas, screwing up, as he stumps along, first his right eye, and then his left. Which is something superfluous in him, for Nature has already screwed both pretty tight.

'If I get on with him as I expect to get on,' Silas pursues, stumping and meditating, 'it wouldn't become me to leave it here. It wouldn't be respectable.' Animated by this reflection, he stumps faster, and looks a long way before him, as a man with an ambitious project in abeyance often will do.

Aware of a working-jeweller population taking sanctuary about the church in Clerkenwell, Mr Wegg is conscious of an interest in, and a respect for, the neighbourhood. But his sensations in this regard halt as to their strict morality, as he halts in his gait; for they suggest the delights of a coat of invisibility in which to walk off safely with the precious stones and watch-cases, but stop short of any compunction for the people who would lose the same.

Not, however, towards the 'shops' where cunning artificers work in pearls and diamonds and gold and silver, making their hands so rich, that the enriched water in which they wash them is bought for the refiners;—not towards these does Mr Wegg stump, but towards the poorer shops of small retail traders in commodities to eat and drink and keep folks warm, and of Italian frame-makers, and of barbers, and of brokers, and of dealers in dogs and singing-birds. From these, in a narrow and a dirty street devoted to such callings, Mr Wegg selects one dark shop-window with a tallow candle dimly burning in it, surrounded by a muddle of objects, vaguely resembling pieces of leather and dry stick, but among which nothing is resolvable into anything distinct, save the candle itself in its old tin candlestick, and two preserved frogs fighting a small-sword duel. Stumping with fresh vigour, he goes in at the dark greasy entry, pushes a little greasy dark reluctant side-door, and follows the door into the little dark greasy shop. It is so dark that nothing can be made out in it, over a little counter, but another tallow candle in another old tin candlestick, close to the face of a man stooping low in a chair.

Mr Wegg nods to the face, 'Good evening.'

The face looking up is a sallow face with weak eyes, surmounted by a tangle of reddish-dusty hair. The owner of the face has no cravat on, and has opened his tumbled shirt-collar to work with the more ease. For the same reason he has no coat on: only a loose waistcoat over his yellow linen. His eyes are like the over-tired eyes of an engraver, but he is not that; his expression and stoop are like those of a shoemaker, but he is not that.

'Good evening, Mr Venus. Don't you remember?'

With slowly dawning remembrance, Mr Venus rises, and holds his candle over the little counter, and holds it down towards the legs, natural and artificial, of Mr Wegg.

'To be *sure*!' he says, then. 'How do you do?'

'Wegg, you know,' that gentleman explains.

'Yes, yes,' says the other. 'Hospital amputation?'

'Just so,' says Mr Wegg.

'Yes, yes,' quoth Venus. 'How do you do? Sit down by the fire, and warm your—your other one.'

The little counter being so short a counter that it leaves the fire-place, which would have been behind it if it had been longer, accessible, Mr Wegg sits down on a box in front of the fire, and inhales a warm and comfortable smell which is not the smell of the shop. 'For that,' Mr Wegg inwardly decides, as he takes a corrective sniff or two, 'is musty, leathery, feathery, cellary, gluey, gummy, and,' with another sniff, 'as it might be, strong of old pairs of bellows.'

'My tea is drawing, and my muffin is on the hob, Mr Wegg; will you partake?'

It being one of Mr Wegg's guiding rules in life always to partake, he says he will. But, the little shop is so excessively dark, is stuck so full of black shelves and brackets and nooks and corners, that he sees Mr Venus's cup and saucer only because it is close under the candle, and does not see from what mysterious recess Mr Venus produces another for himself, until it is under his nose. Concurrently, Wegg perceives a pretty little dead bird lying on the counter, with its head drooping on one side against the rim of Mr Venus's saucer, and a long stiff wire piercing its breast. As if it were Cock Robin, the hero of the ballad, and Mr Venus were the sparrow with his bow and arrow, and Mr Wegg were the fly with his little eye.

Mr Venus dives, and produces another muffin, yet untoasted; taking the arrow out of the breast of Cock Robin, he proceeds to toast it on the end of that cruel instrument. When it is brown, he dives again and produces butter, with which he completes his work.

Mr Wegg, as an artful man who is sure of his supper by-and-by, presses muffin on his host to soothe him into a compliant state of mind, or, as one might say, to grease his works. As the muffins disappear, little by little, the black shelves and nooks and corners begin to appear, and Mr Wegg gradually acquires an imperfect notion that over against him on the chimney-piece is a Hindoo baby in a bottle, curved up with his big head tucked under him, as though he would instantly throw a summersault if the bottle were large enough.

When he deems Mr Venus's wheels sufficiently lubricated, Mr Wegg approaches his object by asking, as he lightly taps his hands together, to express an undesigning frame of mind:

'And how have I been going on, this long time, Mr Venus?'

'Very bad,' says Mr Venus, uncompromisingly.

'What? Am I still at home?' asks Wegg, with an air of surprise.

'Always at home.'

This would seem to be secretly agreeable to Wegg, but he veils his feelings, and observes, 'Strange. To what do you attribute it?'

'I don't know,' replies Venus, who is a haggard melancholy man, speaking in a weak voice of querulous complaint, 'to what to attribute it, Mr Wegg. I can't work you into a miscellaneous one, nohow. Do what I will, you can't be got to fit. Anybody with a passable knowledge would pick you out at a look, and say—'No go! Don't match!' '

'Well, but hang it, Mr Venus,' Wegg expostulates with some little irritation, 'that can't be personal and peculiar in *me.* It must often happen with miscellaneous ones.'

'With ribs (I grant you) always. But not else. When I prepare a miscellaneous one, I know beforehand that I can't keep to nature, and be miscellaneous with ribs, because every man has his own ribs, and no other man's will go with them; but elseways I can be miscellaneous. I have just sent home a Beauty—a perfect Beauty—to a school of art. One leg Belgian, one leg English, and the pickings of eight other people in it. Talk of not being qualified to be miscellaneous! By rights you *ought* to be, Mr Wegg.'

Silas looks as hard at his one leg as he can in the dim light, and after a pause sulkily opines 'that it must be the fault of the other people. Or how do you mean to say it comes about?' he demands impatiently.

'I don't know how it comes about. Stand up a minute. Hold the light.' Mr Venus takes from a corner by his chair, the bones of a leg and foot, beautifully pure, and put together with exquisite neatness. These he compares with Mr Wegg's leg; that gentleman looking on, as if he were being measured for a riding-boot. 'No, I don't know how it is, but so it is. You have got a twist in that bone, to the best of my belief. *I* never saw the likes of you.'

Mr Wegg having looked distrustfully at his own limb, and suspiciously at the pattern with which it has been compared, makes the point:

'I'll bet a pound that ain't an English one!'

'An easy wager, when we run so much into foreign! No, it belongs to that French gentleman.'

As he nods towards a point of darkness behind Mr Wegg, the latter, with a slight start, looks round for 'that French gentleman,' whom he at length descries to be represented (in a very workmanlike manner) by his ribs only, standing on a shelf in another corner, like a piece of armour or a pair of stays.

'Oh!' says Mr Wegg, with a sort of sense of being introduced; 'I dare say you were all right enough in your own country, but I hope no objections will be taken to my saying that the Frenchman was never yet born as I should wish to match.'

At this moment the greasy door is violently pushed inward, and a boy follows it, who says, after having let it slam:

'Come for the stuffed canary.'

'It's three and ninepence,' returns Venus; 'have you got the money?'

The boy produces four shillings. Mr Venus, always in exceedingly low spirits, and making whimpering sounds, peers about for the stuffed canary. On his taking the candle to assist his search, Mr Wegg observes that he has a convenient little shelf near his knees, exclusively appropriated to skeleton hands, which have very much the appearance of wanting to lay hold of him. From these Mr Venus rescues the canary in a glass case, and shows it to the boy.

'There!' he whimpers. 'There's animation! On a twig, making up his mind to hop! Take care of him; he's a lovely specimen.—And three is four.'

The boy gathers up his change and has pulled the door open by a leather strap nailed to it for the purpose, when Venus cries out:

'Stop him! Come back, you young villain! You've got a tooth among them halfpence.'

'How was I to know I'd got it? You give it me. I don't want none of your teeth, I've got enough of my own.' So the boy pipes, as he selects it from his change, and throws it on the counter.

'Don't sauce *me*, in the wicious pride of your youth,' Mr Venus retorts pathetically. 'Don't hit *me* because you see I'm down. I'm low enough without that. It dropped into the till, I suppose. They drop into everything. There was two in the coffee-pot at breakfast-time. Molars.'

'Very well, then,' argues the boy, 'what do you call names for?'

To which Mr Venus only replies, shaking his shock of dusty hair, and winking his weak eyes, 'Don't sauce *me*, in the wicious pride of your youth; don't hit *me* because you see I'm down. You've no idea how small you'd come out, if I had the articulating of you.'

This consideration seems to have its effect upon the boy, for he goes out grumbling.

'Oh dear me, dear me!' sighs Mr Venus, heavily, snuffing the candle, 'the world that appeared so flowery has ceased to blow! You're casting your eye round the shop, Mr Wegg. Let me show you a light. My working bench. My young man's bench. A Wice. Tools. Bones, warious. Skulls, warious. Preserved Indian baby. African ditto. Bottled preparations, warious. Everything within reach of your hand, in good preservation. The mouldy ones a-top. What's in those hampers over them again, I don't quite remember. Say, human warious. Cats. Articulated English baby. Dogs. Ducks. Glass eyes, warious. Mummied bird. Dried cuticle, warious. Oh dear me! That's the general panoramic view.'

Having so held and waved the candle as that all these heterogeneous objects seemed to come forward obediently when they were named, and then retire again, Mr Venus despondently repeats, 'Oh dear me, dear me!' resumes his seat, and with drooping despondency upon him, falls to pouring himself out more tea.

'Where am I?' asks Mr Wegg.

'You're somewhere in the back shop across the yard, sir; and speaking quite candidly, I wish I'd never bought you of the Hospital Porter.'

'Now, look here, what did you give for me?'

'Well,' replies Venus, blowing his tea: his head and face peering out of the darkness, over the smoke of it, as if he were modernising the old original rise in his family: 'you were one of a warious lot, and I don't know.'

Silas puts his point in the improved form of 'What will you take for me?'

'Well,' replies Venus, still blowing his tea, 'I'm not prepared, at a moment's notice, to tell you, Mr Wegg.'

'Come! According to your own account, I'm not worth much,' Wegg reasons persuasively.

'Not for miscellaneous working in, I grant you, Mr Wegg; but you might turn out valuable yet, as a—' here Mr Venus takes a gulp of tea, so hot that it makes him choke, and sets his weak eyes watering: 'as a Monstrosity, if you'll excuse me.'

Repressing an indignant look, indicative of anything but a disposition to excuse him, Silas pursues his point.

'I think you know me, Mr Venus, and I think you know I never bargain.'

Mr Venus takes gulps of hot tea, shutting his eyes at every gulp, and opening them again in a spasmodic manner; but does not commit himself to assent.

'I have a prospect of getting on in life and elevating myself by my own independent exertions,' says Wegg, feelingly, 'and I shouldn't like—I tell you openly I should *not* like—under such circumstances, to be what I may call dispersed, a part of me here, and a part of me there, but should wish to collect myself like a genteel person.'

'It's a prospect at present, is it, Mr Wegg? Then you haven't got the money for a deal about you? Then I'll tell you what I'll do with you; I'll hold you over. I am a man of my word, and you needn't be afraid of my disposing of you. I'll hold you over. That's a promise. Oh dear me, dear me!'

Fain to accept his promise, and wishing to propitiate him, Mr Wegg looks on as he sighs and pours himself out more tea, and then says, trying to get a sympathetic tone into his voice:

'You seem very low, Mr Venus. Is business bad?'

'Never was so good.'

'Is your hand out at all?'

'Never was so well in. Mr Wegg, I'm not only first in the trade, but I'm *the* trade. You may go and buy a skeleton at the West End if you like, and pay the West End price, but it'll be my putting together. I've as much to do as I can possibly do, with the assistance of my young man, and I take a pride and pleasure in it.'

Mr Venus thus delivers himself, his right hand extended, his smoking saucer in his left hand, protesting as though he were going to burst into a flood of tears.

'That ain't a state of things to make you low, Mr Venus.'

'Mr Wegg, I know it ain't. Mr Wegg, not to name myself as a workman without an equal, I've gone on improving myself in my knowledge of Anatomy, till both by sight and by name I'm perfect. Mr Wegg, if you was brought here loose in a bag to be articulated, I'd name your smallest bones blindfold equally with your largest, as fast as I could pick 'em out, and I'd sort 'em all, and sort your wertebrae, in a manner that would equally surprise and charm you.'

'Well,' remarks Silas (though not quite so readily as last time), '*that* ain't a state of things to be low about.—Not for *you* to be low about, leastways.'

'Mr Wegg, I know it ain't; Mr Wegg, I know it ain't. But it's the heart that lowers me, it is the heart! Be so good as take and read that card out loud.'

Silas receives one from his hand, which Venus takes from a wonderful litter in a drawer, and putting on his spectacles, reads:

' "Mr Venus," '

'Yes. Go on.'

' "Preserver of Animals and Birds," '

'Yes. Go on.'

' "Articulator of human bones." '

'That's it,' with a groan. 'That's it! Mr Wegg, I'm thirty-two, and a bachelor. Mr Wegg, I love her. Mr Wegg, she is worthy of being loved by a Potentate!' Here Silas is rather alarmed by Mr Venus springing to his feet in the hurry of his spirits, and haggardly confronting him with his hand on his coat collar; but Mr Venus, begging pardon, sits down again, saying, with the calmness of despair, 'She objects to the business.'

'Does she know the profits of it?'

'She knows the profits of it, but she don't appreciate the art of it, and she objects to it. "I do not wish," she writes in her own hand-writing, "to regard myself, nor yet to be regarded, in that bony light." '

Mr Venus pours himself out more tea, with a look and in an attitude of the deepest desolation.

'And so a man climbs to the top of the tree, Mr Wegg, only to see that there's no look-out when he's up there! I sit here of a night surrounded by the lovely trophies of my art, and what have they done for me? Ruined me. Brought me to the pass of being informed that "she does not wish to regard herself, nor yet to be regarded, in that bony light!" ' Having repeated the fatal expressions, Mr Venus drinks more tea by gulps, and offers an explanation of his doing so.

'It lowers me. When I'm equally lowered all over, lethargy sets in. By sticking to it till one or two in the morning, I get oblivion. Don't let me detain you, Mr Wegg. I'm not company for any one.'

'It is not on that account,' says Silas, rising, 'but because I've got an appointment. It's time I was at Harmon's.'

'Eh?' said Mr Venus. 'Harmon's, up Battle Bridge way?'

Mr Wegg admits that he is bound for that port.

'You ought to be in a good thing, if you've worked yourself in there. There's lots of money going there.'

'To think,' says Silas, 'that you should catch it up so quick, and know about it. Wonderful!'

'Not at all, Mr Wegg. The old gentleman wanted to know the nature and worth of everything that was found in the dust; and many's the bone, and feather, and what not, that he's brought to me.'

'Really, now!'

'Yes. (Oh dear me, dear me!) And he's buried quite in this neighbourhood, you know. Over yonder.'

Mr Wegg does not know, but he makes as if he did, by responsively nodding his head. He also follows with his eyes the toss of Venus's head: as if to seek a direction to over yonder.

'I took an interest in that discovery in the river,' says Venus. '(She hadn't written her cutting refusal at that time.) I've got up there—never mind, though.'

He had raised the candle at arm's length towards one of the dark shelves, and Mr Wegg had turned to look, when he broke off.

'The old gentleman was well known all round here. There used to be stories about his having hidden all kinds of property in those dust mounds. I suppose there was nothing in 'em. Probably you know, Mr Wegg?'

'Nothing in 'em,' says Wegg, who has never heard a word of this before.

'Don't let me detain you. Good-night!'

The unfortunate Mr Venus gives him a shake of the hand with a shake of his own head, and drooping down in his chair, proceeds to pour himself out more tea.

Mr Wegg, looking back over his shoulder as he pulls the door open by the strap, notices that the movement so shakes the crazy shop, and so shakes a momentary flare out of the candle, as that the babies—Hindoo, African, and British—the 'human warious,' the French gentleman, the green glass-eyed cats, the dogs, the ducks, and all the rest of the collection, show for an instant as if paralytically animated; while even poor little Cock Robin at Mr Venus's elbow turns over on his innocent side. Next moment, Mr Wegg is stumping under the gaslights and through the mud.

THE MYSTERY OF EDWIN DROOD

Edwin Drood has been formally betrothed to Rosa Bud since childhood but cares little for her and treats her in a very casual fashion. When Neville Landless and his sister Helena arrive in the town of Cloisterham–she to attend the Nuns' House where Rosa is also a pupil, he to study with the Reverend Septimus Crisparkle–Neville, attracted to Rosa, takes a strong dislike to Edwin for his careless behaviour towards her. Edwin's uncle, John Jasper, who himself nurses an unrequited passion for Rosa, foments the enmity between Edwin and Neville ...

The two young men, having seen the damsels, their charges, enter the courtyard of the Nuns' House, and finding themselves coldly stared at by the brazen door-plate, as if the battered old beau with the glass in his eye were insolent, look at one another, look along the perspective of the moonlit street, and slowly walk away together.

'Do you stay here long, Mr Drood?' says Neville.

'Not this time,' is the careless answer. 'I leave for London again, to-morrow. But I shall be here, off and on, until next Midsummer; then I shall take my leave of Cloisterham, and England too; for many a long day, I expect.'

'Are you going abroad?'

'Going to wake up Egypt a little,' is the condescending answer.

'Are you reading?'

'Reading!' repeats Edwin Drood, with a touch of contempt. 'No. Doing, working, engineering. My small patrimony was left a part of the capital of the Firm I am with, by my father, a former partner; and I am a charge upon the Firm until I come of age; and then I step into my modest share in the concern. Jack—you met him at dinner—is, until then, my guardian and trustee.'

'I heard from Mr Crisparkle of your other good fortune.'

'What do you mean by my other good fortune?'

Neville has made his remark in a watchfully advancing, and yet furtive and shy manner, very expressive of that peculiar air already noticed, of being at once hunter and hunted. Edwin has made his retort with an abruptness not at all polite. They stop and interchange a rather heated look.

'I hope,' says Neville, 'there is no offence, Mr Drood, in my innocently referring to your betrothal?'

'By George!' cries Edwin, leading on again at a somewhat quicker pace; 'everybody in this chattering old Cloisterham refers to it. I wonder no public-house has been set up, with my portrait for the sign of The Betrothed's Head. Or Pussy's portrait. One or the other.'

'I am not accountable for Mr Crisparkle's mentioning the matter to me, quite openly,' Neville begins.

'No; that's true; you are not,' Edwin Drood assents.

'But,' resumes Neville, 'I am accountable for mentioning it to you. And I did so, on the supposition that you could not fail to be highly proud of it.'

Now, there are these two curious touches of human nature working the secret springs of this dialogue. Neville Landless is already enough impressed by Little Rosebud, to feel indignant that Edwin Drood (far below her) should hold his prize so lightly. Edwin Drood is already enough impressed by Helena, to feel indignant that Helena's brother (far below her) should dispose of him so coolly, and put him out of the way so entirely.

However, the last remark had better be answered. So, says Edwin:

'I don't know, Mr Neville' (adopting that mode of address from Mr Crisparkle), 'that what people are proudest of, they usually talk most about; I don't know either, that what they are proudest of, they most like other people to talk about. But I live a busy life, and I speak under correction by you readers, who ought to know everything, and I dare say do.'

By this time they have both become savage; Mr Neville out in the open; Edwin Drood under the transparent cover of a popular tune, and a stop now and then to pretend to admire picturesque effects in the moonlight before him.

'It does not seem to me very civil in you,' remarks Neville, at length, 'to reflect upon a stranger who comes here, not having had your advantages, to try to make up for lost time. But, to be sure, *I* was not brought up in "busy life," and my ideas of civility were formed among Heathens.'

'Perhaps, the best civility, whatever kind of people we are brought up among,' retorts Edwin Drood, 'is to mind our own business. If you will set me that example, I promise to follow it.'

'Do you know that you take a great deal too much upon yourself?' is the angry rejoinder; 'and that in the part of the world I come from, you would be called to account for it?'

'By whom, for instance?' asks Edwin Drood, coming to a halt, and surveying the other with a look of disdain.

But, here a startling right hand is laid on Edwin's shoulder, and Jasper stands between them. For, it would seem that he, too, has strolled round by the Nuns' House, and has come up behind them on the shadowy side of the road.

'Ned, Ned, Ned!' he says. 'We must have no more of this. I don't like this. I have overheard high words between you two. Remember, my dear boy, you are almost in the position of host to-night. You belong, as it were, to the place, and in a manner represent it towards a stranger. Mr Neville is a stranger, and you should respect the obligations of hospitality. And, Mr Neville:' laying his left hand on the inner shoulder of that young gentleman, and thus walking on between them, hand to shoulder on either side: 'you will pardon me; but I appeal to you to govern your temper too. Now, what is amiss? But why ask! Let there be nothing amiss, and the question is superfluous. We are all three on a good understanding, are we not?'

After a silent struggle between the two young men who shall speak last, Edwin Drood strikes in with: 'So far as I am concerned, Jack, there is no anger in me.'

'Nor in me,' says Neville Landless, though not so freely; or perhaps so carelessly. 'But if Mr Drood knew all that lies behind me, far away from here, he might know better how it is that sharp-edged words have sharp edges to wound me.'

'Perhaps,' says Jasper, in a soothing manner, 'we had better not qualify our good understanding. We had better not say anything having the appearance of a remonstrance or condition; it might not seem generous. Frankly and freely, you see there is no anger in Ned. Frankly and freely, there is no anger in you, Mr Neville?'

'None at all, Mr Jasper.' Still, not quite so frankly or so freely; or, be it said once again, not quite so carelessly perhaps.

'All over, then! Now, my bachelor gatehouse is a few yards from here, and the heater is on the fire, and the wine and glasses are on the table, and it is not a stone's throw from Minor Canon Corner. Ned, you are up and away to-morrow. We will carry Mr Neville in with us, to take a stirrup-cup.'

'With all my heart, Jack.'

'And with all mine, Mr Jasper.' Neville feels it impossible to say less, but would rather not go. He has an impression upon him that he has lost hold of his temper; feels that Edwin Drood's coolness, so far from being infectious, makes him red hot.

Mr Jasper, still walking in the centre, hand to shoulder on either side, beautifully turns the Refrain of a drinking song, and they all go up to his rooms. There, the first object visible, when he adds the light of a lamp to that of the fire, is the portrait over the chimneypiece. It is not an object calculated to improve the understanding between the two young men, as rather awkwardly reviving the subject of their difference. Accordingly, they both glance at it consciously, but say nothing. Jasper, however (who would appear from his conduct to have gained but an imperfect clue to the cause of their late high words), directly calls attention to it.

'You recognise that picture, Mr Neville?' shading the lamp to throw the light upon it.

'I recognise it, but it is far from flattering the original.'

'Oh, you are hard upon it! It was done by Ned, who made me a present of it.'

'I am sorry for that, Mr Drood.' Neville apologises, with a real intention to apologise; 'if I had known I was in the artist's presence—'

'Oh, a joke, sir, a mere joke,' Edwin cuts in, with a provoking yawn. 'A little humouring of Pussy's points! I'm going to paint her gravely, one of these days, if she's good.'

The air of leisurely patronage and indifference with which this is said, as the speaker throws himself back in a chair and clasps his hands at the back of his head, as a rest for it, is very exasperating to the excitable and excited Neville. Jasper looks observantly from the one to the other, slightly smiles, and turns his back to mix a jug of mulled wine at the fire. It seems to require much mixing and compounding.

'I suppose, Mr Neville,' says Edwin, quick to resent the indignant protest against himself in the face of young Landless, which is fully as visible as the portrait, or the fire, or the lamp: 'I suppose that if you painted the picture of your lady love—'

'I can't paint,' is the hasty interruption.

'That's your misfortune, and not your fault. You would if you could. But if you could, I suppose you would make her (no matter what she was in reality), Juno, Minerva, Diana, and Venus, all in one. Eh?'

'I have no lady love, and I can't say.'

'If I were to try my hand,' says Edwin, with a boyish boastfulness getting up in him, 'on a portrait of Miss Landless—in earnest, mind you; in earnest—you should see what I could do!'

'My sister's consent to sit for it being first got, I suppose? As it never will be got, I am afraid I shall never see what you can do. I must bear the loss.'

Jasper turns round from the fire, fills a large goblet glass for Neville, fills a large goblet glass for Edwin, and hands each his own; then fills for himself, saying:

'Come, Mr Neville, we are to drink to my nephew, Ned. As it is his foot that is in the stirrup—metaphorically—our stirrup-cup is to be devoted to him. Ned, my dearest fellow, my love!'

Jasper sets the example of nearly emptying his glass, and Neville follows it. Edwin Drood says, 'Thank you both very much,' and follows the double example.

'Look at him,' cries Jasper, stretching out his hand admiringly and tenderly, though rallyingly too. 'See where he lounges so easily, Mr Neville! The world is all before him where to choose. A life of stirring work and interest, a life of change and excitement, a life of domestic ease and love! Look at him!'

Edwin Drood's face has become quickly and remarkably flushed with the wine; so has the face of Neville Landless. Edwin still sits thrown back in his chair, making that rest of clasped hands for his head.

'See how little he heeds it all!' Jasper proceeds in a bantering vein. 'It is hardly worth his while to pluck the golden fruit that hangs ripe on the tree for him. And yet consider the contrast, Mr Neville. You and I have no prospect of stirring work and interest, or of change and excitement, or of domestic ease and love. You and I have no prospect (unless you are more fortunate than I am, which may easily be), but the tedious unchanging round of this dull place.'

'Upon my soul, Jack,' says Edwin complacently, 'I feel quite apologetic for having my way smoothed as you describe. But you know what I know, Jack, and it may not be so very easy as it seems, after all. May it, Pussy?' To the portrait, with a snap of his thumb and finger. 'We have got to hit it off yet; haven't we, Pussy? You know what I mean, Jack.'

His speech has become thick and indistinct. Jasper, quiet and self-possessed, looks to Neville, as expecting his answer or comment. When Neville speaks, *his* speech is also thick and indistinct.

'It might have been better for Mr Drood to have known some hardships,' he says defiantly.

'Pray,' retorts Edwin, turning merely his eyes in that direction, 'pray why might it have been better for Mr Drood to have known some hardships?'

'Ay,' Jasper assents, with an air of interest; 'let us know why?'

'Because they might have made him more sensible,' says Neville, 'of good fortune that is not by any means necessarily the result of his own merits.'

Mr Jasper quickly looks to his nephew for his rejoinder.

'Have *you* known hardships, may I ask?' says Edwin Drood, sitting upright.

Mr Jasper quickly looks to the other for his retort.

'I have.'

'And what have they made *you* sensible of?'

Mr Jasper's play of eyes between the two holds good throughout the dialogue, to the end.

'I have told you once before to-night.'

'You have done nothing of the sort.'

'I tell you I have. That you take a great deal too much upon yourself.'

'You added something else to that, if I remember?'

'Yes, I did say something else.'

'Say it again.'

'I said that in the part of the world I come from, you would be called to account for it.'

'Only there?' cries Edwin Drood, with a contemptuous laugh. 'A long way off, I believe? Yes; I see! That part of the world is at a safe distance.'

'Say here, then,' rejoins the other, rising in a fury. 'Say anywhere! Your vanity is intolerable, your conceit is beyond endurance; you talk as if you were some rare and precious prize, instead of a common boaster. You are a common fellow, and a common boaster.'

'Pooh, pooh,' says Edwin Drood, equally furious, but more collected; 'how should you know? You may know a black common fellow, or a black common boaster, when you see him (and no doubt you have a large acquaintance that way); but you are no judge of white men.'

This insulting allusion to his dark skin infuriates Neville to that violent degree, that he flings the dregs of his wine at Edwin Drood, and is in the act of flinging the goblet after it, when his arm is caught in the nick of time by Jasper.

'Ned, my dear fellow!' he cries in a loud voice; 'I entreat you, I command you, to be still!' There has been a rush of all the three, and a clattering of glasses and over-turning of chairs. 'Mr Neville, for shame! Give this glass to me. Open your hand, sir. I WILL have it!'

But Neville throws him off, and pauses for an instant, in a raging passion, with the goblet yet in his uplifted hand. Then, he dashes it down under the grate, with such force that the broken splinters fly out again in a shower; and he leaves the house.

When he first emerges into the night air, nothing around him is still or steady; nothing around him shows like what it is; he only knows that he stands with a bare head in the midst of a blood-red whirl, waiting to be struggled with, and to struggle to the death.

But, nothing happening, and the moon looking down upon him as if he were dead after a fit of wrath, he holds his steam-hammer beating head and heart, and staggers away. Then, he becomes half-conscious of having heard himself bolted and barred out, like a dangerous animal; and thinks what shall he do?

Some wildly passionate ideas of the river dissolve under the spell of the moonlight on the Cathedral and the graves, and the remembrance of his sister, and the thought of what he owes to the good man who has but that very day won his confidence and given him his pledge. He repairs to Minor Canon Corner, and knocks softly at the door.

It is Mr Crisparkle's custom to sit up last of the early household, very softly touching his piano and practising his favourite parts in concerted vocal music. The south wind that goes where it lists, by way of Minor Canon Corner on a still night, is not more subdued than Mr Crisparkle at such times, regardful of the slumbers of the china shepherdess.

His knock is immediately answered by Mr Crisparkle himself. When he opens the door, candle in hand, his cheerful face falls, and disappointed amazement is in it.

'Mr Neville! In this disorder! Where have you been?'

'I have been to Mr Jasper's, sir. With his nephew.'

'Come in.'

The Minor Canon props him by the elbow with a strong hand (in a strictly scientific manner, worthy of his morning trainings), and turns him into his own little book-room, and shuts the door.

'I have begun ill, sir. I have begun dreadfully ill.'

'Too true. You are not sober, Mr Neville.'

'I am afraid I am not, sir, though I can satisfy you at another time that I have had a very little indeed to drink, and that it overcame me in the strangest and most sudden manner.'

'Mr Neville, Mr Neville,' says the Minor Canon, shaking his head with a sorrowful smile; 'I have heard that said before.'

'I think—my mind is much confused, but I think—it is equally true of Mr Jasper's nephew, sir.'

'Very likely,' is the dry rejoinder.

'We quarrelled, sir. He insulted me most grossly. He had heated that tigerish blood I told you of to-day, before then.'

'Mr Neville,' rejoins the Minor Canon mildly, but firmly: 'I request you not to speak to me with that clenched right hand. Unclench it, if you please.'

'He goaded me, sir,' pursues the young man, instantly obeying, 'beyond my powers of endurance. I cannot say whether or no he meant it at first, but he did it. He certainly meant it at last. In short, sir,' with an irrepressible outburst, 'in the passion into which he lashed me, I would have cut him down if I could, and I tried to do it.'

'You have clenched that hand again,' is Mr Crisparkle's quiet commentary.

'I beg your pardon, sir.'

'You know your room, for I showed it you before dinner; but I will accompany you to it once more. Your arm, if you please. Softly, for the house is all a-bed.'

Scooping his hand into the same scientific elbow-rest as before, and backing it up with the inert strength of his arm, as skilfully as a Police Expert, and with an apparent repose quite unattainable by Novices, Mr Crisparkle conducts his pupil to the pleasant and orderly old room prepared for him. Arrived there, the young man throws himself into a chair, and, flinging his arms upon his reading-table, rests his head upon them with an air of wretched self-reproach.

The gentle Minor Canon has had it in his thoughts to leave the room, without a word. But looking round at the door, and seeing this dejected figure, he turns back to it, touches it with a mild hand, and says 'Good night!' A sob is his only acknowledgment. He might have had many a worse; perhaps, could have had few better.

Another soft knock at the outer door attracts his attention as he goes down stairs. He opens it to Mr Jasper, holding in his hand the pupil's hat.

'We have had an awful scene with him,' says Jasper, in a low voice.

'Has it been so bad as that?'

'Murderous!'

Mr Crisparkle remonstrates: 'No, no, no. Do not use such strong words.'

'He might have laid my dear boy dead at my feet. It is no fault of his, that he did not. But that I was, through the mercy of God, swift and strong with him, he would have cut him down on my hearth.'

The phrase smites home. 'Ah!' thinks Mr Crisparkle, 'His own words!'

'Seeing what I have seen to-night, and hearing what I have heard,' adds Jasper, with great earnestness, 'I shall never know peace of mind when there is danger of those two coming together, with no one else to interfere. It was horrible. There is something of the tiger in his dark blood.'

'Ah!' thinks Mr Crisparkle, 'so he said!'

'You, my dear sir,' pursues Jasper, taking his hand, 'even you, have accepted a dangerous charge.'

'You need have no fear for me, Jasper,' returns Mr Crisparkle, with a quiet smile. 'I have none for myself.'

'I have none for myself,' returns Jasper, with an emphasis on the last pronoun, 'because I am not, nor am I in the way of being, the object of his hostility. But you may be, and my dear boy has been. Good night!'

Mr Crisparkle goes in, with the hat that has so easily, so almost imperceptibly, acquired the right to be hung up in his hall; hangs it up; and goes thoughtfully to bed.

A TALE OF TWO CITIES

During the French Revolution, aristocrat Charles Darnay, known in Paris as Citizen Evrémonde, has been condemned to the guillotine. Sidney Carton, a dissolute English barrister to whom he bears a strong resemblance, is deeply in love with Darnay's wife and, for her sake, has changed places with the condemned man. Having helped Darnay to escape from his prison cell, Carton awaits death …

Sounds that he was not afraid of, for he divined their meaning, then began to be audible. Several doors were opened in succession, and finally his own. A goaler, with a list in his hand, looked in, merely saying, 'Follow me, Evrémonde!' and he followed into a large dark room, at a distance. It was a dark winter day, and what with the shadows within, and what with the shadows without, he could but dimly discern the others who were brought there to have their arms bound. Some were standing; some seated. Some were lamenting, and in restless motion; but these were few. The great majority were silent and still, looking fixedly at the ground.

As he stood by the wall in a dim corner, while some of the fifty-two were brought in after him, one man stopped in passing, to embrace him, as having a knowledge of him. It thrilled him with a great dread of discovery; but the man went on. A very few moments after that, a young woman, with a slight girlish form, a sweet spare face in which there was no vestige of colour, and large widely opened patient eyes, rose from the seat where he had observed her sitting, and came to speak to him.

'Citizen Evrémonde,' she said, touching him with her cold hand. 'I am a poor little seamstress, who was with you in La Force.'

He murmured for answer: 'True. I forget what you were accused of?'

'Plots. Though the just Heaven knows I am innocent of any. Is it likely? Who would think of plotting with a poor little weak creature like me?'

The forlorn smile with which she said it, so touched him, that tears started from his eyes.

'I am not afraid to die, Citizen Evrémonde, but I have done nothing. I am not unwilling to die, if the Republic which is to do so much good to us poor, will profit by my death; but I do not know how that can be, Citizen Evrémonde. Such a poor weak little creature!'

As the last thing on earth that his heart was to warm and soften to, it warmed and softened to this pitiable girl.

'I heard you were released, Citizen Evrémonde. I hoped it was true?'

'It was. But I was again taken and condemned.'

'If I may ride with you, Citizen Evrémonde, will you let me hold your hand? I am not afraid, but I am little and weak, and it will give me more courage.'

As the patient eyes were lifted to his face, he saw a sudden doubt in them, and then astonishment. He pressed the work-worn, hunger-worn young fingers, and touched his lips.

'Are you dying for him?' she whispered.

'And his wife and child. Hush! Yes.'

'Oh, you will let me hold your brave hand, stranger?'

'Hush! Yes, my poor sister; to the last.'

Along the Paris streets, the death-carts rumble, hollow and harsh. Six tumbrils carry the day's wine to La Guillotine. All the devouring and insatiate Monsters imagined since imagination could record itself, are fused in the one realisation, Guillotine. And yet there is not in France, with its rich variety of soil and climate, a blade, a leaf, a root, a sprig, a peppercorn, which will grow to maturity under conditions more certain than those that have produced this horror. Crush humanity out of shape once more, under similar hammers, and it will twist itself into the same tortured forms. Sow the same seed of rapacious licence and oppression over again, and it will surely yield the same fruit according to its kind.

Six tumbrils roll along the streets. Change these back again to what they were, thou powerful enchanter, Time, and they shall be seen to be the carriages of absolute monarchs, the equipages of feudal nobles, the toilettes of flaring Jezebels, the churches that are not my father's house but dens of thieves, the huts of millions of starving peasants! No; the great magician who majestically works out the appointed order of the Creator, never reverses his transformations. 'If thou be changed into this shape by the will of God,' said the seers to the enchanted, in the wise Arabian stories, 'then remain so! But if thou wear this form through mere passing conjuration, then resume thy former aspect!' Changeless and hopeless, the tumbrils roll along.

As the sombre wheels of the six carts go round, they seem to plough up a long crooked furrow among the populace in the streets. Ridges of faces are thrown to this side and to that, and the ploughs go steadily onward. So used are the regular inhabitants of the houses to the spectacle, that in many windows there are no people, and in some the occupation of the hands is not so much as suspended, while the eyes survey the faces in the tumbrils. Here and there, the inmate has visitors to see the sight; then he points his finger, with something of the complacency of a curator or authorised exponent, to this cart and to this, and seems to tell who sat here yesterday, and who there the day before.

Of the riders in the tumbrils, some observe these things, and all things on their last roadside, with an impassive stare; others, with a lingering interest in the ways of life and men. Some, seated with drooping heads, are sunk in silent despair; again, there are some so heedful of their looks that they cast upon the multitude such glances as they have seen in theatres, and in pictures. Several close their eyes, and think, or try to get their straying thoughts together. Only one, and he a miserable creature of a crazed aspect, is so shattered and made drunk by horror that he sings, and tries to dance. Not one of the whole number appeals, by look or gesture, to the pity of the people.

There is a guard of sundry horsemen riding abreast of the tumbrils, and faces are often turned up to some of them and they are asked some question. It would seem to be always the same question, for, it is always followed by a press of people towards the third cart. The horsemen abreast of that cart, frequently point out one man in it with their swords. The leading curiosity is, to know which is he; he stands at the back of the tumbril with his head bent down, to converse with a mere girl who sits on the side of the cart, and holds his hand. He has no curiosity or care for the scene about him, and always speaks to the girl. Here and there in the long street of Saint Honoré, cries are raised against him. If they move him at all, it is only to a quiet smile, as he shakes his hair a little more loosely about his face. He cannot easily touch his face, his arms being bound.

On the steps of a church, awaiting the coming-up of the tumbrils, stands the Spy and prison-sheep. He looks into the first of them: not there. He looks into the second: not there. He already asks himself, 'Has he sacrificed me?' when his face clears, as he looks into the third.

'Which is Evrémonde?' says a man behind him.

'That. At the back there.'

'With his hand in the girl's?'

'Yes.'

The man cries, 'Down, Evrémonde! To the Guillotine all aristocrats! Down, Evrémonde!'

'Hush, hush!' the spy entreats him timidly.

'And why not, citizen?'

'He is going to pay the forfeit; it will be paid in five minutes more. Let him be at peace.'

But the man continuing to exclaim, 'Down, Evrémonde!' the face of Evrémonde is for a moment turned towards him. Evrémonde then sees the Spy, and looks attentively at him, and goes his way.

The clocks are on the stroke of three, and the furrow ploughed among the populace is turning round, to come on into the place of execution, and end. The ridges thrown to this side and to that, now crumble in and close behind the last plough as it passes on, for all are following to the Guillotine. In front of it, seated in chairs as in a garden of public diversion, are a number of women, busily knitting. On one of the foremost chairs stands The Vengeance, looking about for her friend.

'Thérèse!' she cries, in her shrill tones. 'Who has seen her? Thérèse Defarge!'

'She never missed before,' says a knitting-woman of the sisterhood.

'No; nor will she miss now,' cries The Vengeance petulantly. 'Thérèse!'

'Louder,' the woman recommends.

Ay! Lounder, Vengeance, much louder, and still she will scarcely hear thee. Louder yet, Vengeance, with a little oath or so added, and yet it will hardly bring her. Send other women up and down to seek her, lingering somewhere; and yet, although the messengers have done dread deeds, it is questionable whether of their own wills they will go far enough to find her!

'Bad Fortune!' cries The Vengeance, stamping her foot in the chair, 'and here are the tumbrils! And Evrémonde will be despatched in a wink, and she not here! See her knitting in my hand, and her empty chair ready for her. I cry with vexation and disappointment!'

As The Vengeance descends from her elevation to do it, the tumbrils begin to discharge their loads. The ministers of Sainte Guillotine are robed and ready. Crash!—A head is held up, and the knitting-women who scarcely lifted their eyes to look at it a moment ago when it could think and speak, count One.

The second tumbril empties and moves on; the third comes up. Crash!—And the knitting-women, never faltering or pausing in their work, count Two.

The supposed Evrémonde descends, and the seamstress is lifted out next after him. He has not relinquished her patient hand in getting out, but still holds it as he promised. He gently places her with her back to the crashing engine that constantly whirrs up and falls, and she looks into his face and thanks him.

'But for you, dear stranger, I should not be so composed, for I am naturally a poor little thing, faint of heart; nor should I have been able to raise my thoughts to Him who was put to death, that we might have hope and comfort here to-day. I think you were sent to me by Heaven.'

'Or you to me,' says Sydney Carton. 'Keep your eyes upon me, dear child, and mind no other object.'

'I mind nothing while I hold your hand. I shall mind nothing when I let it go, if they are rapid.'

'They will be rapid. Fear not!'

The two stand in the fast-thinning throng of victims, but they speak as if they were alone. Eye to eye, voice to voice, hand to hand, heart to heart, these two children of the Universal Mother, else so wide apart and differing, have come together on the dark highway, to repair home together and to rest in her bosom.

'Brave and generous friend, will you let me ask you one last question? I am very ignorant, and it troubles me—just a little.'

'Tell me what it is.'

'I have a cousin, an only relative and an orphan, like myself, whom I love very dearly. She is five years younger than I, and she lives in a farmer's house in the south country. Poverty parted us, and she knows nothing of my fate—for I cannot write—and if I could, how should I tell her! It is better as it is.'

'Yes, yes; better as it is.'

'What I have been thinking as we came along, and what I am still thinking now, as I look into your kind strong face which gives me so much support, is this:—If the Republic really does good to the poor, and they come to be less hungry, and in all ways to suffer less, she may live a long time; she may even live to be old.'

'What then, my gentle sister?'

'Do you think,' the uncomplaining eyes in which there is so much endurance, fill with tears, and the lips part a little more and tremble, 'that it will seem long to me, while I wait for her in the better land where I trust, both you and I will be mercifully sheltered?'

'It cannot be, my child; there is no Time there, and no trouble there.'

'You comfort me so much! I am so ignorant. Am I to kiss you now? Is the moment come?'

'Yes.'

She kisses his lips; he kisses hers; they solemnly bless each other. The spare hand does not tremble as he releases it; nothing worse than a sweet, bright constancy is in the patient face. She goes next before him—is gone; the knitting-women count Twenty-Two.

'I am the Resurrection and the Life, saith the Lord: he that believeth in me, though he were dead, yet shall he live: and whosoever liveth and believeth in me, shall never die.'

The murmuring of many voices, the upturning of many faces, the pressing on of many footsteps in the outskirts of the crowd, so that it swells forward in a mass, like one great heave of water, all flashes away. Twenty-Three.

A CHRISTMAS CAROL

Old miser Ebenezer Scrooge receives a visit, on Christmas Eve, from the ghost of Marley, his late business partner. In death, Marley is suffering a heavy penance for the selfishness and avarice of his life. He offers Scrooge a chance to escape the same fate. To this purpose, Marley warns his friend that he will be haunted by three spirits ...

Awaking in the middle of a prodigiously tough snore, and sitting up in bed to get his thoughts together, Scrooge had no occasion to be told that the bell was again upon the stroke of One...

Gentlemen of the free-and-easy sort, who plume themselves on being acquainted with a move or two, and being usually equal to the time-of-day, express the wide range of their capacity for adventure by observing that they are good for anything from pitch-and-toss to manslaughter; between which opposite extremes, no doubt, there lies a tolerably wide and comprehensive range of subjects. Without venturing for Scrooge quite as hardily as this, I don't mind calling on you to believe that he was ready for a good broad field of strange appearances, and that nothing between a baby and rhinoceros would have astonished him very much.

Now, being prepared for almost anything, he was not by any means prepared for nothing; and, consequently, when the Bell struck One, and no shape appeared, he was taken with a violent fit of trembling. Five minutes, ten minutes, a quarter of an hour went by, yet nothing came. All this time he lay upon his bed, the very core and centre of a blaze of ruddy light, which streamed upon it when the clock proclaimed the hour; and which, being only light, was more alarming than a dozen ghosts, as he was powerless to make out what it meant, or would be at; and was sometimes apprehensive that he might be at that very moment an interesting case of spontaneous combustion, without having the consolation of knowing it. At last, however, he began to think—as you or I would have thought at first; for it is always the person not in the predicament who knows what ought to have been done in it, and would unquestionably have done it too—at last, I say, he began to think that the source and secret of this ghostly light might be in the adjoining room, from whence, on further tracing it, it seemed to shine. This idea taking full possession of his mind, he got up softly and shuffled in his slippers to the door.

The moment Scrooge's hand was on the lock, a strange voice called him by his name, and bade him enter. He obeyed.

It was his own room. There was no doubt about that. But it had undergone a surprising transformation. The walls and ceiling were so hung with living green, that it looked a perfect grove; from every part of which, bright gleaming berries glistened. The crisp leaves of holly, mistletoe, and ivy reflected back the light, as if so many little mirrors had been scattered there; and such a mighty blaze went roaring up the chimney, as that dull petrification of a hearth had never known in Scrooge's time, or Marley's, or for many and many a winter season gone. Heaped up on the floor, to form a kind of throne, were turkeys, geese, game, poultry, brawn, great joints of meat, sucking-pigs, long wreaths of sausages, mince-pies, plum-puddings, barrels of oysters, red-hot chestnuts, cherry-cheeked apples, juicy oranges, luscious pears, immense twelfth-cakes, and seething bowls of punch, that made the chamber dim with their delicious steam. In easy state upon this couch, there sat a jolly Giant, glorious to see; who bore a glowing torch, in shape not unlike Plenty's horn, and held it up, high up, to shed its light on Scrooge, as he came peeping round the door.

'Come in!' exclaimed the Ghost. 'Come in! and know me better, man!'

Scrooge entered timidly, and hung his head before this Spirit. He was not the dogged Scrooge he had been; and though the Spirit's eyes were clear and kind, he did not like to meet them.

'I am the Ghost of Christmas Present,' said the Spirit. 'Look upon me!'

Scrooge reverently did so. It was clothed in one simple, green robe, or mantle, bordered with white fur. This garment hung so loosely on the figure, that its capacious breast was bare, as if disdaining to be warded or concealed by any artifice. Its feet, observable beneath the ample folds of the garment, were also bare; and on its head it wore no other covering than a holly wreath, set here and there with shining icicles. Its dark brown curls were long and free; free as its genial face, its sparkling eye, its open hand, its cheery voice, its unconstrained demeanour, and its joyful air. Girded round its middle was an antique scabbard; but no sword was in it, and the ancient sheath was eaten up with rust.

'You have never seen the like of me before!' exclaimed the Spirit.

'Never,' Scrooge made answer to it.

'Have never walked forth with the younger members of my family; meaning (for I am very young) my elder brothers born in these later years?' pursued the Phantom.

'I don't think I have,' said Scrooge. 'I am afraid I have not. Have you had many brothers, Spirit?'

'More than eighteen hundred,' said the Ghost.

'A tremendous family to provide for!' muttered Scrooge.

The Ghost of Christmas Present rose.

'Spirit,' said Scrooge submissively, 'conduct me where you will. I went forth last night on compulsion, and I learned a lesson which is working now. To-night, if you have ought to teach me, let me profit by it.'

'Touch my robe!'

Scrooge did as he was told, and held it fast.

Holly, mistletoe, red berries, ivy, turkeys, geese, game, poultry, brawn, meat, pigs, sausages, oysters, pies, puddings, fruit, and punch, all vanished instantly. So did the room, the fire, the ruddy glow, the hour of night, and they stood in the city streets on Christmas morning, where (for the weather was severe) the people made a rough, but brisk and not unpleasant kind of music, in scraping the snow from the pavement in front of their dwellings, and from the tops of their houses, whence it was mad delight to the boys to see it come plumping down into the road below, and splitting into artificial little snow-storms.

The house fronts looked black enough, and the windows blacker, contrasting with the smooth white sheet of snow upon the roofs, and with the dirtier snow upon the ground; which last deposit had been ploughed up in deep furrows by the heavy wheels of carts and waggons; furrows that crossed and re-crossed each other hundreds of times where the great streets branched off; and made intricate channels, hard to trace in the thick yellow mud and icy water. The sky was gloomy, and the shortest streets were choked up with a dingy mist, half thawed, half frozen, whose heavier particles descended in a shower of sooty atoms, as if all the chimneys in Great Britain had, by one consent, caught fire, and were blazing away to their dear hearts' content. There was nothing very cheerful in the climate or the town, and yet was there an air of cheerfulness abroad that the clearest summer air and brightest summer sun might have endeavoured to diffuse in vain.

For, the people who were shovelling away on the house-tops were jovial and full of glee; calling out to one another from the parapets, and now and then exchanging a facetious snowball—better-natured missile far than many a wordy jest—laughing heartily if it went right, and not less heartily if it went wrong. The poulterers' shops were still half open, and the fruiterers' were radiant in their glory. There were great, round, pot-bellied baskets of chestnuts, shaped like the waistcoats of jolly old gentlemen, lolling at the doors, and tumbling out into the street in their apoplectic opulence. There were ruddy, brown-faced, broad-girthed Spanish Onions, shining in the fatness of their growth like Spanish Friars, and winking from their shelves in wanton slyness at the girls as they went by, and glanced demurely at the hung-up mistletoe. There were pears and apples, clustered high in blooming pyramids; there were bunches of grapes, made in the shopkeepers' benevolence to dangle from conspicuous hooks, that people's mouths might water gratis as they passed; there were piles of filberts, mossy and brown, recalling, in their fragrance, ancient walks among the woods, and pleasant shufflings ankle deep through withered leaves; there were Norfolk Biffins, squab and swarthy, setting off the yellow of the oranges and lemons, and, in the great compactness of their juicy persons, urgently entreating and beseeching to be carried home in paper bags and eaten after dinner. The very gold and silver fish, set forth among these choice fruits in a bowl, though members of a dull and stagnant-blooded race, appeared to know that there was something going on; and, to a fish, went gasping round and round their little world in slow and passionless excitement.

The Grocers'! oh, the Grocers'! nearly closed, with perhaps two shutters down, or one; but through those gaps such glimpses! It was not alone that the scales descending on the counter made a merry sound, or that the twine and roller parted company so briskly, or that the canisters were rattled up and down like juggling tricks, or even that the blended scents of tea and coffee were so grateful to the nose, or even that the raisins were so plentiful and rare, the almonds so extremely white, the sticks of cinnamon so long and straight, the other spices so delicious, the candied fruits so caked and spotted with molten sugar as to make the coldest lookers-on feel faint and subsequently bilious. Nor was it that the figs were moist and pulpy, or that the French plums blushed in modest tartness from their highly-decorated boxes, or that everything was good to eat and in its Christmas dress; but the customers were all so hurried and so eager in the hopeful promise of the day, that they tumbled up against each other at the door, crashing their wicker baskets wildly, and left their purchases upon the counter, and came running back to fetch them, and committed hundreds of the like mistakes, in the best humour possible; while the Grocer and his people were so frank and fresh that the polished hearts with which they fastened their aprons behind might have been their own, worn outside for general inspection, and for Christmas daws to peck at if they chose.

But soon the steeples called good people all, to church and chapel, and away they came, flocking through the streets in their best clothes, and with their gayest faces. And at the same time there emerged from scores of bye-streets, lanes, and nameless turnings, innumerable people, carrying their dinners to the bakers' shops. The sight of these poor revellers appeared to interest the Spirit very much, for he stood with Scrooge beside him in a baker's doorway, and taking off the covers as their bearer passed, sprinkled incense on their dinners from his torch. And it was a very uncommon kind of torch, for once or twice when there were angry words between some dinner-carriers who had jostled each other, he shed a few drops of water on them from it, and their good humour was restored directly. For they said, it was a shame to quarrel upon Christmas Day. And so it was! God love it, so it was!

In time the bells ceased, and the bakers were shut up; and yet there was a genial shadowing forth of all these dinners and the progress of their cooking, in the thawed blotch of wet above each baker's oven; where the pavement smoked as if its stones were cooking too.

'Is there a peculiar flavour in what you sprinkle from your torch?' asked Scrooge.

'There is. My own.'

'Would it apply to any kind of dinner on this day?' asked Scrooge.

'To any kindly given. To a poor one most.'

'Why to a poor one most?' asked Scrooge.

'Because it needs it most.'

'Spirit,' said Scrooge, after a moment's thought, 'I wonder you, of all the beings in the many worlds about us, should desire to cramp these people's opportunities of innocent enjoyment.'

'I!' cried the Spirit.

'You would deprive them of their means of dining every seventh day, often the only day on which they can be said to dine at all,' said Scrooge. 'Wouldn't you?'

'I!' cried the Spirit.

'You seek to close these places on the Seventh Day?' said Scrooge. 'And it comes to the same thing.'

'*I* seek!' exclaimed the Spirit.

'Forgive me if I am wrong. It has been done in your name, or at least in that of your family,' said Scrooge.

'There are some upon this earth of yours,' returned the Spirit, 'who lay claim to know us, and who do their deeds of passion, pride, ill-will, hatred, envy, bigotry, and selfishness in our name, who are as strange to us and all our kith and kin, as if they had never lived. Remember that, and charge their doings on themselves, not us.'

Scrooge promised that he would; and they went on, invisible, as they had been before, into the suburbs of the town. It was a remarkable quality of the Ghost (which Scrooge had observed at the baker's) that notwithstanding his gigantic size, he could accommodate himself to any place with ease; and that he stood beneath a low roof quite as gracefully and like a supernatural creature, as it was possible he could have done in any lofty hall.

And perhaps it was the pleasure the good Spirit had in showing off this power of his, or else it was his own kind, generous, hearty nature, and his sympathy with all poor men, that led him straight to Scrooge's clerk's; for there he went, and took Scrooge with him, holding to his robe; and on the threshold of the door the Spirit smiled, and stopped to bless Bob Cratchit's dwelling with the sprinklings of his torch. Think of that! Bob had but fifteen 'Bob' a-week himself; he pocketed on Saturdays but fifteen copies of his Christian name; and yet the Ghost of Christmas Present blessed his four-roomed house!

Then up rose Mrs Cratchit, Cratchit's wife, dressed out but poorly in a twice-turned gown, but brave in ribbons, which are cheap and make a goodly show for sixpence; and she laid the cloth, assisted by Belinda Cratchit, second of her daughters, also brave in ribbons; while Master Peter Cratchit plunged a fork into the saucepan of potatoes, and getting the corners of his monstrous shirt collar (Bob's private property, conferred upon his son and heir in honour of the day) into his mouth, rejoiced to find himself so gallantly attired, and yearned to show his linen in the fashionable Parks. And now two smaller Cratchits, boy and girl, came tearing in, screaming that outside the baker's, they had smelt the goose, and known it for their own; and basking in luxurious thoughts of sage and onion, these young Cratchits danced about the table, and exalted Master Peter Cratchit to the skies, while he (not proud, although his collars nearly choked him) blew the fire, until the slow potatoes bubbling up, knocked loudly at the saucepan-lid to be let out and peeled.

'What has ever got your precious father then?' said Mrs Cratchit. 'And your brother, Tiny Tim! And Martha warn't as late last Christmas Day by half-an-hour.'

'Here's Martha, mother!' said a girl, appearing as she spoke.

'Here's Martha, mother!' cried the two young Cratchits. 'Hurrah! There's *such* a goose, Martha!'

'Why, bless your heart alive, my dear, how late you are!' said Mrs Cratchit, kissing her a dozen times, and taking off her shawl and bonnet for her with officious zeal.

'We'd a deal of work to finish up last night,' replied the girl, 'and had to clear away this morning, mother!'

'Well! Never mind so long as you are come,' said Mrs Cratchit. 'Sit ye down before the fire, my dear, and have a warm, Lord bless ye!'

'No, no! There's father coming,' cried the two young Cratchits, who were everywhere at once. 'Hide, Martha, hide!'

So Martha hid herself, and in came little Bob, the father, with at least three feet of comforter exclusive of the fringe, hanging down before him; and his threadbare clothes darned up and brushed, to look seasonable; and Tiny Tim upon his shoulder. Alas for Tiny Tim, he bore a little crutch, and had his limbs supported by an iron frame!

'Why, where's our Martha?' cried Bob Cratchit, looking round.

'Not coming,' said Mrs Cratchit.

'Not coming!' said Bob, with a sudden declension in his high spirits; for he had been Tim's blood horse all the way from church, and had come home rampant. 'Not coming upon Christmas Day!'

Martha didn't like to see him disappointed, if it were only in joke; so she came out prematurely from behind the closet door, and ran into his arms, while the two young Cratchits hustled Tiny Tim, and bore him off into the wash-house, that he might hear the pudding singing in the copper.

'And how did little Tim behave?' asked Mrs Cratchit, when she had rallied Bob on his credulity, and Bob had hugged his daughter to his heart's content.

'As good as gold,' said Bob, 'and better. Somehow he gets thoughtful, sitting by himself so much, and thinks the strangest things you ever heard. He told me, coming home, that he hoped the people saw him in the church, because he was a cripple, and it might be pleasant to them to remember upon Christmas Day, who made lame beggars walk, and blind men see.'

Bob's voice was tremulous when he told them this, and trembled more when he said that Tiny Tim was growing strong and hearty.

His active little crutch was heard upon the floor, and back came Tiny Tim before another word was spoken, escorted by his brother and sister to his stool beside the fire; and while Bob, turning up his cuffs—as if, poor fellow, they were capable of being made more shabby—compounded some hot mixture in a jug with gin and lemons, and stirred it round and round and put it on the hob to simmer; Master Peter, and the two ubiquitous young Cratchits went to fetch the goose, with which they soon returned in high procession.

Such a bustle ensued that you might have thought a goose the rarest of all birds; a feathered phenomenon, to which a black swan was a matter of course—and in truth it was something very like it in that house. Mrs Cratchit made the gravy (ready beforehand in a little saucepan) hissing hot; Master Peter mashed the potatoes with incredible vigour; Miss Belinda sweetened up the apple-sauce; Martha dusted the hot plates; Bob took Tiny Tim beside him in a tiny corner at the table; the two young Cratchits set chairs for everybody, not forgetting themselves, and mounting guard upon their posts, crammed spoons into their mouths, lest they should shriek for goose before their turn came to be helped. At last the dishes were set on, and grace was said. It was succeeded by a breathless pause, as Mrs Cratchit, looking slowly all along the carving-knife, prepared to plunge it in the breast; but when she did, and when the long expected gush of stuffing issued forth, one murmur of delight arose all around the board, and even Tiny Tim, excited by the two young Cratchits, beat on the table with the handle of his knife, and feebly cried Hurrah!

There never was such a goose. Bob said he didn't believe there ever was such a goose cooked. Its tenderness and flavour, size and cheapness, were the themes of universal admiration. Eked out by apple-sauce and mashed potatoes, it was a sufficient dinner for the whole family; indeed, as Mrs Cratchit said with great delight (surveying one small atom of a bone upon the dish), they hadn't ate it all at last! Yet every one had had enough, and the youngest Cratchits in particular, were steeped in sage and onion to the eyebrows! But now, the plates being changed by Miss Belinda, Mrs Cratchit left the room alone—too nervous to bear witnesses—to take the pudding up and bring it in.

Suppose it should not be done enough! Suppose it should break in turning out! Suppose somebody should have got over the wall of the back-yard, and stolen it, while they were merry with the goose—a supposition at which the two young Cratchits became livid! All sorts of horrors were supposed.

Hallo! A great deal of steam! The pudding was out of the copper. A smell like a washing-day! That was the cloth. A smell like an eating-house and a pastrycook's next door to each other, with a laundress's next door to that! That was the pudding! In half a minute Mrs Cratchit entered—flushed, but smiling proudly—with the pudding, like a speckled cannon-ball, so hard and firm, blazing in half of half-a-quartern of ignited brandy, and bedight with Christmas holly stuck into the top.

Oh, a wonderful pudding! Bob Cratchit said, and calmly too, that he regarded it as the greatest success achieved by Mrs Cratchit since their marriage. Mrs Cratchit said that now the weight was off her mind, she would confess she had had her doubts about the quantity of flour. Everybody had something to say about it, but nobody said or thought it was at all a small pudding for a large family. It would have been flat heresy to do so. Any Cratchit would have blushed to hint at such a thing.

At last the dinner was all done, the cloth was cleared, the hearth swept, and the fire made up. The compound in the jug being tasted, and considered perfect, apples and oranges were put upon the table, and a shovel-full of chestnuts on the fire. Then all the Cratchit family drew round the hearth, in what Bob Cratchit called a circle, meaning half a one; and at Bob Cratchit's elbow stood the family display of glass. Two tumblers, and a custard-cup without a handle.

These held the hot stuff from the jug, however, as well as golden goblets would have done; and Bob served it out with beaming looks, while the chestnuts on the fire sputtered and cracked noisily. Then Bob proposed:

'A Merry Christmas to us all, my dears. God bless us!' Which all the family re-echoed.

'God bless us every one!' said Tiny Tim, the last of all.

He sat very close to his father's side, upon his little stool. Bob held his withered little hand in his, as if he loved the child, and wished to keep him by his side, and dreaded that he might be taken from him.

'Spirit,' said Scrooge, with an interest he had never felt before, 'tell me if Tiny Tim will live.'

'I see a vacant seat,' replied the Ghost, 'in the poor chimney-corner, and a crutch without an owner, carefully preserved. If these shadows remain unaltered by the Future, the child will die.'

'No, no,' said Scrooge. 'Oh, no, kind Spirit! say he will be spared.'

'If these shadows remain unaltered by the Future, none other of my race,' returned the Ghost, 'will find him here. What then? If he be like to die, he had better do it, and decrease the surplus population.'

Scrooge hung his head to hear his own words quoted by the Spirit, and was overcome with penitence and grief.

'Man,' said the Ghost, 'if man you be in heart, not adamant, forbear that wicked cant until you have discovered What the surplus is, and Where it is. Will you decide what men shall live, what men shall die? It may be, that in the sight of Heaven, you are more worthless and less fit to live than millions like this poor man's child. O God! to hear the Insect on the leaf pronouncing on the too much life among his hungry brothers in the dust!'

Scrooge bent before the Ghost's rebuke, and trembling cast his eyes upon the ground. But he raised them speedily, on hearing his own name.

'Mr Scrooge!' said Bob; 'I'll give you Mr Scrooge, the Founder of the Feast!'

'The Founder of the Feast indeed!' cried Mrs Cratchit, reddening. 'I wish I had him here. I'd give him a piece of my mind to feast upon, and I hope he'd have a good appetite for it.'

'My dear,' said Bob, 'the children! Christmas Day.'

'It should be Christmas Day, I am sure,' said she, 'on which one drinks the health of such an odious, stingy, hard, unfeeling man as Mr Scrooge. You know he is, Robert! Nobody knows it better than you do, poor fellow!'

'My dear,' was Bob's mild answer, 'Christmas Day.'

'I'll drink his health for your sake and the Day's,' said Mrs Cratchit, 'not for his. Long life to him! A Merry Christmas and a happy new year! He'll be very merry and very happy, I have no doubt!'

The children drank the toast after her. It was the first of their proceedings which had no heartiness in it. Tiny Tim drank it last of all, but he didn't care twopence for it. Scrooge was the Ogre of the family. The mention of his name cast a dark shadow on the party, which was not dispelled for full five minutes.

After it had passed away, they were ten times merrier than before, from the mere relief of Scrooge the Baleful being done with. Bob Cratchit told them how he had a situation in his eye for Master Peter, which would bring in, if obtained, full five-and-sixpence weekly. The two young Cratchits laughed tremendously at the idea of Peter's being a man of business; and Peter himself looked thoughtfully at the fire from between his collars, as if he were deliberating what particular investments he should favour when he came into the receipt of that bewildering income. Martha, who was a poor apprentice at a milliner's, then told them what kind of work she had to do, and how many hours she worked at a stretch, and how she meant to lie abed to-morrow morning for a good long rest; to-morrow being a holiday she passed at home. Also how she had seen a countess and a lord some days before, and how the lord 'was much about as tall as Peter'; at which Peter pulled up his collars so high that you couldn't have seen his head if you had been there. All this time the chestnuts and the jug went round and round; and by-and-bye they had a song, about a lost child travelling in the snow, from Tiny Tim, who had a plaintive little voice, and sang it very well indeed.

There was nothing of high mark in this. They were not a handsome family; they were not well dressed; their shoes were far from being water-proof; their clothes were scanty; and Peter might have known, and very likely did, the inside of a pawnbroker's. But, they were happy, grateful, pleased with one another, and contented with the time; and when they faded, and looked happier yet in the bright sprinklings of the Spirit's torch at parting, Scrooge had his eye upon them, and especially on Tiny Tim, until the last.

By this time it was getting dark, and snowing pretty heavily; and as Scrooge and the Spirit went along the streets, the brightness of the roaring fires in kitchens, parlours, and all sorts of rooms, was wonderful. Here, the flickering of the blaze showed preparations for a cosy dinner, with hot plates baking through and through before the fire, and deep red curtains, ready to be drawn to shut out cold and darkness. There all the children of the house were running out into the snow to meet their married sisters, brothers, cousins, uncles, aunts, and be the first to greet them. Here, again, were shadows on the window-blind of guests assembling; and there a group of handsome girls, all hooded and fur-booted, and all chattering at once, tripped lightly off to some near neighbour's house; where, woe upon the single man who saw them enter—artful witches, well they knew it—in a glow!

But, if you had judged from the numbers of people on their way to friendly gatherings, you might have thought that no one was at home to give them welcome when they got there, instead of every house expecting company, and piling up its fires half-chimney high. Blessings on it, how the Ghost exulted! How it bared its breadth of breast, and opened its capacious palm, and floated on, outpouring, with a generous hand, its bright and harmless mirth on everything within its reach! The very lamplighter, who ran on before, dotting the dusky street with specks of light, and who was dressed to spend the evening somewhere, laughed out loudly as the Spirit passed, though little kenned the lamplighter that he had any company but Christmas!

And now, without a word of warning from the Ghost, they stood upon a bleak and desert moor, where monstrous masses of rude stone were cast about, as though it were the burial-place of giants; and water spread itself wheresoever it listed, or would have done so, but for the frost that held it prisoner; and nothing grew but moss and furze, and coarse rank grass. Down in the west the setting sun had left a streak of fiery red, which glared upon the desolation for an instant, like a sullen eye, and frowning lower, lower yet, was lost in the thick gloom of darkest night.

'What place is this?' asked Scrooge.

'A place where Miners live, who labour in the bowels of the earth,' returned the Spirit. 'But they know me. See!'

A light shone from the window of a hut, and swiftly they advanced towards it. Passing through the wall of mud and stone, they found a cheerful company assembled round a glowing fire. An old, old man and woman, with their children and their children's children, and another generation beyond that, all decked out gaily in their holiday attire. The old man, in a voice that seldom rose above the howling of the wind upon the barren waste, was singing them a Christmas song—it had been a very old song when he was a boy—and from time to time they all joined in the chorus. So surely as they raised their voices, the old man got quite blithe and loud; and so surely as they stopped, his vigour sank again.

The Spirit did not tarry here, but bade Scrooge hold his robe, and passing on above the moor, sped—whither? Not to sea? To sea. To Scrooge's horror, looking back, he saw the last of the land, a frightful range of rocks, behind them; and his ears were deafened by the thundering of water, as it rolled and roared, and raged among the dreadful caverns it had worn, and fiercely tried to undermine the earth.

Built upon a dismal reef of sunken rock, some league or so from shore, on which the waters chafed and dashed, the wild year through, there stood a solitary lighthouse. Great heaps of sea-weed clung to its base, and storm-birds—born of the wind one might suppose, as sea-weed of the water—rose and fell about it, like the waves they skimmed.

But even here, two men who watched the light had made a fire, that through the loophole in the thick stone wall shed out a ray of brightness on the awful sea. Joining their horny hands over the rough table at which they sat, they wished each other Merry Christmas in their can of grog; and one of them—the elder, too, with his face all damaged and scarred with hard weather, as the figure-head of an old ship might be: struck up a sturdy song that was like a Gale in itself.

Again the Ghost sped on, above the black and heaving sea—on, on—until, being far away, as he told Scrooge, from any shore, they lighted on a ship. They stood beside the helmsman at the wheel, the look-out in the bow, the officers who had the watch; dark, ghostly figures in their several stations; but every man among them hummed a Christmas tune, or had a Christmas thought, or spoke below his breath to his companion of some bygone Christmas Day, with homeward hopes belonging to it. And every man on board, waking or sleeping, good or bad, had had a kinder word for another on that day than on any day in the year; and had shared to some extent in its festivities; and had remembered those he cared for at a distance, and had known that they delighted to remember him.

It was a great surprise to Scrooge, while listening to the moaning of the wind, and thinking what a solemn thing it was to move on through the lonely darkness over an unknown abyss, whose depths were secrets as profound as Death: it was a great surprise to Scrooge, while thus engaged, to hear a hearty laugh. It was a much greater surprise to Scrooge to recognise it as his own nephew's, and to find himself in a bright, dry, gleaming room, with the Spirit standing smiling by his side, and looking at that same nephew with approving affability!

'Ha, ha!' laughed Scrooge's nephew. 'Ha, ha, ha!'

If you should happen, by any unlikely chance, to know a man more blest in a laugh than Scrooge's nephew, all I can say is, I should like to know him too. Introduce him to me, and I'll cultivate his acquaintance.

It is a fair, even-handed, noble adjustment of things, that while there is infection in disease and sorrow, there is nothing in the world so irresistibly contagious as laughter and good-humour. When Scrooge's nephew laughed in this way: holding his sides, rolling his head, and twisting his face into the most extravagant contortions: Scrooge's niece, by marriage, laughed as heartily as he. And their assembled friends being not a bit behindhand, roared out lustily.

'Ha, ha! Ha, ha, ha, ha!'

'He said that Christmas was a humbug, as I live!' cried Scrooge's nephew. 'He believed it too!'

'More shame for him, Fred!' said Scrooge's niece indignantly. Bless those women; they never do anything by halves. They are always in earnest.

She was very pretty: exceedingly pretty. With a dimpled, surprised-looking, capital face; a ripe little mouth, that seemed made to be kissed—as no doubt it was; all kinds of good little dots about her chin, that melted into one another when she laughed; and the sunniest pair of eyes you ever saw in any little creature's head. Altogether she was what you would have called provoking, you know; but satisfactory, too. Oh, perfectly satisfactory.

'He's a comical old fellow,' said Scrooge's nephew, 'that's the truth: and not so pleasant as he might be. However, his offences carry their own punishment, and I have nothing to say against him.'

'I'm sure he is very rich, Fred,' hinted Scrooge's niece. 'At least, you always tell *me* so.'

'What of that, my dear?' said Scrooge's nephew. 'His wealth is of no use to him. He don't do any good with it. He don't make himself comfortable with it. He hasn't the satisfaction of thinking—ha, ha, ha!—that he is ever going to benefit US with it.'

'I have no patience with him,' observed Scrooge's niece. Scrooge's niece's sisters, and all the other ladies, expressed the same opinion.

'Oh, I have!' said Scrooge's nephew. 'I am sorry for him; I couldn't be angry with him if I tried. Who suffers by his ill whims? Himself, always. Here, he takes it into his head to dislike us, and he won't come and dine with us. What's the consequence? He don't lose much of a dinner.'

'Indeed, I think he loses a very good dinner,' interrupted Scrooge's niece. Everybody else said the same, and they must be allowed to have been competent judges, because they had just had dinner; and, with the dessert upon the table, were clustered round the fire, by lamplight.

'Well! I am very glad to hear it,' said Scrooge's nephew, 'because I haven't any great faith in these young housekeepers. What do *you* say, Topper?'

Topper had clearly got his eye upon one of Scrooge's niece's sisters, for he answered that a bachelor was a wretched outcast, who had no right to express an opinion on the subject. Whereat Scrooge's niece's sister—the plump one with the lace tucker: not the one with the roses—blushed.

'Do go on, Fred,' said Scrooge's niece, clapping her hands. 'He never finishes what he begins to say! He is such a ridiculous fellow!'

Scrooge's nephew revelled in another laugh, and as it was impossible to keep the infection off; though the plump sister tried hard to do it with aromatic vinegar; his example was unanimously followed.

'I was going to say,' said Scrooge's nephew, 'that the consequence of his taking a dislike to us, and not making merry with us, is, as I think, that he loses some pleasant moments, which could do him no harm. I am sure he loses pleasanter companions than he can find in his own thoughts, either in his mouldy old office, or his dusty chambers. I mean to give him the same chance every year, whether he likes it or not, for I pity him. He may rail at Christmas till he dies, but he can't help thinking better of it—I defy him—if he finds me going there, in good temper, year after year, and saying, Uncle Scrooge, how are you? If it only puts him in the vein to leave his poor clerk fifty pounds, *that*'s something; and I think I shook him yesterday.'

It was their turn to laugh now at the notion of his shaking Scrooge. But being thoroughly good-natured, and not much caring what they laughed at, so that they laughed at any rate, he encouraged them in their merriment, and passed the bottle joyously.

After tea, they had some music. For they were a musical family, and knew what they were about, when they sung a Glee or Catch, I can assure you: especially Topper, who could growl away in the bass like a good one, and never swell the large veins in his forehead, or get red in the face over it. Scrooge's niece played well upon the harp; and played among other tunes a simple little air (a mere nothing: you might learn to whistle it in two minutes), which had been familiar to the child who fetched Scrooge from the boarding-school, as he had been reminded by the Ghost of Christmas Past. When this strain of music sounded, all the things that Ghost had shown him, came upon his mind; he softened more and more; and thought that if he could have listened to it often, years ago, he might have cultivated the kindnesses of life for his own happiness with his own hands, without resorting to the sexton's spade that buried Jacob Marley.

But they didn't devote the whole evening to music. After a while they played at forfeits; for it is good to be children sometimes, and never better than at Christmas, when its mighty Founder was a child himself. Stop! There was first a game at blind-man's buff. Of course there was. And I no more believe Topper was really blind than I believe he had eyes in his boots. My opinion is, that it was a done thing between him and Scrooge's nephew; and that the Ghost of Christmas Present knew it. The way he went after that plump sister in the lace tucker, was an outrage on the credulity of human nature. Knocking down the fire-irons, tumbling over the chairs, bumping against the piano, smothering himself among the curtains, wherever she went, there went he! He always knew where the plump sister was. He wouldn't catch anybody else. If you had fallen up against him (as some of them did), on purpose, he would have made a feint of endeavouring to seize you, which would have been an affront to your understanding, and would instantly have sidled off in the direction of the plump sister. She often cried out that it wasn't fair; and it really was not. But when at last he caught her; when, in spite of all her silken rustlings, and her rapid flutterings past him, he got her into a corner whence there was no escape; then his conduct was the most execrable. For his pretending not to know her; his pretending that it was necessary to touch her head-dress, and further to assure himself of her identity by pressing a certain ring upon her finger, and a certain chain about her neck; was vile, monstrous! No doubt she told him her opinion of it, when, another blind-man being in office, they were so very confidential together, behind the curtains.

Scrooge's niece was not one of the blind-man's buff party, but was made comfortable with a large chair and a footstool, in a snug corner, where the Ghost and Scrooge were close behind her. But she joined in the forfeits, and loved her love to admiration with all the letters of the alphabet. Likewise at the game of How, When, and Where, she was very great, and to the secret joy of Scrooge's nephew, beat her sisters hollow: though they were sharp girls too, as Topper could have told you. There might have been twenty people there, young and old, but they all played, and so did Scrooge; for, wholly forgetting in the interest he had in what was going on, that his voice made no sound in their ears, he sometimes came out with his guess quite loud, and very often guessed quite right, too; for the sharpest needle, best Whitechapel, warranted not to cut in the eye, was not sharper than Scrooge; blunt as he took it in his head to be.

The Ghost was greatly pleased to find him in this mood, and looked upon him with such favour, that he begged like a boy to be allowed to stay until the guests departed. But this the Spirit said could not be done.

'Here is a new game,' said Scrooge. 'One half hour, Spirit, only one!'

It was a Game called Yes and No, where Scrooge's nephew had to think of something, and the rest must find out what; he only answering to their questions yes or no, as the case was. The brisk fire of questioning to which he was exposed, elicited from him that he was thinking of an animal, a live animal, rather a disagreeable animal, a savage animal, an animal that growled and grunted sometimes, and talked sometimes, and lived in London, and walked about the streets, and wasn't made a show of, and wasn't led by anybody, and didn't live in a menagerie, and was never killed in a market, and was not a horse, or an ass, or a cow, or a bull, or a tiger, or a dog, or a pig, or a cat, or a bear. At every fresh question that was put to him, this nephew burst into a fresh roar of laughter; and was so inexpressibly tickled, that he was obliged to get up off the sofa and stamp. At last the plump sister, falling into a similar state, cried out:

'I have found it out! I know what it is, Fred! I know what it is!'

'What is it?' cried Fred.

'It's your uncle Scro-o-o-o-oge!'

Which it certainly was. Admiration was the universal sentiment, though some objected that the reply to 'Is it a bear?' ought to have been 'Yes'; inasmuch as an answer in the negative was sufficient to have diverted their thoughts from Mr Scrooge, supposing they had ever had any tendency that way.

'He has given us plenty of merriment, I am sure,' said Fred, 'and it would be ungrateful not to drink his health. Here is a glass of mulled wine ready to our hand at the moment; and I say, "Uncle Scrooge!" '

'Well! Uncle Scrooge!' they cried.

'A Merry Christmas and a Happy New Year to the old man, whatever he is!' said Scrooge's nephew. 'He wouldn't take it from me, but may he have it, nevertheless. Uncle Scrooge!'

Uncle Scrooge had imperceptibly become so gay and light of heart, that he would have pledged the unconscious company in return, and thanked them in an inaudible speech, if the Ghost had given him time. But the whole scene passed off in the breath of the last word spoken by his nephew; and he and the Spirit were again upon their travels.

Much they saw, and far they went, and many homes they visited, but always with a happy end. The Spirit stood beside sick beds, and they were cheerful; on foreign lands, and they were close at home; by struggling men, and they were patient in their greater hope; by poverty, and it was rich. In almshouse, hospital, and jail, in misery's every refuge, where vain man in his little brief authority had not made fast the door, and barred the Spirit out, he left his blessing, and taught Scrooge his precepts.

It was a long night, if it were only a night; but Scrooge had his doubts of this, because the Christmas Holidays appeared to be condensed into the space of time they passed together. It was strange, too, that while Scrooge remained unaltered in his outward form, the Ghost grew older, clearly older. Scrooge had observed this change, but never spoke of it, until they left a children's Twelfth Night party, when, looking at the Spirit as they stood together in an open space, he noticed that its hair was grey.

'Are spirits' lives so short?' asked Scrooge.

'My life upon this globe is very brief,' replied the Ghost. 'It ends to-night.'

'To-night!' cried Scrooge.

'To-night at midnight. Hark! The time is drawing near.'

The chimes were ringing the three quarters past eleven at that moment.

'Forgive me if I am not justified in what I ask,' said Scrooge, looking intently at the Spirit's robe, 'but I see something strange, and not belonging to yourself, protruding from your skirts. Is it a foot or a claw?'

'It might be a claw, for the flesh there is upon it,' was the Spirit's sorrowful reply. 'Look here.'

From the foldings of its robe, it brought two children; wretched, abject, frightful, hideous, miserable. They kneeled down at its feet, and clung upon the outside of its garment.

'Oh, Man! look here. Look, look, down here!' exclaimed the Ghost.

They were a boy and girl. Yellow, meagre, ragged, scowling, wolfish; but prostrate, too, in their humility. Where graceful youth should have filled their features out, and touched them with its freshest tints, a stale and shrivelled hand, like that of age, had pinched and twisted them, and pulled them into shreds. Where angels might have sat enthroned, devils lurked; and glared out menacing. No change, no degradation, no perversion of humanity, in any grade, through all the mysteries of wonderful creation, has monsters half so horrible and dread.

Scrooge started back, appalled. Having them shown to him in this way, he tried to say they were fine children, but the words choked themselves, rather than be parties to a lie of such enormous magnitude.

'Spirit! are they yours?' Scrooge could say no more.

'They are Man's,' said the Spirit, looking down upon them. 'And they cling to me, appealing from their fathers. This boy is Ignorance. This girl is Want. Beware them both, and all of their degree, but most of all beware this boy, for on his brow I see that written which is Doom, unless the writing be erased. Deny it!' cried the Spirit, stretching out its hand towards the city. 'Slander those who tell it ye! Admit it for your factious purposes, and make it worse! And abide the end.'

'Have they no refuge or resource?' cried Scrooge.

'Are there no prisons?' said the Spirit, turning on him for the last time with his own words. 'Are there no workhouses?'

The bell struck twelve.

Scrooge looked about for the Ghost, and saw it not.